Over the Line

Faye Sultan

AND

Teresa Kennedy

Over the Line

● ●

DOUBLEDAY

New York   London   Toronto   Sydney   Auckland

PUBLISHED BY DOUBLEDAY
a division of Bantam Doubleday Dell Publishing Group, Inc.
1540 Broadway, New York, New York 10036

DOUBLEDAY and the portrayal of an anchor with a dolphin are
trademarks of Doubleday, a division of Bantam Doubleday Dell
Publishing Group, Inc.

Library of Congress Cataloging-in-Publication Data

Sultan, Faye.
    Over the line / Faye Sultan and Teresa Kennedy. — 1st ed.
        p.   cm.
    I. Kennedy, Teresa, 1953–   . II. Title.
    PS3569.U359609   1998
    813′.54—dc21   97-20653
    CIP

ISBN 0-385-48525-5
January 1998
First Edition

10 9 8 7 6 5 4 3 2

TO HORACE BENJAMIN BEACH, WHO CALLED ME DR. TRICKS AND
TAUGHT ME HOW WE TURN A LITTLE BOY INTO A MONSTER.

Acknowledgments

Special thanks to our families, for their patience and
    understanding . . .
To all the "Sophies" . . .
And to our dedicated readers for their help and suggestions.
You know who you are. Thank you.

Courage is fear that doesn't control you.

—ELEANOR ROOSEVELT

Dixon, South Carolina
May 1992

Prologue

● ●

LILA MOONEY stood wearing a faded print housedress with three buttons missing at the throat, watering her window garden of African violets, and thinking of the pills.

It was three days after her birthday and she still wasn't over it. She could tell by the way her thoughts kept going back to the precious amber bottle stashed in her medicine chest, circling like buzzards in the bright summer sky. She had stored them so carefully over the past months, telling Dr. Avery how she'd dropped the bottle and needed more, doing without them even when the pain got bad, just so she'd be sure—when the time finally came—that she would have enough.

"Oh, you don't need to worry," she said grimly, addressing the plants. "I got a week's worth of groceries comin' from Ed's Market. Waste not, want not, as they say."

She peered down at the row of potted violets—the hairy leaves and the timid look of the blossoms filling her with a dim, formless sort of rage. Somehow, without her knowing about it, the African violet had become the ultimately appropriate gift for an old lady; worse even than orchids. But try as she would to stop the custom, people had been giving Lila violets for years—on her birthday, at Easter, sometimes for no reason at all.

Still, she reasoned silently as she refilled the can and started on a second sill of pots, she herself would have to admit orchids were more for grandmothers. There was something more esteemed about orchids; they commanded respect and care. African violets, on the other hand, were ordinary—nothing special about them. All they needed was water and light. Maybe a little talking to now and then. If they lived, they lived. If they died, well—who cared?

She snatched at a shriveled leaf, scowling. The latest, a white one, had arrived from the florist in Charlotte for her birthday. The hastily scrawled card still dangled from a curled purple ribbon.

> Many Happy Returns on your 83rd!
> Love and Kisses, Diana.

The old woman glanced at the signature just as water overran the rim of the pot, causing the ink to run in blurred rivulets.

"The hell with you, too," Lila muttered in the silence. No matter how often she'd been invited, her niece hadn't taken the time to make the drive from Charlotte to Dixon in nearly three years. Oh, Diana was always full of promises to visit—talking big about lunch and a matinee, but it never happened. Never would, either.

Lila sighed. All she really asked from her niece was a bit of company—news of the world going on outside. A little visit would have been nice. What she got instead was violets. Lots of them. The old woman stared absently down at the plants. It was her own fault, she supposed. She had never inspired much love in people, just a sense of obligation.

And again, without meaning to, she thought of the pills.

"Where in blazes are those groceries?" she demanded of the pots. "I called over there to Ed's more than two hours ago." Done with her watering, Lila set the long-nozzled can precisely in the center of a tatted antimacassar, so as not to leave a ring on the polished table. There had been a place for everything in Lila Mooney's house for more than sixty years. And she aimed for it to stay that way.

She scuffed across the floor toward the ancient black wall phone, wincing in advance at the thought of putting her crooked, arthritic finger to the dial. She could have got touch tone, of course. The telemarketers from the phone company were always calling her with some new deal. But thus far Lila had resisted what she considered to be the foolishness of small conveniences.

She let it ring twelve times before hanging up. Either Ed's Market had burned to the ground or they were too lazy to answer the phone.

"Lord save us," she said irritably, trying to ignore the sudden conviction that she'd gotten the number wrong. It happened more and more of late, forgetting things like phone numbers, or whether the bills were paid. Her mama used to tell her that's what dying was like—the harder a body tried to keep things real, the more unreal things became.

"Just my mind turning loose of it," her mama had said those many years before, her face and hands wasted above a faded patchwork quilt. "Little by little, turning loose of the world."

Lila shivered and shook her head to clear it of the image of waxy, yellowed skin and skeletal hands. She didn't want to think of her mama this morning. It was those pills, that was all. Just pills and age and foolishness.

"I'll give them twenty minutes," she went on to the empty room, reluctantly replacing the receiver. "Twenty minutes more and that's all. It's that boy Jimmy doing the deliveries, I'll bet. I'll bet it's him that got it wrong."

Jimmy Wier was no boy—he was a grown man and then some, from the size of him, but you didn't have to be an old lady Sunday school teacher to know he wasn't right. Most times he was fine, like a big old kid on that bicycle of his. But there were other times, too. Those times his eyes would get a funny look, sly like, with little twitches around the mouth. You could see the drifter in him then, the secrets. Lila would see it in his eyes and know the kid stuff was just an act. There was danger in Jimmy Wier. You could see it if you tried. Jimmy had been delivering groceries for Ed's for almost three years, but that didn't mean she had to trust him. He could fool the whole town for all Lila cared. He might as well have been invisible for all that folks paid him any mind. But he wasn't going to fool Lila Mooney. The old woman turned and stared fretfully out the window. Lila Mooney knew only too well what it was to be invisible. How it was to smile and go through the motions and nod and say the right things until you choked on them—until you thought you might die from being so unnoticed, so unseen. People only saw what they wanted, mostly. They never saw the rage underneath.

Lila sighed heavily. There was no use thinking about it. Ed's was the only market in town that delivered and Jimmy was the only person who delivered for Ed. And since the blessed state of North Carolina had seen fit to take away her driver's license, Jimmy Wier was the best she could do.

Lila scowled at the strange white of the summer sky, thinking of the 1955 Chrysler New Yorker Deluxe parked in her garage. Bright as a new penny and only thirty thousand miles on it. Up until two months ago, she'd driven it back and forth every morning for nearly forty years to her job as a secretary at the Presbyterian school. Every day and Sundays, too, for Bible classes. But that job was gone now, even the Sunday school—along with her license. It wasn't fair—not fair. Sudden tears sprang to her eyes and she clenched her fists until the pain in her hands made her gasp. She ought to do it—find those pills. Get it over with. If this was all that was left of her life, she should do it today.

Taking a life is a crime against God. She could hear the words as clearly as if she'd said them herself at Sunday school. The body is a temple and killing is wrong. Doesn't make no difference to God if it's your own temple or someone else's. Lila brushed at her eyes and sank miserably into a nearby chair.

"What about your crime against me?" she asked of the emptiness, and shuddered at the blasphemy of the words.

The mantel clock chimed hollowly, making her jump; it was just before ten.

She absently fingered the place on her dress where her buttons were missing, trying to forget the pills, trying to think; there was something she had meant to do.

The early morning sunshine had given way to a close, clouded sultriness that seemed to threaten not rain but something less specific. The air that managed to penetrate the fly-specked screen was heavy and oddly still. As though the day were already lost, as though it were already late in the afternoon instead of ten in the morning.

Three miles away, at Ed's Market in the Friendly Mall on West Friendly Avenue, in a tiny loft office perched above the cashier's line, Ed Derman lit his fourth Pall Mall of the morning and enjoyed the sudden silence created as Lila Mooney finally gave up pestering him and hung up the phone. He'd heard it ringing, of course, but he'd simply chosen not to answer, knowing in advance who it was. Lila Mooney had been bothering him about her grocery deliveries for two years now. They always got there, rain or shine, but that had never made a difference to Lila. She pestered him just the same. And on that particular morning, Ed figured himself to be fresh out of oil to pour on those waters.

He squinted out the grimy window, scanning for the Schwinn with the baskets on the back. Jimmy wasn't much—he was slow and lazy and something else, too. Maybe a little crazy, Ed had never really been sure. He'd just taken him on when Jimmy rolled into town and asked for a job. Nobody seemed to know where he came from, and nobody seemed to care. Ed Derman least of all.

From the looks of him, Ed had it figured, Jimmy was some old country boy running from his folks. Even a fellow as many bricks short of a load as Jimmy got tired of folks working him to death. The woods were full of boys like him—come out of nowhere and nowhere to go. Jimmy lived in the loft of what once was a tobacco barn on the outskirts of town. He got to stay there free in exchange for keeping the place up to the point where it didn't fall down, and he had a job that paid close to a hundred a week. He kept on Ed all the time about saving his money to get an apartment in town. But Ed wasn't too worried. Jimmy Wier probably lived better in that barn than he ever had in his life outside of jail. Or so Ed had it figured.

Tired of his view of the parking lot, Ed returned to his desk and thumbed idly through an old issue of a skin magazine he kept to amuse himself when the Friendly Mall got too much to stomach.

"Y'all come back," chirped Denise from the cash register below. Ed glanced down at sixteen-year-old Denise Johns as she waved to Mrs. Higgs, who was trying to drag her brat through the door and carry her groceries at the same time.

Ed smiled lazily at Denise as she chatted amiably with another customer. He glanced again at the magazine, his mind superimposing Denise's sweet head on those lush lovely bodies, thinking of how it would be when she came to him. She was his niece, sure. But she wanted it, Ed could tell. He knew it from the way she wore that perfume to work or teased him in that flirty way she had. Little Denise had something in mind for her old uncle Ed. It was only a matter of time. A matter of a little planning.

He lit another cigarette and sighed, dreaming his dreams.

Downstairs, another customer, Constance Bennet, came down aisle three. Ed hurried to duck before she saw him, but he was too late.

"Hey there, Ed! Yoo hoo, Ed Derman?"

Ed lifted his head and smiled thinly. Connie Bennet had to be close to ninety, but was always bubbly as a schoolgirl as she went about her never-ending string of good works in the community.

She grinned up at him, her eyes enormous behind thick glasses, her teeth the color of marigolds. "I've got you down as a substitute elder at the Church of Christ next month, Ed. Ben Philpott is going over to his sister's in California for a long vacation and we're all counting on you."

Ed felt a headache coming on. "That's just fine," he answered. "I'll be there, Miz Bennet, you know that."

The elderly woman flashed what she thought was a charming grin. "I just wish more men in this town were as good Christians as you, Ed. Honestly, I do. How's everything otherwise?"

Ed shrugged. "Oh, you know. About the same. I was just waiting on Jimmy to take a delivery over to Miz Mooney's."

At the name, Constance Bennet's face clouded over. "Oh, my goodness. Poor Lila. Here her birthday came and went and I didn't do a thing about it. I clean forgot. Do you think she'll ever forgive me?"

"Oh, sure she will," Ed replied, not much caring one way or another.

"I should drop over there in a while. I should. On my way home from the post office. I'll bring her something." Constance took a moment, glancing over the aisles, trying to think of something appropriate to the occasion.

"Devil Dogs!" she cried after a moment. "I just know she loves Devil Dogs. And it'll be like a little birthday cake, too. You think she'd like that, Ed?"

Ed mustered another wan smile. "Sure she will. She'll appreciate that, Miz Bennet. Devil Dogs."

As Mrs. Bennet disappeared down the aisle, Ed glanced through the fly-specked window and spotted his delivery man huffing his way through the parking lot with an expression of supreme concentration, moving his lips as if conversing with an invisible friend. Ed tucked the magazine back under the seat cushion of his chair, watching through the glass as a stray dog came up to sniff at Jimmy's heels. Jimmy's face broke into an easy smile. He hunkered down to pat the dog's head and was presented with immediate and frantic enthusiasm. Ed gazed at them, man and dog, as they frolicked together in the parking lot. After a moment, he rose heavily to his feet. Someday he was going to have to fire that boy. Ed stubbed out the cigarette and made his way down the rickety stairs. If he didn't go out and get him, Jimmy would play with the damn dog all morning.

"You take care of them bags, Jimmy?" he called as he walked through the glass double doors.

Jimmy raised his head toward the voice and rose to his feet, uneasily plucking at the strap of his overalls. "Yeah, I did. They all got measles over there. Everyone. Even the babies got 'em. I felt bad for them kids, Ed. So I let 'em ride the bike. They liked it. Even with their spots. I ain't late, am I, Ed?" He fixed Ed with an almost fierce expression in his pale blue eyes. "I didn't think it would make me late to play with 'em."

Ed turned away, oddly conscious of the younger man's physical advantage. Jimmy Wier stood six foot four to Ed's five ten and had thirty hard-muscled pounds on him to boot. He glanced at the crude bracelet of jailhouse tattoo that circled Jimmy's huge right wrist.

"Naw, you ain't late. But you will be if we stand out here in the parking lot all morning."

As they moved together through the doors and into the store, Ed caught sight of Denise stretching toward a case of canned string beans, exposing the wide pink satin ribbon of midriff between her T-shirt and jeans, adorned with a small circle of gold glinting from her newly pierced navel. It made Ed shiver a little to see it, as though the wire were embedded somewhere in his own flesh. "Goddamn," Ed breathed. "What'll they think of next?"

Jimmy could not help following Ed's gaze. Seeing Denise, his blue eyes went oddly flat, as if he were seeing nothing at all. "Oh," he said by way of acknowledgment. "It don't hurt much. Once you get used to it."

Catching his expression, Ed came back to himself all at once. Sometimes, with Jimmy, it was easy to see why his folks had whupped him. "And how the hell would you know that?"

Jimmy didn't look at him. "Some guys I know fooled with that one time. Body piercing. I got a pierced ear, you know? This one here. I thought it would grow over. But it never has."

Ed felt himself blush for no reason at all as he caught the glint of cheap silver hanging crookedly from Jimmy's meaty earlobe. Even to his own ears his laughter was too loud, forced-sounding. "A pierced ear?" he hooted. Remembering himself, he glanced around to be sure no customers stood within earshot. "A fucking pierced ear? What're you, Jimmy, some kind of faggot? I got to tell you, boy. We can't have no faggots around here. You ain't a queer, are you, Jimmy?" Ed blustered, knowing how obnoxious it was, and somehow unable to stop himself in time. Jimmy looked down at him, his eyes gone cold, his mouth an unreadable line.

"No, Ed," he answered softly, "I ain't no faggot. You figure what somebody wants to stick in you makes you something? You think that, Ed? You think somebody pricked a little hole in Denise and made her all different? Like she can't be yours no more?"

Ed stared up at Jimmy, something like terror spreading through his bowels. Did he know something? The notion that this big dumb cluck could actually know something of the dark desire that swirled through Ed's fantasies made it suddenly difficult to breathe. He peered at Jimmy uncomprehendingly. How could he have known? How could he have fucking known?

But Jimmy's eyes betrayed nothing—not understanding, not vengeful glee—just a vague bewildered emptiness. And Ed drew a shaky breath. Jimmy didn't know, then—about what he wished—planned— for Denise. Jimmy didn't know anything.

"Aw, Jimmy," he said, showing his teeth in a phony grin. "I was just funnin', okay? You're straight as my own daddy's razor, anybody can see that. Why, I wouldn't be surprised if old Miz Bennet over there comes in here all the time just to get at you." Ed chuckled in spite of himself. "You know women, Jim. They never get enough."

Jimmy seemed to draw in on himself. "Yeah," he answered. "They never do."

"Get on with them groceries now, Jimmy. Jim? You got two bags for Miz Mooney. Over by the door. She'll be fit to be tied if you don't get a move on. Hear?"

He made to clap Jimmy on the shoulder, then stopped himself. "Miz Mooney's—" Ed drew himself up to as great a height as he could muster, catching the sudden, unpleasant smell of something on the other man's breath. "Two bags. Double time."

Jimmy came back to himself all at once. "Two bags. Yessir. Two bags." Nodding emphatically, he hoisted Mrs. Mooney's order in his arms, edging through the doors with a beefy shoulder. "Double time," he called and hurried toward his bike.

Ed stood in the doorway, struggling to reassert some sense of his own authority. "And don't you break them eggs in there, you hear? They're right up top. Break one and I swear I'll dock you for the dozen." He sighed and glanced over his shoulder, watching for Denise to reappear and check out the elderly Mrs. Bennet and her Devil Dogs. "Fuck," he said tiredly. But he didn't have a choice, overhead being what it was, and the boy working practically for free.

· · ·

Almost ten-thirty. Fretfully, Lila moved away from the window and ran a hand through her hair, fresh from a new blue rinse and permanented into tense little curls. She'd forsaken her usual hairdresser and gone to the more expensive BonTon on Main, intending it to be a birthday gift to herself. Miss Kit, the beautician, had cooed to her all the while about giving her a whole new look, but it hadn't come out right. When Miss Kit had confided that she moonlighted on the Bon-Ton and fixed the hair of the dead for the funeral home, Lila's hairstyle had been ruined forever in her mind. No matter which way she turned when she looked in the mirror, she couldn't help thinking those tense little curls made her look dead too. Irene, the cashier, told her it was nonsense; it was just birthday blues, and not the hairstyle at all. But Irene eyed her so sympathetically that Lila was compelled to tell her to mind her own beeswax, and had stalked out of the shop in tears with the smell of permanent wave solution lingering in her nostrils.

Birthday blues, indeed. She brushed the notion aside as she heard the Schwinn Roadmaster wheezing up the driveway and around to the back, under the weight of two bags of groceries and two hundred and fifty pounds of Jimmy Wier.

"Well, I guess it took you long enough, didn't it?" she called through the back door screen. Irritation made her lie. "I called the store. Ed said you were going to be late."

It took a moment for the statement to register, and a few more for Jimmy to find words for a reply. His broad face was as flat and empty as the moon. "I ain't late," he told her. "I asked Ed and he even said I wasn't."

The big man swung the grocery bags effortlessly from the basket, dwarfing them against his chest as he made his oddly graceful way to the back steps. He smiled at her through the screen, guileless as a boy. Lila held the screen door, a sudden spasm in her hands making her wince.

"Well, I don't know about Ed Derman's clocks. But that clock on my kitchen wall there's telling me you're plenty late, Jimmy Wier."

"Oh," he assured her. "The Robertses had me bring over four bags, on account of they all got the measles and couldn't get nowhere in the car. I had to bring all their bags first and then go back to the Friendly Mall and get yours next. And that's what I did. I asked Ed if I was late and he told me not. Not late, I mean." He paused and peered at her, squinting uncertainly. "If you called Ed at the store, that's what he told you, I bet. Same thing as he told me."

Annoyed at being caught in a fib, Lila set her mouth and swung the door wide. "Well, I am certainly not going to argue about it. Since you finally got here, you may as well bring them in and help me put them away. I can't do it myself. I got a misery in my hands this morning."

Jimmy bowed his head low as he passed her, clutching his burden tightly in his arms. The breath from his massive chest made a sound in the empty kitchen like bellows and she caught the scent of sweat on him from the morning's exertions, close and offensive in the stifling air. Lila shrank from him, then suddenly began to shout. "Well, my sweet Jesus! What in the world have you got? Is that an—earring? Oh my lord, have mercy! Just wait till I tell Ed Derman!" With clawlike fingers, she pointed at his earlobe as if to snatch it from the rest of him. Startled, Jimmy countered the move, clutching the bags so tightly that the dozen eggs resting on top rolled and shattered over the floor.

"Now you've done it! Why can't you watch what you're doing?"

Panicked, Jimmy was already on his knees trying to contain the mess in his hands. Little desperate gasping sounds escaped his throat. "Oh nonono. Nonono. He said not to and then I did and oh no, oh no no."

The old woman dropped to the floor beside him, furious, and unaware that one withered breast was completely exposed as she stooped, thanks to her missing buttons.

"Get a rag, damn you!" she shouted shrilly. "You're just making it worse! Over by the sink. And don't think Ed isn't going to hear about this either! I'm going to see to it that you're fired! What do you mean coming in here like that? My God—an earring, no less. You think I don't know about things like that? You think I don't know what that means? It means you're sick, and—and—dirty. You know that? Dirty and sick and disgusting. You hear me, Jimmy? You hear?"

But Jimmy wasn't listening anymore. Instead, he knelt upright beside her, his eyes glazing as he fixed on the old woman's breast, hanging forlornly from her faded housedress. A huge hand fumbled toward a vague throbbing in his pants. His breath came faster. He licked his lips with a wet, pink tongue. Sweat glistened on his forehead and his eyes were flat and clear.

She glanced up at him, spitting with rage. "Get the rag! By the sink.

And the mop, too. It's in the broom closet. You understand me, Jimmy? You're going to stay here and clean this up. Every bit of it."

Jimmy smiled distantly and got to his feet. On crippled knees, Lila struggled to contain the slippery mass with the hem of her dress, her knotted fingers snatching at fragments of eggshell.

Across the room, near the sink, Jimmy stood by the window, transfixed by the violet plants that lined the sill.

"Hurry up, damn you! I just cleaned this floor!" Lila shouted again. "It's right there, you idiot! Right in front of you!"

Jimmy found the rag and found the knife block too, right in its place. Right where she told him. He selected the butcher blade, wide and sharp. It looked like the best one, he thought. It looked like the one he needed.

"Pretty," he said, turning around.

At the same moment that Lila noticed the escaped breast and was frantically covering herself, she saw the rounded, steel-reinforced toe of Jimmy's workboot out of the corner of her eye. She felt it meet her jawbone in the next instant, a crack that sent a white-hot flash of pain into her skull and threw her backward against the floor. She lay there uncomprehending, blinded by stars of pain as the taste of blood filled her mouth. Jimmy loomed over her. She saw the knife turning over and over in his hands as he played with it, used the tip of it to catch the zipper of his fly and pull it down, so slowly, so carefully. His penis—swollen and red—poked obscenely through the opening as he crouched over her. He was smiling.

And even as her vision dimmed, she knew from the sly look that shone out of his eyes that it was not Jimmy at all coming to do this thing. There was another. You could see it if you tried.

And in that moment, Lila Mooney knew she wasn't going to need those pills after all. And the dark surprise of it almost made her smile.

One

● ●

"OPEN AND SHUT is what it is."

Sheriff Dwight Glass gnawed intently on the wet
end of a two-dollar stogie and looked away from the ruins of Lila
Mooney's kitchen. He never smoked anymore, at least not on duty,
but from the moment that morning when the call had come in from a
canvassing Jehovah's Witness about the bloody horror glimpsed
through the late Lila Mooney's starched front curtains, the cigar had
never left his lips.

He gazed morosely through a window lined with pots of African
violets as the state forensics team went about the grisly business of
bagging the bodies. Or what was left of the bodies. The two victims,
Lila here in the kitchen and in the living room Constance Bennet, had
been cut from hell to breakfast.

The sheriff drew some deep breaths, allowing himself to be momentarily hypnotized by the lazy whirl of red cherry lights from the
ambulance and state police vehicles. The rain that had threatened
earlier had come down in torrents about noon, leaving the air outside
the window smelling as though it had just been made.

Shit, Dwight, he told himself. Get a grip.

It was important to concentrate—important not to drop the ball in
these first crucial hours following the crime. But the images of the old
ladies' torn dresses and spread legs—of the way their severed nipples
had been placed so carefully in the center of their chests, continued a
mad dance in back of his eyes. What had been done here today was so

far beyond Glass's experience that the force of seeing it up close had sent the sheriff into a kind of furious argument with himself. His mind kept insisting that such things were impossible here on the quiet roads of his jurisdiction; his heart knew better though, and forced him to turn around.

He set his teeth into the wet comfort of his cigar. Forty years ago, Lila Mooney had been his Sunday school teacher.

"What'd you say, Sheriff?" Deputy Justin Chitwood glanced up from his laptop, his eyes darting from the sheriff's face to the unholy mess on the floor. The Chit, as Glass referred to him when he was out of earshot, had been to some hot-shot Ivy League school up North and was so unendurably full of the latest in criminology and forensics that the sheriff couldn't help wondering why the kid hadn't chosen a more demanding job. There wasn't much to do in Dixon except lock up drunks and write traffic tickets and scare the bejesus out of teen-aged shoplifters. At least, not until today.

Now, the junior deputy was frantically entering the specifics of the official report into a sleek computer no bigger than a magazine. When he glanced up to speak, his restless fingers never left the keys.

"I said," Dwight began in a carefully controlled voice, "that what you ought to be doing is helping the boys round up that grocery man from Ed's Market instead of settin' here on your butt playing Nintendo. Ain't nothing to this—" Sheriff Glass stopped and made a weak gesture toward the chalk outline of Lila Mooney's remains. "We know who it was done this. That Wier fella. The grocery man. Had to be. Pick him up and that's all she wrote. Open and shut."

Chitwood raised an eyebrow, finished his entry, and snapped the computer closed. "Wier's the obvious choice, of course," he agreed cautiously. "Neighbor across the way placed him here a little after ten this morning. But—"

Glass's face flushed with irritation. There was nothing in particular about Justin Chitwood that pissed him off—it was everything in general. The fair good looks, the tough, young man's physique, the calm intelligence. And then there were the buts. Couldn't a thing happen in Dixon his deputy didn't feel the need to qualify.

Glass reminded himself to give the boy his head. On a case like this one, all that fancy book learning might turn out to count for something. From the quiet, reflective expression on the young deputy's face as he glanced at a forensics man bagging Lila Mooney's female organs, he might have been eyeing a pile of leaves. He met the sheriff's glare with the same implacable calm.

"I just meant that at first look there's some interesting discrepancies. Things to think about."

Glass narrowed his eyes and slid the cigar to the other corner of his mouth. "Like what?"

"The jewelry box, for one thing," Chitwood answered simply. "Mrs. Mooney was killed right here in the kitchen, while Mrs. Bennet was done near the front door, right?"

"Yeah, so?"

"So why did he go to the bedroom last instead of first? You can see that from the blood we found in there."

"Robbery."

"Don't think so," Chitwood answered. "I called the niece over in Charlotte. Read her the content inventory. Says she don't know for sure, but she thinks there might be a few things missing. Costume stuff mostly. There's a gold watch left in there and a pretty good diamond ring. So if it was robbery, why didn't he take the good stuff? And the one in the front room—?"

"Miz Bennet . . ." the sheriff said a little sadly, thinking that his wife—a Church of Christer—was going to take it awful hard about Miz Bennet.

"She still had her jewelry on—money in her wallet, too."

Another image swam up in the sheriff's mind, unbidden and unforgettable. Ninety-year-old Constance Bennet, hog-tied with her own panty hose, ankle to wrist, neck broken at a hideous angle, eyes blank and somehow surprised, with pearl earrings poised underneath her crisp white curls.

It made him want to vomit.

"What's your point, Chitwood?" he demanded instead.

Chitwood gave a small shrug. "Don't know—" he answered. "Just that it don't seem as simple as it looks, I guess."

Sheriff Glass swallowed hard. "You think too much, you know that? Fact is, he was here and we got to be pretty sure he's the one killed these old women and raped 'em, and he—" Glass paused and fought back the urge to shout. "These here ladies died hard. Real hard. I just hope they didn't have to feel too much of what he done to 'em before they went. And I hope to God I never have to see anything like this again."

Chitwood studied him intently, and the sheriff felt himself color amid the confusion of his emotions.

"I'm not saying I disagree, Sheriff. I just don't know why he took the trouble to make it look like robbery. I'm just saying maybe it's something to think about."

Glass found himself fumbling in his pockets for a match and found none. "Shit, Chitwood. Give it up." He set his mouth around the cigar. "You think there's got to be a reason for everything. I mean, it ain't as though Jimmy Wier's a goddamned mastermind. I seen him down at Ed's. He's just another no-account, redneck drifter. Smarts of a tree stump, know what I mean?"

Chitwood's gaze was bloodless and level, as though he might be making comparisons. "Whatever you say, Sheriff."

The sheriff rubbed his chin. "Don't work so hard, Sherlock. There ain't no mystery here."

Chitwood looked at the floor. "Everything about this crime indicates a sort of—ritual. The placement of the nipples, the way the bodies were cut—" He glanced up again and met the sheriff's eyes full on. "Don't tell me that doesn't mean something."

"Sure it means something," Glass interrupted. "It means those old ladies are dead. It means the boy they trusted to deliver their groceries for 'em got his dick up and a goddamned knife in his hand. And the sooner he gets what's coming to him, the happier I'm going to be."

The young deputy shook his head. "There's always a reason, Sheriff," he answered quietly. "Whether you want to see one or not."

Glass took two quick, angry strides to the entrance to the living room. "Y'all about finished with that?" he called to the remaining forensics team. "We could stand to get outa here."

One of the team murmured from the bedroom and Glass turned again to face his deputy. "They'll be a few minutes," he said, and sank heavily into a nearby chair, the claustrophobic silence of the kitchen closing around the two men like a shroud. He watched the color subside in Chitwood's face before he spoke again.

"I'll tell you something about crime, Chitwood. About there being a reason." He met the deputy's eyes for a long moment. "You ever go to Sunday school?"

Justin Chitwood looked momentarily bewildered by the question. "Yeah, for a while. Mostly I played hooky, if you want to know the truth."

Glass smiled thinly. "I thought so. Because if you'd hung around more, Chitwood, you'd know that something like this here—these murders—they don't need a reason to happen. You know how come?"

"Why?"

"Because they're evil, that's why. Pure and simple. You believe in evil?"

Chitwood looked uncomfortable. "I don't know."

"Well, you ought to think about it. Because it's there. Out there in the world. Just waitin' on a chance. Hell, they probably even got evil up there at that fancy college you went to. It's in the papers and it's on the news every goddamned night. Mark it down, Chitwood. You've seen evil today—right here in this house. You looked right into its face when you looked at them bodies."

Chitwood said nothing, but only sat, examining the backs of his hands as they moved restlessly in his lap.

"Way I see it, everybody's got to choose. Everybody, man or woman, smart or dumb. They got to pick for themselves—right or wrong, good or evil. This Wier boy had that choice today and he chose evil. And for him to make that choice is all the reason evil ever needs. And even if he's outa his dumb fuck mind, it was his choice made him that way. 'Cause once evil gets ahold of you, it can make you do anything. The rest"—Glass paused and gestured wearily around the room—"the rest is just crap and lawyers."

A sudden silence yawned as they waited, each man lost in his separate thoughts, watching the last of the forensics squad file like ghosts through the rooms and out into the yard.

"Hey!" Chitwood called after one of them. "Did you note the missing plant?"

A tired-looking man with a notebook edged in the direction the deputy was pointing, to the window over the sink.

"Say what?"

"There," Chitwood said. "You can see the space where it was, there with the others. There's a trace of fresh soil, so it was removed recently. I checked around in the garbage and the rest of the house, and it wasn't there, so maybe you got to figure it was part of the robbery."

The man made a hasty notation followed by a question mark and left as Chitwood met the sheriff's eyes across the kitchen. They were silent for a long moment before Chitwood spoke again.

"Just tell me this, Sheriff. What does this evil want with an African violet plant?"

Now it was Glass's turn to shrug, but the look in his eyes was wary. "Maybe you weren't listenin', son. Like I said—evil don't need a reason. It just—is."

At that moment, the cellular unit attached to Chitwood's belt grumbled to staticky life. Glass watched as he answered and an expression of grim understanding passed over the young deputy's features. He signed off and picked up his hat from the scarred expanse of Lila Mooney's kitchen table.

"Johnson and Stevens picked up Jimmy Wier about a half mile from here," he said. "They say he was crying and trying to bury something under a tree."

Glass went a shade paler. "Oh, sweet Jesus, more body parts?"

Chitwood shook his head. "Nope," he answered. "But there was some jewelry. And a shirt with blood on it. And—" He paused and looked directly in the sheriff's eyes with an unreadable expression, as if trying to decide whether to tell him the rest of it.

"And what?"

Chitwood sighed. He placed his hat squarely on his head and gave a last glance around the tired little room. "And a package of Devil Dogs," he said, and headed out into the open air.

They strode across the lawn toward the state police car parked at the back. Sheriff Glass breathed deeply and slid into the shotgun seat, leaning back against the upholstery with the air of a man who had done all he could for the day.

"Just drop me down there and you can go on home," he said after a moment. "Your shift's up anyways."

Chitwood turned to him. "If it's all the same to you, I want to be there for the interrogation. You're gonna need a hand with the booking."

Glass shrugged. "Have it your way," he said.

"There's some things I think we should ask—" he began, then fell silent as the sheriff held up his hand.

"Stevens and Johnson brought him in. Besides"—Glass finished with the ghost of a smile—"I'm gonna handle the questioning myself."

"Sheriff, I—"

"You just keep your eyes open, Chitwood. And your mouth shut. You might learn something," Glass answered. "Enter it all into that fancy computer of yours. But this one's mine. Understand?"

"Whatever you say, Sheriff," Chitwood replied grimly. He fired up the engine and Glass could see his jaw muscles working as they pulled slowly away from Lila Mooney's tidy yard and onto the silent street.

"Like I said, boy," Glass said softly. "There ain't no mystery. Just open and shut."

And Sheriff Dwight Glass tasted the bitterness of the wet end of a two-dollar stogie against his tongue and wished very hard for a match.

Two

• •

THE DREAM was always the same.

Nothing but sound at first; footsteps down an endless corridor. A pair of stout boots leading the way—one two, one two—slow march to the room at the end of the hall. Then a whisper of paper slippers, sighing along the floor. Sshhh—shhh, the footsteps told her, light and anonymous—a worried little dance of anticipation, coming from behind. A drone of words after that, echoing in the darkness, monotonous and utterly resigned.

ThelordismyshepherdIshallnotwant.Hemakethmetoliedowningreenpastures . . . heleadethmebesidethestill waters . . . Herestorethmysoul. . . .

The darkness shattered by blue-white light. Blinking, blind, trying to breathe, being pushed forward into that room. It was so small, that room. Barely space to turn around, barely space to—breathe.

Her chest is tight and she knows it will be hard trying to breathe, trying to think. Panic rises up and beats against her with black wings as she sees the room. The big man in the boots, the skinny priest. She stares at him, holding his book. He looks up and smiles; his eyes are empty and cruel.

This is wrong, she thinks desperately. It was not supposed to be like this—they knew that.

"Hey, baby," the big man whispers. There is the feel of his hot breath on her skin, smelling of onions. *"Go toward the light, baby. Go toward the light."*

Need to breathe. If you took deep breaths it would be all right. The

brain works on oxygen; if you can breathe, you can think. A few deep
breaths and—and—

It would be over.

Someone said that—before. She tries to remember but cannot. She
cannot do anything but try to breathe. It's so much harder now because of the room. Breathe, breathe. She doubles over, still trying,
swallowing, gasping, gulping air. But there is only that ragged
whistling in her chest, and it sounds like someone screaming. Someone only she can hear.

The telephone, she thinks. There would be the telephone. And her
eyes search the tiny room frantically, knowing it is there, must be—
should be—

There! And then she sees the skinny priest holding up the wires,
sees how they have been cut, the ends hanging in colors to the floor.

"God forgives everything," he tells her.

Arms all around her. They lift her up, feet kicking helplessly. She is
lighter than air, giddy for air—weightless, without power.

"No!" She tries to scream, to tell them they're wrong, but there's
no air. No air.

They put her in a wooden chair. She stares at them. Oh sweet
God—the Chair.

It's me?

The knowledge makes her want to laugh, but she can't get the air
for it. She stays very still instead, feeling through her skin the hardness
of the wood against her back, the rough splintered wood of the arms.
And a voice in her head is jibbering with glee.

*No sense fighting anymore, is there? You knew this would happen. You
knew it all along. It's not like you needed a Ph.D., is it? All that work,
all those lies . . .*

She struggles helplessly against the voice, trying to silence it with
the sound of her own hollow gasps.

It's all over now, she thinks. Only thing to do now is wait. Just wait.
Close your eyes and try not to think. A clock ticks somewhere. But
she doesn't need to see it; she already knows what time it is. One
minute after midnight.

The night is when the fun begins. It's all in fun, isn't it? Secret fun.

She sees the executioner then. She wonders if it is the same one—
the big man who brought her in. He bends low and tightens the
restraints—wrists, legs, ankles—so tight, biting into her flesh. Hands
and feet first burn, then grow icy cold. She stares at her fingers and

thinks she is dying in little pieces first—before the gas will come to finish it. She looks at the executioner, searching for a face behind the soft black hood, and she sees one eye is gone, the socket shrunken in folds of purplish skin. The other is pale blue and bloodshot, full of tears.

"An eye for an eye," he whispers.

Now, now, you don't want to think about that, do you? No point in overthinking it. Must breathe—not think. Just breathe.

But there is no air at all. The room is too small and the straps are too tight. She knows again the awful smothering in her lungs—as though she had been stuffed with filthy rags. Must—must—she thinks, and her gasping is low and thin—like sobs.

Come on! It takes too long if you hold your breath. Much too long. And your eyeballs burst and the foam comes out of your mouth and it hurts, oh God, it hurts so much, and you . . .

Breathe or die. Breathe and die.

Deep, deep breaths, they all said that. All the books, all the lawyers, even. The quicker the better. Over in a minute. Justice is done and we all can get on with our lives.

She sees the window, then—the row of smiling silhouetted heads watching through the glass.

Mouth dry, gasping, she mouths soundless questions. "Why are you here? Why are you watching me?"

The heads begin to laugh. She struggles against the straps, but she has no strength, no air. A woman flies up out of her chair and presses her face close to the window, and she can see the foggy smear of breath on the glass.

"You can't save everybody!" the woman shouts, and the others scream their laughter.

Then blackness again as the thick leather mask slides over her face, tearing at the roots of her hair. Blind again. The leather stinks and scratches. They will watch her, but she will not see them.

Only a hole to breathe.

And she cannot. Can't move—can't breathe. And her lungs are on fire with the need. One goddamned breath—just one, please . . .

Please, God, let me breathe.

They are gone then. The door slams, locks turn—bolted with an oily metal sound. All alone now; left to die—helpless. So helpless.

She can feel their eyes through the glass. Waiting. Wanting to see it. Needing to see it done.

Deep breaths, deep, pleaseplease, Jesus, let me die, let me breathe so I can die quickly.

Sissss! The gas—oh God, the gas sounds like breathing—the scent of almonds—no—not that. It smells of sweet slow rot—of death.

She waits, dead fingers clutching. Let me—her lips move soundlessly, lungs bursting in the stinking dark. Let me—

Breathe!

Portia McTeague sat bolt upright in bed, clawing at her throat, taking great, shuddering gulps of air. Cold with her own sweat, she coughed hoarsely and shook her head, breathing, making herself breathe again and again until she was light-headed and the darkness of her room swam with brilliant-colored spots that floated before her eyes.

She kicked aside the twisted sheets and reached up to wipe away the last traces of icy tears on her cheeks. Still stupid with sleep, she swung her legs over the side and almost jumped at the sudden, extraordinary comfort of the thick carpeting under her feet, the solidity of the floor beneath. Her long fingers clutched the edge of the bed as she forced herself to come fully awake.

It's only a goddamned dream, she told herself. Only that dream. Again. That mother-of-all-dreams dream.

Furious at her own vulnerability, she stared uncomprehendingly at the red glow of numbers from the bedside clock; it was four forty-three in the morning.

Shivering, Portia snatched a light robe from the bedpost and threw it over her shoulders. She knew these nights well enough to be aware that any hope of sleep was gone. The moon shone bright as a dime in the gorgeously eerie blue of the pre-morning sky, and she walked unsteadily toward the window, the light tangling in the tousled length of her hair.

The dreams had been worse lately; she knew that. Expected it, even. With her testimony in the Warren case coming up in a few hours, she could have predicted her nightmares the way a weatherman predicted rain. But after today, she hoped they would go away again. No more bad dreams and no more George Warren, at least as far as she was concerned. Whatever the jury decided in the end, Portia McTeague had already decided there would be no more George Warrens in her life—at least not for a while.

The execution had done it, she knew that. Sammy. She closed her eyes tight as the image of his arched back and the sound of his last gasping screams tore at her memory, forcing her to sit on the edge of the rumpled bed, her head bent nearly to her knees.

She never could have believed it would be like that—watching a man die. Sammy Dean Parker had been executed for murder by the state of North Carolina six months before. And she had been a witness. He wanted her there, he'd told her—he wanted her to be able to tell folks what it was like after he was gone. He'd chosen the gas chamber over the needle, even tried to have it televised. Just so people could see what happened when the state turned executioner.

"They bought the ticket," he'd said a few frantic days before he died. "I figure it's only fair to let 'em watch the movie." Portia and a team of lawyers and sympathizers had taken Sammy Dean's fight all the way to the Supreme Court before a weekend justice had refused to hear the case. But finally, only a few had seen Sammy Dean Parker die. Only a few had come to hear his last gurgling gasps as the cyanide gas came and took him.

He'd asked her to come with tears in his eyes. And she'd gone willingly, never imagining in advance what it would mean to sit in that claustrophobic theater along with his lawyer, a few members of the press, and the family of the victim, a high school senior named Dawn Marie Lowry. The Lowrys had sat to one side, away from the rest, almost leaning toward the window that revealed Sammy Dean strapped to the chair. When it was done, Dawn's father had gotten to his feet and clapped his hands. Five claps that echoed in the terrible aftermath of the twisted agony they had witnessed; five claps and Sammy Dean was gone.

She had wondered since, on nights like this, what made a man applaud the sickening spectacle they had witnessed that night. She had wondered what god he served that demanded a serving of such terrible revenge. Sammy Dean Parker was a tattooed, smartass scrawny little son of a bitch from Florida who'd murdered a prom queen in the backseat of a stolen Pontiac in 1980. What brains he had were fried on cheap bourbon and crack cocaine. But it was never his brain that had defined Sammy Dean—it was the rage coiled up in him like a rattlesnake—waiting, ready to spring, hungry for some opportunity. Sammy Dean Parker stood five feet six inches tall and weighed 130 pounds soaking wet. And he'd snapped her neck and all but severed her spinal cord with his bare hands. Sammy Dean Parker was as quick and mean as a junkyard dog, with—thanks to some regular head injuries at the hands of his father—a memory and attention span to match. When they came to arrest him, Sammy hadn't even remembered the crime. He'd tossed Dawn Marie's nude body out on the side of the highway like a sack of meal. And he hadn't even remembered doing it.

As his psychologist of record, Portia McTeague could have recited a family and criminal history that told the thousand reasons why Sammy Dean Parker had turned out a killer. But she'd never quite managed to convince the jury that history didn't make a man into an animal; it just made him act like one.

Portia frowned and hugged herself, trying not to let her thoughts go down what she knew to be a dead-end road. But a high, persistent inner voice rose up in spite of herself.

"He was only the first one you'll see die. Three death sentences came after him. It'll all turn out the same, you know. No matter how you testify. Not exactly a great batting average, is it? And now Warren. Sure, he's nuts, but that doesn't change what he did, does it? You saw those pictures. How can you spend your time defending scum like that, anyway?"

Portia closed her eyes and sighed. On nights like this, that good old inner voice had a way of sounding suspiciously like her mother's. And her mother was one of the reasons she'd become a shrink in the first place.

She needed more sleep; just an hour, maybe two. She glanced at the tangled bed and knew it from the heavy, hot feeling behind her eyes. Sleep disorders, she thought. That's a symptom. One of the top ten. Maybe it was time to haul out the old green-and-whites. Dr. Prozac. Maybe it had been a mistake to take herself off again. Three times on, three times off. Three strikes and you're . . . clinically depressed.

"Shit," she said aloud. "This line of work could depress Mother Teresa."

She gazed mournfully around the bedroom, finding little comfort in its tasteful simplicity. White-on-white wallpaper, bleached oak floors, a king-size bed that suddenly seemed ridiculously large. And empty. The room looked—and was—expensive. It also looked anonymous, oddly impersonal. Almost like a hotel room. And not a very clean one, at that. Never much of a homebody, Portia nevertheless chided herself for the lack of creature comforts in her surroundings. It wasn't that she held no taste or love for beautiful things—she did. What she found hard was owning. The more you had, after all, the more you had to lose. And, at forty, Portia McTeague had already lost too much not to appreciate the value of keeping things simple.

She made her way down a silent hall to the next bedroom where her daughter, Alice, was sleeping undisturbed. That room was more human anyway, and she nearly smiled as she crept through the doorway toward the small bed where Alice was curled under the covers, snoring softly. So much of her life was changed since Alice had come. Portia drew a measure of comfort from the cheerful, childish paintings that covered the walls, the toys and stuffed animals that cluttered every available surface. She went to the bedside and gazed for a long time at the dark angel's profile against the Minnie Mouse pillow slip. Portia loved to watch her sleep like that. It filled her with a kind of hope.

Alice sighed unexpectedly and turned on her back as Portia edged silently out of the room and made her way downstairs to the kitchen for a long, predawn session with the coffeepot.

It was better anyway, she told herself as she fumbled for the filters. Dream or no dream. There would be time now to go over her testimony again. Once more before her court appearance that morning. She had one more chance to make sure the jury understood that George Warren was insane—completely unresponsible for his own actions. George Warren had psychoses that would fill the textbooks for years to come. Your basic psychologist's dream, she thought, and smiled grimly.

The coffeepot gurgled and dripped, filling the kitchen with the sharp, comforting scent of morning. Portia shivered against a sudden chill.

She could draw the court a picture of George Warren's mind that would frighten an Inquisitioner. Warren was sick and he was dangerous. He should be put away somewhere, kept suitably medicated, and never, ever let out. She could tell them all that, and maybe even convince them—all in the cool, authoritative style that had earned her a reputation as one of the best forensic psychologists in the country.

She only hoped that it would be enough to keep George Warren from a death sentence. Just this once.

Because the nightmare was always the same.

Mecklenburg County Courthouse
September 1992
People v. George Henry Warren

Three

• •

ASSISTANT DISTRICT ATTORNEY Amy Goodsnow
cleared her throat as she eyed the witness on the stand.
The young ADA was angry and she was more than a little scared. Two
long years on the job trying DWIs and delinquent fathers until
George Warren had fallen into her lap—the biggest case in Mecklenburg County in fifteen years. This day, this case—it should have been
a high point in her career. Instead, the prospect of questioning the
witness on the stand filled her with a cold apprehension. Her glasses
slipped further down her small nose in the brutal September heat.
Even with the air conditioners running full blast, the confidence with
which she'd begun that morning's hearing had ebbed steadily in the
rising humidity, making her fingers clumsy as she scanned her pages of
notes, slowing her steps as she approached the cool, well-dressed
woman in the witness box.

Amy took a deep breath and tried to steady the fluttering in her
stomach. The testimony of Dr. Portia McTeague could ruin her case.
And Amy Goodsnow knew that better than anyone.

The morning's hearing was for one purpose only: to determine
whether George Warren's confession had been coerced by the arresting officers, one of whom had had the poor sense to lead Warren in a
prayer to get him to talk. The officer had testified already; it had taken
nothing more than some hand clasping over "The Lord's Prayer" to
get Warren to sing like a bird. The problem was, this particular bird
hadn't had a lawyer present at the time. If the defense could prove

that the confession hadn't really been "voluntary," it was back to square one. Everything—all the state's evidence—even the body of the brutally raped and murdered nine-year-old Lisa de Veau, would be rendered inadmissible. Warren had given them everything—even led them to the desolate spot where the little girl had been buried, deep in the piney woods. Without the confession they had no body; without a confession and without a corpse, they had no case.

And for Amy Goodsnow, who was not so far out of the piney woods herself, that could very well mean no job. Life at the DA's office was hard enough on her as it was. The pay wasn't really good enough for someone who had so many student loans to repay, the hours were long, and she'd taken the job in the first place because it was the only one she was offered after passing the North Carolina bar. Losing Warren would mean an end to all the work and all the dreams that had lifted her out of the poverty of a childhood spent in trailer parks and sawmill camps. Getting him, on the other hand, would be the cherry on her sundae, maybe a ticket out of the District Attorney's office and into a private law firm.

The auburn-haired woman on the stand sat easily, crossing her long legs and nodding slightly at the judge. Though Portia McTeague had a formidable reputation as a forensic psychologist and expert witness, Amy had been utterly unprepared for the flawlessly cut designer dress and chiseled features of the woman on the stand. Rumor around the courthouse said McTeague came from money somewhere down in Mississippi, and seeing her face to face, Amy did not doubt the speculation. But it wasn't the clothes or the looks that gave her away—it was something else. You could buy clothes, you could probably even buy those cheekbones if you wanted them badly enough. Amy allowed herself another quick glance as McTeague was sworn in, her voice low and warm and utterly at ease. From the look of her, Portia McTeague didn't even seem like someone who indulged much in ladylike airs. No, it was worse than that. This was a woman who had it, whatever "it" was, but she was also somebody who never flaunted it.

Amy shifted uncomfortably in her poorly fitting burgundy suit and sneaked a look down at her cheap shoes, feeling like a mongrel dog sent to yap at the heels of a thoroughbred.

Great, she thought miserably. And they say there's no such thing as class in a democracy.

But the young ADA had no time for self-indulgent comparisons.

She had to concentrate on Lisa—to think about what she'd been through before she died. She had to see to it that George Warren fried in hell before he could ever do that to another little girl.

The thought gave her courage and Amy strode to the stand, squaring her skinny shoulders and clearing her throat once more.

"Dr. McTeague," she began in a high nasal tone, hating the flat sawmill accent she'd never quite been able to lose. "Would you please clarify for the court just what it is that you do? I know you explained your background some for Mr. Dylan over there." Goodsnow paused and made a weak gesture in the direction of the defense attorney, Declan Dylan, who was idly jotting notes. He and McTeague looked as though they were cut from the same piece of cloth. Even stuck in that wheelchair, he had the same natural elegance. "But I'd like to hear it again for myself."

Portia McTeague leaned slightly toward the microphone, her voice low and her manner confident. "I'm a clinical and forensic psychologist for the state of North Carolina."

"And are you in professional practice in that capacity, Doctor?"

"Yes, my practice is in Charlotte."

"So, people come and tell you all their psychological"—Goodsnow placed an unpleasant little emphasis on the word—"problems and you get paid just to listen, is that about right?"

Portia McTeague leaned back slightly, seeming to swallow the young lawyer in a glance. Then she smiled.

"My clients come to me for help and treatment for a variety of problems, which I do provide, and like most professionals I get paid for that, yes. In addition, however, my practice is about fifty percent forensic work."

Goodsnow glanced at the judge and continued. "Would you explain that part of your work, please?"

McTeague continued in a steady, patient teacher's voice, as if she were instructing the young ADA. "I consult to the criminal justice system here in North Carolina and elsewhere around the country, doing evaluations like this one, where I've been asked to examine either the victim of a crime or an alleged"—here the doctor paused for only an instant, yet it was somehow long enough for emphasis—"perpetrator of a crime, and I present the results of my evaluation to the court just as I'm doing today."

"And are you paid for those services, Doctor?" Flustered, Goodsnow could feel the blood rising to the surface of her pale cheeks.

"Sometimes, sometimes not."

"Meaning what, exactly?"

The witness seemed to focus her even gaze somewhere just above the prosecutor's straw-colored hair. "Meaning that in some cases my clients or their families or the state are able to offer a fee for my services as a witness."

"And did that happen in the case of George Warren?"

"Yes it did."

"Objection, irrelevant." Declan Dylan's silky drawl rose over the proceedings. Amy turned around, still blushing. He didn't even look up.

"Overruled," the judge intoned. "You may continue, Ms. Goodsnow."

Amy began to breathe a little easier. She could still make this go her way; she could. By establishing McTeague as nothing more than a hired gun, she could taint her testimony in the eyes of the court. Little did she know how often the woman in front of her had traveled down that particular road, led by prosecutors with a lot more experience than Amy Goodsnow.

The younger woman drew a short, sharp little breath. "How much?"

"Objection," Dylan intoned again in a bored voice. "The witness's personal finances are not at issue."

Amy shot him an irritated glance. From his place at the table, the defense attorney looked almost as bored as he sounded. Their eyes met, and he began to tap his pencil lightly on the desk.

Don't look at him, Amy told herself. He's trying to psych you out. Defense attorney Declan Dylan had a reputation for being one of the best criminal lawyers in the South—as smooth as silk and as deadly as an adder in the courtroom. Amy suppressed a little sigh. It was easy to see how he'd come by his image.

The judge appeared almost troubled. Clearly, he found the question marginal. He glanced down at the witness, noting not for the first time her extraordinary auburn hair, just beginning to show threads of gray. "I'm going to allow you to answer that question, Doctor. But, Ms. Goodsnow, try to keep in mind that there's no jury here to impress, will you? So let's move along after this. Doctor?"

"Certainly, Your Honor," Portia replied evenly. "I was paid five hundred dollars. That was the amount allowed by the judge for this initial evaluation."

Seeing the expression of genuine surprise in the ADA's eyes, Portia hid a grin. Since Dec had taken her on as the expert, and the judge himself had approved her fee, it appeared that, of the principal players in the courtroom that morning, Amy Goodsnow was the last to know. Still, it wasn't the first time she'd seen a prosecutor blanch at discovering how little an expert witness was actually paid for an opinion. Especially when Declan Dylan was the one arguing the fee. Like most of those born into wealth, money meant nothing to him. And she'd learned from experience that if he paid at all, almost nothing was generally what you actually got. Still, she never refused him if she could help—they went back too far for that.

She eyed the young attorney, now struggling to regain her composure. The bad burgundy suit only highlighted her paleness, and Portia saw she'd somehow managed to run her stockings in the course of the morning's proceeding. But Amy Goodsnow was tougher than she looked, and whatever sympathy the doctor felt for her evaporated with the next question.

"Are we to understand that you're the kind of expert who would sell your testimony for a mere five hundred dollars?"

Oh lord, thought Portia. Here we go.

"Objection!" said Dylan. "Badgering."

"Sustained," said the judge. "Ms. Goodsnow, mind your manners. Either rephrase that or I'll have it stricken."

"Sorry, Your Honor." Amy ducked her head and made an attempt to look suitably humbled. "Let's just continue." Once more, she faced the witness, her pale eyes unnaturally bright.

Portia shifted in her chair, trying to identify the look on the younger woman's face. From somewhere, unbidden, came the image of a single eye, looking out of a soft black hood. Pale and bloodshot. Like Amy Goodsnow's eyes. Portia reached for a sip of water.

"Dr. McTeague," the attorney went on in a more casual tone. "In looking over your CV here, I see you have a particular interest in children, most particularly victims of sex abuse. There's a number of articles here on the subject, appointments to various committees, all concerned with that area. Victims of sexual abuse, domestic violence, etcetera. Is that right?"

"Yes," Portia answered slowly, wondering where she was going with it.

"And yet I also see here that in your former position as co-chair of a committee on crime and public safety you were a major force behind the methods now used by the prison system to evaluate and consider sex offenders for community placement in treatment programs, is that also correct?"

"At the time—I believe it was from 1988 to January of 1990—I worked with a board of psychologists and other mental health experts in designing the programs and methods that are now in place to evaluate some cases, yes."

Amy silently counted to three before asking her next question. "Wasn't George Warren placed in one of your programs?" She glanced down at her notepad. "Up in Durham, in June of 1991?" Goodsnow's voice shook with sudden emotion. Her eyes met the witness's for a single instant. And Portia knew suddenly that there was something more than winning a case at stake for Amy Goodsnow. For the young assistant district attorney, this morning—any morning—was all about survival. For any victim, it was always about survival.

"That seems counterproductive doesn't it, Doctor?" Amy hurried on. "I mean, to be interested in the victims and the children on the one hand, and to be turning loose the criminals on the other? Warren's record is full of indications, isn't it? There's a number of priors. Lewd and lascivious, exhibitionism . . ."

Portia watched the prosecutor carefully, never changing the expression in her deep green eyes. Funny how she could spot them so easily. In Amy's case it might have been beatings, sexual abuse—but something had happened to the young woman in front of her. Somewhere along the line, something had happened to give her that rage—that desperate need for validation. She would do anything to get it, anything to win. Even if it was wrong. Portia shot a quick glance at George Warren, who sat with his head bowed, oblivious to the proceedings, moving his lips in a litany of silent prayers. George's battle with rage was already lost. Amy Goodsnow's went on every day. And that made her dangerous.

Nevertheless, Portia's reply was as cool and liquid-sounding as a glass of sweet ice tea. "Mr. Warren's previous record is a matter of public knowledge, just as it is also a matter of public knowledge that abused children frequently become abusers as adults. The release program was carefully monitored."

"We're all aware of the abuse excuse, Doctor," Amy countered acidly. "How do you explain Mr. Warren's being out on the street? Apparently he wasn't monitored carefully enough."

Portia's voice remained calm. "I don't explain it. Though I helped to design the programs used by the state's prison system in evaluating sex offenders, I personally had no part in the decision to release him to community placement. That decision was made by his parole board."

Amy faced the witness defiantly. "But it was your program that was responsible, wasn't it, Doctor? You designed it? So wouldn't you honestly admit to the possibility that Lisa de Veau would be alive today if it wasn't—"

"Objection!" This time Dylan's voice rumbled like low thunder through the room. "The witness is not on trial here, Your Honor. This line of questioning is purely speculative and entirely irrelevant to the matter at hand."

The young prosecutor whirled to face the judge. "I'm simply trying to establish the witness's credibility in a larger context, Your Honor. If her evaluation programs are shown to be flawed or personally biased, then her psychological evaluation of the defendant might prove equally lacking."

Nice save, thought Portia with a certain appreciation. She sneaked a glance at Dylan, who was beginning to look as near to disturbed as he ever got. Clearly, he hadn't counted on the rookie ADA's grit. Portia offered him a sympathetic nod. The defense attorney was a good man and a good friend, but like most good people, he tended to be a rotten judge of character.

There was a breathless little silence. The judge passed a weary hand over his eyes.

"There was a group in here last week," he said. "Son was killed in a wreck with a blood alcohol of two point something. The parents were all set to charge the bartender of the place where he'd been drinking with murder." He glanced at the lawyers, then at the witness, his old eyes moving restlessly from one face to another. "I got to tell y'all, I don't hold with that line of reasoning. If folks could be sent to jail for not having perfect foresight I expect we'd all get there sooner or later." He paused and looked at Amy, his face set.

"Now, Ms. Goodsnow, I suggest you give us all a break here and get on with what you got to talk about. The doctor here designed the evaluation program for the state of North Carolina. If it was good enough for them it ought to be good enough for you. And if she wasn't around to evaluate this man before he was released into the community, well, she's done it now, so why don't you stick to asking her what she found out?"

"All right, Your Honor." Amy nodded abruptly, clasping her hands in front of her to hide their trembling. For a moment Portia almost felt sorry for her. It was obviously not easy to be Amy Goodsnow on a good day. And with any luck, this certainly wasn't going to turn out to be one of her best.

The prosecutor's thin soprano wavered. "Let's move on, then. Dr. McTeague, how many times have you interviewed Mr. Warren since his arrest?"

Portia glanced down at her notes. "I began seeing Mr. Warren in April. Since then, I have met with him a total of eighteen times. That is excluding his psychological testing, which was performed by my colleague, Dr. Isabel Waters."

"And as I understand it, you rely on the results of these various psychological tests to form some sort of opinion or diagnosis of your—uhh—clients?"

"In part. Yes, I do."

"And these are standardized tests? You didn't—design them?"

Portia felt a blush rising from her collar. "No, I did not. They are, in essence, diagnostic tests used all over the country to determine psychological problems, intelligence, areas of concern, and so forth."

"So—these are the kinds of tests where they ask you if you're afraid of germs on doorknobs, that kind of thing?" Amy glanced around the room and offered a thin smile.

Jesus, thought Portia. Spare me. "They ask a variety of questions," she answered. Suddenly tired of the sparring, she wanted to jump up from the witness stand and shout. What's the matter with you people? Can't you see the man's crazy? Can't you see he's not responsible? He doesn't even know where in hell he is! Look at him! Instead, she swallowed a sigh and steeled herself for the young prosecutor's next question. It didn't matter how many times she'd been through it, it never got any easier, trying to make them understand.

"But the standardized tests are considered important, are they not? Diagnostically speaking?"

Portia nodded. "Yes. They help to complete the patient's psychological profile."

"And Mr. Warren was given these important standardized tests?"

"Yes, he was."

"But by your associate—"

"Yes."

Amy did her best to look confused. "So, even though you'd spent all this time with Mr. Warren as his doctor, you handed these critical psychological tests off to one of your colleagues. How come you didn't give Mr. Warren the tests yourself?"

From her place on the witness stand, Portia shot Declan Dylan a knowing glance. This was how they'd hoped it would go. By deliberately leaving some gaps in the defense's questions about the results of Warren's psychological tests, Dylan had set a nice little trap for the young prosecutor. And Amy Goodsnow, unbeknownst to her, had just fallen in.

Portia took a sip of water from the glass at her elbow.

"My initial observation and consultation involved trying to establish a relationship with Mr. Warren," she said. "It's important that my clients trust me enough to confide in me as their doctor, and so forth. But it's equally necessary in conducting an intensive or thorough psychological evaluation for the person who gives these types of tests not to be the same person the client is used to, and with whom they spend a lot of time. What is known is that people will alter their responses, or attempt to perform well if they're interested in pleasing the person they're performing for. Given Mr. Warren's psychological condition"—here Portia paused to take another sip of water, her eyes meeting the prosecutor's in a long, unwavering look—"that is especially true."

Portia was baiting Amy, but still and all, it seemed only fair. Lawyers spent most of their lives trying to elicit the right answers from witnesses; in her years of testifying in cases like this one, with Declan Dylan's help, Portia had learned a trick or two about manipulating her answers to get them to ask the right questions. Turnabout wasn't always fair play, but hell—it was the only game in town.

Amy's pale eyes narrowed. "Especially true, Doctor? And just why is that?"

Bingo! thought Portia. Her long fingers tightened in anticipation as she gripped the edge of the box and leaned toward the microphone. "Meaning simply that Mr. Warren's psychological disorders are such that he experiences terrible rage and feelings of isolation from other people."

"Did you discover that from these tests of yours?"

"And from my interviews with him, yes."

"What else did you find out from those tests?"

Portia took a deep breath. "For the most part, the test information we gathered was not helpful."

"Why? Because he's not insane?"

"Objection!"

"Sustained. You want to rephrase that?"

Amy began to pace. "Dr. McTeague, would you please enlighten us all here on the results of Mr. Warren's standard psychological tests?"

Portia managed a small smile. "That would be difficult to do. For the most part, Mr. Warren's test results were outside of what is generally considered statistically probable. He was off the scales."

Amy's eyes flashed and she clutched her notepad closer to her chest. "But you've already stated that he will do almost anything, including manipulating answers on a test, to please people and try to form a bond with them, is that right?"

"Yes."

"So isn't it possible that Mr. Warren somehow manipulated your associate? Or deliberately answered in such a fashion as to skew the results?"

Portia considered her response. "That is possible, but doubtful, because, as I've mentioned, Mr. Warren is very anxious to please. Particularly when he encounters those he considers authority figures. Like a doctor, or the police, or—" she paused and glanced up at the judge uncertainly, indulging in another little bit of legal theater.

Seeing the look, Amy scowled and moved closer to the stand, her little heels clicking on the floorboards in a light staccato.

"Or what?" she demanded suspiciously.

Portia met her eyes. "Or a religious person," she answered sincerely. "Like a priest or minister. As his records indicate, Mr. Warren is a cult survivor, and—"

"I object!" Amy, blushing more furiously than ever, appealed to the judge. From the corner of her eye, Portia caught the flash of Dylan's delighted grin.

"Ms. Goodsnow," the judge answered patiently, "I believe you asked the question. You can't object to your own question."

"I meant—I want the witness's response stricken from the record. That last part. It's not pertinent."

"Let her finish. I'm the one who's going to decide what the jury will hear and what it won't, and before I do, I want to know what she has to say. Is that all right with you?"

Stunned at the judge's tone, Amy stood rooted to the spot, her eyes darting uneasily around the room. "But—"

"Just be quiet and collect yourself a minute," the judge warned, then turned back to Portia. "You were saying?"

Portia took a deep breath, carefully wording her response. "I was saying that George Warren is the survivor of a religious cult. Therefore, religious people and things act as psychological triggers for him. Based on what I have learned of his background, I would have to say he considers religious people authority figures."

"Thank you," said the judge. "Ms. Goodsnow?"

Shaking, Amy tried to rescue her line of inquiry. "We are all aware of the evils of cult-type worship, Doctor. We all know how it can go to extremes. But a police officer is not a minister. And Officer Franks over there"—she gestured to the cop who'd testified earlier that morning—"is no more an authority on religion than you or I. Surely you don't equate the kind of thing that goes on in a cult with a simple Christian prayer?"

"I don't at all," Portia replied smoothly. "But Mr. Warren does."

Goodsnow fairly danced with annoyance. "I don't see how, Doctor. It's clearly a case of apples and oranges, isn't it?"

"Objection," intoned Dylan. "Calls for speculation on the part of the witness."

"Sustained. Ms. Goodsnow?"

Amy drew a deep breath. "Sorry, I meant only that even as a psychologist, Dr. McTeague wouldn't be privy to Mr. Warren's exact state of mind on the day of his arrest, would you, Doctor?"

"Not entirely. However, I have been able to reconstruct his state of mind to some extent after my interviews with him."

"You've heard the officers here testify that they led Mr. Warren in 'The Lord's Prayer' before he made a confession?"

"Yes."

"And it is your opinion that this simple act of Christian faith, this common prayer, was enough to cause George Warren to tell them anything he thought they wanted to hear?"

"Objection," Dylan intoned.

Judge Hamlin sighed. "Overruled. She's here to give her opinion, so let her give it. Answer the question, ma'am."

Portia nodded, feeling a headache just begin to take shape behind her eyes. "It is my opinion that from a psychological standpoint, Mr. Warren understood the prayer as a command to confess, not as an invitation. And that his desire to please resulted in his telling the officers what he thought they wanted to hear."

"Did he say that to you in those words?"

"No."

"Then how do you account for the fact that the information he gave was entirely accurate?"

"Objection! Calls for a conclusion on the part of the witness."

"Sustained."

Amy wet her lips. "Did George Warren tell you he was innocent of the rape and murder of Lisa de Veau?"

"Objection! She is asking the witness to compromise confidential information."

"Overruled. Answer the question."

"No. Mr. Warren has no memory whatever of the crime."

From his place at the defense table, George Warren sat, apparently oblivious to the uproar around him, his handcuffed hands clasped together, his lips moving in some mute supplication.

"Did he tell you that the officers had tricked him into praying with them?"

"No."

"But if I understand you correctly, what you're claiming here is that the simple fact of Warren's having belonged to some questionable religious cult way back when has affected him psychologically to the point where somebody could get him to do whatever they wanted just by saying 'The Lord's Prayer'?"

Portia set her jaw. "Under certain conditions, that would probably be true."

Amy managed a cynical smile. "Doctor, what was this cult that George here was supposed to have belonged to? Some kind of guru thing? Satanist?"

For the first time that day, Portia had to fight to keep the emotion out of her voice, as the childish sobs of a shattered, helpless George Warren echoed in her mind. She took a long moment to glance through her notes and regain her composure. "Mr. Warren's family were members of a Christian fundamentalist organization whose practices included starving, beating, and the ritual exorcism of children they believed to have been possessed by the devil. Those exorcisms included physical abuse, burning, and other forms of torture for victims they believed were possessed. Mr. Warren himself endured no less than six such rituals between the ages of five and twelve years of age. In addition, Mr. Warren has recollected between nineteen and twenty-three separate incidents of sexual abuse, genital mutilation, and torture by both male and female members of that cult, resulting in what I consider to be permanent psychological and personality damage. One characteristic of that damage is that in certain situations, under certain kinds of stress, he is unable to respond to prayer as anything other than a command." Portia gulped back the lump of rage that rose up in her throat. "They would have killed him if he had."

There was a stunned silence. Even Amy Goodsnow's face seemed to have gone paler than usual, the shadows under her eyes suddenly apparent. "But we have—we have only Mr. Warren's word for that, don't we? Have you corroborated any of this?"

"The report issued by the forensic evaluation team at Dorothea Dix hospital that was ordered by you indicates evidence of scarring that might be seen to corroborate his story, at least in part," Portia answered.

"But that is still only a matter of opinion, isn't it? I mean, scars can be caused by any number of injuries, can't they? The truth is, we really don't have anything to prove this far-fetched tale of Mr. Warren's background, just his word, isn't that true? The word of a man whom you have just told us will say almost anything to please an authority figure—including a doctor."

Portia gripped the witness box. "My relationship with Mr. Warren—" she began, and was almost immediately interrupted by the ADA's high thin voice working her nerves like fingernails on a blackboard.

"Is one of words, isn't it, Doctor? All we have here is Mr. Warren's word for what happened to him. Just that." Amy turned away, looking out over the courtroom. "That and your—expert—opinion," she added sarcastically.

Portia opened her mouth to respond, but just at that moment she caught the look in Declan Dylan's eyes from across the room. Don't lose it—the look implored her. Don't lose it now.

She took a deep breath. "That's right," she said quietly.

Amy's smile was as thin as a knife blade. "No further questions," she said.

Four

• •

AH, DON'T WORRY about it. You did a great job," Declan Dylan drawled as they emerged from the courthouse and made their way to the parking lot. The heat and humidity hit them like a slap in the face, rising in shimmering waves from the newly paved parking deck. The mauve-tinted marble on the new Federal Reserve building gleamed in the harsh midday sunlight. Seemingly oblivious to the strangling air, Portia made her way down the steps adjacent to the wheelchair ramp, her mouth set in a line and her eyes steely.

"Hot enough for you?" Dec asked innocently, after another moment of silence. She glanced at him as he displayed a row of white, movie-star teeth in his most charming grin.

"Oh stop it, Dec," she snapped, still smarting from her clash with the prosecutor. "You look like FDR."

"And you look like a June morning," he replied, throwing a hand theatrically over his heart. 'And she is fair, and fairer than that word of wondrous virtue—' "

Portia shot him a warning look. "Spare me the Shakespeare, okay? The quality of mercy was pretty damned strained this morning, if you ask me. Did you believe that little rookie?"

Dec shrugged. "Not bad. Get a few years on her and she could turn out to be a player."

Portia turned to him. "Sure. But what about Warren?"

"It'll be all right. Hamlin is a fair man, as judges go, and I've got a good feeling about this one. In spite of Goodsnow's shenanigans." Without meaning to, his tone lost some of its conviction, and his dancing eyes grew serious. "You want to get some lunch or something?"

"No," the psychologist answered. "Thanks anyway. I just want to get in my car and drive somewhere where they don't have lawyers."

Dec laid an expensive, butter-soft leather briefcase across his knees. In a casual tone, such as he might have used to discuss something as trivial as the weather, he asked, "Dreams again?"

She faced him, momentarily nonplused, nodding a silent assent.

"I can always tell," he answered, his voice dropping a notch. "You can't let it get to you, hon. Parker's dead."

Portia sighed. "And, more than likely, Warren's going to be dead too," she answered bitterly. "So what good does it do?"

At the bottom of the steps, Portia turned her gaze out over the parking lot, running a distracted hand through the humidity-curled tangle of her hair.

Declan eyed her sympathetically. He, too, had sat through the sad spectacle of Sammy Dean Parker's execution, and had had his share of nightmares afterward. But Sammy Dean Parker had been in the ground for six months, and Declan Dylan had put him in that place in his mind where he put all such things—the same place he'd put his beautiful wife and the use of his legs and the drunken missed turn on a long-ago moonlit highway. Those things were never coming back any more than Sammy Dean was going to rise up from his grave. They'd done the best they could to save him. And in the end, they'd lost. There was nothing to do but go on.

"Never mind. You did good up there," he said comfortingly. "What's important is that Hamlin got the information. And you didn't lose that famous temper of yours in giving it either." He winked, still trying to lighten her mood.

She shot him a skeptical smile. "Talk about damning with faint praise. I can't afford to lose my temper up there and you know it."

He held her eyes for a moment longer than was necessary. "Nonetheless," he answered, "I was proud of you. But, as you well know, I'm your biggest fan."

She smiled for the first time that day. "Then why do I always have the feeling I'm the first one you'd throw to the wolves?"

"Because against you," he replied, laughing, "no self-respecting wolf would stand a chance. Take me, for example." He spread his arms wide and shrugged. Portia shook her head, still smiling. Dec was one in a million. Not many women could boast a male friend like him. She only wished he would find someone. His wife had died in the accident that crippled him. And even after all these years, Portia could not help thinking that more than his legs had died that night. Lily's death had taken a part of his heart. She was sure of it.

"Of course," Dec continued, carefully steering the conversation back to the Warren case, "I can't say for sure how it'll go. Maybe Hamlin will throw out the confession and maybe he won't. But we did the best we could. These days, that's winning all by itself."

"Oh yeah?" Irritation quickened her steps as she walked along beside him. "You know as well as I do how many cases I've testified in. And how much good did it do? Do they care? Expert witness—hell." She paused and shook her head. "As far as psychology in the courtroom goes, I might as well be selling snake oil and tarot card readings."

They approached a blue Volvo parked under a line of shade trees at the far end of the lot. Portia opened the door and rested against the car for a moment, trying to let some air into the stifling interior. She looked down at her old friend, her eyes unreadable.

Dec sighed. "Well—I got to admit, a jury that's in the mood to hang is never too interested in psychology. But cheer up. With any luck at all, this is one confession the jury won't get to hear. I still think we won this round. And if not—" He made a small gesture of dismissal. "There'll be another round. You have to take it by the day."

Portia folded her arms across her chest and held herself, glancing back at the courthouse uneasily. "That little girl's still dead, Dec. And Warren's still crazy. He needs to be locked up—probably forever. Nobody won anything. That's the hell of it."

Dec's face grew serious and he reached out and placed a hand lightly on her arm. "Maybe not," he agreed. "But at least maybe he won't have to die for being crazy. Maybe because of you he just goes to the hospital where he belongs. Maybe he'll get some help. And maybe, if we say it enough times, somebody will get the message that the state's putting him to death isn't going to bring that little girl back. That's what we're here for, isn't it? A little justice for everybody."

The lines of tension in her face softened somewhat. "That's what you're here for, Dec. Me, I'm not so sure," she answered. She paused for a moment, and drew a deep breath.

"It all seems so useless. I think I ought to quit. I need some—perspective. Maybe it's me. My presentation—my being a woman. I don't know! I just think you ought to find somebody more convincing." She faced him, her eyes dark and serious. "Warren was the last one, Dec. I can't do it anymore. I'm burned out." She fell silent, waiting for his response. Dec Dylan was the most ardent opponent of the death penalty she'd ever known. Conviction came so easily to him that she envied him sometimes. It kept him going against all the odds. But Portia, though she shared many of her old friend's opinions, couldn't help feeling a little like Sisyphus rolling his rock up the hill. One step forward, two steps back.

Now Dec's handsome face didn't change. "Oh," he said softly. "Well, now, that's a shame, that is."

"It's everything—the politics, the extra workload. And now, with Alice—well—maybe I should be a little more responsible, you know? Beef up my practice, start saving for her college. I can't be traveling all the time—getting stuck in lockdowns. Half the time she doesn't even know where I am! And she needs me, Dec. I'm all she's got."

She trailed off uncertainly as, oblivious to her protests, Dec plunged a hand deep into his expensive briefcase and withdrew a thick file. He thumbed through it. "I understand," he told her in an even tone and allowed himself a little sigh. "I had something else for you, but I guess it doesn't matter now."

Portia frowned. "What?" She regretted the word as soon as it was out of her mouth.

Dec refused to meet her eyes. "Oh, nothing. Really. Just a case down in Dixon. I had Deb Yarborough on it, but she quit on me. Walked out yesterday afternoon. It was the client, I guess. He uhh—"

"He what?"

The lawyer shrugged. "Can't say for certain. She just said she was scared."

Despite herself, Portia felt a sudden spark of curiosity. "Scared? Scared of what? Of the client? How come?"

"She didn't get into specifics. She just—walked." Dec glanced up from the file. "Maybe she was burned out," he offered.

Portia slid sideways into the front seat of the Volvo, ignoring the hint of sarcasm. "She's damn inexperienced is what she is. Yarborough's too young to be burned out.

"What kind of case is it?" she demanded in the next breath.

Dec did his best to hide the beginnings of a smile. It was like hooking a catfish. Once they bit, they never let go. "Oh, multiple murder," he answered casually. "Along with a trumped-up kidnapping charge and first-degree assault, but that's window dressing. I just thought that, seeing as she left me in a bind like this, you might be willing to have a look. You know, just to help out. But I'll call Harry Falcone. Maybe he'll be willing to testify."

Portia's eyes narrowed. "Falcone? You must be kidding, Dec! He's under investigation. Falcone's so corrupt, half the judges in Carolina have barred him from their courtrooms. He'll say anything for a few bucks. And screw the oath."

Dec sighed heavily and tapped the file on his knees. "Beggars can't be choosers. Too bad, though. It's a juicy one. And who knows? Falcone might come through."

Portia looked pained. "Ahh, Dec! The only thing that one comes through for is himself. He couldn't care less about these guys!" In spite of herself she reached across the space between them and snatched at the file. "Just tell me who it is."

Now, at last, Dec allowed himself a small, triumphant smile. "Jimmy the Weird, no less. Ring a bell?"

Portia's eyebrows shot up in surprise and she hastily thumbed through the file. "I remember it from the papers . . . The old-lady killer, right?"

"Alleged old-lady killer, if you don't mind. But yes—one and the same," Dec replied. "They've got him down at Columbia. The Death Penalty Resource Center down in South Carolina contacted our office for some help. Strictly pro bono. Interested?"

Portia began to read, her face intent. "I don't know—" she murmured reluctantly. All at once she paused. "What do you mean pro bono? Two minutes ago you were ready to pay Falcone!"

Dec grinned. "He won't do it for free," he answered smoothly. "You will."

"In a pig's eye—"

"Check out the police photos—" Dec urged. "There's lots of guts and feathers."

"Jesus," Portia breathed, glancing through the file. She squinted at one of the photos. "What's that?"

"If you're looking at what I think you're looking at, it's a nipple," Dec answered. "They don't call our boy weird for nothing."

Portia peered at the photos, shuddering with distaste. "Could be some ritual aspect. So, what do you know? What's the story?"

"That's what we want you to find out. All we know for sure is that the state police picked him up in the neighborhood as he was trying to bury a bag containing a package of Devil Dogs, and some costume jewelry taken from the scene. Go figure."

"What did you say—Devil Dogs?" Portia stared at him.

Dec shrugged, his eyes dancing. "Like Twinkies, only chocolate. Honestly, you have led a sheltered life, haven't you?"

Portia waved him silent as she continued to scowl over the file.

Dec observed her from his wheelchair, grinning from ear to ear.

"Police could also place him at the scene because he stole one of the victim's African violet plants," he went on after a few moments. "Had it on him, buttoned up in his shirt. Yarborough didn't get much. And neither has anybody else. He won't talk and he doesn't test out in any of the standard stuff. Won't cooperate."

Dec's voice grew suddenly low and urgent in the heat of the early afternoon. "We need you, McTeague. South Carolina's going for the death penalty as soon as they can get it. We're working with a team down there and going for insanity, but the DA's in no mood to bargain. Wier's already been deemed competent to stand trial, and unless we can get this guy to open up, he's a dead man."

Portia did not answer, the implications of Dec's statements reverberating in her throbbing head like a brass band. If Dec's team was going for not guilty by reason of insanity, they were in serious trouble. In murder cases, that plea was the longest shot there was—which meant it was probably the only one they had.

"When's the trial start?" she asked in a low voice.

"Begins on the twelfth of next month."

"Dec—that's less than six weeks!"

He nodded. "We won't need you until the sentencing phase, but it's still not much time. We'll have to move with what we've got. The murders got a lot of press, and the prosecution doesn't want to lose momentum."

"But what difference does that make? Who's prosecuting?" Portia asked, unnerved by the expression in his eyes.

Dec looked uncomfortable. "No bright young whippersnapper assistant on this one. Folks are too upset about those little old ladies. Pillars of the community and all. Donny Royal's going for the big time. He thinks he can pull a senatorial nomination if he can win an execution for some poor son of a bitch delivery boy like Jimmy Wier."

He gazed out over the simmering asphalt, heat waves the only motion in the torpid air. "I expect he's right about that much," he sighed. "Besides, Wier's white. Sending a white man to the death house looks real good up in Washington these days." He uttered a short harsh laugh. "That way, they can't accuse you of racism."

Portia groaned. "Royal? Say I didn't hear you right. You know Royal, Dec. He gets me up there and it'll set the cause of equal rights for women back a hundred years. Or don't you remember the last time we met? All those headlines?"

"I remember 'em," Dec agreed. "Especially that one—'High Noon for Hired Gun'—I loved that one. I had it framed."

"Oh shut up—you know what I'm talking about. Aside from being a drunk and a bigot, Donny Royal can also lay claim to the distinction of being a world-class misogynist."

Dec's eyes twinkled with mischief. "So as a world-class psychologist you ought to know better than to take it personal, darlin'. The man's just doing his job."

Frustrated, Portia gnawed a little on her lower lip. She knew what he was asking; she also knew he wouldn't be asking if he didn't already believe she might take the case. Unbidden, a little voice piped up through the clamor of her thoughts, sounding suspiciously like Sammy Dean's. You know lawyers, it chided. They only ask questions they already know the answers to.

"Dec—I was—humiliated!" she finally managed to protest. "If it was anybody but Royal—anybody."

Again he flashed her that presidential grin. "You got creamed all right," he agreed. "But you fought back, didn't you? Just like you did today. And just like you're gonna do for this old boy down in Columbia." He leaned forward, blue eyes steely in the light. "You trying to tell me you're losing your fight, Pokey?"

All the air went out of her lungs in a rush. Dec had sworn never to use the nickname bestowed on her by her daughter. Never, of course, unless he was feeling extremely manipulative. She eyed him warily. Or extremely desperate.

"Shit. Okay—I'll look. But no commitments, understand? Just an initial evaluation and we'll see." She threw the file across the front seat of the Volvo and slid behind the wheel. "So, when do I see him?"

Dylan propped an elbow on the handle of the car door. "I took the liberty of scheduling an appointment for this very afternoon. You never schedule sessions for court days, and you can make Columbia by two-thirty."

Portia stared at him incredulously. "Damn you, Dec. You're a conniving bastard, you know that?"

His handsome face moved closer, barely brushing the air above her cheek with his lips. "Of course I know it," he answered. "That's what makes me such a fine attorney." He met her eyes then, his smile gone. "It's going to be all right. You'll see. There's a big space between the living and the dead, Portia. You just have to keep trying to fill it. And the only thing to fill it with is more living."

She stared at him for a silent instant. "No promises," she insisted.

"None expected. Just go have a look."

Abruptly, she turned the ignition key, placed one hand on the wheel and the other on her car phone. "I'm not committing to the whole case, understand? I'm just doing the initial evaluation. No guarantees."

Dec nodded. "No guarantees," he said. "Scout's honor."

She allowed herself a small smile. "Since when were you ever a Scout?"

He feigned offense at the remark. "Two whole months before they threw me out for buying merit badges," he replied. "Read the file."

She waved as she backed the car out of the lot and into the street. Dec watched her until the sleek blue Volvo turned at the far corner and disappeared behind some trees, an odd half smile on his face that reflected a combination of relief and concern. Portia McTeague might insist she was burned out, but she hadn't looked it. As he memorized the last glimpse of her profile and thought about the grim determination in the line of her jaw, he decided she didn't look burned out at all. She looked instead like a woman on fire—someplace inside her that no one could reach.

And he wondered, for a moment, if he'd done the right thing. When it came down to fighting for those who couldn't fight for themselves, nobody worked harder than Portia McTeague. And nobody took it harder when they lost.

"Be careful out there, Pokey," he whispered to the empty air, and turned his chair slowly in the deserted parking lot.

Portia eased the Volvo into the flow of traffic along the interstate with the contents of Jimmy Wier's file spread over the seat next to her, reading with one eye and driving with the other. Even in the early afternoon, traffic was heavy—what seemed like hundreds of cars and trucks swam through the lanes of traffic like fishes, vying for a place in the never-ending current.

North Carolina, Portia thought, merging faultlessly into the right-hand lane—the promised land. More like the land of promises, considering the pace of progress in these parts, at least insofar as progress might be measured in the halls of justice. But then, the population of the Carolinas wouldn't be the first in the history of the world to learn the difference between wanting change and actually getting it. Progressive as it was in some ways, it seemed woefully backward in others. Still, ever since the sunbelt boom of the early eighties, the state's population had grown at an astonishing rate. People from all over the country were moving to the New South in search of better jobs and better lives. Lured by all those politicians' promises, most of them probably didn't find life any better here than it had been anywhere else. The schools weren't good, businesses came and went, and now even the tobacco industry was listening to the bell toll. But the politicians and the promises kept coming and so did the people, bringing their stress, their crazies, and their crimes. Portia sighed heavily, looking down at the thick file. That was one thing about evaluating criminal psychotics for a living. Business was booming.

She punched the number for her office into her car phone and waited for the ring.

"Lori?" she asked.

"Oh it's you." Her assistant never failed to sound a little disappointed to hear from her, as though Portia's calls were an utterly unnecessary interruption of routine. "You're not supposed to be here until tomorrow. What's up?"

Portia smiled indulgently. Lori Stone was as reliable as a revenuer and just about as warm.

"Just checking in to tell you I'm on my way to Columbia. I promised Dec I'd do a preliminary on a client of his."

Lori was not impressed. "Yeah, I know. Jimmy the Weird, right? Dylan's office called yesterday after you left to say that's where you'd be. I got it on the calendar."

"They did? But I didn't even know myself until twenty minutes ago. He just handed me the file!"

"Hhmm—I guess maybe he just had his assistant call me in case you took it," Lori responded dryly. "I don't recall. But Deb Yarborough's assistant's looking for a job. Earlene Wilson told me at lunch. Dr. Yarborough's decided to close up the office and go back into research."

"You don't say," answered Portia, who knew for a fact that there was no information network on earth more formidable than the one made up of assistants, secretaries, and people like Lori, who made the professional lives of their employers run.

There was a little pause, punctuated only by a hissing of air on the line, as Portia digested this new bit of information. Was Yarborough really quitting practice for research? And how much of that decision had to do with Jimmy Wier?

"Was there something you wanted done?" asked Lori after another moment.

"Not exactly, I just wanted to ask—"

"—You know where you're going?"

Portia hesitated. "Sure—uhh, Columbia." The fact was, she was notorious for her poor sense of direction. Despite the fact that her glove compartment was stuffed to overflowing with state and county maps, Lori had received hundreds of phone calls over the years as the eminent Dr. McTeague got hopelessly lost on the road.

Lori sighed heavily. "Check for a folder from Dylan's office that says 'directions' on it. Is it there?"

Hastily, Portia flipped through the file. "Yeah. How did they know to do that?"

"I told 'em when they called that you'd need it. So please use it, okay? I got to pick up my kids at three so I ain't gonna be here if you manage to get yourself lost."

Portia grinned. "Bless you," she answered.

"And no shortcuts," Lori warned. "I mean it. There's folks livin' out in the backwoods you don't want to meet."

"I promise. When do I see you tomorrow?"

"Nothing until eleven. Then a staff meeting."

"Right," Portia answered. "Oh, wait!"

"What?"

"Did you remember to call Aggie?"

Lori snorted derisively. "Course. Don't I always? She'll pick up Alice after school and keep her till you get home. Whenever."

Portia smiled with relief. It didn't matter that she and her adopted daughter, six-year-old Alice, had been together for two years now, she still experienced moments of panic as a working mother, always a little unsure of her nurturing skills. Thank God for Aggie, her next-door neighbor, a stay-at-homer who didn't mind filling in the gaps.

"Hang on," Lori said. "Phone's ringing."

Portia waited for some minutes until Lori came back on the line. "Hey, my cellular bill's as big as my mortgage, all right? What was that? Anything important?"

"Search me. But his timing's good. That was somebody name of Justin Chitwood. Deputy sheriff. Said he'd called in at Dylan's office and was referred. He knew all about you coming on the Wier case. He was at the scene in Dixon, and wanted you to know he was available if he could be of any help."

Portia frowned out the window. "Why would he do that? I mean, it's not like the guys with the badges are usually on my side."

"Maybe he's looking to change careers," Lori answered. "Wants to be a shrink when he grows up. He sounded about fourteen."

Portia was still puzzled. "You get a number?"

"Of course. You want it?"

Portia fumbled in her purse and sighed. "Save it," she told her. "I can't find a pen and I don't have time to talk to him now, anyway. Okay, hon, I guess that's it. I just hope I don't get stuck in another lockdown." Portia eased the Volvo past an ancient Dodge that was chugging along at about thirty-five.

There was the barest hint of a smile in Lori's reply. "If you do, it'll be your third this month. Have a real nice day."

Despite a certain propensity for getting lost, Portia was an accomplished driver. It soothed her for the most part; the endless hours on the road were the only time in a crushingly busy schedule that seemed to belong entirely to her—she could think, catch her breath, and catch a little distance between horrors. But mostly she enjoyed driving because it freed her to do nothing else but drive. The endless details that tend to clutter a mind all fell magically away as she traveled asphalt ribbons of Southern highway, and she felt her worries of the morning unraveling along with the miles.

She wedged the Volvo alongside a trucker from Florida and smiled graciously as he allowed her to pass. He flashed her a lascivious answering grin in her rearview mirror, wearing the road warrior's uniform of sweaty bandanna, feed cap, and mirrored aviator shades. She waved and accelerated to put some distance between her and the semi. There were no better drivers on the road than most of these truckers, she knew, but she also knew the majority of them would flunk every drug test known to man. And whatever else the day might bring,

Portia didn't aim to get her Volvo rear-ended by an eighteen-wheeler, no matter what the commercials had to say about their safety record.

With one hand, she plucked a folder labeled WIER OFFICIAL PSYCH EVAL—STATE OF SC from the file on the seat. Edging easily back into the right-hand lane, she hit the cruise control and began to read, her eyes moving automatically from the page to the road and back in a long-practiced rhythm.

The first of the official reports was dated shortly after Wier had been apprehended while trying to bury a grocery bag in a vacant lot in Dixon. She hastily scanned the page for the name Chitwood. He was not listed as one of the arresting officers. Weird. Whoever this guy was, he had a reason for wanting to talk to her. The problem was, Portia knew the game well enough to know an expert witness had to be very careful of other people's reasons. Still, she had to agree with Lori—whoever he was, his timing was perfect. Maybe too perfect.

But first, she had Wier to think about.

Confused and obviously disoriented by his arrest, Wier had been remanded to the county prison hospital by the court for observation and an initial psychiatric evaluation to determine his competency to stand trial. There, a Dr. Jonathan Keene had found him "of average or below average intelligence," "nervous," and otherwise "nonresponsive" when questioned about the murders. After just one interview, Dr. Keene had prescribed Benadryl, the antihistamine, as a tranquilizer in roughly four times the amount dispensed in over-the-counter dosages, and deemed him competent.

Portia looked up and scowled fiercely as a red Mazda pulled out in front of her, top down and speakers thumping.

"Hey! Use the fast lane, why don't you?" she yelled. The driver waved cheerily over his shoulder and sped out of sight.

"Asshole," she cursed under her breath, though whether to the driver or the signature on the report was uncertain. She read on, gnawing her lip thoughtfully. Keene had done the initial workup then. Terrific. In terms of Wier's actual psychological condition, that could mean just about anything.

As a state employee for the prison system, Dr. Jonathan Keene had long ago stopped doing anything more than going through the motions of his job. Portia had come up against him more than once over the years, and knew for a fact that his signature on an initial evaluation like this one might mean Jimmy Wier was as sane as a Sunday school teacher or as crazy as they come. Keene wouldn't know because he wouldn't have cared to know. He was a well-paid paper pusher, and that was all.

So there was no telling Wier's real mental condition during the arrest and arraignment proceedings, especially considering the Benadryl. Prison psychiatrists like Keene routinely prescribed the allergy medication for their charges for everything from insomnia to full-blown paranoid delusions. It was cheap and, taken in huge amounts like those prescribed for Wier and other inmates, it kept them sleepy enough to be docile. It did nothing for their psychological problems, of course, save to mask a few symptoms, but on the other hand, prison officials liked nothing better than a docile inmate population.

In any event, any real information about Wier's psychological condition just after the murders was probably lost forever. If someone had just gotten to him in time, before he shut down, it might have made a difference, Portia reflected. If a diagnosis had been attempted, she would have had something to go on, a starting point. Even if it was wrong.

She knew from experience that all the passions look alike—love and hate, fear and rage, envy and helpless need—they all resemble each other, especially when a person can't tell for himself what he feels. But if someone had cared enough they might have been able to reach in and pull Jimmy Wier back from the place he'd gone to escape what he'd done. From what Dec had told her, Wier's current condition was more than a simple refusal to cooperate; she'd seen it too many times before. It was more than likely Wier had withdrawn to that place in the mind where George Warren was now, mumbling his endless prayers—a prison stronger than anything built of metal and brick. And faced with the enormity of what he had done, there was no telling when, or if, he would ever get free again. Maybe Yarborough could have helped, but Yarborough had been frightened. Frightened enough to quit. If Jimmy could still scare the dickens out of a rookie psychologist, maybe he was reachable.

Or maybe, she thought without meaning to, he's dangerous as hell.

Portia glanced out the window as the gentle hills of the Piedmont began to give way to sandy flatlands. God's country—she thought ruefully—the Bible belt. And not for the first time, her agnostic's heart wondered if God wasn't just a little disappointed by all the things that went on down here.

Taking the next exit south, she thumbed through the rest of the file, trying to piece together a preliminary impression of Wier's case.

The two-part trial system was used in nearly every state that had the death penalty. The first part of the trial determined guilt or innocence according to the law. Wier was charged with a total of three counts of murder, all elderly women, the two in Dixon and one older case involving a rural woman who matched his so-called pattern. Each had been killed, mutilated, and sexually violated, in that order. Blood found on Wier's clothes matched that of the two Dixon victims, Lila Mooney and Constance Bennet, and he was also found in possession of some jewelry and an African violet plant that had been taken from Mrs. Mooney's home, though he claimed to have no idea how he got those things. Subsequent DNA matches of tissue, blood, and semen found at the scene all but proved him the killer.

The second part of the trial, the sentencing phase, was when the jury got to hear testimony that sought to establish mitigating circumstances surrounding the crimes—evidence such as she might offer that spoke to a criminal's mental state, motives, and background, all of which might affect a jury's decision on the sentencing.

Or at least, she reminded herself ruefully, that was the optimistic view. Portia smiled grimly at the windshield-tinted landscape. The fact was, she had been through the process too often to be optimistic. But even though she'd promised to quit forensics a hundred times since coming to it, she always went back. Dec knew it, Lori knew it—maybe everybody knew she couldn't quit. Maybe it was the need to help and maybe it was something darker—some part of her that had grown used to the terror and the violence of murder and murderers and was drawn back to it again and again like some terrible narcotic. She needed to learn from it, of that she was aware. But she didn't always know what.

And now, rolling down the highway with Jimmy Wier's case file spread out over the seat, she knew she had to try again to discover what had gone on in that mind and to put those findings before a jury. Dec had been right. Without a strong presentation of mitigating circumstances, Wier would fry for sure. Even though the trial hadn't yet begun, the chances of his being found innocent were terribly slim, given the evidence. The insanity plea was all the defense they had, and in South Carolina, it wasn't much. That left the sentencing phase, where she came in.

She shuddered involuntarily, images swimming up in her mind. The severed nipple placed so carefully in the center of the old woman's chest, the expression on her face. What was it about dying, Portia wondered, that made so many of them look surprised?

According to the reports, Jimmy Wier had been seen regularly by state psychiatric personnel throughout the course of his initial evaluation. The strange part was, no one seemed to have put the pieces together.

Portia searched the folders remaining at her elbow for the pertinent psychiatric reports. At first, he was reported to have no memory of the crimes themselves, though one report noted that Wier had admitted to a ward nurse that he could see "pictures in his head" of some of the women's corpses. Nevertheless, he still experienced complete dissociation from having committed the actual murders. In an interview with a social worker, he'd spoken of having "seen some things at Mrs. Mooney's," implying his presence at the scene. Of Constance Bennet, the second victim, he apparently remembered nothing, and there was no mention at all of the third homicide. No confession, nothing.

But the "pictures in his head," along with the blood and tissue samples, would be enough to convict. Portia flipped through page after page, deep in thought, looking for something—anything—that would give her a place to begin.

She frowned out over the road. What was it Dec had said? That Royal was going for the chair because Wier was white? That meant something.

She scanned the documents for a physical description. There it was: male Caucasian, blond, blue eyes, six feet four inches, two hundred and fifty pounds. A big guy, then. Really big. Tall, blond, and heavily muscled. Or fat.

Well, she thought. At least tall and blond were good. But fat was bad. Jurors tended to think fat people had a problem with self-control. She swung the Volvo onto the exit ramp that would carry her over the state line into South Carolina, plucking through the file, struggling to recall if she might have seen a picture in the papers or on the local news. There was no photo of the man himself. Still, how Wier looked could mean the difference between living and dying.

She glanced again at the pages, trying to put a face to all the facts and statistics.

"Well, Jimmy," she said aloud. "I hope for your sake you look to be as crazy as you are."

That, all by itself, could save his life. Jurors felt sorry for a crazy-looking man, especially if he was white. Sorry enough, anyway, to give him life in prison over the death penalty. But there was no calling this one, Portia knew, especially with Donny Royal and his senatorial ambitions at stake. Unless the defense team worked fast and well, the prosecutor would probably succeed in winning the death penalty for Wier, and tie himself up a senate nomination too. Son of a bitch. That Jimmy Wier wouldn't be executed until his appeals were exhausted didn't mean all that much to a man like Donny Royal. He knew that public opinion could be capricious, and he knew the votes would come his way as a law and order candidate. Up until recently, the appeals process could add as much as fifteen years to the life of a man on death row. Now, nobody could be sure. Too many variables came into play—the mood of the public, the belt tightening of the legislature, the harebrained cheerleading going on in Washington as politicians sought to exploit voter fear and unclog the overburdened court system. Appeals of a death sentence could go on for years. Or they could be cut very short, very soon. Portia herself could be certain of only one thing— Donny Royal would throw the switch himself if it meant a senatorial nomination. And he'd smile and sign autographs while he was doing it.

She flipped through more, even less enlightening reports, searching for anything that might give her a clue to Jimmy Wier.

"The prisoner appears increasingly dissociative," one intern had noted, less than three weeks after his arrest. By July, a new psychiatric nurse on the ward had *"informed officials of the subject's complaining of hearing voices"* and *"engaging in bizarre repetitive finger and hand movements."* Still another notation from a staff physician Wier had seen recently for a stomach ailment said Wier *"worked his lips throughout the interview."* He had recommended Mellaril, an antipsychotic, which appeared to have alleviated Wier's symptoms, at least temporarily.

During the last weeks of August, Dr. Keene had evaluated Wier again in preparation for his trial, deemed him once again competent, and increased his Benadryl prescription. He was now taking almost nine times the normal over-the-counter amount.

Portia closed the folder, silently wishing the good Dr. Keene transported to the farthest reaches of hell. To call a man like Keene corrupt was almost beside the point—to call him an incompetent psychiatrist even more so. Keene's so-called reports were almost always the same. Yet he was so deeply entrenched in the state's network of good old boy politicians, lawmakers, and state specialists, she knew in advance that to call his findings into question would never do any good. She could only hope to discredit Keene's reports with better, more cohesive, more intelligent work. Extensive psychological testing, interviews, testimony, maybe months of work would be needed to discover the real nature and extent of Jimmy Wier's psychoses. She had the talent, the dedication, and even, in some circles, the power. What she didn't have was time.

She glanced again at the thick collection of folders. There was more, much more, but first she had to think. Whatever was going on with Jimmy the Weird, it was clear even from what she'd read that he was deteriorating—fast. But it was almost impossible to identify his principal disorder; it could be any number of things; schizophrenia, paranoia, bipolar disorder, fixation, not to mention the probability of a sexual quirk or two.

She frowned through the tinted windshield, thinking hard. It was now September and she had a little more than a month before the trial was due to begin, maybe eight weeks at the outside before the sentencing phase.

She snapped on the radio to give herself some sound to concentrate against, and was met with a public service ad from the local sheriff's office on how they "didn't truck with drugs in Hicksburg County." She snapped it off again.

"Just another example of your taxpayer dollars at work, folks. They're prescribing Benadryl for schizophrenics! What's next? Alka-Seltzer for sex offenders?"

The turn to Columbia was right where Lori's directions had promised it would be, and Portia swung the car onto the ramp. Just ten miles to go. Dylan was right, of course, he nearly always was. She would take this case. But it was not because Jimmy Wier had been given short shrift in prison or the county hospital, or because the forces were already in place to see that he died for his crimes. In the end, it was not because she felt anything like horror or pity looking at the bloodied bodies in the police photos, or even because she wanted the chance to bust Donny Royal's butt in court.

The flat red brick of the prison compound rose up out of nowhere, looking like some odd farming community somewhere on the moon. She swung the Volvo through an unimposing main gate and down the narrow roads dotted with parking areas. Each building announced its purpose with a small solitary sign, and Portia drove a little uncertainly, squinting in the glassy afternoon light—Mental Health, women's prison, and there on the left, the men's, the largest of the buildings. Farther down the road stood what she presumed to be the death row building, and last the tiny death house at the end, smaller than the rest, and set well apart.

Electrified fence and curls of razor wire surrounded each building, but except for that the buildings in this compound might have been anything—erected for any vague government purpose, anywhere in suburbia, each one of them square and anonymous and ugly as sin.

Portia swung the car into the parking lot near the Visitor's Center, ignoring the sudden irregular thumping of her heart. It didn't matter how many times she'd made this trip or others like it—coming to prison always felt the same. She slipped on a pair of tortoise-framed sunglasses and grabbed a shapeless linen jacket from the backseat to wear over her flattering green silk dress. In another instant, she pulled her hair into a demure knot at the back of her neck, and grabbed the file from the front seat, pausing for only another second as she glanced at the page on top of the pile.

In the end, she smiled as she headed up the well-trimmed walk, the grass frying brown in the Carolina sun. A few scraggly flowers tried to flourish in a tired window box outside the Visitor's Center, and she smiled again when she saw them.

She was still smiling as she presented her credentials to the gray-haired guard at the Visitor's Center. She turned over her keys and briefcase and emerged again into the light, her eyes unreadable behind the glasses. In the end, she could ignore the uneasy feeling she got seeing the dark silhouette of the guard stationed in the watchtower, and the feeling of the other guards' eyes upon her as she made her way to the next security checkpoint.

For in the end, Dr. Portia McTeague was looking forward to her first meeting with the killer they called Jimmy the Weird. Not because of what he had done, or what had been done or might be done to him inside a faulty system. Even though it was certain he had killed, and was sick enough to warrant her attention, those things alone were not sufficient to force her decision to take on his case. Not even Dec could make her do that.

Instead, it had been decided by something entirely different, something another doctor or lawyer might have missed. She wanted to meet Jimmy Wier, to take his case for the same reason she had taken on all the other cases of her career—he interested her. Inside all the twisted workings of a mind and soul that drove him to do what he had done was something she wanted—somehow needed to know.

In the end, just one thing had made up her mind.

She wanted to ask him about the African violet.

Five

• •

S HE PRESENTED her credentials at the final security
checkpoint, sliding her identification into a metal box fit-
ted into a slot in the cinder-block wall. The guard on duty, obscured
by the dark-tinted glass of a small window, did not acknowledge her
except to note that her face was the same as the one pictured on her
driver's license. He motioned to a metal door on the left and she
passed through into a small chamber that held only another set of
doors, which in turn opened on a tiny elevator. The doors slid silently
apart and she entered. The elevator itself had no controls, no indicator
lights; the guard ran it from a panel at his station.

Portia's shoulders tensed and her breath came a little faster. She felt
an all-too-familiar tightening in her chest as the elevator began its
ascent. Her claustrophobia had been long ago traced to its origins in
therapy, but knowing where your phobias come from wasn't always
the same as knowing how to make them go away. Her palms wet, she
drew a deep, cleansing breath. She could handle it, but there was still
the uncertainty, the niggling fear that her brief moments in confined
spaces wouldn't end before her measure of control ran out.

The doors slid soundlessly open on a corridor, dim in the forty-watt
illumination that characterized the prisons of America. The state press
releases assured voters that it was economical and energy-efficient and
that low light had a tranquilizing effect on a restless inmate population; what it was was cheap, and more than a little depressing. An
exhausted-looking woman pushing a baby stroller made her way past

Portia in the hall. Portia smiled and the woman turned her head away, her eyes downcast.

Another benefit of suicide lighting, the psychologist thought disgustedly. Even the visitors got to feel they were being punished. Midway down the corridor, she tapped sharply at the window glass of yet another guard station.

"Excuse me? I think the guard downstairs made a mistake. I'm Dr. McTeague. I have an evaluation scheduled for James Wier."

The guard gave her a lazy appraisal with a slow, conspiratorial wink at the end of it. The lady doctor was good-looking in a bitchy sort of way. "So?" he asked.

She set her mouth in a stiff smile and her eyes betrayed nothing of her impatience. "So," she answered slowly, "I always try to evaluate in a conference room."

The guard thumbed through his appointment listings. "Not according to this here," he said. "This here says you meet Wier down the hall. Fourth door to your right. Only primary counsel gets a conference room."

"The attorney's office was supposed to request—"

The guard shrugged. "I don't know what's supposed to be, ma'am. I only know what is. Warden's got Wier in max, and that means no private conferences."

"But I can't do an evaluation with half the guards on the block standing around!"

The man behind the window was unmoved. "It's all the same to me, ma'am," he answered. "I reckon you can take it or you can leave it." He snickered a little. "Hell, old Jimmy won't care anyways. Not the way he's playin' possum. Playing crazy, I mean. Now, if you want my opinion—"

"Thanks," snapped Portia, swallowing the hot retort that bubbled up in her throat, and feeling her color rise. "Thanks anyway." It didn't matter if every guard on the block felt free to offer a diagnosis; she had no choice but to play along. The fact was, she was completely dependent upon these guards for access to the prisoner—any prisoner. One word from the man behind the desk, and she wouldn't get to see Jimmy at all. So she turned on her heel and made her way down the bleak stretch of corridor. The game of negotiating prison regulations had rules. The first of them was that the warden and guards could change the rules whenever and why ever they pleased. Arguing with the moron at the end of the hall would only have wasted valuable time. She'd let Dec fight it out with the warden, for her next visit. For today, she'd have to make do.

The fourth door was open and she found herself in a closetlike booth, the window in the door affording the only view of the poorly lit corridor. She sized up the arrangements in one instant; the tiny room was halved by a Plexiglas and wire partition over a narrow countertop; both were old and scarred, with only a smattering of tiny holes in the Plexiglas to serve as a speaker opening. She glanced around again—no panic buttons—and somewhat reluctantly slid into a molded plastic chair on her side of the chamber. She set the yellow legal notepad on the narrow ridge of chipped Formica that served as a countertop and tapped a number two lead pencil lightly against the edge, waiting for them to bring in Jimmy the Weird from the other side. In the hallway behind her, guards patrolled idly, pretending not to notice she was there. The sight of a woman was rare enough on the block; the sight of a good-looking one rarer still. Their covert glances through the window at the back of her head made her feel like a zoo specimen.

It was several more minutes before they brought him. She twisted in her chair at a rhythmic metallic clanking in the corridor, holding her breath as the bulk of him filled the small chamber. Shackled hand and foot, Jimmy Wier was a huge man, yet he looked somehow boneless and defeated in his ill-fitting prison jumpsuit. Portia studied him carefully. He might have been anywhere from twenty-five to forty. His fair hair was oily and unkempt. His huge hands dwarfed the circles of steel around his wrists, and she shifted a little in the chair. What was it the guard had said—that he was playing possum? Despite herself, she felt a tickle of fear in the small of her back.

The big man's head was bowed low, his eyes fixed on the floor. She caught the scent of masculine sweat and prison laundry hanging in the stale air. For the second time that day, Portia had to struggle with a dizzying little rush of claustrophobia.

As his escort secured him behind the partition, Wier began to shuffle back and forth on his side of the room, never looking at her, the shackles making an eerie sound as the chains dragged over the linoleum. Portia studied him in silence for a few moments. They hadn't been kidding when they said he was nonresponsive. His affect was totally flat, the soft lines of his profile without animation.

Then, without warning, he raised his head and looked at her. And the eyes that met her own held an expression that sent flocks of panicky butterflies swirling through her innards. For one long, indescribable moment she felt the rest of the world falling away. For the prisoner's eyes held nothing of fear or hatred or hostility at her presence—all of those things she might have expected, even prepared for. Instead she found herself looking into twin voids—blue and empty as a whole wilderness of sky. They were eyes that held nothing, no spark of recognition, no flicker to betray the fact that he was seeing her, or the room, or anything at all. It seemed almost like blindness, but the lock of his eyes on her own was unmistakable, viselike and inescapable. And she could not look away. He'd caught her like a rabbit with a single look; something in that vacuum sucking her down into a vast emptiness as she searched in vain for a spark of life or thought or humanity, the eyes daring her to turn, daring her to blink. She did not even think to be afraid. For the madness in Jimmy Wier's eyes was huge and hypnotic and insanely seductive, beckoning her into a bottomless, jibbering chaos where nothing mattered anymore. Not good nor evil nor guilt nor innocence nor death. Everything was equal in those eyes. Everything was free.

And at last, almost without meaning to, she glanced away, catching some movement by the guard outside the window in her peripheral vision. The game was ended, the spell broken.

She drew a ragged breath and steadied herself. If the eyes were truly the windows of the soul, then Wier's were looking out from a rare and special kind of hell.

She wet her lips and reached for something to say, aware suddenly of the sound of her own heartbeat, the whisper of papers on the countertop.

"Mr. Wier," she began in a measured tone, raising her voice a little to make herself heard through the window. "You like violets?"

The huge head twitched, as though listening to some unseen instruction. He did not look at her, though, and that relieved her a little.

"Do you know who I am—what I'm doing here?" she began again.

For all he noticed, or was pretending not to notice her, the man might have been alone in the room. Still shaken, she struggled to regain his attention, to make some relevant contact. The first few minutes were important. If she didn't break through in the first few minutes, it might never happen. Portia tapped her pencil against the edge of the counter, the sound unnaturally loud in the cramped quarters. Still nothing.

"Do you know why you're here?" she went on. Sometimes they didn't. Trapped in some internal world, the changes in the details of the outer world failed to register. Oftentimes the psychosis was such that a criminal had no memory at all of how he'd come to prison—nor any notion of where he was.

Now, though, there was the barest moment of hesitation before the shuffling resumed. So brief she might have missed it if she'd blinked. But he had paused—he'd heard her, anyway. Something had registered. That meant a lot.

Slowly, the psychologist got to her feet and leaned toward the Plexiglas shield that separated them. She placed her hands, palms flat, against it. "They sure have you locked up tight," she offered.

A guard immediately came to the window at her back, but sensing his presence, she turned and waved him off.

"I'm a doctor, Mr. Wier," she went on, leaning casually against the counter while keeping her tone low and musical. McTeague's voice was one of her best professional assets. She knew it and she used it well. An internship on a buzzing suicide hotline had forged its low, soothing tones, full of reassurance and peace.

"Your lawyers asked me to come over here and talk to you a little bit."

Miraculously, Wier nodded slowly without looking at anything.

Yes! she thought with a little rush of elation. Good start. "People are saying you did some pretty terrible things. Do you know that, Mr. Wier? Jimmy? Can I call you Jimmy?"

Wier resumed his pacing, unable—or unwilling—to respond.

Portia sank easily down into her chair, careful to make no sudden moves. "Okay," she went on soothingly. "I'll call you Mr. Wier for a while.

"They say you killed three women. You know about that?"

Wier cast her a furtive glance as he paced. Portia relaxed a little. It wasn't much, but it was a whole lot better than nothing. She struggled to fan the tiny flame of acknowledgment.

"You're in deep shit, Jimmy Wier." She paused, allowing the statement to sink in. "You know that?"

Abruptly, Wier paused in his shuffling and looked at her. Once again straight in the eye, daring her to fall back into that weird bottomless void. Portia felt an unexpected chill. Jimmy Wier might be nuts, but not so nuts that he didn't know his power.

"This is a bad place," he whispered. The voice was low and strange and rumbling. "Why would you come here?" He paused and gazed upward, momentarily entranced by some invisible spot on the ceiling. "That other one went away. I made her. I always make them go away." He slowly lifted his huge hands as far as the shackles allowed and began to mime a choking motion. Then he smiled.

Portia took a breath and countered the gesture with a smile of her own. "I don't think I'm going to go away," she said matter-of-factly. "You know why? Because I might be able to help you. I might be able to help people understand how you got into this trouble you're in. But you have to help me first. You need to talk to me a little. You think you can do that?"

He fixed his strange stare at some space just above her hair, his head utterly still, cocked slightly to the side as though he were listening to something far away. Then, all at once, the expression in his eyes changed, like a light going on somewhere, and Wier began to make a low humming sound, big lips moving in a gray, doughy face.

"Will you talk to me, Jimmy?" Portia leaned closer to the glass but he backed away, so she withdrew, easily resuming her place. "Your lawyers told me you wanted to talk to a woman. You said that? Remember? Remember Dr. Yarborough?"

Unexpectedly, Wier uttered a high-pitched, evil-sounding snicker and in that instant Portia silently took back any uncharitable thoughts she might have harbored about Deb Yarborough. This one was enough to send anybody back into research.

In the next moment, the eerie laughter ceased as suddenly as it had begun. Wier leaned closer, his blue eyes mad and bright behind the Plexiglas shield.

"Women know the truth," he offered in a low voice. "They always know the truth."

Portia noted the statement on her pad without looking down, her hand moving rapidly over the paper. She gave an encouraging nod. "Why do you say that, Jimmy?" she asked.

Wier shook his huge head from side to side as if amazed by the question. "They always get it out of you," he went on, as if it were somehow obvious. "No matter what. That's why they know it. 'Cause they take it away from you and keep all the truth for themselves so you have to ask them for everything. Everything. It's how they keep you," he finished, his voice dropping to a conspiratorial whisper. "They steal the truth and keep it in their panties."

Portia wrote carefully, enclosing the notation in neat quotation marks. Then, in the margin, she placed a single exclamation point.

"Is that what happened with those ladies, Mr. Wier?" she responded, trying again to meet his eyes. "They stole the truth? Did you think you could get it back by hurting them?"

Jimmy paused, frowning, then resumed his shuffling pace. "They keep telling me things. They say I did things, but the truth got stolen, so how should I know? It's gone, now. All used up."

The psychologist maintained a calm, open expression while inwardly her thoughts were racing. Even as she watched him, Wier seemed almost to shrink under her gaze, the glimmer of interaction retreating once again under a flat affect—the low atonal humming that might have been a song. She observed him in silence for another few moments, listing the tests she was going to need in order to be able to rule out physical causes for his condition. She made another note to ask Dec whether there was any money left for an evaluation by a neuropsychologist. That look in his eyes might be a head injury or a tumor. At any rate, she had to rule out the physical causes first. She included a note for a CAT scan and an MRI series. And she'd have to send somebody in to do the standard tests, too. Clearly, Deb Yarborough had missed a few things.

When she glanced up again, Wier was obsessively picking at a place on the back of his hand, trying to open the scab on a skinned knuckle. "Mr. Wier?" she asked. "Jimmy? Can you hear me?"

Nothing save the humming that went on and on. Portia never took her eyes off him as she scribbled hasty notes. The file stated Wier was a longtime drifter. That meant she was going to have a hell of a time tracing records and corroborative sources. Still, there was always a chance. Whatever was going on with Jimmy Wier, she could be reasonably certain it had been going on for a very long time. And maybe, somewhere, there had been other victims.

The odd humming rose suddenly in pitch, making for a kind of sigh that seemed to come from everywhere at once. He wanted her attention, she thought, he wanted it back.

"Jimmy," she continued, as if there had been no break in their conversation. "Let's talk some more about those women. Do you remember, Jimmy? You remember what happened at Miss Mooney's?"

The prisoner's expression grew troubled. "Poor ladies," he said, then, in the next instant, managed an odd smile. "It was an accident, I bet. They die so easy—women I mean. You wouldn't believe it." He flexed his hands again, fingers moving inside the steel cuffs.

"The police think somebody wanted them to die on purpose," Portia responded.

Wier slowly shook his head, as though she had spoken of something impossible to imagine. "I think you ought to be going now," he announced abruptly. He heaved his bulk toward the partition, so close she could smell his breath, see the fog of it form and evaporate again against the plastic. His voice trembled with secret excitement. "Terrible people live in here."

Portia steadied an unruly thumping of her heart. Stay with it, she told herself. Stay with him. "Jimmy," she said evenly. "What does it feel like when I ask you questions? What's it like?"

The question seemed to bring him up short. He leaned back, working his mouth in a supreme effort. When he spoke again, his tone was utterly changed—odd and exaggerated and falsely bright.

"That's a beautiful dress," he said. "Why in the world would you cover it up with that jacket? They don't go together at all."

Portia stared at him, momentarily distracted. "Uhmm. Thanks," she answered, and made a quick notation. His affect had changed so quickly, it was like throwing a switch. "But I want to talk about you, Jimmy. Why did you suddenly notice my dress? Was it because I was asking too many questions?"

Wier did not reply, only turned to look at the guards slowly patrolling the corridor outside the window. "Can they see us?" he asked in the same bright voice. "I can see everyone, but I never really know if they can see me."

"They can see us," the psychologist answered. "Same way we can see them."

With that, the huge prisoner continued his restless shuffling, head bent, the slow clinking of his shackles punctuating the silence. He continued to work the scab, wincing a little.

"What made you notice my dress, Jimmy?" she insisted. "Jimmy? Mr. Wier?"

He glanced up vacantly as she called him by name. "I don't remember," he replied, and stared at her. "I don't remember anything at all." With that, he gave an enormous yawn.

Fighting to maintain contact, Portia kept talking. "Can you sleep much in here? A lot of people I talk to say they can't sleep in jail because it's so noisy." She flipped a page of the legal pad, trying to regain his faltering attention. But his eyes were again fixed on his knuckle, worrying it raw.

"You know you're in jail, don't you, Jimmy?"

The scab was free now; she could see the bright spot of fresh blood on his knuckle. He flexed the fingers, watching, fascinated, as the spot grew larger.

"They came and bit me the other day," he told her. The high notes were gone, replaced by a distant monotone.

She leaned forward, bewildered. "Who bit you, Jimmy? Is that what happened to your hand?"

The prisoner smiled distantly. "Oh, it was a vampire, I think. In a white hat . . ." He paused, frowning. "But maybe I shouldn't be telling you that." He froze then, his mouth clamped down in a line. Only the hands kept moving, frantically clenching and unclenching inside the cuffs.

McTeague wanted to reach through the Plexiglas and shake him—anything to keep him talking. She'd discovered practically nothing. And she was running out of time. Desperately, she tried to get the dialogue going again—disjointed as it was. "You can tell me anything you want, you know that? Anything."

All at once a thick hand gripped the edge of the table and Wier slid his huge frame into a chair. Slowly, Portia stretched her hand toward the partition between them and let it rest there with her palm against the plastic. Unable to meet her eyes, Jimmy sat slumped, his head bowed in resignation.

"Don't be afraid, Jimmy, okay?" Her voice was low and urgent. "If you talk to me I can help you. Me and your lawyers. You remember, Jimmy? You remember your lawyer? Mr. uhh—?" For one frantic moment, the name of Wier's court-appointed attorney was a blank. Then it came to her. "Evans," she hurried on. "You know Mr. Evans?"

At the name, he raised his head and looked at her, an odd smile playing around his mouth. "He wants to fuck me," he whispered. "They all want to fuck me."

Portia wanted to scream with frustration. Dave Evans was a small, harried, fiftyish attorney with four kids in college, and a list of good works so long that Dec frequently referred to him as a saint-in-waiting. She shook her head slightly; it was already clear that Jimmy Wier could toss out delusions like beads from a Mardi Gras float.

Thwap! She jumped as a huge beefy hand slapped against the partition and slid down the plastic, sending her halfway out of her chair.

Wier grinned wildly, trying to touch her, smearing the partition with blood and slapping his thick, sausage-like fingers against the tiny air holes.

She drew back instinctively as the prisoner leaned closer, his terrible eyes shining with anticipation, as though they were about to share some unimaginable secret. Then, as she watched openmouthed, he began to slowly lick away at the trail of blood, leaving behind a disgusting sheen of slick saliva.

"Blood," he mumbled in a low singsong. "Blood can make you sick and die. From AIDS. You'd better be careful, girlie. This is a bad place."

She watched, paralyzed, as in the next mad instant Jimmy Wier went somewhere deep inside himself, those terrible eyes gone abruptly blank and expressionless, jaw slackening as he dissociated, falling back awkwardly in his chair.

Portia began to breathe again, her mind struggling to absorb what she'd just witnessed as the prisoner sat motionless, gazing at nothing. Dissociation. It was a good trick, she knew—one she'd seen many times before. The mind shutting itself off from too many questions, from the possibility of any more pain. Yet, the change had been so fast—so complete. The minutes ticked by as she sat there, feeling the thumping of her own heart slow down to something resembling normal. Wherever he'd gone, it didn't appear he'd be coming back any time soon.

She rose unsteadily, convinced that her interview had come to an end, and began to gather her notes. Relief made her legs rubbery as she realized just how frightened she'd actually been.

And at that moment, Jimmy the Weird spoke once more.

"You go to jail for being bad," he said. "They lock you up and throw away the key."

Portia made herself speak, her mouth dry. "Is that how you got here? Did you do something bad?"

But Wier only slumped in his chair, his face expressionless, like some huge, unfinished statue.

"Jimmy?" Portia said softly. "Are you still with me, Jimmy?"

He blinked and stirred a little. "Oh," he answered, "I come and I go."

The sudden closeness of the tiny chamber bore down on her and she had to fight with herself not to bang on the door and begin yelling for the guard. There were still a few seconds left—a minute, maybe two. She could last that long. She would make herself last. "Is that right? How does that feel?"

He moved his hands, staring at the opened scab as though he'd never seen it before. "I don't know," he admitted. "It feels like—nothing. Most things feel like nothing."

She leaned forward, trying to close the distance between them. "Has it always been like that?"

"Oh no," he assured her. "You have to do something an awful lot before it feels like nothing." He focused on her, confused. "I can't say any more. I thought I told you. I don't remember."

His huge moonlike face again betrayed the ghost of a smile, and she had to fight the uneasy sensation that he was playing with her, moving from menace to befuddled confusion with frightening speed.

"I got a hole in my head," he whispered. Wier reached up and shook his finger, putting on a mock frown. "You got a hole in your head, boy," he mimicked, and again Portia felt a chill.

"Who told you that, Jimmy?" she asked, grasping at the straw. "Was it your mama? Somebody like that?"

The answer came coldly, distantly back, finding its way through the thin shield of Plexiglas to strike a place deep inside her. A place so guarded, so carefully covered in scars, she wouldn't have thought it possible to hurt there anymore.

"Anybody could have been my mama, girlie." He stopped and fixed her with those mad blue eyes. "Even you."

With that, they both drew away from the partition as if by some unspoken agreement. "You have to go now. Your time is up." Wier looked at her and flashed an odd, meaningless smile. "I know all about time. Everything. I know just how long time is. Always. And yours is up."

Portia stared at him for a last long moment, frustration and bewilderment and something like amazement all vying for a place in her thoughts. She wanted more—something more than this to go on.

At her back, a guard tapped lightly on the windowpane, signaling the end of her interview.

"You're right, Jimmy," she told him gently. "I do have to go now. But we'll see each other again. All right? I'm going to come back here. Soon—so remember me. My name is Portia. Portia McTeague."

He glanced back at her over his shoulder as a guard led him away. "Oh," he said, softly. "Don't worry. I'll remember."

Her eye caught a bright drop of blood glistening on the counter.

"Hey!" She turned and called after the guard and his charge. "Get him a Band-Aid, will you? He hurt his hand."

She watched, frowning, as they made their slow way back to the cell block.

Suddenly exhausted, Portia gathered up her notepad, anxious to get free of the oppressive atmosphere. She headed to the security check-point at the end of the corridor, her mind restlessly running through the fragments of thoughts and impressions she'd managed to gain from her all-too-brief interview with Jimmy the Weird.

At the end of the hall, the guard's grin was broad and sly. "Ole Jimmy's a piece of work, ain't he? Professionally speakin', I mean. So what'd you think? He tryin' to fake us out?" He fixed her with such an expectant expression that she had to fight a sudden urge to giggle. The day had been long, her encounter with Wier so harrowing that a good belly laugh might have provided a wonderful avenue for release. Inappropriate yes, but wonderful anyway. She slid the register back to him and gave him a long look.

"Sorry," she told him. "I'm not allowed to talk about it." She flashed him a smile and headed toward the elevator.

When she emerged again into the open air, she paused and drew deep gulps of it into her lungs, treasuring the sensation of freedom. She headed hurriedly toward her car, anxious to get behind the wheel and put some miles between her and Jimmy the Weird. Most of all, she wanted to get home. She needed to see Alice—needed to hold her and feel the strength of those small skinny arms around her waist, clinging as if she'd never let go.

As she turned the key in the ignition, she glanced back toward the sad brick compound, wondering at the mystery of the huge crazy man they called Jimmy the Weird. That he was crazy was obvious—the question was why. She drove through the main gate, with conflicting impressions and theories crowding her thoughts. The mystery of it worked on her like a drug—examining the possibilities, all the reasons why and how a personality could warp and twist itself into the strange monstrous man Jimmy Wier had managed to become.

Portia's green eyes shone with excitement underneath a frown of concentration as she glanced in the rearview mirror and took the ramp onto the interstate. Mentally, she made an inventory of the things she had gleaned from the afternoon's session. The eyes, the dissociative episode, the way he'd flipped from a totally flat affect and back again with dizzying speed. Though it was still too soon for any kind of real diagnosis, she tried to fit the things she'd read in the file together with the puzzle pieces of impression she'd gained from the man.

She blinked back the sudden vivid image of his tongue against the blood on the Plexiglas. Clinical distance notwithstanding, Jimmy the Weird could be one scary schizoid son of a bitch. So many explanations were possible—family history, genetics, sexual abuse—the list went on and on. She glanced at the pile of folders and wondered. Even Keene's judgment of competency began to become clear—Wier knew who he was and where he was. On some level, she was certain, Jimmy Wier even knew what he'd done. But none of that came together as an explanation for the crime.

And all the way home she wondered what horrors locked in Jimmy's past might have turned that mind in on itself, twisting and adapting and warping to the level of personality damage she'd seen that afternoon. She wondered what had caused the terrible blood-thirsty rage that found its way out of him on the afternoon of the murders, and wondered too if he would ever be cogent enough or trusting enough, or even if he would remember enough, to help them both find the answers before Donny Royal pushed his trial through to a death sentence.

But most of all, as she swung the Volvo off the highway heading toward the old Dilworth neighborhood in Charlotte where Alice would be waiting at Aggie's and demanding to know where she'd been—most of all Portia wondered, with a stab of regret so intense it brought sudden tears to her eyes, how he had found that place within her where so many of her own ghosts lay hidden. She wondered how he could have known to say it—the single thing that would open an old wound so deeply and cleanly, the pain as fresh as if it had never healed.

Most of all, she wondered how he could have known about the baby.

He was back in his cell now, safe again. It was better here, better than in the glass room with the lady in it. She had hungry eyes, that one, hungry to get inside. Talking, talking all the time in that sweet low liquid voice of hers, telling him she was going to help him. There was honey in that voice, or maybe it was booze. The voice could make you drunk and trusting; it could make you say things you'd regret. Voices like that could steal the truth from you like candy from a baby. Sweet honey woman voice, talking so slow.

He held himself against the memory, his great arms wrapped over his chest, pinching his nipples between thumbs and forefingers until his eyes squeezed shut tight in flashes of pain. He turned against the wall as the other voice came rising in his head, commanding him. It got so hard to listen to all the things she said. It got so hard to resist. And he fumbled in his pants and squeezed, feeling himself get harder, stroking himself and listening.

Then there was a sound from somewhere in the block—a howl of pain, laughter. Somebody got it tonight. Snuck up on, pants ripped down, and cheeks spread wide. He knew about that. It felt like nothing. He always wondered why it made them scream. After so many times, it just felt like nothing. You had to keep changing it to make yourself scream.

That was how she wanted it tonight. He'd been listening. He knew. It had to hurt or she wouldn't leave him alone.

No sound now but the last of the guard's footsteps down the hall, fading into the dull, ceaseless roar of the cell block. The sound comforted him; it was like hearing the ocean in a shell. He would be safe here for a while. Safe in the dark.

He caught the dark spot of blood on his knuckle out of the corner of his eye as he masturbated, and he heard the voice coming out of the darkness, hissing at him from the dark corners of his mind.

"Dummy. Did you see her hair? Whores have hair like that, don't they? And whores deserve to die. They want to die, Jimmy boy. Even if they don't say it, they want to die. Bitch doctor. She was too smart for you, wasn't she? Dummy! You and your big disgusting thing. She knew you thought she was pretty. The pretty ones always know, don't they? Even her. Got to take care of this now, don't we? Pretty is as pretty does. You know what happens now, don't you? You know what happens now."

Jimmy stood hypnotized in the center of the floor, his great blue eyes fixed on the slit of Plexiglas in the concrete that served as his window, drawing endless little circles in the air with his cock as he worked to the voice's command.

And Bonnie Jean began to chant, escalating in excitement. "The straw, Jimmy. The one in your pocket. Stick that up your cock and see how it feels."

With trembling fingers, he obeyed, unwrapping a small plastic drinking straw he'd smuggled from the cafeteria at dinner, the cellophane crackling in his shaking hands.

"Like that . . . yes, like that. Stick it in, Jimmy. That's what it feels like. It has to hurt. Please, yes, Jimmy. Harder—yes. I have to make you learn, don't I? I have to see that you don't talk. Rub, Jimmy, squeeze it. It hurts! Oh God, it hurts!"

And somewhere in the darkness, Jimmy screamed.

The big man shook himself awake in a blur of tears, his ravaged penis lying bruised and throbbing in his hand. Bonnie Jean's voice was loud and clear and strong, so strong. Strong enough to drown out everything. The ocean of other noise receded around him until there was nothing anymore but Bonnie Jean, crooning to him in a low voice—satisfied now—sweet and strong in the half darkness, rocking him to sleep.

Jimmy raised a hand to wave at the slit of window. "Bye bye, pretty," he murmured. Then, all at once, he rose in the darkness and moved across the cell like some great cat, lithe and silent and powerful. He fumbled in a box on the shelf, and removed a single glass earring, studded with curled metal leaves and a great glittering stone. He put it on and lay down on his bunk, smiling a little, sliding his bulk sensuously over the rough bedding as though it were made of satin or silk. He pursed his mouth and kissed the darkness, his eyes half-closed as he gazed at the ceiling, his hands roaming easily over his thighs.

He didn't have to worry anymore. Not about the doctor or the guards or those bad, bloody pictures in his head. They would go away now. Now that he'd done what the voice had told him.

Six

●●

THAT NIGHT, after a light supper and what Portia esti-
mated to be the eighteenth run of the Pocahontas
video, she and Alice curled up together in Portia's big bed, an assortment of storybooks scattered around their slippered feet. Alice's tilted,
exotic eyes were already at half-mast, but after the tumult of the day's
events, Portia couldn't help feeling a little selfish, wanting to extend
the sweetness of their few hours together a little longer. Alice yawned
hugely and stretched out, snuggling deeply into Portia's armpit, and
she felt such a flood of emotion at the sight of that dark, perfect
profile that it came near to bringing her to tears. Alice's presence had
completely altered the fabric of what she'd always thought life was
supposed to be. Watching her grow and learn and grasp all those
wonders that adults took so much for granted instilled in Portia a kind
of love she had never before known, never once believed possible—a
love rendered somehow all the more precious because their coming
together was not so much destiny as accident.

"Sing, Mommy," Alice whispered, the last of her resistance to sleep
already ebbing away.

Portia softly stroked her hair. "Which one, honey?" she asked.

"Fox," Alice replied, and closed her eyes.

Portia began to sing, the verses of the old song coming back in fits
and starts from some long-forgotten place in her own childhood
memory.

. . .

"The fox went out on a chilly night. He prayed for the moon to give him light. He'd many a mile to go that night before he reached the town-oh."

Alice turned a little and sighed. "Pokey," she whispered, using their private nickname as she did whenever she was chiding Portia for the measured slowness of her pace. And then, in the next breath, fell fast asleep.

Portia gazed down at her, relishing the rare peace of the moment. Raising Alice had given her so much that was precious, had added so much to her life, that sometimes she could not help fearing it would all be snatched away, that something would happen—some unforeseen catastrophe would overtake the small peaceful family they had made together. The little girl had her share of fear too. Even at six, Alice had ghosts of her own. Her mother, grandmother, the terrible day when they had found her baby sister drowned in the tub and her grandmother face down at the kitchen table—a bullet in her neck. Alice had never seen it, and even now Portia silently blessed whatever or whoever it was that had saved the little girl from witnessing these things that might never have been erased.

Alice's mother had done it, of course. Killed the child and her mother too, caught up in some wildfire of rage and drugs, crazy with depression and poverty and hurt. Portia had evaluated her mental state for the courts prior to her trial. She'd killed the baby because she hadn't wanted to watch it suffer and die; there hadn't been money or health insurance to cover the correction of a congenital heart defect. She'd killed her mother for trying to stop her from doing it, though the cancer in the older woman's belly would have finished her off in a matter of weeks. She'd likely have killed Alice too, if the child hadn't been out trying to scavenge something from the neighboring vegetable gardens for them all to eat. The police had gotten there before Alice, spiriting her off to the juvenile authorities while her mother was taken away to await trial on two counts of first-degree murder.

Portia closed her eyes against the memory, lulled by the rhythm of the child's soft breathing. Even after all this time, more than two years now, it never failed to amaze her. How things could move so slowly when lives were still at stake, how the oceans of paperwork and red tape and government agencies all plodded through their endless forms

and procedures and welfare incentive programs for months and sometimes years while the lives of those who so desperately needed help
were left hanging by a thread. And when the thread simply broke, as it
had with Alice's mother, when it was too late, all those same systems
came together with what seemed like astonishing efficiency, to take
away the criminals and mop up the messes and bury the dead.

She'd gotten a death sentence in the end. But in the end even that
hadn't mattered. For two weeks after her trial was over, Alice's mother
had seen Portia every day while awaiting transfer to the overcrowded
state prison in Raleigh. The only thing she'd asked in those meetings,
those same tilted eyes she'd passed on to her daughter bright with
need, shining from the same bronze skin, was that Portia take Alice in
a formal adoption. There had been no other relatives, no friends. And,
as reluctant as she'd been at the outset, in the end that was exactly
what had happened. Because in the end, there had been nothing else
to do. The day after Portia filed the initial application, Alice's mother
hung herself in the prison laundry. She was twenty years old.

The next morning, with the bright September sun shining through
the curtains, they awoke in almost the same position in which they'd
fallen asleep. Portia chided herself for not having carried Alice to her
own bed. Once established, letting a child sleep in a parent's bed was a
hard habit to break. All the family therapists said so. Yet, as Portia
herself had discovered in the past two years, there was a lot more to
child rearing than could be found in clinical studies. And sometimes,
when the need for the simple comfort of the other's presence was
great, as it had been last night, it seemed only right to let her stay.

Besides, Portia reminded herself ruefully as Alice jumped up from
the rumpled bedclothes and scampered off to the bathroom, it wasn't
as though there was anything or anyone else to occupy her bed these
days.

She shook off the last vestiges of sleep as she fumbled for her worn
Filofax on the nightstand. In fact, she had an appointment this morning to discuss that very aspect of her life. At their previous session,
Sophie had insisted Portia begin to think about the reasons for her
lack of interest in establishing any real relationships with men. And,
running somewhat true to form when it came to her therapist's instructions, Portia had forgotten about it completely.

. . .

Sophie Stransky had her offices in an old Victorian not far from Dilworth, off one of the main arteries that led to downtown Charlotte. The house was huge, comfortable, and agreeably cluttered with relics and mementos from Sophie's travels and explorations of the globe. Feathered dream catchers dangled in the tall bay windows, while two forbidding African fertility masks hung haphazardly on one wall. Hundreds of books spilled in no particular order from floor-to-ceiling bookshelves, and a pretty good Persian Heriz rug covered most of the polished hardwood floor. Rain sticks and drums and gongs abounded; there was a red leather camel saddle embellished with Egyptian brass work in one corner, while in another stood an assortment of modern electronic biofeedback equipment, strangely out of place in this passionately eclectic setting.

Portia settled herself on the rusty velvet of an old wingback and smiled at the diminutive woman perched like a plump brown sparrow behind an antique desk whose mahogany surface was cluttered with pencils and blotters and all manner of papers and publications. Sophie Stransky, a Jungian by training but a self-described humanist by disposition, had a formidable reputation for taking on only those patients she felt she could help. She enjoyed what she did and she did it for love, not money. Independently wealthy, she was as comfortable and expressive as her surroundings might suggest, and Portia silently thanked her stars that during the two years she'd been seeing her, their therapeutic relationship had proved among the most productive she'd ever had. Sophie was intrusive, curious, and demanding—always forcing Portia beyond the surface of her cool, carefully crafted professional exterior to the reality of the woman beneath. She could relax with Sophie, she could trust her. And neither had ever come easily for her.

"So," Dr. Stransky began, the barest trace of a European childhood coloring her inflection. "What's going on—what's happening inside that head of yours this week? Did you do your assignment?" The older woman's black eyes were alive with interest. "Did you think about men?"

Portia could feel the color rise a little in her cheeks. "No," she admitted, feeling a little like a reluctant schoolgirl. "I—got busy. I had a preliminary hearing yesterday."

Sophie nodded. "How did that go?"

Portia shrugged. "It's always so hard to know—to gauge—how any of them go. I tried to give them the facts, that's all." She paused and stared for a moment at her hands before glancing up to meet her therapist's eyes. "But the facts don't make the difference. It makes me wonder why anyone even bothers about the law. There I was, testifying as to the mental condition of a man who's so obviously psychotic—so obviously damaged that he has no awareness at all of what's going on around him—who's deteriorated till he's so far gone there's nothing to do but lock him up in a high-security mental hospital for the rest of his life, and all the prosecution—all anybody wants—is revenge. They want their eye for an eye, his blood for the victim's blood. They don't want the facts, it's all about emotion."

Stransky fixed her with an intense, birdlike stare. "Why are you talking about everyone else? You tell me about the criminal's condition, you tell me about the courts, you tell me about 'them.' I thought we were here to talk about you."

Portia nodded acknowledgment of this gentle reminder. "I just feel so frustrated by it all," she went on. "I've been thinking—had been thinking—of quitting. At least the forensics aspect. The court consultation."

"Quitting? Only because of frustration? At this point in your career as a therapist, I should have thought you understood the value of patience," Sophie responded wryly. "If frustration were grounds for walking away from our responsibilities, tell me, who would work at anything?"

Portia couldn't help smiling. "You're right, of course. You're right. It's more than frustration." She paused, gazing through the window as she sought the appropriate words for the tangle of her emotions.

"So, what are we talking about here? Are you questioning your abilities because you meet a patient who is beyond a psychologist's help? Who is—too crazy to ever get well? Are you questioning testifying on such a man's behalf? Or is it that you question the value of that life?"

Portia stared across the expanse of mahogany that stretched between them. "No, at least I don't think so. I mean, I don't think he can be helped anymore, that's true. At least, not significantly. But I don't think he ought to be executed for being crazy. For being *driven* crazy. I've always believed that. But I have to question why I do it—why I submit myself to the punishment of sitting up there on the stand and giving my testimony over and over in these cases."

"Why do you call it punishment?" Sophie wanted to know.

"Because it is! Some of those prosecutors make it their personal business to make a fool of me. I keep trying to distance myself from it, but—I'm not trying to tell anybody they're not guilty, I'm trying to make them understand what happened to these people! Criminal behavior follows predictable patterns. I try to make people understand that—to understand why. And the courts, the juries—they just don't give a—"

"Shit," Sophie answered firmly. "You think no one gives a shit. And perhaps many of them don't. But in the collective mind, the idea is quite simple. Kill the killers and the killing will stop. The problem will go away. And each of those people in the courtroom won't have to be quite so afraid when they go to sleep at night. They believe, when they vote for execution, that they are doing right, just as you believe you are doing right."

Portia shifted in her chair. "They don't know," she answered. "They haven't seen—"

"A man die in the gas chamber?" Sophie peered hard at her patient as Portia flinched at the indirect reference to Sammy Dean. "Not so long ago a whole nation, a whole world, saw hundreds of thousands die in gas chambers. They watched the newsreels as the bulldozers uncovered mass graves. Many simply refused to believe it; but those who had seen—those who had witnessed, those who had survived—cried out for those responsible to be brought to trial for their crimes. And what happened?"

"Nuremberg."

"And what happened to those who were found guilty under the law?"

"They were executed. A lot of them, anyway." Portia frowned uncertainly.

Sophie leaned back, the soft leather of her chair squeaking softly. "What did the world and the law demand of the Nazis, Portia? Was it justice? Or was it revenge?"

Portia looked at her, a little bewildered. "After the Holocaust, I guess I'm not sure how those two things could have been separated."

"Exactly," Sophie replied. "All anyone knew was that they wanted to be sure such things would never happen again. And now, there are many, many people who don't believe it ever happened at all. None of it. They insist it is simply a myth of history, despite the evidence. Despite the facts. Why do you think that is?"

Portia shook her head. "Ignorance? Denial? I can't honestly say. Maybe it's because they didn't live through those times. They didn't see it with their own eyes."

Sophie smiled sadly. "Because this great tragedy is not personal. You're right. Those juries of yours haven't seen a man die in the gas chamber the way you have. They did not see a tortured boy gunned down in front of their eyes as he tried to give himself up."

Portia leaned into the velvet upholstery, her knuckles white against the curved arm of her chair. Suddenly she hated Sophie a little for reminding her of that long-ago day that had forever changed the path of her life. But Sophie wanted to remind her, she knew. She wanted to make sure Portia never forgot the simple bank robbery, ill-conceived and poorly executed by a nineteen-year-old boy, that had turned into a hostage crisis. Twenty-seven people face down on the floor; she could still feel the coolness of the tile against her cheek. Two shots and the boy's partner was dead, along with a security guard. Two shots and the boy, hysterical with rage and grief, started screaming that he would kill them all. She'd been working the hot lines then, finishing her master's and considering a practice in child psychology.

But all that changed the day at the bank when she heard that screaming rage and felt the terror as a nineteen-year-old kid suddenly found himself in way over his head. And she'd known, better than anyone, just how far he'd go before he let himself drown. So she'd started talking to him—that was all. Not screaming at him, not pleading for her life or anyone else's, but just talking to him, trying to find a place where they could meet and somehow trust each other.

Four hours later, with police and SWAT teams poised around the building in a small army, soon-to-be-psychologist Portia McTeague had persuaded the young man to give himself up. They'd walked to the entrance together, and in the next horrific moment, she'd watched her first real patient fall with a single gaping hole in the center of his forehead as a sharpshooter brought him down. And she knew then that no matter what he'd done, however huge his mistakes, in the end, he was only a kid with a gun, confused and more desperate than he'd ever been in his life. He shouldn't have died for that; no one should have to die for that. And she'd been working in forensics ever since.

"The courts, the juries, do not know the people behind the crimes," Sophie was saying. "But they have seen the police photos, the corpses of the victims, the tortured faces of their families. They want to make sure it doesn't happen again. And in doing that, they believe they are right. It is perfectly natural to want to distance oneself from these horrors."

"So where does that leave me?" Portia made a helpless little gesture with her hands. "I knock myself out to give them the facts, the statistics, and if I'm lucky, a little insight into the reasons why desperate people commit desperate crimes—and in the end, I feel completely ineffective!"

"Let me see if I understand," Sophie interrupted smoothly. "Would you agree that you got into this line of work for personal reasons?"

"Sophie," Portia responded. "Don't play games; you already know that. And I might add, made a point of reminding me of it not two minutes ago."

"Right." Her therapist's eyes drew up in a network of spidery lines at their corners. "And have we not established that many juries respond the way they do because their reasons for doing so are also, ultimately, personal reasons?"

Portia sighed. "Yes."

"And isn't at least part of your perception of your work that it is your job to make a jury understand that criminals are simply people. Damaged people, crazy people, troubled and desperate to be sure, but people after all—subject to the things all people are subject to? Isn't part of your therapeutic approach to make real contact with a person—no matter what they've done?"

Again Portia had to agree. "Sometimes I even succeed. At least where the clients are concerned. But it's futile in the courtroom," she added. "The juries, the prosecutors, even the judges—they don't get it. And I always feel responsible—guilty even—when they don't. It's tearing me apart."

Sophie Stransky faced her with a long, unwavering look. "Perhaps you feel torn because you're trying to get people to understand a person by giving them the opinion of an expert. Perhaps you feel conflict because you're trying to paint a picture of a man that will be as vivid as a police photo of a corpse, and you use only your facts and statistics and opinions to do it."

Portia looked down, and began worrying the edge of a hangnail. It was a long moment before she spoke. "Professionalism," she reflected. "I feel so strongly that I have to really come off as an expert. It's someone's life on the line when I'm up there."

Sophie shot her an intense look. "And if you cope with that sense of responsibility in court by distancing yourself behind a perfect professional facade, you're doing everyone a disservice. Yourself, the patients you are trying to help, and even the jurors. Facts don't decide cases, people do. And they don't always decide on the basis of the facts; they decide with their hearts—those emotions you resent so much. But how can you resent that reality if you keep sacrificing the person you are—your own emotions—to the expert you want to appear?"

Portia moved her shoulders to release some of the tension she'd built up in the course of their exchange. "You're saying I need to get more of myself—of my heart—up there on the stand with me," she answered softly. "God, that's risky. I feel like I put everything on the line as it is." She paused and smiled ruefully. "And you're saying I should do even more."

"I'm saying that a murder trial is a very emotional game. You might consider playing on their terms rather than expecting them to come to yours. Yes, it's risky. But showing genuine emotion can be very convincing. I've always known you to have a great passion for your work. Maybe it's time you allowed the rest of the world to see some of that passion."

"That's good advice, but as it happens it might be very bad timing."

Peering hard at her, Sophie said, "You mentioned earlier you had been thinking of giving up, but you put it in the past tense. What changed your mind?"

"Well—nothing. Something. Someone. A consultation. It was unusual for me, though. I—he made me afraid."

"Afraid how?"

And with fifteen minutes left on the clock, her thoughts about the session whirling uncertainly at the edge of her story, Portia began telling her therapist about Jimmy the Weird.

Seven

• •

TWO DAYS LATER, at precisely one-thirty in the after-noon, Portia crossed the pleasant, fern-bedecked dining area of the Pewter Rose in Dilworth toward a table on the far side of the room. As always, she appreciated the atmosphere of the old ware-house. With its brick walls, softened by hanging Victorian lace and tapestries and pleasantly partitioned for privacy, its bright flowers in crystal vases on each small table, this had always been a special place for her. Alan Simpson smiled appreciatively and rose to his feet as she approached, and Portia couldn't help basking a little in the warmth of his welcome.

"Hey, you," he said, taking her hand in both of his own as she reached the table. "Glad you called."

Portia withdrew her hand a little reluctantly. "Glad you could make it on short notice."

Alan grinned as he pulled out her chair with an easy flourish. "How could I not?" he asked. "Never let it be said that I'm not always at the disposal of a beautiful woman."

Portia smiled easily. Alan Simpson might be full of it, but he was nice to be around. Tall, blond, and smart as they came, private investi-gator Simpson was a man who made no bones about the fact that he genuinely enjoyed the company of women. All women. Tall, short, blond, brunette, leggy, or curvaceous, Alan made every one of them feel as if she were possessed of something very special. He consciously exuded a breezy, lighthearted charm and the sort of sexy sophistication that was never threatening. For all of the five years or so they'd worked together, Alan had never once indulged himself in any overtly seductive behavior. Nevertheless, he'd always managed to convey the unmistakable message that he was utterly available to her—wherever, whenever, and for whatever. Portia had always marveled a little at Alan's gift for wearing his sexuality like a pair of favorite jeans—stylish, casual, well used, and oh-so-comfortable.

She busied herself with the menu in order to avoid for a moment the lively expectant expression in his dark blue eyes. The truth was, Portia found the opportunity to bask in the glow of Alan's unabashed appreciation a little too comfortable. Despite the boundaries of their well-established professional relationship, she knew herself to be no more immune to Simpson's considerable charms than any other red-blooded American female. They were both good-looking, fortyish, and decidedly not in the market for a long-term commitment. And that alone had always raised the possibility between them of some rather interesting distractions.

"Crab cake appetizer and a salad," she told a waiter hovering nearby. "And tea. Plenty of ice."

"I never eat crab except in Maryland," Alan said, referring to his Baltimore childhood. "Can't trust the Carolina stuff. I'll have the hickory-smoked strip steak. And another glass of cabernet. Or whatever it is." He grinned as the young waiter, obviously offended, huffed off in the direction of the kitchen.

"I really ought to insist that you join me in a glass of wine," he continued. "To celebrate. It's been too long, Portia."

"Can't," Portia answered rather more shortly than she intended. She ran a hand through her hair and paused mid-gesture, intensely aware of the message of that particular bit of body language. "I have patients this afternoon. Sorry."

Alan gazed at her with all the frank attention of a man admiring a work of art, a small smile playing under the handlebars of his honey-blond mustache. "That's okay. I'll take a rain check," he answered easily. He paused just a moment to let the implication sink in. "But, since you're going to insist on exploiting me for purely professional reasons, I have no choice but to oblige. What's up?"

Portia withdrew a sheaf of papers from the briefcase at her elbow. "Case in Columbia," she told him. "James Wier. Probable schizophrenic. Cut up two old women down in Dixon."

Alan nodded. "I remember reading about it in the *Observer,*" he said. "My, my, our Mr. Dylan does like to hand you the biggies, doesn't he?"

Portia glanced up. "I took it by choice, Alan," she told him. "Besides, Dec was in a spot."

"Spot or not, he got you to do it, didn't he? Not that I mind the business, you understand. But I thought you'd eased off on the forensics."

Portia sipped from her water glass. "I had. But well—this came up and—"

"Dylan roped you into it," Alan finished.

"I wouldn't say that."

Alan grinned. "I wouldn't expect you to," he went on. "But Dylan will do anything for a win—use anybody. Hell, why do you think he puts up with me?"

"I thought it was because you're the best," Portia countered.

Alan accepted the compliment with an easy smile. "I am, but as you well know, there's not much love lost between me and the counselor. My concern is about you. Or am I misremembering our last meeting?"

Despite herself, Portia blushed. She'd run into Alan quite by accident in the first dark days following Sammy Dean's death. She'd taken the day off to do some shopping and he'd found her in the parking lot of the mall, leaning against the side of her Volvo and crying her eyes out. They'd wound up doing nothing that day but riding around for hours as Alan drove and listened and let her weep. That meeting had opened a door in their relationship, but what that door would lead to was a question Portia preferred to leave unasked.

"No," she answered quietly. "I was in bad shape and you were very kind. But that was six months ago, Alan. People do recover."

"I don't care about people. I care about you," he replied softly, and reached across the table to take her hand.

She glanced down at the contact, and withdrew her fingers. "I appreciate that."

Alan leaned back in his chair. "But you wish I'd shut up, right? Look, all I'm saying is that maybe your gut reaction was the right one. Fact is, there's a lot of people out there who're just not worth the trouble."

Portia met his eyes. "So how come you do it?"

He laughed, the moment of seriousness passing like a cloud over the sun. "For the money, of course. Besides, the forensics is just a sideline for me. I prefer divorce cases."

"I'll bet," she answered. "All those wronged women to comfort. You bring them the bad news and then provide an oh-so-willing shoulder to cry on."

"I resemble that remark—"

"Yes, you do," she told him, smiling. "Now, could we get on with this?"

Alan half bowed from his chair. "Like I said, ma'am. At your service."

She breathed a small sigh of relief. "Wier won't—or can't—talk. I got practically nothing on his background from the preliminary evaluation. He's really disoriented—very nuts. I've contacted a private psychiatrist, Charlie Carter, down in S.C. to change his medication to Haldol. State's approved the change, so that ought to help. In a few days, he should be able to string some coherent thoughts together. But it's still no guarantee he'll open up."

"Does he know they're going for the death penalty?"

Portia shook her head slowly. "I doubt it. Even if his lawyers explained it, I don't think he got it. We'll try again with the new meds."

"It would certainly make me a little more forthcoming, knowing there was a potential noose around my neck."

"Yeah, but you're sane." Portia sipped her tea. "Not to mention incorrigibly self-serving."

Alan smiled. "Depends on who you talk to, Madam Doctor. What else?"

Portia flipped through the files. "I've already got him scheduled for the physical stuff and Jayne Patten from my office is going to administer the standardized tests. But so far he hasn't given a lot of clues to his history. Nothing, really. All they've been able to turn up is a Social Security number issued in California in 1961. A town called Twentynine Palms. The Twentynine's all one word—ring any bells?"

Alan nodded. "I know of it—it's attached to a Marine base. The usual assortment of transients and trailer park trash. Quite the breeding ground for a deranged killer, I suspect."

Portia glanced up from the paperwork, protesting, "Alan—"

He held up his hands. "Okay, okay—no further editorializing. But you know as well as I do what base towns are like. Pretty tough places, most of 'em."

Portia frowned and scribbled a note to herself. "His father may have been in the military. Start there, then. It's not much, I know, but it's all we've got. I have no idea how old Wier was when he got the SS number or how long he lived there, but see what you can find out. I need everything, Alan. Family members, school records—anything. So far, the state agencies haven't even turned up a birth certificate."

"Hey," Alan responded. "Not that unusual—especially if he happened to be born in the back of a truck."

Portia shot him a glance. "Or if his mother wanted to keep the birth a secret. I don't know—" Her eyes wandered to the far end of the room, but the expression in them traveled farther than that, focusing sadly on something Alan couldn't see. He studied her for a moment, filing the change in her expression for some future discussion.

"Sorry," she said, abruptly coming back to herself.

"No apology needed. What were you thinking about?" he probed gently.

"Just—Wier," she answered, hesitating. "Whatever—wherever he came from, whatever your prejudices might be, Alan, there's something about this guy. I don't know the background, but the genes are good, you know? You can see it. He's huge, healthy. He doesn't have that look. You know what I mean?"

Alan nodded, encouraging her to continue. They'd both been at this long enough to know what she was talking about. Three or four generations of violence and incest showed up in the genes. "You thinking he was adopted?"

She faced him, her eyes intent. "I don't know for sure, but yes—he even said it. Something like it, anyway. He said that anyone could have been his mother, even—" She broke off abruptly as the waiter came to fill their water glasses.

"Even what?" Alan prompted when he had gone.

"Nothing. But yes. Check adoption records out there. Now that I think about it, that's a definite possibility. What he said—that anybody could have been his mother. Something like that. It could be a clue." She passed Simpson a folder across the table and went on.

"Pretty much everything we've got is in here. But there's got to be more. I've seen him, Alan. He didn't get this sick overnight. It's been going on for a long, long time. Check the hospitals, mental institutions. There have to have been other episodes—a progression."

"Don't worry so much, Portia. Hey, I know the drill," Alan replied.

"I know you do," she told him. "But we can't afford any oversights." She passed a weary hand over her forehead, trying to think whether there was anything she might have forgotten. "Wait! He has a tattoo. Here." She reached across the table and encircled Alan's wrist with her fingers, then instantly snatched her hand back to the safety of her lap.

"Strictly jailhouse issue," she continued. "So maybe there's something there. If not in California, then somewhere else. I can't be sure, but there might be other victims. I don't know. It's just that the women he killed were quite elderly, both of them. Maybe some kind of pattern. I'm guessing—but he might have been reared by a grandmother, rather than by his natural parents." She leaned back in her chair, sighing heavily.

"Something about those old ladies was the trigger. I just don't know what."

"Unsolved old-lady murders," Alan reflected. "Okay, I'll check. But it's a long shot linking this guy up that way. The cops put that kind of crime down to simple robbery and close the books. You say he's a slice and dicer?"

"I said nothing of the kind," Portia answered wryly. "But yeah, a definite cutter. No special surgical skills though. He removed the female organs from one victim, not from the other. Both had a nipple removed and placed in the center of the chest, and both had their vaginal areas mutilated with the murder weapon. A butcher knife. I can get you copies of the file photos if you want."

Portia paused as she looked up and saw that their waiter had reappeared, and was obviously eavesdropping on their conversation, his jaw hanging slightly open, his eyes wide. He set a bread basket down in a little flurry of activity and started to leave when Alan stopped him with a hand on his arm.

"I'll take that steak rare, by the way, son. Blood rare."

Portia shook her head as the waiter all but ran to the kitchen. "Honestly," she said. "You don't know when to stop, do you?"

Alan flashed a grin, his teeth white against his golden tan. "Oh," he told her, "I know when. I just don't always know how. Never mind him anyway," he continued with a dismissive little gesture. "Serves the boy right for eavesdropping. You were saying?"

Portia sighed resignedly. "There's not much more to say. I need information. Anything that might help me fill in a profile. You see, part of Wier's delusional system dictates that women know the truth."

Alan leaned back, chuckling. "Mine too, actually."

Portia felt herself blushing again. "Never mind," she chided him. "The point is that to get him to open up and trust me, I'm going to need to confront him first with some facts about himself. If he thinks I know about him already, chances are he'll give me more. Enough to get a real picture of him. Maybe even enough to provide some substantial mitigation at sentencing." She faltered a moment. "I just hope it works."

Alan leaned forward over the table and she could feel the sheer warmth of his physical presence. "Oh, it'll work," he assured her. "Don't worry. I'll get you the stuff. I'll begin by working the web this afternoon and fly west in the morning. I presume this is on Declan's nickel?"

She nodded as the waiter slid their plates in front of them, expertly moving the files to one side. "He okayed the usual budget," she told him. "But if you need more, let me know. I'll talk to him."

Alan tore into his steak, chewing appreciatively, and she couldn't help noticing that he ate the same way he did everything else, with a certain indefinable sensuality.

"Better you than me," he went on, swallowing. "You know Dylan. Anytime I come in on a case, he's pretty much convinced the business expenses of private investigation include squandering his private funds on fast women and riotous living." He paused, eyes twinkling. "Or is that fast living and riotous women? I can never keep them straight."

Portia grinned. "Either way," she answered. "We both know it's about half true. So save your receipts this time, all right? After all, Dec has been known to use his own money for this stuff. There's not a lot of public money out there anymore. So go easy, okay?"

"Yes'm. I promise," Alan replied in mock seriousness. "Though it won't be hard to keep expenses down. I got to tell you, from what I know of Twentynine Palms, there's hardly a riotous woman to be had. Besides, it's California, so it's probably been taken over by raging vegetarians and alien worshipers. Still, it's only sixty miles or so from Palm Springs. I can always stop there to restore my sense of reality."

Portia grinned in spite of herself. No matter how hard she tried to keep their discussions on a professional level, Alan had a way of making light of things. It provided a welcome relief from her own intensity. She envied him his sense of humor, even if she didn't entirely trust the man who hid behind it.

Alan pointed his fork in her direction. "Why couldn't you just once come up with a crazy from Paris? Or Rome? Somewhere interesting?

Why're you always sending me off to godforsaken burgs like Twentynine Palms? I tell you, McTeague, you ought to go international. There'd be much more for a devoted profligate like myself to turn up in the way of fast living."

Portia shook her head, still smiling. "Men," she murmured.

Alan shot her a slow, meaningful smile that sent an unexpected warmth down her arms, making her fingertips tingle as she met his eyes, making her feel as if she'd joined him in that glass of wine after all.

"Ahh," he sighed. "Women."

Portia tried to make herself as inconspicuous as possible as she slipped into the reception area of her office, hoping that her three o'clock would be a few minutes late. Her meeting with Alan had left her feeling lighter inside, more hopeful in a way she knew she ought to sit down and examine in the privacy of her own company. But as she passed behind the reception window, Lori motioned to a seat in the far corner of the waiting room where Evelyn Endicott sat poised on the edge of her chair, as though the slightest unexpected movement might shatter her into a million pieces. And Portia resolutely pushed any thoughts of Alan Simpson aside. She snatched up a sheaf of pink message slips and called out to the waiting area in a bright, encouraging voice.

"Evelyn?"

The patient looked up from her magazine, her expression a little frightened under the too-careful makeup. "Yes?" she answered anxiously.

"Three minutes, Evelyn. I just have to make one phone call and then we'll start. Okay?"

Evelyn peered at the wall clock in a concerned way. It read four minutes to three. She glanced at her own watch, then back at Portia, who was smiling reassuringly. "All right," she answered. "I'll be here."

Portia's smile fell away as she rounded the corner into her own bright office, making a mental note to check on the status of Evelyn's antianxiety and hormonal medications. Evelyn had experienced a number of paranoid delusions since the onset of menopause, not the least of which was that her husband was trying to sell her into white slavery.

She sank gratefully into her chair, sorting through her messages. Three were from Declan Dylan's office, and she punched in the number from memory.

He answered the phone himself. "Dec?" she asked when he came on the line. "What's up?"

"I just wanted to let you know, you've been cleared for Wier visitation. Evans got on the warden about it yesterday and you can have all the time you want until the trial date."

"Hallelujah," said Portia with a grateful sigh. Setting up regular consultations could sometimes take weeks, depending on who was in charge. And weeks were something they didn't have. "Conference room consult, right?"

"If you say so," Dec replied. "But I don't know if that's entirely wise. Wier's dangerous."

"Dec," she said, trying to steer him away from the beginning of an oft-fought argument. "We are talking about prison here. There are guards all over the place."

"Many of whom would consider it nothing less than poetic justice if Jimmy Wier decided to attack you. You want to see him alone, most of those boys figure you're just asking for whatever happens."

"Dec," Portia replied patiently. "I can't try and get through to Wier as a human being if he's locked up in a cage. I have to make contact. You know that."

"I know it," Dec admitted. "But I don't pretend to like it."

There was another little pause while Portia waited for him to continue. When he didn't, she asked, "So what else is up?"

"That's it, I guess. I was just touching base."

She frowned at the receiver. "That's it? Three phone calls just to touch base?"

Dec breathed noisily over the line. She thought she could hear him tapping something on the edge of his desk.

"So?" she insisted after another moment.

"I told you. Nothing. Your girl said—"

"—Woman. Assistant. Receptionist, if you don't mind," she corrected him. "Or you might even want to call her Lori. It's not like you haven't been speaking over the phone for years."

"Fine," Dec replied. "Lori said you were having lunch with Simpson. And you ran late, so I . . . did you fill him in?"

"I did," she answered. "He's on the case. He said he'd work the computer records tonight and fly out in the morning. He said he'd call the moment he comes up with anything."

"I daresay—" Dec said acidly.

"What's that supposed to mean?"

"Nothing at all. You wanted him, you got him. I just hope he can handle it."

"He's always come through for us before—what is it with you today anyway?"

Their conversation was abruptly punctuated by an insistent electronic dinging from Declan's intercom, and Portia heard a faraway voice informing Mr. Dylan of a call on line five.

"Nothing. Nothing. Listen, I gotta go. I'll check in tomorrow, okay? We may want you to do a deposition later in the week to see if we can get the trial date pushed back. Could you do that? Recommend postponement pending effects of the new medication or something?"

"Well, sure I could," she told him. "But so can Charlie. He's writing the prescriptions."

"I just meant—you don't have—other plans or anything?"

"Not really," Portia answered, thoroughly puzzled.

"Great," Dec said. "Later." And hung up.

Portia sat for another long moment, staring at the telephone, reviewing the uncharacteristically strained conversation. It almost seemed as if Dec were deliberately wasting time. Only Dec was a man who never, ever, wasted time if he could help it. She rifled again through the message slips on which Lori had dutifully recorded the times of the incoming calls. The first of Dec's calls had come in around one, shortly after she'd left for lunch. The second had come in at two-fifteen, and the last at two thirty-five, just twenty minutes later. Odd, she thought. Really odd.

And all at once the realization dawned, surprising her so completely she could only stare down at the message slips spread out on her desk like a hand of playing cards.

"Well, I'll be damned," she said aloud. "You knew I was having lunch with Alan Simpson and you were flat out jealous! I'll be damned! Checking up on me—"

Portia glanced up and all but jumped out of her chair as she saw that Evelyn Endicott had planted herself firmly in the doorway, her back ramrod straight, heels together, her handbag held out in front of her almost like a shield. Evelyn fixed her with a worried, vaguely accusatory look as Portia flashed what she hoped was a welcoming smile. Wonderful, Portia, she thought. Nice to have your patients see you talking to yourself. Very professional.

"Evelyn," she called brightly. "Come in."

"You said three minutes," Evelyn answered uncertainly. "Three. And I waited exactly three minutes. Then I came back. Is that all right?"

Portia smiled and rose to usher Evelyn Endicott into a chair, guiding her around the desk like some delicate, breakable vase. "Evelyn, honey," she assured her, "that's just fine. Just fine."

Eight

● ●

THE DRIVE to the prison seemed arduously slow as traffic on the interstate wound wearily around five miles of
construction. Portia, maddened by the delay, sat insulated in the coolness of the air-conditioned Volvo, her thoughts circling wildly over
the possibilities of her upcoming meeting with Jimmy the Weird. It
was crucial not to expect too much, she knew. Establishing a therapeutic relationship took time, trust, and patience. Yet she couldn't
avoid a tingle of anticipation as she crept her way to Columbia. Wier's
Haldol should be working by now. With some of his symptoms under
control through medication, Wier would be able to speak more—to
respond more coherently to the bits and pieces of information she had
managed to pick up about his past. Alan Simpson had called the previous evening with a possible hit from the computer files: There had
been a Marine named Horace Wier based at Twentynine Palms, California, from 1961 to 1967. Alan was flying in that morning to check it
out. It wasn't much—but it was a start.

She sighed heavily and frowned at the line of cars moving slowly
ahead of her. Even though it was little more than shooting in the dark
at this point, she felt she had to play her hunch that Jimmy's father
had been in the military. He would be able to respond, at least.
Whether or not he would was another story.

After what seemed like hours, she swung the car onto the exit ramp
and glanced uneasily at the dashboard clock. She had ten miles to go
and it was already close to the hour. Ordinarily it wouldn't matter if

she was a few minutes late, but today showing up on time was important. It gave a man like Wier something to depend on at a time when
his whole universe was coming apart. He had said it himself—he knew
all about time. In some part of his twisted consciousness, he would
know if she were late.

She parked the car and all but ran through the security check at the
Visitor's Center where a sleepy-eyed guard checked her belongings
without much interest. She dashed up the brown-edged walk to the
main entrance of the men's prison. Once inside, as the doors to the
minuscule elevator slid closed behind her, she stifled a little sigh. They
hadn't stopped her downstairs. If they'd wanted to they could have
canceled her scheduled session just for being late. But they'd let her
through without comment. And the thought made Portia smile a
little. Dec and Evans had them on the run, then. Too much interfer-
ence from the warden or the guards and Wier's defense team would
find a way to use it in court.

Upstairs, she made her way to the last security checkpoint and
flashed her identification. The guard studied it for a long moment,
eyeing her up and down in her plain outfit of T-shirt and chinos.

"Says here you got a conference room," he said after a moment.

"That's right."

"Wier's dangerous," he offered. "You might want to change your
mind about that."

"Thanks," said Portia, forcing herself to smile sweetly. "But I'll be
okay."

"They have you sign a waiver?"

"It's all with the warden," she replied. "I'll be fine."

"Whatever—" The guard shrugged. "Long's we got the waiver.
It's your a-as—" He stopped and changed his mind. "It's your neck,
ma'am."

"Thanks. I'll be careful."

He directed her down a corridor opposite the one she had taken on
her first visit. "First door on your left. He'll be in directly."

The conference room was, if anything, smaller than the rooms used
for ordinary visitation. Those at least held the advantage of being
divided and windowed, giving at least an illusion of space. But the first
door on the left gave way to a chamber of perhaps five by five feet,
housing only a small chipped table and a couple of plastic chairs. She

shivered a little against the familiar tug of claustrophobia. The room had no windows and only one door. That meant that in order to observe Wier properly when they brought him in, she would have to place herself on the other side of the table—away from that door and away from any possibility of a fast exit should there be trouble.

The sound of shackles in the corridor made her decision. She took the chair on the far side of the table and sat waiting, facing the door, for them to bring in Jimmy Wier.

The change was there. One look told her the Haldol was working almost better than she had hoped it would. The light blue eyes that met her own as he entered were clear, nearly free of the flat emptiness that had characterized them at their first meeting.

"Hi, Jimmy," she said warmly. "Do you remember me?"

The prisoner nodded once and began to settle his huge bulk into the empty chair when, almost on impulse, Portia called out to the guard.

"Please unlock him." She looked hard at Jimmy. "How about it, Jimmy? Don't you think you'd be more comfortable talking to me without those chains on?"

The eyes that met her own held a curious mixture of astonishment, gratitude, and mistrust. "I guess," he answered softly.

"Do it," she told the guard.

The guard stared at her and started to protest. "Ma'am, I—"

Portia shot him an unwavering look. "This man is my patient," she told him in a carefully even tone. "And I'd like you to unlock him now, please."

The guard's eyes narrowed. "You got a waiver?"

"I do," she answered. "It'll be all right. Won't it be all right, Jimmy?"

"Hands only," the guard responded, "I can't be responsible for—"

"Fine," Portia broke in. "That'll be fine."

"Well, if you say so. I'll be right outside." The guard moved to unlock the manacles that circled Jimmy's wrists. As they fell away, leaving bright red indentations in the flesh, Jimmy sat staring at the marks in mute concentration.

"I can't feel my fingers," he said when the guard had closed the door.

"I know," Portia told him. "I could see the cuffs were too tight."

There was a little pause. "Jimmy," she began softly. "Do you remember me? Do you remember who I am?"

"Tricks," he replied. "You're Dr. Tricks."

Portia smiled. "Yes, I am a doctor. But I'm not going to trick you, Jimmy. I promise you that. I just thought we could talk a little. Okay?"

He gazed down at the now-fading marks on his wrists, still fascinated. "Why?"

"Because if we can talk a little, maybe I can help you remember what happened."

Wier smiled to himself. "Oh," he answered. "I don't think so. I don't think I would like to do that."

Portia made a hasty note. He was tracking, anyway. Logically, he seemed well oriented. "Why not, Jimmy? Are you afraid you might remember something bad?"

There was only silence for an answer. He looked at her without meeting her eyes, his gaze fixed somewhere just above her forehead.

She decided to proceed more cautiously. "Have you seen Mr. Evans, Jimmy? Or Mr. Dylan? Have you talked to your lawyers?"

He shook his head, perturbed. "There was two of them. Two men. I remember that. One was in a wheelchair."

"Yes," Portia replied. "Yes. Those are your lawyers, Jimmy. Mr. Evans and Mr. Dylan. Mr. Dylan's the one in the wheelchair. What did they tell you, when you talked to them? Do you remember?"

"He's lying, I bet," Jimmy reflected. "I didn't like him. Not one bit. He's nothing but a faker."

Portia stared at him.

"Who's faking?"

"That one. In the chair. He has to be faking that he can't walk."

"But I know him, Jimmy. He really can't. He was in an accident a long time ago. Why did you think he was faking?"

"All men are liars," he whispered, more to himself than to her. "Only women know the truth." Jimmy paused and inclined his huge head. He began to drum his fingers nervously on the tabletop. All at once he looked at her.

"I'm sorry," he said. "Did you say something? There was somebody talking."

She wrote, "command voices," followed by a question mark on the legal pad in front of her. When it came to schizoid symptoms, hearing voices was near the top of the list. "Do you hear voices a lot, Jimmy?" she went on smoothly. "Are they inside your head or outside?"

"Depends—" he answered softly. "It just—depends."

Uneasily, she shifted her weight in the chair. "What did your lawyers tell you?"

He raised his head and his face assumed an entirely new expression, one that Portia recognized as familiar but couldn't pinpoint until Jimmy the Weird opened his mouth in a spooky imitation of Declan Dylan that was so accurate it raised the hair along her arms.

"You're coming up for trial on two counts of murder here, Jim. Help us out. You've got to talk to us and you've got to take your medicine and you've got to talk with your doctors. You've got to do your best, Jim, because if you don't—" He broke off and the mimicry ended as abruptly as it had begun.

Portia leaned in closer. "If you don't what, Jimmy? What did Mr. Dylan say after that?"

"He told me a lie."

She peered at him, searching his broad face for clues. "What did he tell you? How did you know it was a lie?"

Jimmy looked over his shoulder uneasily, then back at Portia. He leaned across the table so close that it took all her strength not to draw back from that huge frame—not to give him any sign she might be afraid. She looked into his eyes and looked away again and saw the golden hairs curling across the knuckles of his meaty fingers. For one faint, dizzying instant she could smell his breath.

"They said they would—they said—" he stammered painfully, and she knew suddenly that whatever Dylan had told him, it had frightened Jimmy Wier to the depths of his being.

"Easy, Jimmy. It's okay. Just take your time and tell me what he said."

He looked at her for a long moment, his eyes tortured. "He said they would kill me if it was true," he said. "He said I had to remember, or—"

Damn Declan, she thought, as the sense of what Jimmy was saying suddenly took root in her mind. "Oh, Jimmy. They're not going to kill you, nobody's going to. What they were telling you was that you're going to trial for murder. For those old women. But Mr. Evans and Mr. Dylan, they're your lawyers, Jimmy. They're on your side. It's the other side that wants—" Now it was her turn to falter as she struggled for words. "The other side—the prosecution—wants to give you the death penalty. Do you understand what that means?"

He settled back in his chair, eyeing her. "Yes."

The word hung between them like an accusation. Portia took a deep breath. "We're going to do our best to see that doesn't happen, okay? Me and your lawyers. We're going to try and see to it that you get—that you get the help you need. That's why you have to try very hard to talk to your lawyers, Jimmy, and me. Because the more information we have, the more we can help you when we go to court."

He faced her squarely, his face both suspicious and sad. "How can you help me?" he asked. "How can you keep me off the Row?"

She swallowed hard. "I don't know, Jimmy. All I can do is try to understand you. And then tell the jury about you so they'll be able to understand."

He stared off at the blank wall, his hands lying limp in his lap. There was no threat in him now, no menace. He looked suddenly very young, very confused. Like a lost child waiting to be comforted. She started to reach for his hand, then stopped herself.

"Tell me about those ladies, Jimmy. I can help you if you tell me."

He slumped even further in his chair. "They tell me I killed them."

"Did you?"

He glanced around the room fitfully until his eyes came to rest on her once more. "I don't know. I don't know the difference between what they tell me and what happened. If they say it, it probably happened. I probably did those things. Maybe I did them afterward—after they said I did. I don't know."

Portia felt the air go out of her lungs in a rush. Poor boundaries—another of the prime symptoms. Not being able to distinguish yourself from other people, fantasy from reality, what was said from what occurred. In Jimmy's case, they seemed almost nonexistent.

"How long have you felt like that, Jimmy?" she asked quietly.

"Always," he answered dreamily. "Always always . . ." Suddenly he began to sing in a high, wavering tenor. *"I'll be loving you, always. With a love that's true, always . . ."*

Portia observed him carefully. He was smiling as he sang. He was remembering. It was a chance she couldn't afford to miss. "You're a good singer, Jimmy. Really good."

"Oh," he replied. "I like to sing."

"Where did you hear that song? Do you remember where you were when you first heard it?"

He nodded, eyes closed, a little smile playing around his mouth. "On the radio. Jukebox radio. I liked that. Listening to the radio."

"It's an old song, Jimmy," she coaxed. "It was written a long time ago. Do you remember how old you were when you heard it?"

"Pretty young, I guess. I don't know." He frowned uncertainly, gazing off into the distance at something she couldn't see.

"Try, Jimmy," she urged softly. "Try to remember."

There was a long silence in which she all but held her breath. She could feel him struggling to capture the images in his mind, trying to relive some long-ago moment. The silence seemed to stretch for minutes, until she began to think she'd lost him.

"There was a patch of light from the window," he announced in the same faraway voice. "I used to play with it. Making shadows, moving in and out. I thought that piece of light belonged to me. Like it was a toy that was all mine. I can hear the radio. If you listen to the radio, you can't hear the rest."

"What's the rest, Jimmy?" Portia spoke very softly, hardly daring to disturb his recollection. "Was there something else going on then? Something you didn't want to hear?"

The answer came slowly, sadly, little more than a sigh. "Just them."

"Who's them?"

"I don't know—the voices." He began to hum.

Portia fought down a flurry of impatience as a thousand questions rose up in her thoughts. Let him talk, she reminded herself. Let it come. Don't force it.

"What are the voices saying, Jimmy?"

"Nothing. No words. Just sounds. Those sounds they make. Sounds like—hurt." He reached up and covered his ears against the echoing memory. "I listen to the radio. I like the radio."

A moment passed, then two, as Portia noted the connections. Sex equals pain equals punishment equals murder? She underscored the last word, her own question mark recorded on the page, mirroring the hundred other questions coursing through her mind.

Suddenly, Wier turned in his chair and looked at her, blinking rapidly as if he had just been roused from a nap. "What was I saying?"

"You were talking about the radio," she prompted him.

He nodded vaguely. "I hadn't—hadn't thought about that. For a long time. Radio. There was one."

"Where was there a radio, Jimmy? Where? Do you remember?"

He shook his head. "It's gone—all gone now. First there was something. Now there's nothing. It was—a sort of picture. In my head. Like a dream."

Portia looked at him for a long moment. He'd come so far since their first meeting. And yet it was still so far from where they needed to be. She also knew they were running out of time.

You're not here to be his therapist, damn it, she reminded herself silently. It's your job to rip him open.

She gazed for a long moment at the huge man slouched inside the orange jumpsuit, trying to calculate the unknowns. She took a breath and braced herself, struggling to maintain a professional distance she wasn't sure she had. She was digging for gold—the kind of information that could save his life.

"I don't think it was a dream, Jimmy. I think the picture in your head was real. I think it was a real place. In California. You lived in California for a while, didn't you, Jimmy? And your father was in the Marines. Do you remember that? Do you remember the base, Jimmy? The town—Twentynine Palms?"

Jimmy jumped to his feet, knocking the plastic chair to the side with a crash. He began to pace, pounding his freed hands together, palms flat, over and over, in a way that made her stomach churn.

"You're tricking me!" he cried, his voice rising in agitation. "You're tricking me you're-tricking-me, you're-tricking-me-you're-tricking—me—"

"Jimmy, no!"

But it was too late. The guard outside, hearing the disturbance, burst through the door just as Jimmy began to pound on the wall—first palms, then fists, and finally head—the impact of flesh and bone against concrete punctuating his agonized litany. "Tricking-tricking-tricking me . . ."

She could only watch, openmouthed, as they led him away, handcuffed again and shuffling back to the block, his cries still ringing in her head. Shaking, she gathered her notes and eased around the table and out the door.

On her way down the hall, she paused and drank lukewarm water from a grimy fountain, horribly aware of her dry mouth, her trembling knees. At the floor desk, she stopped and made a brief call to Charlie Carter's office, advising him to up the Haldol dosage slightly and to order Wier a suitable round of tranquilizers to get him through the night.

She closed her eyes and leaned heavily against the wall as the elevator doors closed silently behind her, trying to get her breath, not thinking—not allowing herself to feel anything about the terrible anguish she had just witnessed. Once outside, she headed for the Volvo, unlocked it, and slid into the comfort of the interior, safe again behind the steering wheel. And it was only then that she began to fully absorb the enormity of her mistake. She had promised not to trick him—she had promised. And then—then. . . .

She leaned her head against the wheel and squeezed her eyes shut tight, a sudden well of tears burned beneath her eyelids.

"Shit!" she said to no one. And fumbled for the keys.

Nine

●●●

S HE HEADED NORTH on Interstate 77, driving for
some minutes almost without thinking, happy to sub-
merge herself in the familiar rhythms of the highway, only dimly aware
of the rest stops and weigh stations and tired billboards falling away as
she placed some distance between herself and the events of the morning. After a few more minutes, she punched her office number into
the car phone. Lori's voice answered with characteristic efficiency.

"What's on for the rest of today?" she inquired wearily.

"Good morning, yourself," Lori answered dryly.

"Sorry, Lori. I had a rough session with Wier."

"Hold a minute, the phone—" Lori abruptly put her on hold as she
went to answer the other line. "Well, let me see—" she said after
another moment. There was the sound of paper as Lori flipped
through the day's appointments. "You've got the Wilsons at two-
thirty; you're due at Mr. Dylan's office at four; back here till six-thirty.
And a parent-teacher conference at Alice's school at seven-thirty."

"Yikes—" Portia gulped.

"No rest for the wicked," Lori offered wryly.

But Portia was in no mood for banter. "Okay—see if you can
reschedule the Wilsons for later in the week. Tell them—something—
anything."

"You all right?" Lori inquired.

Portia stifled a derisive little laugh. "Yeah—it's nothing. Like I said.
Rough session. I'll call Dylan's office myself. He wants me there for a

deposition, but after this morning—well—never mind—I'll talk to him. Who's on at five-thirty?"

"Louise."

Portia closed her eyes and opened them again as a semi passed her in the left-hand lane, the momentary blast of diesel fumes filtering through the air conditioning, making her nauseated and light-headed.

Louise Denton had been in therapy only a few weeks. She'd been referred after her eighth round of plastic surgery had failed to correct what Louise felt were highly visible defects in her appearance. To date, Louise Denton had had a nose job; an eye job; a cheekbone enhancement; breast enlargement; and a chin job. She'd had liposuction on her cheeks and collagen in her lips and a couple of skin treatments whose names Portia didn't even remember. Louise Denton, at the ripe old age of twenty-seven, had all the mannequin-like appeal of a Barbie doll. And a sense of self-loathing so acute she felt it could be cured only with a surgeon's knife.

"Okay—" Portia sighed. "I'll be there for Louise. What I need now is for you to go back through the log and see if you can find the number of that guy who called a few days ago—what was his name? The one who wanted to talk about Wier."

After a few more moments, Lori spoke over the line. "Got it. Justin Chitwood—555–3752. Okay? He's at the sheriff's office near Dixon."

"That's the one," Portia replied, taking one hand off the wheel to scribble down the number. "I'm just out of Columbia. Maybe ten minutes. What exit do I take to get to Dixon? I'm going to try and get over there this afternoon if I can cancel Dec."

Lori paused before answering and Portia knew she was planning a suitable route. God bless her, Lori was a walking road atlas. The woman knew the highways and byways of the Carolinas by heart. "Okay. Look out your window. You're on the interstate, right?"

"Of course."

"Check the signs. You see exit twenty?"

Portia peered through the windshield. "No. I'm—wait a minute. I'm at sixteen."

"Okay—so what you do is, you get off at twenty, take the first left off the ramp to Route 402. Dixon's about fifteen minutes down that road. You'll have to ask where the sheriff is, though. I don't know. You got that?"

"Got it," replied Portia, easing over into the right lane.

"If you miss the exit, go on to twenty-one, turn right off the ramp; double back and take the old Highway 4 into Melville. It's a two-lane—cuts through a lot of nothing, but five miles on you'll come to a sort of dogleg. Veer left and that takes you into Melville. You should be able to get to Dixon from there. But it's more complicated."

"Don't worry," said Portia. "I'll get there."

"I hope so," said Lori and rang off.

Her next call was to Declan Dylan's office. As she passed exit eighteen, she pulled off onto the shoulder as a precautionary measure. First, she wanted to be able to concentrate; second, she didn't want to miss her exit. Lori's second set of directions had sounded rather more involved than she cared to contemplate.

Maris Beasley, Dec's executive secretary, answered the phone. "Mr. Dylan's office. How may I help you?"

Portia couldn't help smiling. Maris Beasley was a relic of some past age; the sound of those clipped, almost robotic tones on the phone conjured up precisely the same image Maris presented to the world in person. Dyed, beehive hair, penciled eyebrows, and a sense of fashion that had been forged somewhere in the heyday of Sid Caesar and Uncle Miltie. Maris was tough, utterly unflappable, and could type 120 words a minute on an old-style IBM Selectric. What she could do in front of a computer keyboard was anybody's guess. Thus far, she'd refused to allow Declan to get her one.

"Hello, Maris," Portia said warmly. "This is Portia McTeague. Is he in?"

"He's always in to you," Maris replied. "As if you didn't know. How're you keeping?"

"Don't ask, Maris. It's been a rough day. And it isn't half done."

"I know what you mean," Maris answered. "Hold on, I'll get him."

"Great news, Portia," Declan announced when he came on the line. "I was just on the phone with Royal's office. They've agreed to drop the third murder charge. Lack of evidence. Apparently Royal doesn't want to risk his reputation by trying to pin the earlier case on Wier based only on the MO. So—we're down to two counts of murder one."

"That's great, Dec," Portia answered without enthusiasm.

"I'll say it is. Without the third charge, we'll have a much better shot at insanity. Even temporary insanity. So, how did it go with Wier?"

Portia gnawed a little at her lower lip. "It went," she answered.

"What does that mean?"

"It means I just don't know, Dec. I may have blown it. For real. I thought I could get him to open up and—well, let's just say it backfired. And it was my own stupid fault. I should have known better."

Dec's voice deepened with concern. "What happened, Portia, did he get violent?"

"Yes. Well—no. Not to me, anyway. He had a violent reaction to some statements I made. About his family."

"But that's good, isn't it? Doesn't that prove you've made contact?"

Portia laughed ruefully. "Sure," she answered. "Assuming he'll ever speak to me again. I don't know, Dec. I may have gone too far, too fast. He may not trust me ever again. We have to be prepared for that. It's not like the guy has a great history."

There was a short silence as Declan, ever the attorney, absorbed the information and calculated his response. She could almost hear the wheels turning. "Will you be able to give us anything?" he asked after another moment. "Officially?"

She had to fight a sudden impulse to scream at him—to accuse him of having no emotions, no feelings at all for the people he tried so hard to save. With him, it was all the case—the mechanics, the strategy.

But in the next instant the flame of her anger died as suddenly as it had blossomed. After all, she reminded herself silently, when you got right down to it, couldn't she accuse herself of all the same things? The memory of Jimmy Wier banging his head against the wall floated up in her mind and she resolutely pushed it back. It was her fault, wasn't it? Her mistake. If she wasn't able to testify for Wier in the end, it wouldn't be on Dec's head. It would be on her own.

"Well, I know what we've got, anyway," she answered finally. "I can give you a provisional diagnosis of chronic schizophrenia, undifferentiated type. He may be hearing command voices, experiencing some visual hallucinations, and he's responded reasonably well to medication. The rest—the rest I can only guess at. He's got to be retested. I've got that scheduled, but I need more interview time. Pull some strings and see if you can get me unlimited visitation, will you?"

"Royal won't like it," Dec said doubtfully, "but I'll try." There was a little pause on the line before he pressed further. "But what do you think? Is Wier crazy? Legally?"

"He told me you and Evans met with him. What do you think?"

Dec sighed. "Poor bastard," he said. "But in order to make the plea stick, we've got to have more."

"I know," she answered softly.

"I wanted you to come in today and give your deposition about the effects of the medication. We were going to try and buy some time, say something about how you needed a couple of extra weeks to see if it was working. Or state the necessity for further investigation of his background."

Portia frowned through the windshield. "Carter should be the one to make the statement about the meds, Dec. He's the one who wrote the scrip."

"On his way to Bermuda," Dec replied. "What about your needing further investigation time for proper evaluation?"

"Sure, I'll come in and swear to that. You think it'll do any good?"

"Of course it won't," Dec answered. "But I can't help being tickled at the thought of inundating Donny Royal's office with paper. The thought of his wide polyester butt parked behind stacks and stacks of defense documents and I—"

"Ordinarily I'd agree with you," Portia interrupted. "But since the court's going to deny the motion for a delay and since my coming in there isn't going to accomplish anything useful, I'd like to pass for today, if it's all the same to you. Can we do it next week? There's something I want to check out on my own."

"On your own? What have you got?"

"Maybe nothing," she replied. "But a man named Justin Chitwood called my office. Said he'd heard I was on the Wier case."

"So?"

"He said he was with the sheriff's office in Dixon. Apparently he was at the scene. I'm just about thirty miles from there now. I thought I'd go over there and see what he had to say."

Dec made an irritated little noise. "What about Simpson? Isn't that precisely the kind of lead a private investigator is supposed to check out? What the hell am I paying him for anyway?"

"First, I want to check it out myself because Chitwood contacted me, okay? That probably means he wants to talk to me, not somebody else. And secondly, Alan's in California. He's got a lead on a man with the same last name out of a Marine base. Horace Wier. It may be nothing, but it's a place to start. The years of service are close enough, anyway. So I'm going to Dixon."

Dec's voice was interrupted by a sudden blast of static. Portia thumped the cell phone lightly against the dashboard. "You still there?"

"Yeah, I'm here. But look, Portia, I don't like this at all. There's no reason for you to be hauling down there. This guy might be some crackpot. He might—"

"He was at the scene, Dec," she interjected. "That could mean something. He might be able to offer some information on the arrest. I've got no information on Wier's mental state at the time. It could mean a lot."

"Or this Chitwood might be some nut case—" Dec rejoined. "If he was one of the arresting officers, there's not a chance in hell he's on our side. They just want to make the charges stick."

"Fortunately, I know how to handle a nut case," she answered dryly. "I have a degree—"

"Nevertheless—"

"I'm going," said Portia as she eased the Volvo back into the right-hand lane. "I'll call you if I find out anything."

"But—"

"Bye, Dec. Have a nice day," she told him. And hung up.

The sheriff's office in Dixon, South Carolina, was a squat red brick building at the tail end of a rapidly deteriorating downtown. What had once constituted the main drag of a sleepy little Southern town had clearly fallen victim to the age of strip malls and suburban spread. What was left of Main Street consisted of little more than a branch bank, a coffee shop, and a used-furniture emporium, all looking deserted and sad. Portia glanced around as she angled the Volvo into a parking space on the opposite side of the street. Main Street in Dixon might have been lifted straight out of *The Last Picture Show*. All it needed was a couple of tumbleweeds to complete the impression of general godforsakenness.

She crossed the street and headed down to the end of the block, eyeing the office a little apprehensively. The two calls she'd made from the road had yielded no answer, and she wasn't at all sure she'd find anyone around. Then, as she drew nearer the corner, she spied an official-looking police vehicle parked in the alley just off the street.

The door to the office was propped open, and a huge, old-fashioned wooden ceiling fan creaked tiredly overhead. An overweight man with an unlit cigar clamped between his teeth sat with his feet propped up on a scarred desk, leisurely perusing a worn paperback novel.

Portia knocked softly on the open door. "Excuse me?"

The feet came down off the desk and the man got up with surprising alacrity.

"He'p you, ma'am?" He spoke in an elaborate countrified drawl of a kind rarely heard anymore, and sized her up in the same split second it took her to realize that the drawl was at least in part put on for her benefit—the quintessential Southern lawman faced with an obvious outsider.

Portia managed a little smile. "Hope so," she drawled back. "I wasn't sure there'd be anyone around. I called a couple of times from the road but got no answer. You open for business?"

The lawman gave her the benefit of an aw-shucks kind of a grin. "Always open. Not much business though. I reckon we ought to be thankful for that. You called from the road you said? I been here since nine. Phone didn't ring."

"Maybe I copied the number down wrong," she answered. "I was looking for somebody named Justin Chitwood. Are you him?"

There was a slight change in the man's expression, a fleeting moment of wariness that she might have missed had she blinked at the wrong moment. Then the lawman's smile grew just a shade wider.

"No, ma'am," he answered. "You missed old Chitwood. The boy up and quit on me. I'm Dwight Glass, sheriff."

The name rang a bell. She recalled that Glass had been one of the names on Wier's arrest report. "I'm Portia McTeague," she told him. "Dr. McTeague." She made a little gesture in the direction of a chair. "Mind if I sit?"

"Please," the sheriff replied and resumed his own seat behind the desk, his small eyes bright with curiosity.

She eyed the man uncertainly, figuring that as long as she was here, there was nothing to be lost in a little further conversation. "Well," she went on, "I don't know quite what to say. Seems Mr. Chitwood called my office some days ago. Something about a case I've been working on."

"A case?"

"Yes, I'm a psychologist. I've been called in by Jimmy Wier's defense team to evaluate him. You were listed as one of the arresting officers, weren't you?"

"That's right." Most of the drawl fell away with his answer, and the moment of silence that followed was chilly with disapproval. "Booked him myself. Terrible thing. Downright sickening. I never would have believed it. You say you're with the defense?"

"In a manner of speaking," she told him. "I've been asked to give my opinion of Mr. Wier's mental state in court."

"Oh." The sheriff's eyes narrowed almost imperceptibly. "You one of them hired guns?"

If she minded the term, she didn't allow it to show. "Something like that." She was going to offer him an explanation, but was interrupted before she could continue.

"I got to tell you, ma'am. I saw what that boy done and I questioned him and I booked him and Jimmy Wier is as sane as you or me." He looked as if he had quite a bit more to say on the subject, but was thinking better of it.

Portia continued to smile sweetly. "I'm really not allowed to discuss his condition," she said. "But I guess I found the right man, after all. You say you did the booking?"

"Yes'm, I did."

She feigned a fascinated expression as she observed the sheriff. "Was there anything—you know—unusual about Wier when they brought him in? Did you observe anything out of the ordinary about him—his behavior?"

The sheriff appeared to consider the question. "He was crying quite a bit. But I took that to be remorse. He'd done murder. And he knew it."

They stared at each other for a long, uneasy moment before Glass spoke again. "I expect all the details you need are in the report. I reviewed it myself, you know. It's all in there. We might be a small town, but we do our job."

"Of course," Portia replied evenly. "It doesn't hurt to ask, though, does it? Sometimes things slip by. Terrible crime like this—people get upset. Sometimes they won't remember something till afterward."

"Not this time," replied Glass, still smiling.

"Uh-huh." Portia got to her feet. "To tell you the truth, I was a little surprised to get the call from Mr. Chitwood. Seeing as how your report was already so—thorough. Do you have any idea what he might have had to say to me?"

"Nope," Glass admitted. "But it was always pretty hard to tell what Justin was thinking. Might have been anything. He was a loose cannon all the way around. I wouldn't put too much stock in what he had to say one way or another. Only reason I had him sit in on the questioning was so he could observe. Boy's a rookie. I wanted to let him get his feet wet. Guess he flat out couldn't handle it. Anyways, he's up and quit on me. Week or so ago."

"Is that right?"

"Oh yeah." Glass nodded. "I wasn't sorry to see him go, neither. Chitwood got real strange after that night. Uncooperative, unreliable. Only reason I kept him on was the computer. You got to have that now. Keep up with the times. But I wasn't sorry when he gave his notice. I'd been training one of my other men for the computer part of it anyway."

The sheriff paused and sucked the end of his cigar. "I expect I would've had to fire old Chitwood before too long, anyhow. He had no feel for the law, y'see. No talent for peacekeeping. And the Wier case—well—it just put him over the top. If a lawman can't look at the worst of it, he's got no business in the uniform."

"I see what you mean," said Portia. What she saw was a pack of lies that threatened to get bigger and more colorful the longer she stayed and listened to them. Whatever Chitwood's reason for calling her, she was willing to bet it had nothing to do with the things she'd just heard.

"Well, Sheriff," she said, rising and making her way to the door, "I want to thank you for the information. But you know how these things are. You have to check them out."

"I know it," Glass replied, resuming his country boy drawl. "That's what you get paid for," he added with a little edge of contempt. He rose, signaling the end of the conversation.

She let it pass, despite a number of withering retorts that came to mind. As she reached the threshold, she paused and turned around. She stood eye to eye with the sheriff and pasted on an expression so charming she all but batted her eyelashes. "I don't suppose I could find Mr. Chitwood in town anywhere?"

The cigar rolled to the other side of his jaw. She could smell the wet tobacco on his breath. Glass flashed a surprisingly toothy smile. "Used to could," he acknowledged. "He and his wife lived in that complex near the Friendly Mall. You know where that is?"

She allowed that she didn't.

"It's off Friendly Avenue. Just two rights and a light past Main here. They had a place in there. You'll see it right away. From what I know, they moved out the day he quit. Left town. The manager might know where they went, though. Give you a forwarding address or something. I seem to recall the wife had folks somewhere in Tennessee. I figure they moved off up there. Some family business."

Bullshit, thought Portia. "Thanks," she said aloud. "I'll check it out."

As she had suspected, the manager of the apartment complex, a fat, middle-aged woman who insisted that Portia call her June, was less than helpful. June also insisted, with characteristic Southern hospitality, that she stay for a glass of tea. As Portia sipped and nibbled on a shortbread cookie of indefinable pedigree alongside the complex's postage-stamp-size swimming pool, June explained that Justin Chitwood and his Missus had just packed up and went. No address, no nothing.

"I can't say I was surprised, though. I see a lot of it. Being a landlady like I am." June peered at Portia over the tops of her sunglasses, puffing with self-importance.

"You see a lot of what?"

June waved in the direction of a row of identical-looking doors that faced the pool opposite where they sat. "Rootlessness," she answered ponderously. "Everybody's like that now—don't care a fig for settling down anyplace. You know what I mean? They go around like they ain't got no family, no past. They're all like that now—all the young folks. They never build nothing—just start over with a brand-new slate. That Chitwood was like that. You could just tell. And his wife told me he went to Harvard College. I blame that. Too much education makes people restless. I got five units standing empty, and I got to put it down to that."

Portia looked at her and wished fervently that she were somewhere else. Clearly, June had quite a lot by way of opinions to offer on the migratory habits of the young. She finished the last of her tea and smiled.

"Thanks, June. That was lovely, but I really do have to be going."

June peered up at her as Portia rose stiffly from a nylon-webbed aluminum chair. "I bet you know where you come from, don't you?" she said. "I bet you got roots."

Portia managed a wan little smile. Oh, June, she thought. You have no idea.

June stared into the depths of the bilious-looking pool water. "I just don't know what to do about their security deposit, either. The Chitwoods, I mean. Of course, I would return it to 'em, seeing as how they were paid up till the end of the month. But considerin' as they up and left that way, I suppose I'll have to keep it."

She'd looked at Portia as though she were asking permission for something that Portia, in her turn, declined to give. Their brief interview ended, the psychologist smiled and thanked the landlady for her time. She even went so far as to ask if June had ever encountered Jimmy Wier, but June had only shaken her head.

"I seen him around of course. But we never did have a conversation at all. He worked for Ed over there at the mall," she offered darkly. "I got no use for Ed Derman, never did. Highway robbery is the only business he's in. I shop at Harris Teeter. Better prices and double coupons, too."

As she swung the Volvo out of the parking lot and onto the service road that would lead her to Ed's Market, Portia waved at June's squat little form ensconced at poolside—looking as forlorn as an old mother hen bereft of her chicks.

Inside Ed's, a girl of about sixteen sat idly thumbing through a magazine at the front register. She didn't look up until Portia stood directly in front of her and cleared her throat.

"Hey," the girl responded in a bored voice.

Portia smiled again. Too much more of this cultivating the locals and she felt as if her face would crack. "Hey—" She caught sight of an almost illegible nameplate pinned at an angle over the girl's heart. "Denise?"

"That's right," the girl replied.

"I was wondering if you could tell me if the owner is around? Ed Derman?"

The girl moved her head from side to side. "Nope. Today's Thursday," she added by way of explanation.

Portia nodded as if she understood. "Oh?"

The girl's pale green eyes flitted over Portia's plain T-shirt and chinos with all the expression of the average lizard's, then settled for a moment on her hair. Her hand moved up to her own hair then, self-consciously yanking at a few bleached tendrils that looked to be in need of a good shampoo.

"He's gone on Thursdays."

"I see." Portia paused and measured the possibility of gleaning any real information about Jimmy Wier from the girl in front of her, figuring her chances to be anywhere from slim to nonexistent. Sensitivity to others didn't seem high on Denise's list of cognizant capabilities.

"So it's okay if we talk a little, then?" Portia coaxed.

The girl shrugged. "About what?"

"I wanted to ask you about somebody who used to work here. Jimmy Wier."

The lizard eyes came unexpectedly alive at the name and Denise's expression hovered somewhere between awe and amusement. "That was something, huh? The way he did those old biddies?" She stopped, remembering herself. "I mean, Miz Bennet and Miz Mooney. Are you a cop?"

"No," Portia replied. "I'm a psychologist. I was called in to evaluate—"

"A psychologist? Like a headshrinker?"

"Yeah, like that. You worked here when Jimmy was around, didn't you?"

"Sure. Uncle Ed gave me the job. My mom made him."

"Okay. Now, Denise—" Portia leaned closer, her tone urgent and confidential. "You could be real important to this case, okay? On account of you working with Jimmy. You understand?"

Denise grinned stupidly. "You mean I might have to testify, right? Like on Court TV?"

"Maybe—I don't know. But for now I just want you to think, okay? I want you to try and remember if you noticed anything about Jimmy while you were working here together that seemed—" Portia broke off and searched for the right words. It was important not to lead her, she knew. Important not to taint any memory this girl might have by the wrong choice of word or inflection. "Just tell me what you thought of him," she finished.

Denise puzzled over the question for a long moment. Portia didn't blame her. Denise didn't look as if she'd been encouraged to do very much thinking at all, much less to express herself.

"Well, at first I thought he was fine, you know?"

Portia nodded, feeling a little sinking in the pit of her stomach. Fine was an all-encompassing, quintessential Southern word used to describe any and all conditions from the weather to complex emotional impressions. In this context, it probably meant that Denise had only been dimly aware of Jimmy Wier as he moved around the periphery of her life. Portia forced another smile.

"Denise, can you be a little more specific? Can you tell me anything about him?"

"He was mostly—fine. Like I said. But sometimes—well—" She glanced up, frowning, clearly at a loss to articulate what she meant.

"Sometimes?" Portia prompted.

"I mean, I never noticed anything much about him. He was big and sorta dumb like. But then all of a sudden he'd turn out to know things. You know what I mean?"

"Know things? You mean he was smarter than you thought he was?"

Denise began chewing on a cuticle. "Yeah, but not smart like in school. It was another kind of smart. It was like—he knew about stuff in magazines. Like he'd been around, you know? I dunno—it was just like—Jimmy was just Jimmy—humping around—doing the deliveries. And then all of a sudden you looked up and there he was. And you could tell he really was there, that he was paying attention. It gave me the creeps."

Portia struggled to make sense of what she was hearing. "Why did Jimmy make you uncomfortable, Denise? Did he ever approach you—touch you?"

"You mean sex? Naw, not Jimmy. But once he killed those women—well, when I heard that, a lot of things started to make sense."

"Like what?"

"Well, what I heard about it, I couldn't help thinking, all this time I been working with this—killer." Denise grinned self-consciously.

"I mean it could have been me, right? And I started to think about if he ever watched me or thought I was sexy, you know. And I figured out that he did. Once I thought about it, I could have told you he was a pervert way back. Only I never thought about it till after the murders. It was only after they happened that everybody realized what kind of guy Jimmy was. But once I did—well, it all made sense. He was just waiting for a chance, I guess. I'm glad it wasn't me. But it could've been, you know? Like—it was so obvious."

The last vestiges of the psychologist's smile fell away as Denise trailed off, seemingly amazed with herself for having gotten out so long a speech at one go. The ego, Portia thought, is a wonderful thing. Like its old buddy, hindsight, the ego is able to adjust reality almost at will. It was just too damn bad this girl hadn't made a distinction between celebrity and victimhood. Somehow in her mind, being a might-have-been corpse by virtue of her proximity to Jimmy was almost as good as the real thing.

"Thanks, Denise. Thanks a lot. You've been real helpful," she lied.

Denise's face became as animated as it probably ever got. "You think they'll call me as a witness?" she asked. "I bet if I thought some more, I could remember a whole lot of stuff."

Portia shook her head and paused, one hand on the double doors. "I bet you could, Denise. I bet you could."

Ten

●●●●●●●●●●●●●●●●●●●●●●●●●●●●●●●●●●●●

T HE NEXT TWO DAYS passed in a merciful refuge of
routine. Alice lost a front tooth and insisted she would
not place it under her pillow until she had some assurance that the
Tooth Fairy was prepared to bring her a kitten in exchange. Portia
promised to relay the message, but nothing beyond that. Cats, all cats,
belonged to another part of her life—one that she had no interest in
resurrecting.

The news from Columbia that filtered into her office indicated that
Wier had no obvious physical anomalies and that, save for high blood
sugar, he was in reasonably good health. With the physical reports out
of the way, Portia confirmed the schedule for him to get a number of
standardized psychological tests. Two calls to the prison infirmary had
confirmed that he was continuing to respond well to his medication,
and that the slight increase in Haldol had been to his advantage.
There had been no further episodes or outbursts, so on Friday Jayne
Patten would make the long drive to Columbia to administer the
standard Wechsler Adult Intelligence Scale and the MMPI to the prisoner. That left the weekend before Portia would have to face him
again.

Friday morning in her office, she briefed Jayne on the case with
more than a little trepidation. Though Jayne was a veteran psychologist, there was no telling how Wier might react to a new face at these
early stages of evaluation.

"Just keep your cool, Jayne," she offered lamely after the briefing. "He may try to scare you."

At six two and one hundred and eighty pounds, the graying Dr. Patten didn't have the look of a woman who frightened easily. She offered Portia a tight smile as she gathered up the last of the testing materials and stuffed them unceremoniously into a battered briefcase. "Hey, I know the routine," she said. "Don't worry so much."

"Can't help myself," Portia replied.

Jayne shot her a quizzical glance. "Look, he's on his meds—he'll get through it. What's got you so uptight about this case, anyway? It's not like you've never done this before." She frowned a little. "You giving the TAT yourself?"

Portia nodded. "I think I'd better," she answered. The TAT or Thematic Apperception Test was a series of pictures about which patients were asked to tell a story, or describe what they saw. Though none of the standard tests were usually given by the psychologist of record, hearing and recording Wier's TAT results was an opportunity Portia didn't feel she could let slip by.

"Good," Jayne answered abruptly. "I hate giving that one. Either they decide they don't see anything or they see the damn ceiling of the Sistine Chapel. Takes forever."

Portia grinned, protesting, "Jayne!"

"Well, it's true!" Jayne answered, rising to her feet. "I had a patient go on for hours once. Couldn't stop talking about number six. Made me nuts."

Portia shook her head at her colleague's kidding. "This whole job makes me nuts sometimes," she answered.

"So get a shrink," Jayne said, heaving the briefcase under one arm and heading for the doorway. "Listen, I'll call when I've got something, okay? I know his date's coming up. If all goes right with the world, I'll get to the scoring this weekend."

"Thanks, Jayne," Portia answered. "I appreciate this." If nothing else, the standard profiles would be something to analyze, real data she could bring to the witness stand. With a little help from Jimmy's test results, she might even be able to narrow the category of "undifferentiated" schizophrenia to a more specific type. That could help him in court. All she had to do was hang in there.

Jayne gave her a long look. "Take it easy," she said. "And the hell with a shrink. Take a vacation." With a wave, she disappeared down the hall in long strides.

As she watched Jayne go, Portia couldn't help feeling some misgiving. Her formidable appearance might prove too intimidating for Jimmy Wier. Worse, Portia feared Jayne's age or graying hair might set him off in some way she didn't yet understand. After all, his victims had been women. Women far older than Jayne it was true, but the niggling fear that Wier would react violently or in some way she'd failed to anticipate still worried her.

Yet, Portia reminded herself to be patient. At least with medication, Wier had reached a point where he was coherent enough to be given the standard tests. Before Haldol, that would have been impossible. Nevertheless, her own feelings of inadequacy as a therapist continued to gnaw at her as she played and replayed her last session with Jimmy Wier.

As it turned out, that was the principal topic of conversation at her appointment with Sophie Stransky Friday afternoon.

"He called me Tricks, Dr. Tricks," Portia concluded after giving Sophie the specifics. "Of course he did. Why not? I did trick him. I think I'm so damn smart. I tricked him right into losing what little bit of mind he had left. Some genius. First, I capitalized on his vulnerability, then I confronted him with something that was more than he could stand. It was completely irresponsible on my part. I feel like a monster. I wasn't helping him—I was pushing for the sake of my investigation."

Portia paused and looked at Sophie, her eyes confused and full of pain. "I don't know what's happening to me. I used to think it was okay!"

The soft afternoon sun had begun to take on the lavender tinge of a fast-approaching autumn. It touched Sophie's hair as she sat in the light of the window, turning it from crisp white to beautiful silver, the way Portia might have imagined an angel's hair would look, had she been the kind of woman to believe in angels. The room was filled with its usual genial clutter, smelling of old books and sandalwood, but today she could draw none of the feelings of refuge and safety she usually found there. Her mind continued worrying at her treatment of Jimmy Wier, and her heart would not let it rest. As Portia paused in her self-flagellation, Sophie attempted to soothe her.

"You took a gamble, that was all," she offered mildly. "And you lost. It happens. From what you've told me, this man is clearly schizophrenic. And schizophrenics are not famous for their predictability. You need to find out about his background or you can't help him. That's your job. You aren't his therapist."

Portia set her mouth in an unhappy line. "But I had no right— when I confronted him with that stuff about California, I knew he wasn't ready to tell me."

Sophie nodded, understanding. "From what you've told me, his reaction would indicate that your poking around was pretty valuable."

Shifting uneasily against the velvet chair, Portia made a dismissive little gesture. "That's hardly the point," she answered curtly, then composed herself. "I'm sorry. I'm not irritated with you—it's me. My own insensitivity to his condition. How can I call myself a healing person and knowingly cause so much pain?"

Sophie placed her delicate, knotted fingers lightly against the edge of the mahogany desktop. "Are you telling me that you would be feeling differently right now if you had confronted your patient with what you suspected and he had not exploded? I imagine that the truth of his past would be terribly painful no matter when you approached him with it. What's the real problem here?"

She smiled gently at Portia's obvious discomfiture. "I'm not so sure we're talking about poor Mr. Wier, after all. I think maybe we're talking about your pain—the fact that you know you need to expose your own pain in order to move forward."

She paused only a moment at the sound of Portia's sharp intake of breath. "You have hidden yourself from me—your shadow side, the parts you fear the most—for a very long time. We have discussed your 'story,' some details of your early life. But, I really know very little about how you have managed these agonizing truths within yourself. Perhaps you are weary of hiding. Or maybe it's only that digging around in Mr. Wier's past reminds you of your own."

"No . . ." Portia tried to protest and faltered as the truth of Sophie's statements reverberated in her heart. "I—I—it's just the job— just the lousy job."

"You know as well as I do that you were free to turn down this job as you call it. You're hiding behind your professional veneer. You pretend that you are different from your Mr. Wier. None of us is different. We all have pain—dark sides that we are afraid to see. This is what keeps each of us from becoming fully integrated."

Portia fidgeted. "I know all that," she acknowledged. "But, I . . ."

Sophie peered at her intently. "Why are you making so much of this?" she wanted to know. "Wier's reaction was unfortunate, I grant you. But that doesn't mean the evaluation process cannot be rescued. It doesn't mean he will never speak to you again. Unless that's what you want. Do you want your relationship with this patient to end? Are you trying to stop it before the process has truly begun?"

"I'm not so sure," Portia replied sadly. "I don't think so. But I don't know anymore! I looked over my notes from that first session. It should have been obvious to me that he perceives women—all women—as unreasonably powerful. It's the whole key—to the murders, to everything about this man. And his psychoses."

"And—?" Sophie's bright birdlike eyes never left Portia's face.

The younger woman moved her hands restlessly in her lap. "I feel like I used my power over him to hurt him. I blew it. On the one hand, I tried to establish trust; on the other hand, I wanted him to perceive me as powerful because I knew things about him. It was so stupid! I can't explain it, but I honestly thought that confronting him with something about his past would enable him to trust me—that it would ease the way for his confiding in me."

"Is that how it works for you?"

"What?" Portia stared at her doctor, caught off guard by the question.

"I asked if that is how it works for you," Sophie replied patiently. "When people confront you with some piece of information about your past, something you are trying to suppress or that you find painful, how does it make you feel? When they have power over you because they know things that you can't allow yourself to feel, does that make you trust them? Confide in them? What happens to you?"

Portia drew back from the sudden insistence of Sophie's tone. "We've been through all that," she answered. "I've told you about my past. What happened."

"You've told me about a young girl who was repeatedly raped and abused, yes. But it happened to you, Portia. You were that girl. And yet you continue to describe these things to me as though they happened to someone else. Tell me, what do you feel when you talk of such things?"

The question hung between them like a challenge. Portia glanced uneasily at the clock; there were almost fifteen minutes left to the hour. "I'm not sure I—" she answered nervously.

But the older therapist pressed on. "Does it inspire your trust when people confront you with the past? What do you do when you see someone you grew up with? Someone from Mississippi? Do you smile and put out your hand? Or do you run? To protect yourself from a confrontation?"

Portia stiffened against the broad wingback, her eyes moving restlessly around the room to the feathered dream catcher swaying gently in the mauve-tinted light of the window. "I'm not sure what you mean," she answered carefully.

Sophie shook her head slowly, her voice low and resigned. "Oh, my dear, I think you know exactly what I mean. There is a great deal about your past that you are not yet willing to feel with me. I know it and you know it. So why aren't we talking about it? Why is the past a subject to hide your feelings about? I'm talking about you, Portia. Not your professional life, not your day-to-day problems. I'm talking about the hidden past—your emotional life. Your shadow side."

Portia stared at the dream catcher, thunderstruck, as a thousand thoughts and images rose up in her mind, fighting for acknowledgment—all the terrible secrets within her fighting for a voice, fighting to be told. She took a shuddering breath and faltered, overwhelmed by a sense of humiliation so acute she could only push it away, her thinking self ripped away in a hurricane of feeling, her body all but frozen in her chair.

Sophie sat unmoving, watching her, and Portia could feel her eyes, unrelenting, waiting her out, waiting for the feelings to come, to be confessed, exposed, explored. She tried and failed to find a word, some way to describe the horror within her. And still she could feel Sophie waiting, patient and immovable as stone.

Then, in the next instant, in the time it took to take a breath and blow it out, in the pause before the next, the air was gone. She struggled against the panic, gasped and tried again. And still she could not make herself speak. She panted, bracing herself against the velvet upholstery, struggling for air, while the desperate need within wrapped cold fingers tighter around her heart. She fought the need—looked frantically for some distraction, some way to stop the questions from coming. Panic rose and the breaths came shorter; her hands shook violently as she grabbed for the box of tissues that teetered on the edge of the desk—tissues that the dry-eyed Portia did not appear to need. The room fell so suddenly silent, she could hear the clock ticking as the moments fell away, punctuated with the now-familiar whistling in her throat as she began to gasp and bright spots floated before her eyes. Her hand flew to her neck and she stared at Sophie helplessly, terror in her eyes.

"Okay," Sophie soothed. "Breathe. Look at me, Portia. Just me, okay? Just Sophie, that's it. You can breathe—you can. Do it, Portia. Let yourself breathe. Relax. Now breathe, just breathe. That's right. Keep it up—good. You're okay—deep—from the diaphragm."

Silent—all but paralyzed—Portia could only do as she was told, forcing air into the pit of her stomach, inhaling again and again, drawing great gulps of it until she could feel the terror begin to subside, the awful tightness in her chest begin to ease.

"Again," Sophie directed. "Deeper. Don't think about anything but your breathing for a moment. Once more. Let the tension out of your shoulders as you exhale. Feel it—feel it go?"

"Yes," Portia managed after long minutes. Sophie poured her a glass of spring water and Portia sipped silently, trying to recover herself. Her voice croaked with effort when she was once again able to speak.

"I'm—sorry. I don't know what happened. All you did—was mention—my past. I can't believe I had such a strong reaction. I thought I was through with being a victim."

"You have nothing to apologize for," Sophie told her. "I pushed a bit just now. More than I have before. Perhaps I believed your discomfort about confronting Mr. Wier meant you were ready to confront yourself."

"No—Sophie—it was me—I couldn't get—"

"No." The therapist interrupted her with a wave of her hand. "It was me. I take the responsibility. I confronted you with something I suspect you are not ready to deal with. I used my power in this relationship. We all use our power. And yes, I caused you pain and terrible discomfort. But that is sometimes necessary for you to get better. Just as it might be necessary for your Mr. Wier."

As the implication of Sophie's words began to take hold, Portia was suffused with embarrassment. She felt a hot blush creep up her neck. "Oh God—" she sighed.

"And when I confronted you with this power of mine, you froze. You began to develop the symptoms of a full-blown panic attack." Sophie relaxed a little on her side of the desk, and a hint of mischief played in the twinkle of her eyes. "So tell me, Doctor," she went on. "What happened? What were you feeling a moment ago?"

Portia ducked her head, and began to slowly tug the tissues from the box in her lap, one by one, crumpling them in her hand. "I was—afraid," she said in a low voice. "Obviously."

"Yes," Sophie answered firmly. "You were afraid. But of what, Portia? Of me?"

"No—I'm not sure."

"Say it—work to identify the fear. Were you afraid of me?"

Portia took a deep, shuddering breath, trying to sort out the jumble of thoughts and impressions, trying to find some way to articulate the crippling panic that had overtaken her.

"No," she went on. "No, not of you. I know that there are—things—issues that maybe we haven't talked about. And I just—couldn't—didn't feel ready." She paused and looked at Sophie, her eyes filled with unspoken pain. "I was afraid because I felt—so many things. All in a moment. And I didn't feel ready to talk about them. I wanted time—to—I don't know," she trailed off helplessly.

Sophie observed her patient with a mixture of empathy and frustration. There were only so many places to hide from oneself. And Portia McTeague was running out.

"You said you wanted time. What for? Was it time to analyze your feelings? Or was it that you wanted time to distance yourself from experiencing the pain of those feelings?"

"Ahh—" Portia opened her mouth and shut it again. In answer, she licked the tip of one index finger and scored one mark for Sophie in the air.

"Exactly," replied Sophie. "Ahh—and while you're at it, consider that your panic attack—this shortness of breath—functioned in you as a protection against the experience of pain. You panicked just now because you understood on some level that if you couldn't breathe, I wouldn't ask any more questions. You effectively removed yourself from the possibility of pain. You panic in your nightmares in the same way. You can't breathe—and so you must wake up in order to make the dream end."

Portia sat for a long moment, staring at the mess of tissues in her lap, outwardly silent and resistant, while inwardly she was filled with protest.

I'm a therapist—I'm aware, damn it! The nightmares are about trauma—nothing else! I saw somebody killed!

But Portia said nothing at all. Instead, she lifted her eyes and stared at Sophie in wounded silence.

Sophie was not to be deterred.

"I push a button, your internal alarms go off," she continued. "Someone is trying to climb the walls you have built within yourself, Portia. And not being able to breathe is a kind of security system to prevent that. A behavior that takes place whenever someone is climbing the wall."

"You make it sound like the personality is a prison," Portia countered.

The older therapist didn't miss a beat. "Given your chosen profession, I'd say that was an interesting choice of words, wouldn't you? You reacted the same as your prisoner. He sought to keep you outside by behavior that prevented any further exploration of his pain. He effectively prevented you from getting in, just as your panic prevented me from going any further with you. The only difference is that he is a schizophrenic. You are not."

Portia's jaw went slack with astonishment as the full implication of Sophie's observations hit her head on. At that moment, an old-style butler's bell pull tinkled softly, signaling the arrival of Sophie's next patient. Sophie might have let it end there, but she pressed for a little bit more.

"So. What do you think?" she asked, coming around the desk to stand beside her patient as Portia stood on unexpectedly shaky legs. "Will I see you next time, or are you going to fire me now?"

Portia, who was looking for a place to toss the handful of crumpled tissues, paused and looked down at her diminutive therapist incredulously. "Fire you? Why would I do that?"

Sophie shrugged and plunged her hands deep into the pockets of her worn cardigan. "Because I played a hunch. Because I didn't have those facts that you are so fond of. Because in playing my hunch I caused an unfortunate reaction in my patient—a panic attack. In attempting to make a discovery about you, I caused you pain. Just as you did with your Mr. Wier." She paused and uttered a long, mock sigh. "So, if you want a referral or anything—"

Portia, still reeling, could only stare at her. "Sophie, are you serious?"

The older woman smiled benevolently, dropping the ruse. "Of course I'm not. But according to the standard you're setting for yourself, I should be. I played a hunch, with bad consequences—I didn't get the results I was looking for. By your standard, that makes me a poor therapist."

Tired, but oddly elated, Portia took her handbag and slung it over her shoulder. "Don't be ridiculous. You're a wonderful therapist. And you know it."

They made their way to the door and paused, reluctant to end what they both knew to have been a very important session. Sophie looked hard at her patient. "So are you," she told Portia. "So are you."

Portia started to open the door, but Sophie stopped her once more. "Just think about something else for me, won't you? For next time?"

Portia swallowed hard, wanting to know, and yet unable to stop herself from dreading whatever the formidable little woman in front of her might ask. Finally she nodded. "Of course."

"You spoke of the personality as a prison. But try to remember, my dear, security systems are not merely a protection against those who are trying to get in. Maybe—just maybe—they were put in place to keep something from trying to get out."

Twentynine Palms, California
September 1992

Eleven

• •

O F ALL the godforsaken burgs, Alan Simpson thought as he swung a rented eggplant-colored Ford Contour through the peculiar desolation that characterized the wide, abandoned-looking streets of Twentynine Palms. Stuck smack between a Marine installation and an Indian reservation, the town itself seemed to have sprouted out of some other landscape entirely. The flat vistas and dust and squat scattering of buildings held all the ghostly appeal of some lost space colony from a vintage science fiction epic. What were once two main neighborhoods seemed to have spilled into one another over the years. The better part of town, consisting mostly of cheap, but reasonably functional government-issue tract houses, once duly constructed nearer the base, had eroded more or less into the depressing landscape, the houses' small yards now dotted with rusting cars and the odd, abandoned toy. A quarter mile on, Alan found long stretches of falling-down apartment buildings nestled among a fistful of trailer parks and a scattering of tough-looking roadhouse bars. He supposed that at its best, Twentynine Palms had been a pit stop for transients, men and their families stuck there by the government, whose best hope was of leaving. At its worst, housed in the flimsy apartments and broken-down trailers, were those who had no hope of leaving, caught somehow and forced to stay in this place that was, Alan figured, just somewhere to the west of no place at all.

He flipped the sun visor to snatch at a piece of paper stuck behind it. An address was scrawled diagonally in his own clean, angular script.

He glanced at a collection of what looked to be plywood-paneled apartment dwellings, the architecture of which seemed to have been directly blueprinted from the butt-ugly rows of barracks of the military base from which he had just come. He pulled up beside the manager's office next to a blue Pinto wagon that somehow managed to look well maintained in the face of its immediate surroundings. From somewhere inside the thin walls of the complex, a television blared and an infant wailed mournfully.

All in all, he speculated idly as he paused in the broiling sun, it seemed like as good a place as any to bring up a maniac.

He rang the bell and stood, staring upward, momentarily transfixed by a spider's web that had managed to survive just above the doorjamb.

"Yeah?"

The woman in front of him was somewhere between fifty and a hundred; in the merciless light, with her hair tortured with peroxide and her skin tanned the color of shoe leather, it was impossible to tell.

Alan flashed a slow, easy grin and shifted his muscular frame in a way that he was well aware women were wont to notice. "Hi," he said simply. "I was wondering if you might be able to help me."

The woman tugged a little at the pair of short shorts that rode up over the tops of her thin, sinewy thighs. Alan allowed his eyes to wander at the sight, another little smile playing under his moustache.

"Maybe and maybe not," the woman answered. "I can't know until you ask, now can I?"

Despite the glare, Alan slid his sunglasses up into his hair and gave the manager the full benefit of his golden-lashed ice-blue eyes. "I'm a private investigator. Name's Alan Simpson. You want to see some ID?"

The woman nodded, and as she leaned a little into the doorjamb to study the official-looking card that he flipped open his wallet to display, her low-cut halter top fell open to display some of her own credentials. A suffocating perfume rose from her body, something that seemed to Alan to be a cross between coconut, jasmine, and ether. He smiled again. "Mind if I come in?"

"Not if you don't," the woman answered shortly and proceeded to usher him through a miserably small office area into an equally miserable main living room. The odd pieces of furniture were disguised here and there with tired-looking chenille bedspreads and throws, and through the shuttered blinds, slits of yellowish light played against walls painted a tired, tropical green. Hanging just above the console television was an enormous velvet painting of a pale, bleeding Christ figure with arms outstretched, golden flocking peeling from his thorny crown. He was smiling down at the world in a tragic, bemused way, as though there were so much more he'd meant to say.

"Sit," the woman directed. Alan made his way to what appeared to be a lump of recliner crouching beneath a chenille disguise. "Not that," the woman said. "That's got a bad spring. There. I'm Dot, by the way."

She watched him as, having no real choice, Alan settled himself in one corner of a small sofa, knowing she would come to join him there.

"You want a drink?" she asked. "I ain't got much, but I'll share it if you want." She hoisted a bottle of vodka in his direction, two inches of liquid left swirling on the bottom.

"No thanks," he assured her. "But you go ahead."

"Well," she said, coming back into the room, her plastic mules flapping along the floor. "What can I do you for?"

Alan showed his teeth in a benevolent grin, as though the turn of phrase was something he'd never heard before. She settled into the sofa, a little closer to him than was really necessary.

He drew a deep breath and said, with all the sincerity he could muster, "Well, Dot. I need your help. At least, I thought I did back at the base. But now that I'm here, I don't think you can give it to me."

Dot peered at him. "Why not?"

Alan hung his head. "The truth of it is, I'm looking for somebody who might have lived here a while back. A long time ago. A family that might have been stationed at the base out here. But, looking at you, I realize that you couldn't possibly be—well—old enough to know who I'm talking about."

She tossed back a little vodka and smiled at him, revealing uneven teeth stained the color of old bones. "I guess you get pretty far with that stuff, don't you?"

Alan grinned on. "Pretty far," he agreed. "How far am I gonna get with you?"

"Depends," she answered. "I've been cleaning this rathole for thirty years. Didn't get to manage it until my husband ran out on the alimony and the court give it to me." She paused and gestured around the room. "Some prize, huh?"

"So your husband owned the place?"

Dot looked at him. "I just told you. I own the place now. So supposing you tell me just who the hell you're looking for and why?"

Alan considered it. Apparently, Dot's days of falling for the fatal charms of smooth-talking private-eye types were long gone. He withdrew a small notebook from his back pocket and flipped through it for the page he sought.

"It was a family named Wier," he told her. "The husband, Horace Wier, was stationed at the Marine base from '61 to '66. He and his wife were divorced after he was sent to Germany for eight weeks in the fall of '64." Alan looked at Dot, who was, in her turn, looking at him through the bottom of her now-empty glass.

"Says nothing about why you're looking," she said, settling the glass on a kidney-shaped cocktail table in front of them. "Don't they keep records out there? Addresses and such?"

Alan shook his head. "Horace Wier died of heart failure at the age of fifty-eight in San Diego—three days after his retirement from active military service. He was a career officer."

Dot nodded. "Poor bastard. Guess he liked what he did for a living, huh?"

"I don't know, Dot. That's where his record ends."

"So?"

"So—the Marines say his family, or at least his wife, may have lived here sometime during that period. Does the name ring any bells? Would there have been any rental records—leases, anything like that? Something to show a forwarding address?"

"Rental records? Hah!" Dot snorted. "My old man took cash. Only cash. No records, no taxes. And no leases. My tenants are kind of leery of making anything too legal, if you know what I mean."

Alan leaned closer, placing a hand lightly on Dot's bony shoulder. "Think, Dot. Do you remember anybody named Wier? Maybe just a woman? They had a son; we think he might have been adopted. But there aren't any records of that, either."

Dot looked at the hand, then at Alan. Seeing the look, he removed it.

"Wasn't all that unusual back then," she reflected. "Adoptions, if you know what I mean. Girls stuck out here, husbands in boot camp or getting shipped off to God-knows-where, and a whole base of other guys to keep 'em company in the meantime. Happened all the time. Girl finds herself in the family way unexpected, husband's out on maneuvers maybe for months. They just give that baby away and pack up for the next base. Join up with the husband and he's none the wiser. Or leave the kid with a neighbor to baby-sit and just never come back. Happened all the time." Dot shook her head. "You won't find no papers for that kind of adoption," she assured him. "Never happen."

Alan settled back into his corner of the sofa, already knowing that what Dot said was true. "You still haven't told me if you remember anybody," he said. "Anybody named Wier."

She stood, a little unsteadily, and patted her bleached blond hair. "You still haven't told me why you're looking," she countered.

Like his hostess, Alan, too, rose to his feet, sensing that their interview was about to come to an end. He took a deep breath, feeling suddenly exhausted. "There's a man named Jimmy Wier coming up for trial in South Carolina next month. I've been hired by his defense lawyers to investigate his background."

Dot smoothed the shorts down over her hips. "Oh yeah? What'd he do?"

"Murder," Alan replied. "Two uhmm—elderly women. Wier is—disturbed. He can't tell us anything about his background. The defense is going to plead insanity, but in order to keep him from the death penalty we need to find evidence—family history, previous mental illness. His lawyers believe it will help save his life."

Dot fired up a Marlboro from a pack on the television and squinted at him through a cloud of blue smoke. "Huh," she said. "Well, I wouldn't know about that. But—"

Alan was already at the door when he heard the word. "But?"

Dot shrugged. "Might be nothing. But now I think about it, I seem to remember somebody like who you're talking about over at the Sherman's Arms. You know where that is?"

Alan didn't and took notes as she described a place that sounded even worse than the one he was already in.

"Same address as this, two blocks over. We get mail for them all the time. Only it's on Palm Court and we're on Palm Road. I used to know a gal ran it for a while back in the sixties. It was trashy, though. Sherman's Arms took wetbacks even, Indians too." She grinned at him, once more displaying her frightening teeth. "That's where you rented if you were too trashy to get with the trash in my place," she chuckled. "Maybe they'll know something, though. Wouldn't exactly be the first time the government got an address wrong, would it?"

"Thanks," Alan replied. "Thanks."

They paused in the doorway and once again Alan caught a whiff of her perfume, now intermingled with vodka and tobacco. Dot looked up at him. "You say this guy's crazy?" she asked him. "The one you're investigating?"

"Pretty much," Alan told her. "He did a crazy thing, that's for sure."

Dot considered it. "And you're trying to keep him from a death sentence?"

"More or less. I was hired by the defense, anyway."

Dot stood in the doorway as he entered the hall, her silhouette haloed in a billow of smoke. As he made to leave, she called after him, "Kill 'em all, is what I say."

He turned to look at her as she jerked her thumb over her shoulder, back toward the Jesus dying on a black velvet sea. "Let God sort 'em out."

Two hours later, in the sizzling heat of the desert afternoon, Alan made his way along a desolate strip of road dotted with the remains of blown-out tires and the twisted, eerie branches of sentinel Joshua trees. His trip to Sherman's Arms had not yielded anything so substantial as a record of a family named Wier, but the hard-eyed Indian who ran the place recalled a woman from the area named Sawtelle who'd married a Wier around that time. One of her brothers had lived on the outskirts of the desert, twenty miles outside of town. As far as the Indian knew, he was still alive.

So Alan, sweating bullets in the air conditioning and dreaming of spending the night in nearby Palm Springs, pulled into the ratty-looking strip of grit that passed for a driveway outside a decrepit mobile home set on blocks. An eroded-looking Pontiac was sinking in the sand near the front door like some archaeological relic. From somewhere around the back of the place a distracted rooster kept crowing, eternally confused by the desert's glassy light. Alan stared at the place with some misgiving and reached for a newly licensed .22 he'd been keeping under the driver's seat. Nothing about the desolation of the place alerted him especially, but as he peered through the tinted windshield, he found himself wanting it near. Tucking the gun safely into his belt, so that just a suggestion of the handle showed above his waistband, he got out of the car and made his way toward the cinder-block steps that perched unevenly near the front door. He knocked, waiting in the sun.

The door swung inward to a surprising blast of cold. A man of about seventy, dressed only in a stringy T-shirt and a pair of filthy boxer shorts, peered warily at him through the screen.

"Your name Sawtelle?" Without waiting for an answer, Alan introduced himself and flashed his license, with two fifty-dollar bills displayed prominently across the fold. "I'm a private investigator," he finished.

Wordlessly, the man opened the screen door and motioned Alan inside. The dark air-conditioned interior was a blessed relief from the heat, and he sank gratefully into the plastic-covered kitchen chair the old man shoved in his direction. An ashtray overflowed with unfiltered cigarette butts and the air was suffused with the chemical stench of the trailer's rudimentary toilet facilities. The old man stuck a hand in his direction and Alan shook it.

"I'm looking for somebody, Mr. Sawtelle," he began. "They told me in town it might have been your sister."

The man leaned closer in, cupping a hand to his ear, and indicating that Alan would best speak up. Alan slid the fifties across the table's surface in the old man's direction and began again. "I'm looking for information about a family named Wier. The woman's name was Elizabeth—Elizabeth Wier," he went on. "She was married to a Marine named Horace Wier. Back in the early sixties sometime. They told me you might be Elizabeth's brother. Back in town. Only they weren't sure. You know anybody like that, Mr. Sawtelle?"

The old man covered the fifties with his palm and slid them back across the table. When he looked up, he met Alan's eyes with a long, unreadable expression, as though he were not seeing him at all but someone else, as though that short speech had conjured a whole vision of someone long forgotten and only recalled with a terrible effort. He met Alan's eyes and nodded, his expression caught somewhere between pity and contempt.

"I knew somebody like that," he said after a long moment. "But back when I knew her, she didn't have no name."

Twelve

● ●

THE DRIVE to the prison was long and strange. The blue Volvo seemed to fight her steering as the four lanes of the interstate spread out before her in numbed desolation. The sky was dull and leaden gray in the sunless morning. The blank sky asked its questions and she felt the gray answers deep in her body, her limbs heavy and unwieldy as though they belonged to someone else. She wanted to pull off the road, to lean her head against the wheel and sleep. But there was no time for that now.

And so she could only keep driving, unable to concentrate, knowing she must, knowing, too, how easy it was to get lost on the road. Lost. The idea of it filled her with unreasonable fear. It would be terrible to get lost now. Now that she was so close. Her eyes searched the roadside for some sign, some direction, but found nothing to point her way. She had to find the right exit and not miss her turn, and she gazed through the tinted windshield at the endless stretch of road, wondering and afraid.

Nothing looked familiar. She glanced sideways as she passed a wreck—a jackknifed semi rolled on its side like some huge burned insect, the metal twisted and smoldering. She knew she ought to stop—tried to stop—but there was no stopping now. There was no time. Her eyes followed the ruined, smoking heap in her rearview mirror as it shrank and finally disappeared. She had to hurry and not get lost. Time—time was running out.

Jimmy was waiting.

She had to jerk the wheel violently to the left to avoid a black cat, which watched her as she passed it, eyes glowing emerald, then red. Hissing and snarling, its back arched as its hackles rose. She saw it and felt an answering chill on the back of her neck and along her arms.

The radio came on, the announcer's voice troubled and sickly sweet, expressing concern in a high, androgynous whine.

"Please be careful out there, folks. There's been an unusually high incidence of black cats in the paths of motorists today. We know what that means, don't we? Bad luck if one crosses your path—just think of what might happen if you killed one. Bad luck," the announcer sang. *"The worst luck there is, killing a cat. There's more than one way to skin one, oh yes. But you want to be careful about getting them killed, don't you? Don't you, Doctor?"*

She couldn't think about that. She had to hurry. Jimmy was waiting.

Tires screamed as she swerved onto the exit ramp and the buildings of the prison rose up on the left. She pressed her foot down on the gas pedal, relieved and confused, blinking in the strange white light. It was the same place, but it was altered, changed. The razor wire glinted eerily along the fence; the parking lot was deserted. For a long, terrifying moment, she thought she was too late.

The crouching buildings beckoned her, and the short walk to the Visitor's Center seemed to take forever in the strangling, sodden air. Her breathing grew labored and she could feel the humidity like a solid thing against her skin, warm and cool at once, the temperature of a fever chill.

The guard behind the desk smiled secretively as she showed him her identification.

"Who are you?" he asked. And the question made her afraid. "Who are you really?"

She leaned against the desk, panting in the torpid air. She was so tired—too tired to explain. Unable to respond, she could only point to the small square of her driver's license picture, her finger trembling with effort—

There.

The guard's grin grew wider and she saw suddenly that his eyes were familiar—green and flat, like lizard's eyes.

Friend or family? he wanted to know. *Family or friend?*

And she breathed, hearing the whistling start deep in her chest. She coughed to clear it, managed to speak. "I'm her! There! Can't you see me? That's who I am—why can't you see?"

Who have you come for? he insisted. *Who is it this time?*

She leaned against the counter, light-headed and sick. Her eyes traveled dizzily to the guard's nameplate—Chitwood. She tried to place the name and couldn't, her memory vanished in the struggle for air. And she bowed her head to the guard and began to weep.

"He's my—child."

The guard takes her by the arm and leads her, and she cannot fight him anymore. She knows there's no use in fighting anymore.

We knew it all along, he whispers. *No one does anything for nothing, do they? There's always a reason—always a reason. Facts are facts, aren't they? No hiding from that . . .*

He takes her face in his hand then, and she feels the pressure of his fingers against her jawbone, deep in her flesh. And as he makes her look at him she sees herself reflected in those lizard eyes—trapped and afraid as they study her face, bright and strange and merciless.

You think you can save him now?

And she cannot answer, can only look, falling deeper into the green, green eyes. Green eyes—like a lizard's—like a cat's.

It's bad luck if you look too long, the guard cautions and drops his hands, whirling her around to march in front of him.

This way. This way—Jimmy's waiting.

And he is dragging her then—her feet sighing along the ground. He opens the doors, and from somewhere deep inside the prison walls, she hears cheering as they welcome her.

The guard is grinning now, a wide cat's grin, full of secrets. *You're no different, are you? They all know that. Blood calls, doesn't it? Blood calls.*

She wants to run, but she cannot fight him. She is captured—her face wet with tears.

You gave away your secrets like candy. And the voice was like a hissing in her ear.

No! Portia begins to moan, the sound coming up from somewhere deep within her, her sobs doubling her over in agony.

Lies . . . all lies. The guard tells her. *It's too late now though— Jimmy's waiting.*

She raises her head and tries to make him out through the wet blur of her weeping. "Please—"

He shoves her roughly ahead of him, into a hallway that has no end, marching her forward. And she hears their footsteps keeping time to the weeping, hears the sighing of paper slippers as they march along the floor.

You couldn't take the truth and you couldn't take the consequences, the guard murmurs. *Happens all the time.*

She stares at him over her shoulder as she stumbles on into the darkness of the endless hall. "I had no choice—I had no choices left."

The guard throws back his head and laughs, the sound coming from deep within him, as he delights in her pain.

Lies! All lies! The penalty for lying is death, don't you know? They changed it. Come and see.

He shoves ahead of her, bursting through a set of heavy metal doors, and the hall is filled with a blinding light. She falls to her knees, blinking—and from somewhere, everywhere, comes the ringing of the alarms. Bells, bells everywhere, so many bells, and she cowers against the sound, covering her ears against that terrible ringing. The guard begins to shout and dance ahead of her, pointing his finger as he goes.

Jimmy is waiting! Come and see! You knew the truth and you never said a word. Time to go tell them. They're all waiting.

And the bells began to scream.

Portia sat up, bathed in sweat, her face and hair damp with weeping. Reflexively she fumbled toward the telephone on her nightstand, already knowing with some part of her mind what it would take to silence the terrible ringing that still echoed through the last vestiges of sleep. She lifted the receiver and glanced toward the clock, the red digits glowing in the dark. It was almost three.

She swallowed once and groped for a word, closing her eyes as she swam into consciousness. "Hello—yes?" Her voice sounded unfamiliar to her—a soft croak, little more than an exhausted whisper.

"Portia?" a voice on the other end wanted to know. "Is that you?"

"Alan—God." At the sound of his voice, Portia sank groggily back on the pillows. "Yes, it's me. I was asleep, that's all. Where are you?"

Alan's voice fairly crackled with excitement. "Palm Springs. I'm sorry about the time. But I figured it couldn't wait. You have a fax machine at home?"

Portia sat upright, fully awake now, hardly daring to form a question. "Sure I do—Alan—?"

"Well, make some coffee and fire it up," Alan replied gleefully. "You have a long night ahead of you."

She swung her feet over the side of the bed and fumbled for a robe. "Alan—my God. Tell me. Is it Wier? Did you find something?"

Alan's reply was so warm with affirmation it sent an answering heat through her own veins as she responded to his quiet intensity from somewhere deep in her solar plexus.

"Oh my darling," he told her. "We just might have hit the mother lode."

Even though it was only the beginning, the deposition that was clicking through her fax machine, signed by one Larry Sawtelle, spoke volumes. He was not the brother, but a first cousin of the woman who had taken the name Elizabeth when she was married to a Marine named Horace Wier in 1961. Before that, Elizabeth Wier had never been given a name, and was referred to by the rest of her family only as Sister. She was the only girl child in a family consisting of a father and three boys, all of whom believed that females were chattel, to be used for household duties and as sexual outlets for their male relatives. The mother of the family had committed suicide with a shotgun shortly after the birth of her youngest child, a boy named Jack. As far as Larry Sawtelle was aware, the woman known as Elizabeth Wier had never been to school and was kept chained in the yard of the family home until the age of eight. By the age of thirteen, it was decided by the Sawtelle males that she was mentally defective, and she was sent to the state institution for shock treatment. While there, she underwent an involuntary sterilization procedure at the request of her family. She was returned to them after a little more than a year, and after six more months was once again sent back to the state mental hospital after stabbing one of her brothers with a knife. Upon her release, she had run away and taken to prostitution, working the bars around the base until she met Horace Wier, whom she married shortly thereafter.

The deposition went on to state that the couple had continued to live in the area in an apartment off the base, for a little more than five years. Elizabeth maintained some contact with her relatives, though not with her brothers or her father. This contact consisted mostly of begging for money and food, and Mr. Sawtelle recalled being sent by his own father to Elizabeth's apartment on more than one occasion to break up some violent domestic dispute between Horace and his wife.

As Sawtelle explained, Elizabeth was "never quite right," but the family had come to accept her emotional problems.

In Sawtelle's view, Horace Wier believed that his wife's emotional problems stemmed from her not being able to have children of her own. He went on to state that Horace himself had gotten her a baby from a neighbor in town, though he was not aware of any specific details of the adoption. It appeared that Elizabeth was happier having a child to raise, and Sawtelle did not recall any arguments for the three months or so that the couple continued to live in town before moving to San Diego in the early spring of 1967. Of the child Sawtelle recalled very little, except for the fact that it appeared to be about six months of age when the Wiers took it in, and secondly that ". . . she was a pretty little thing. Elizabeth kept it dressed up just like a doll."

Having spent the rest of that night and the following morning pouring over the Wier file and cross-referencing the information in the deposition with earlier police and psychiatric reports, Portia decided to return Alan's favor by rousing him out of bed at the crack of dawn, Pacific Time.

"You up?" she asked the sleepy voice on the other end of the line.

"For you, always," he answered, managing to sound both sleepy and sexy at once.

Portia shook her head, smiling into the receiver. "You never miss a trick, do you?"

"I take the fifth," Alan answered groggily. "It is the fifth, isn't it? So, what'd you think of our Mr. Sawtelle? Is this our family or just a rabbit trail?"

"I've got to believe it's them, Alan. Background fits. Jesus, the mother's history reads like a how-to manual for raising psychotics. Those poor kids—"

"Kids? As in kids plural?"

"Well, if Sawtelle says the child was a girl. I've got to assume, if this is the same crew, that Wier was adopted into the family after they went to San Diego."

"Possible . . ." Alan replied doubtfully.

Portia frowned into the receiver. "Alan, what're you thinking?"

"That I need to call room service," he told her. "I need coffee."

"Alan, be serious—"

"Okay, okay. Give me a minute. I'm trying to figure out what I am thinking. You can be really demanding, you know that?"

"Look, I've got a session with Wier in less than two hours. I don't even know if he'll talk to me. The man is so nuts he can't even tell me enough to save his own neck. So if you've got a good idea, spit it out, okay? I don't have time for games." Without meaning to, Portia's voice shook a little over the last words, and Alan caught the desperation in her tone.

"Hey, take it easy," he said. "I'm on your side, remember?"

"Sorry, Alan, I—there's just a lot of pressure . . ."

"I know that. But it isn't going to save anybody if you go round the bend now, is it?"

Portia bit back the hot retort that bubbled to her lips. She wanted to shout that she wasn't in any danger of going around any bend and if Alan Simpson wanted to take up psychology, he could at least sign up for a correspondence course. But the words never came, cut off as they were by Alan's next remark.

"Look over Keene's initial diagnosis and evaluation. You got it in front of you?"

"Of course I do," Portia almost snapped.

"If memory serves, there was something in there about a possible gender-identity disorder, wasn't there?"

"What—?" Portia flipped hastily through a number of pages, reading silently until she came across the phrase that Alan had mentioned. "It's not part of the initial evaluation at all," she said. "It's just a note by the head psychiatric nurse at the Columbia hospital. Somebody named Melanie Durant. My God, Alan, how in the world did you remember that?"

"God is in the details. Or so they said at detective school. But, given that we don't exactly have the most reliable source in Mr. Sawtelle, and seeing that our Elizabeth was pretty obviously crackers anyway you crumble it—what if that baby really was our Jimmy?"

"But he said it was a girl."

"Yeah, I know what he said. But that doesn't mean he was right."

"You mean she just treated the baby like a girl? Dressed him like one?" Portia scowled over the accumulation of papers on her desk, thinking hard. "It could fit," she went on uncertainly. "From what the cousin says, Elizabeth would certainly hate males. Still, I don't know, Alan. I can't put the gender thing with what I've seen of Jimmy. I can't see how it fits."

"But," Alan interjected, "wouldn't something like cross dressing a toddler give rise to your basic gender-identity disturbance? If the nurse at Columbia was right?"

Portia was silent for a moment as her mind turned over the implications of Alan's statement. "I've got to see Elizabeth's hospitalization records," she said. "It's the only way to find out anything for sure. If I know more about her psychoses, I can get a better handle on what she might have done to Jimmy." Then, with her next breath, "How soon can you get them to me?"

Alan laughed aloud. "It's going to take some time, Portia. Remember, California isn't open yet. I'll get my act together and head for San Diego as soon as I get off the phone. Whoever these people are, the records there have got to be better than the military's. So I'll get on it. Okay with you if I get breakfast first?"

Portia grinned, her good humor restored. "Continental," she told him. "And eat standing up."

"I'll get back to you tonight. And chin up, okay? As my own dear mother used to say, 'Don't let the bastards get you down.' "

Portia had the fleeting thought that Simpson's mother must have had quite a bit more than that by way of snappy repartee to have forged a character like Alan, but she let it pass.

"After Wier, I'm going to check out that nurse, Melanie Durant. She'd still work there, right? It's only been a few weeks. Maybe she can give me something."

Alan was noncommittal. "If the prosecution hasn't gotten to her first," he answered. "Why don't you throw Big Nurse off onto some wide-eyed clerk in Mr. Dylan's employ? Take a couple of hours. Go see a movie."

"Sorry, Alan," she replied. "I'll be right around the corner from the prison hospital. No reason I can't do it myself. Besides, I'm your basic Type A personality, remember?"

"Hmmm," Alan reflected. "What's that A stand for, anyway? Adorable? Auburn-haired? Angelic? Aphrodisiac?"

"Ascetic," Portia broke in, laughing. "As in celibate, self-flagellating. As in hair shirts and lots of penance."

"Whatever rings your bells," Alan replied dryly. "But it all sounds very dreary."

"Bye you," Portia answered warmly. "And, Alan—thanks. This gender thing. It could be something."

"No thanks necessary, darlin'. Just a thought. I'll call you tonight. You promise to miss me?"

"No," she said. And hung up, shaking her head as she fumbled for her files, bag, and car keys. If she hurried, she'd be able to make it to Columbia with enough time before her scheduled session with Jimmy to locate Melanie Durant.

If she hurried, she wouldn't have to think about Alan Simpson any more than was necessary.

Thirteen

● ●

HALFWAY DOWN THE ROAD to Columbia prison, Portia's car phone chirped, making her jump. She'd been uneasy on the drive, pushing back both her rising anxiety over her upcoming session with Wier and a hangover mood from the previous night's nightmare. Fragments of dream images kept fighting their way up from her subconscious into the glassy, unforgiving light of day. She reached for the phone almost gratefully, thankful to be distracted from the tumult of her thoughts.

Maris Beasley's flat, efficient voice greeted her calmly. "You sound like you're in a cave," she offered. "You charge that thing recently?"

"It always sounds like that, Maris. It's a car phone. What's up?"

"Stupid," Maris reflected. "How is anybody supposed to get away from anybody anymore? Anyway, himself wants to talk to you. We got that fax deposition from California. Hold on."

Portia waited until Dec's voice came on the line. "At least Simpson coughs up a piece of paper once in a while," he began grudgingly. "What I want to know is, does it mean what I think it means? Is it the right family?"

"Looks like it, Dec. I'm going to try and find that out this morning. I'm on my way to Columbia now. If these people in California were really Jimmy's folks, the mother's abuse history means a lot. More than a lot. From what you can read there, a kid wouldn't stand a chance. Anyway, it's what we've got for the moment. That and the physical tests. No real surprises there. He seems to be of average intelligence, and the only thing the early inventories show is that he's making an attempt to hide how nuts he really is. There's evidence of disorientation, paranoia—''

"Never mind. I mean, thanks, but tests results don't go very far in the jury box. Where's Sam Spade now?"

Portia smarted unexpectedly at Dec's reference to Alan. "He's in San Diego. He's going after the hospitalization records for the mother, and he'll try and trace any children from there. School records, foster care even. But it looks good, Dec. If these are the same people, this woman—Elizabeth—she'll have been in and out of state hospitals quite a bit. And once in the system, there's always paperwork. We can trace from there."

"We?" Dec tried and couldn't quite manage to keep the acid from his tone.

"Yes, we," Portia responded testily. "You remember us, right? The members of your defense team?"

Dec hastily tried to cover his tracks. "I just know how busy you've been, Portia. I don't want you to feel as though you have to oversee every detail of the background investigation. That's Simpson's job. Let him do it."

"He is doing it, Dec. But you know as well as I do that until I get Wier to give me something substantial, anything Alan can throw my way is necessary to that investigation. I need it to get through to Jimmy. My lord, what is the matter with you? You'd think you'd made a deal with the devil himself when you hired Alan. You two have worked together before."

She heard only a rush of air as Dec exhaled noisily on the other end of the line.

"I'm sorry, Pokey. It's been a bad day already, and it's still morning. We got a call from Royal's office. No bargains, no deals. Since we won't back off on the not guilty by reason of insanity plea, and they won't bargain off the two counts of murder one, they've come up with their own expert psychologist. He went in to evaluate Wier over the weekend—that's the real reason I'm calling. Warden gave him some sort of special weekend rate, or something. They're faxing over the results of his consultation after lunch."

For a moment, the road in front of her blurred a little as Portia absorbed the impact of Dec's statement. Royal had planned for all the bells and whistles—a war of expert opinion to top off the usual war of words and evidence. "Shit," she replied after a moment. "Who is it?"

"Portia," Dec went on. "I don't think you really—"

"Who?"

"I don't want you to feel any additional pressure over this—"

"Too late," snapped Portia. "Who did they get?"

Dec hesitated only a moment. "It's Falcone. Harry Falcone."

Unexpectedly, Portia began to laugh, a high, harsh sound that made Dec wince on the other end of the line.

"Portia," he broke in. "Pokey—"

"My, my, you should have hired him when you had the chance, Dec. At least then you wouldn't have had to deal with Falcone's brand of bullshit coming at you from the other side."

"Don't be cynical, Portia. Even Falcone can't ignore Wier's clinical condition. And who knows, he may even corroborate."

Portia fought a sudden urge to turn the car around, drive all the way back to Charlotte, go home, and cash in her retirement funds. Harry Falcone. It really was too much. And now Dec, ever the optimist, ever the professional, telling her that a hack like Falcone just might be turned to their advantage. The odds against saving Jimmy Wier from the death penalty had suddenly grown immeasurably worse.

She sighed heavily into the handset. "Yeah, Pollyanna, but due to the fact that I've finally got him medicated, Wier's going to look and act a whole lot less crazy than he did before. Get it? Hey, he probably can speak in complete sentences by now. Who knows how Falcone will read it."

"Shit," said Dec. "I forgot about that."

"Shit is right. Deep shit. Royal's cooked himself up a real little sleaze fest this time, hasn't he? I can't wait. Never mind that Falcone is a complete hack. Never mind Jimmy Wier. It's all to get Royal grinning in front of the voters. Mr. Law and Order." Portia paused as their connection was momentarily interrupted by a shiver of static. "I think I'm going to be sick," she finished miserably.

"Well, pull over first. Puke stains are a bitch to get out of leather upholstery," Dec answered wryly. "Look, we're doing what we can. The rumor is, Falcone's climbed on Royal's bandwagon for the same reason Royal got up there in the first place. Wants to make a big virtuous comeback after being investigated by the Psychology Board. Maris even heard he's chasing a book deal."

"Forgive me," Portia interjected. "But just how is this supposed to make me feel better?"

"Oh," Dec answered, chuckling. "Since you're working pro bono, I petitioned the court that the prosecution not be allowed to exceed fees paid to the defense experts. Who knows? Poor Harry Falcone might wind up working for free. He can't afford to back out in the face of his current image problems, and even if he does, Royal's team will have to come up with somebody else. And they don't have any more time than we do."

Portia couldn't help smiling. "Dec Dylan," she said, "I have to hand it to you. You do have style. But it won't work and you know it. They'll give Falcone any price he sets."

"Thank you, I thought it was rather stylish myself. But the point is, I can make the fee discrepancy a big deal when I get him on the stand. Self-sacrificing single-mom expert who only wants the truth to get out versus scum-sucking bottom feeder. Motivation like that, Falcone might surprise us all and tell the truth."

"Presuming he would know what that was. Personally, I wouldn't let him evaluate the psychological condition of a house cat."

"I thought you hated cats," Dec replied.

And again, without warning, a shred of last night's dream floated like a corpse from beneath the waters of her consciousness. "I do," she replied after a moment. "That's what I meant. I do."

"By the way, you didn't tell me—you manage to run down anything on that deputy? What was his name?"

"Chitwood," Portia replied. "Justin Chitwood. And the only thing I managed to run down was the fact that he left Dixon very suddenly, shortly after he called me. I talked to the sheriff out there though, who went out of his way to let me know that anything I needed to know could be found in the police report. Period."

"Anything else?"

Portia sighed. "I had a talk with Chitwood's ex-landlady—more nothing. The only thing I know for sure at this point is that the number he left with Lori was not the number of the Dixon County Sheriff's Department. I tried a couple of times, but wherever he is, he's not answering the phone."

"Strange," Dec mused. "I wonder what's up with him."

"Don't know, but I'm not going to find out until he decides to call again."

"Maybe not," Dec agreed.

Portia scowled as she headed over a rise and saw that traffic was slowed down for what appeared to be miles. Some accident ahead, no doubt.

"One more thing, Dec," she added, burrowing into a good-looking spot in the center lane. "I spoke to the checkout girl at the grocery where Jimmy worked. She seems to have some pretty interesting rape fantasies, but that's all."

Dec's tone was instantly troubled. "What's her name?"

"Denise something. I don't know, why?"

"I think she just came in on the prosecution's preliminary list of witnesses. You think she'll hurt us? Denise Johns?"

Portia scanned the lanes of traffic. "She's very suggestible. Depends on Royal's line of questioning."

"Wonderful," Dec replied distractedly. "Listen, we better break this up. Give me Chitwood's number, and I'll have someone here track him down. You got anybody else? I forgot to tell you, I have a new hireling."

Portia raised an eyebrow. "You? Actually delegating responsibility? I don't believe it."

"Look who's talking. The little red hen—what's the number? Maybe the phone company can turn something up."

Portia scattered papers over the front seat. "I don't have it, Dec. Call Lori. And let me know what you find out. The only other thing I've got is a note from a psychiatric nurse at Columbia hospital. And I want to talk to her myself."

There was a moment's hesitation on the other end of the line. "Whatever. Look, Portia, I'm sorry about all this. How about I make it up to you? Dinner? Say Friday?"

Portia debated silently. The fact was, a comfortable dinner with an old friend like Dec sounded like just what she needed. "I don't know," she demurred. "Let me check what's going on with Alice."

"Bring her along," said Dec.

"Maybe—"

"I'll cook," he wheedled. "Something Mediterranean? Lots of garlic?"

Portia smiled. The truth was, Dec was a fabulous cook, and the prospect of one of his specialties was hard to resist. "Okay," she said at last. "A tentative okay—like I said, I have to see about Alice."

"Great. And listen, don't get so wound up over this stuff. I have confidence in you, Pokey. If anybody can get Wier to give it up, it's you. Just go in there with your therapeutic guns blazing. Pull out all the stops.''

"That's what they call a mixed metaphor, isn't it?'' She swung the car into the left lane, avoiding a twisted black piece of tire rubber hulking in the road.

"Whatever. Just give him everything you've got. He'll come around. It's just that with Falcone in the soup, I'm afraid it's got to be sooner rather than later—okay?''

"Okay,'' Portia answered, thinking the situation was very far indeed from okay. "Pull out all the stops. I'll call you, Dec,'' she said, abruptly bringing their conversation to a close. "After I've seen him. But I've got to hurry.''

"I'll be here—good luck.''

"And, Dec?''

"What?''

"Don't call me Pokey,'' she told him. And hung up.

By the time she'd swung the car onto the exit ramp thirty minutes or so down the road, the morning's confusion had resolved itself into a new kind of resolve. For better or for worse, she'd made a statement of authority in her last session with Wier and it was a stance she would have to stick to if she intended to stay in the game. If anything, she only had more to back it up this time. Dec was right; even Sophie had been right. She had to go in with both guns blazing if she intended to get inside Wier's head. The mention of his family had provoked an extreme reaction, that much was obvious. And even though she'd been shooting in the dark, she'd come very near some sort of mark. If she didn't want to lose him, she'd have to stay on Jimmy Wier's case no matter whom it hurt.

She grinned as she made the turn that would take her the last ten miles to Columbia prison—talk about mixing metaphors. Then, suddenly, without warning, in the time it had taken her to finish her last thought and begin another, came a flash of insight so startling and complete it took her breath away.

Wier perceived women as unreasonably powerful. That was the reason he'd killed, that was probably even the reason he'd scared off Deb Yarborough. He saw women—all women—as powerful, and he was both compelled to evade and compelled to answer to that power. In that moment, Portia saw with utter clarity the source of her own conflict in dealing with him as a patient.

The bottom line was, power was what she wanted. More than anything, she wanted to be effective, to be helpful and trusted. She wanted power over Jimmy Wier—she wanted to be right about his history, to know enough to be able to help him. She wanted to be powerful enough to make a jury see what he was, enough at least to spare his life. That all came down, finally, to a question of power.

Then on the heels of that thought came another. Portia McTeague knew with utter clarity that she had the power to help Jimmy Wier—all she had to do was to find the strength to use it.

She pressed down on the accelerator and swung out to pass an ancient horse trailer limping along behind an equally ancient Ford. She was right. Even the dream had been right. She did have to hurry. Time was running out. And Jimmy was waiting.

She paused at the Visitor's Center to inquire if a psychiatric nurse named Melanie Durant was on the premises, and was told she didn't come on shift until noon. As she passed through the usual security checkpoints and made her way up to the appointed conference area, she found herself feeling strangely cheerful, almost liberated.

Jimmy was already there. He sat like some huge statue in the airless conference room, watching her as she made her way through the door and sat with her back to it, sliding a clean yellow legal pad between them. Portia observed him for a long moment, suddenly not sure where to begin. That he'd improved on the increased medication was beyond question. His eyes were clear, and he no longer exhibited any bizarre or repetitive movements. He watched her almost lazily as she settled herself into the chair, but beneath his feigned disinterest she sensed an almost predatory watchfulness—like a cat pretending to doze in front of a mouse hole. The memory of their last session lay between them, and Portia could feel Wier's silent accusation as clearly as if he had raised one meaty finger and pointed it in her face.

She wet her lips, her mouth suddenly dry. "I heard some people came to see you, Jimmy. Do you remember the woman, Jimmy? Jayne? She gave you some tests. Do you remember the tests?"

Nothing. Wier sat motionless, mute and unforgiving, punishing her with his silence. He was manacled this time. It occurred to her to call the guard and have the cuffs removed, but she thought better of it.

Somehow her safety mattered a bit more today. Wier was going to feel pretty stressed in a few minutes and there was no telling what might happen. She shifted a little in her chair, aware of the rush of adrenaline coursing through her.

"Jayne Patten is a doctor, too, Jimmy," she went on conversationally. "Just like me. What'd you think of her?"

She watched carefully as the prisoner's eyes flicked over her. He was responding then. Whether he knew it or not. Portia debated a moment whether to bring up the subject of Harry Falcone's consultation, then decided to take another tack. She leaned almost casually back into the molded plastic chair. "As a matter of fact," she went on, "about the only thing your tests show is that you're trying to hide just how crazy you really are. You want to tell me about that, Jimmy?"

A sound then—a ghost of a sound, so faint she could not be sure she'd heard it at all.

She leaned forward a little, trying to get him to meet her eyes. "That's the thing about those tests, Jimmy. You really can't hide anything, can you? Not from me."

The stubborn silence deepened between them and she saw him flex his huge hands inside the cuffs, working the fingers in a slow infuriated rhythm.

Portia swallowed hard. Pull out the stops, she told herself. You've got nothing to lose. And Wier has everything to gain. She took a breath and steadied herself. It wasn't going to be easy.

"I'm Dr. Tricks," she continued brightly. "You said so yourself. Do you remember that? Women know the truth—didn't you say that, Jimmy? Remember?"

Wier looked away, pretending to study the ceiling tiles.

"What about that other doctor, Jimmy? Dr. Falcone? Did you try and hide how crazy you are from him, too?"

He shot her a glance then, clearly confused. She pressed the momentary advantage.

"Oh yes," she said almost idly. "I know all about him, too. I know that he came and saw you over the weekend. It was the weekend, wasn't it, Jimmy? Did you know what day it was—what time it was—when Falcone came? That was because of me, too. Because I was the one who ordered your medicine. They only give it to you because I say so. You know that, don't you? You only feel the way you feel now because of me. I saw what you needed and I got it for you. How does that make you feel, Jimmy? That I know so much about you?"

His glance lengthened to a long stare, the pale eyes so full of hate and pain it shook her. Yet she met the look without flinching, her voice rising clear and falsely confident.

"I do know, Jimmy. I know about you. I know about pain." At the word, the false confidence of her tone fell away. She looked at him; Sophie had been right. There was no difference between them. And no grandstanding, no show of false confidence or power playing would change that. Pain always felt the same, no matter where it came from.

When she spoke again, her voice was soft, choked with emotion as she reached across the gap between them. "I know that some of that pain is caused by things we don't have any control over. Like our families. My family caused me a whole lot of pain, Jimmy. So did yours. I can tell that, too. I can tell just by looking. I can tell because I know what it's like. I can tell because we're just the same, Jimmy. You and me."

He wanted to answer; she could feel his need to answer her rising up from somewhere deep within him. And she watched his face as he fought it back, pushed it away—down deep to the dark place where he kept it to fuel the fires of his rage.

She continued to speak in a singsong, soft as a lullaby, reaching not for any button this time, but only for the softness in him, that desperate vulnerability that lay buried like a corpse beneath the craziness and rage.

"You killed two old women with your bare hands and a butcher knife. You tied them up like animals and you cut them open and you raped them. Their names were Constance Bennet and Lila Mooney. Do you remember?"

He was sweating now, the perspiration running in rivulets from his forehead, coming out in dark patches on his orange jumpsuit. He stared at her, his expression caught somewhere between horror and mad relief.

"My hands—"

He'd spoken. Inwardly Portia cheered. "Yes, yes, Jimmy, your hands. You did this thing. No one else. And then you took some jewelry and some other things from the house. And you showed all the things you took to the police when they found you. You remember, Jimmy? There was jewelry and an African violet and—"

But she'd lost him again. In less than the time it had taken to speak the words, his eyes had drifted from her face, gone blank and unseeing and utterly hopeless as he stared down at the tabletop, where drops of his own sweat still glistened on the scarred surface, bright as tears.

Portia watched him closely. She was so stunned at the change, she could not absorb it immediately, slowly taking in the details of his face, his condition, until her mind began to form the thought, then the words. She'd gone too far—again. She'd taken the gamble and lost. Made the same mistake again, even knowing in advance that it wouldn't—couldn't—work. Even with the medication, he hadn't been able to handle a direct inquiry. In less than a moment, Jimmy Wier had dissociated as completely as he had at their first meeting, the only difference being that, on Haldol, he didn't hum.

Portia sighed and sank wearily back into her chair, and the silence in the room settled over them like a shroud. From somewhere inside the prison walls, there came a low chuckle as the guards paused in their perpetual patrol. Portia stared at her charge helplessly. In confronting him, she'd been prepared for rage—even violence. Anything was better than the hulking, defeated ruin in front of her. The old guilt rose up within her as she watched him, but she managed to resist it. Instead, almost on impulse, she reached for one of his manacled hands, covering it with her own.

"Jimmy," she called softly, urgently. "Jimmy, if you can hear me, damn it, don't do this! I'm on your side, don't you know that? I'm trying to help you—but you've got to help me."

She squeezed the hand more tightly, aware of the coldness of his fingers. It was like touching a corpse. Portia rattled on, suddenly breathless, desperate—not knowing if he could hear her, not knowing or even caring if she was right—as bits of facts and information flew apart in the face of this terrible isolation. In that moment nothing else mattered. Not power or facts or even psychology. She knew only that she had to reach into the void between them and try to bring him back from where he had gone.

"You once lived in California, remember, Jimmy? You told me about the sun. I think you were adopted by a family named Wier. Your mother's name was Elizabeth and your father's name was Horace. And you played with the sun and you thought it was your toy and you listened to the radio. Please remember, Jimmy—God. Please try."

Nothing. Desperately, she went on.

"What happened with your parents, Jimmy? Did they hurt you— what happened? There's so much pain in you, Jimmy. So much anger—I can feel it. You don't have to be afraid to tell me. I know all about secrets. I know what it's like to feel ashamed. The pain comes from your family, Jimmy—the pain, the craziness. The killing. You can tell me, trust me. Was it your mother, Jimmy? I heard your mother was crazy, Jimmy. Was she? Was she crazy? Did she hurt you? What happened in California? Jimmy—please. They can't hurt you now. Nobody can hurt you. So it's all right. You can tell me what they did to you to make you so crazy. Crazy enough to kill those old ladies."

She stopped all at once, her passionate pleas dying as suddenly as they had begun. There was nothing. No response, no flicker of contact. Wier only sat there motionless, defeated, his eyes as absent of light and understanding as if someone had thrown a switch. She might have been alone in that room, save for the huge, lifeless bulk sitting so terribly still in the chair opposite her. Portia stared miserably at the blank sheet of legal notepad in front of her, the neat blue lines of it mocking the chaos of her thoughts.

She had never expected victory, but neither had she expected defeat to come so quickly. The minutes crawled by, five then ten. There was no point in staying, she knew. From the look of Jimmy Wier, the episode might continue for hours. And even if he came out of it, he wasn't going to talk to her or to anybody else.

In less than one month's time, the state of South Carolina was going to try Jimmy Wier for the crime of murder and sentence him to death. The merciless inevitability of the next few weeks filled her with an unspeakable sense of dread. Jimmy Wier would be strapped to a table and injected with drugs to paralyze his muscles and slow his respiration and, finally, stop his heart. The people would have their justice and Donny Royal would have his sound bites on the six o'clock news. And sitting in front of her was a man so completely out of his mind that he was going to die without ever understanding what had happened to him—neither the nature of his crime nor the nature of his punishment.

And Dr. Portia McTeague, forensic psychologist and expert witness, wasn't going to be able to do anything about it. Because, for all of her training, all her understanding, all her knowledge of the workings of the human mind, and all her good intentions—she hadn't been able to reach him. Because, in the end, Jimmy Wier was too crazy even to save himself.

She stood, finally, gathering up the blank legal pad and single pen. And Jimmy did nothing at all. At the last moment, she turned in the doorway and looked at him once more, feeling her chest tighten with a profound sorrow. For him, for herself, for the women he had killed so brutally. And finally, for the little boy who had played in a spot of sunlight, listening to the radio.

"Sorry, Jimmy," she whispered. "I guess I'm out of tricks."

She tapped lightly on the small window of the room to let the guard know she was ready to leave. She heard the heavy footsteps turn and make their way back down the corridor in her direction.

And then she heard, so faintly at first that she was not sure the sound was real—a high alien voice, strange and false and pleading.

"Do you, do you, do you?" the voice sang.

Portia waved the guard away and swung around, astonished to find that Jimmy had spoken, and seeing in the same instant that it was him and yet not, as though that great body were possessed by some spirit. He fixed her with eyes that were devious and bright and demanding. His huge hands moved in airy gestures as he marked the space between them.

"Do you know what time it is? Do you know what day it is? Do you know why you're here? Do you remember? Do you do you do you? Bitch! Bitch doctor, witch doctor. Do you?"

"Jimmy—"

"They always ask the same questions," Wier told her. "All the bitch doctors. I think I know the answers by this time, don't you?"

Portia slid hastily into her chair and leaned toward him. "Jimmy, goddammit. Talk to me. You said there were other doctors—where was that, Jimmy? Where were the other doctors? When did you see them? Was it in a hospital? In jail? Tell me—you've got to tell me!"

Portia drew back suddenly, shocked at herself. She could have reached out and slapped him if she thought it would make him talk. But it wouldn't. Only Jimmy could decide when to speak. Only Jimmy would decide who won the battle for his soul.

She could only hold her breath and wait for some answer.

And finally it did come, the words filling her with a strange dark triumph. And when the answer came, it was in his own voice again, low and tired—marked with an awful resignation.

"Her house was filled with violets," Wier began. "There was nothing I could do."

Fourteen

● ●

Portia's voice was little more than a whisper. "Whose house, Jimmy? Lila Mooney's?"

His eyes were troubled and faraway. "Lila?"

"The old lady, Jimmy. The one you killed. You remember? When you delivered the groceries?"

The big head moved back and forth. "No. No. Lizzie's house—home. In San Diego."

Portia could have shouted. Lizzie—Elizabeth. The one who'd had no name. It meant everything. She shifted in the chair and swung her notes around in front of her, never taking her eyes from the big man's face.

"Tell me about Lizzie. What happened at Lizzie's house?"

Jimmy's breath sounded noisily as he struggled to explain.

"She had them everywhere, those flowers. Purple and white." He raised his hands clumsily inside the cuffs and brought his index fingers and thumbs together for her to see. "They had little eyes—" he said. "In the middle. Little yellow eyes that were always looking at you. No matter what you did. No matter how you tried to hide, the little eyes would always see you and then they would tell her. And then—"

Portia could feel her own heart beating wildly in her chest. "Then what, Jimmy?"

He shrugged noncommittally. "Whatever she wanted. You had to do whatever she wanted." His eyes focused suddenly, meeting her own, and the desperation hidden in their depths made Portia want to cry out. His voice dropped to just above a whisper. "It was because I was so bad—bad boy, disgusting, dirty."

Portia leaned closer. "Did Lizzie tell you that? Did she say you were bad?"

The prisoner managed a wan, thoughtful smile. "I suppose—but she didn't have to, after a while. I always knew. Everyone knew."

Portia began to take notes as fast as she could write, filling the yellow paper with cramped, closely crowded words. "Was Lizzie your mother, Jimmy?"

"Sort of. She adopted me. Her and Horace."

"When was that, Jimmy? Do you know how old you were?"

He leaned back. "She said six months. I don't know. But that's what she told me. She said—she said my real mama didn't want me either. Because I was so bad—you know. She told it how my real mama left me like a sack of garbage on the kitchen table."

"She and Horace told you you were adopted?"

Jimmy laughed. "Oh yeah—oh yeah. I never didn't know that. That I was—I always knew."

Portia shook her head. "What else do you remember? Just let it come, Jimmy. Don't even think about it. Just let it come."

There was a long uneasy pause before he began again, whispering, so that she had to lean her head forward to hear him.

"She didn't want me. I know that. She wished I was a girl. She even tried to make me a girl. Grew my hair long and made me wear dresses. I was maybe eleven, twelve when she stopped. I got too big and I wouldn't let her do that no more."

Portia's mind was reeling, but she forced herself to stay calm. "What else can you tell me about Lizzie?" she asked quietly.

Jimmy nodded, more to himself than to her. "She—she was kind of crazy I guess you'd call it. She—I—" He began to stammer helplessly and Portia reached for his hand, the fingers damp and clammy.

"It's okay, Jimmy. You don't have to be afraid."

Jimmy snatched his hands away from her touch. "I ain't afraid. I'm—I'm—it's just hard. I don't like to say the words."

"I know it's hard, but say them, Jimmy," Portia urged. "Tell me. We have to talk about what happened to you."

He took a deep breath and went on sheepishly. "She took my—" He stopped and pointed between his legs. "That."

"Your penis?"

He nodded. "She put it away between my legs, tucked way up

inside. And I'd have to walk with my legs squeezed together to hold it there."

Portia paused, her heart aching for the child Jimmy had been. "Oh, Jimmy. I'm sorry. I'm sorry she hurt you like that."

Jimmy nodded, his big face sad and resigned. "I got a little older, she used to tape it down. You know, in case I got a hard-on or anything. She done that a lot."

"Do you know why she did those things, Jimmy? Did she ever tell you?"

There was a moment of hesitation—a breathless little silence as Jimmy's face seemed to turn in upon itself, slackening, changing in some indefinable way. He looked younger, a strange vulnerability coming over his features.

Jimmy giggled childishly. "She told me all the time. She told me she had to do it because my thing was so ugly. She said that when I grew up, I'd fuck people 'cause that was all boys cared about." He leaned toward Portia, his voice dropping to an odd, confidential whisper. "Boys was born dirty and mean. You can't change that. No matter how hard you try."

Portia took an unsteady breath. "Did Lizzie say that?" she asked him.

He nodded mutely.

"What did you think when she said those things, Jimmy? How did you feel?"

Again, the deprecating sneer played around his mouth. He snorted derisively. "I didn't think nothing. I mean—I—she was right. Cocks ain't so pretty to look at, are they?"

Portia studied him for a long, silent moment, trying to think of how to answer. "Wanting to have sex isn't wrong, Jimmy. It doesn't make you bad or mean."

She watched the light in his eyes changing even as she said the words, like a cloud passing over the sun. When he looked at her again, the look in them was lewd and dangerous, and she saw the pink flicker of his tongue as he passed it over his lips. Wier began to snicker suggestively.

"It does if you don't get any for a while. You get real mean if that happens. But I guess you wouldn't know about that, would you?" His tongue lolled from his mouth, pink and shiny with saliva, as he gave a long predatory look from beneath lowered lids. His voice, when he spoke again, was soft and suggestive.

"Bet you're getting it real regular, ain't you, Dr. Tricks?"

She stiffened in spite of herself, and she heard Jimmy chuckle softly.

Her voice was steady in the silent room. "Are you trying to frighten me? Show me what a bad boy you are?" She met his eyes fearlessly—staring him down, daring him to speak. Until he blinked and it was over.

"Here's the deal, Jimmy," Portia went on evenly. "I can stay here or I can leave. I can walk through that door and never come back. And if you scare me, I will leave. Only if that happens, then I won't be able to get close enough to give you any help. If I leave, there's going to be nobody to help you make some sense of what happened to you. Maybe, if you give me some effort here, we can save your ass. But if I stay, I need to ask the questions, all right? I ask and you give me the answers. No bullshit. No games. You got that?"

She snapped back a page of the legal tablet so abruptly it sounded like a thunderclap in the stifling room. She sat with her pen poised above the paper, watching as Jimmy slumped deeper in his chair. His eyes narrowed and he began to rock silently, his arms pressed against his massive chest.

Portia rose suddenly and leaned toward him, her eyes blazing, hands on the table. "Do you want me to go?"

He shrank a little from her sudden proximity, and in that moment, Portia could see again the terrible vulnerability in him. All the jail-house macho, all the sly craziness—evaporated with the terror rising in his eyes. She eased herself back into her chair, afraid for a moment that if she pushed him now, she would lose him for good.

"Who's Larry Sawtelle?" she asked.

"My cousin. From California."

"When was the last time you saw him?"

Jimmy sucked his teeth and thought hard. "I was maybe six, seven. He was picking crops up and down the coast. And he came and got me."

"Got you? Why did he get you?"

Jimmy shook his head. "Don't know. He just came, and I went with him and picked for a while. And then I was back."

Portia took a deep breath. "He told us some things about you, Jimmy. About your mama and daddy. You listen, and then you tell me if Larry told us right. Okay?"

There was no answer, only a little jerk of Jimmy's head from the other side of the table.

"You are the adopted son of Horace and Elizabeth Wier," she told him, her voice sounding odd and strangely cold in the closeness of the room. She softened her tone with some effort and went on. "You lived in Twentynine Palms, California, and then moved to San Diego when you were between two and three years old. Is that about right?"

"I don't remember," Jimmy answered.

She glanced up, aware suddenly of the ghost of the blue-lined paper dancing through her field of vision as she looked at him. He wasn't lying; he didn't remember. He closed his eyes and rocked, waiting for the next question.

"Larry told us your parents had some pretty bad fights, Jimmy. Is that right?"

Jimmy winced at the question, but made no effort to reply, as though the answer were so obvious it wasn't worth saying aloud.

"Did your mother and father live together after that? After you moved to San Diego?"

"Couple years. I was maybe four years old when Daddy left. Maybe five. He went away someplace. With the Marines. And he never came back. She said it was me that made him go. She said he couldn't stand to have me around."

Portia took a note and silently cursed mad Elizabeth Wier. "Did you love your father?" she went on. "Did you miss him?"

"I don't remember it like that." Jimmy's tone flattened as he answered. The greater the emotion behind the words, the less he was able to express. "He was there. Then he was gone. I don't remember much else. But . . ."

Portia glanced up and saw that Jimmy was thinking hard, his eyes closed, agony etched in the lines of his mouth. "What, Jimmy?"

"I wanted him to know—about Mama. About what she did when he wasn't around."

"What did she do, Jimmy? Did you tell him?"

"Yes. Some things. I told him about my pecker. How it hurt to pee."

"What did he do when you told him?"

"He beat on me."

Portia bit her lip. "What about your mama, Jimmy? Did you love your mama?"

There was a long silence before the answer came, full of bitterness and confused regret.

"I tried."

Portia felt rage boiling up deep inside her as a thousand questions flooded her thoughts, each begging an answer, some explanation for all the horror those two words implied. Who could have so abused a little child? Why? Oh God, why—why—was there no one to notice, to see what was happening to the little boy? Jimmy Wier had been left alone with only a psychotic to provide for him. She stared at him, knowing that he was waiting, that some part of him wanted that next question to come.

Portia fought back her own emotions. Jimmy Wier did not need her grief or her horror or her tears; he needed her help. There was nothing to do but go on.

"Did you want to hurt her?"

"Oh, yeah," Jimmy answered. "All the time. I was bad that way. I was always bad."

"Did you ever try to hurt her?"

"I don't know—maybe. It was hard."

"Why, Jimmy? Why was it hard?"

He grinned then, and the look was eerie and strangely unnerving under the fluorescent light. "She knew," he went on, almost matter-of-factly. "Like she knew things before they happened. So if I hit her or something, it was all like she said. It was proof—like all her crazy dreams were coming true. And she'd tell me I was bad and disgusting and I wanted to hurt her and fuck her because I was a boy and all boys were bad. And she'd prove it. She'd make me watch her—and I'd see her and—"

"And what, Jimmy?"

The air left Jimmy's lungs in a rush, as though he had been holding it against the question. "And it would be true." Jimmy paused and stared at Portia helplessly. "It was true, see? All of it. She knew everything. All she had to do was say it and it would be true. Everything was just the way she thought it was."

Portia made herself ask, not wanting—not needing even to know the answer. "Did you sleep with her, Jimmy?"

She waited as he struggled with his answer.

"She—couldn't sleep, sometimes. Most times. And we only had the one bed. So if she didn't have no man, I did. Sleep there." He looked at her then, his eyes pleading for understanding. "Mama—she needed somebody. She needed somebody all the time. So she wouldn't be alone."

"Did she make . . ." Portia faltered, and began again. "Did you have sex with her, Jimmy? With Lizzie?"

Jimmy hung his head and stared into his lap for a long moment, the sudden silence ringing between them. "I never knew that. Never. I tried to remember—for a long time. But it's like a dream. They kept asking me, though."

Portia's head snapped up as though she'd been slapped. "Who asked, Jimmy? Who?"

Jimmy glanced at her, seemingly surprised by the question. "The other doctors. And so I tried to think about it. But the harder I tried, the further away it got. Like a dream."

Portia's mind snatched desperately at the bits of fact that filtered through Jimmy's speech, trying to listen, trying to grasp the meaning behind the words. "Where, Jimmy? Can you remember that? Where were the other doctors?"

Jimmy shrugged. "Oh, lots of places. But these ones who wanted to know—that—about the sex. They were at Atascadero. I got sent up there. There was a rape charge."

Portia wrote the name, her hand trembling with excitement. "What did you tell them, Jimmy?"

He gave a short, unpleasant laugh. "Whatever they wanted to hear," he answered. "I had to get like—cured, you know? So I just told 'em. You know—so they'd let me out."

"How long were you there?"

"Maybe four, five years. I served the time, you know? So they let me out. But I don't think they ever thought I was cured." He paused and stared hard at the ceiling.

"This rape charge, Jimmy. Can you tell me when it happened?"

He shrugged noncommittally. "Nineteen-eighty maybe. In there. It's not clear."

"Did you rape somebody, Jimmy?"

Jimmy faltered uncertainly. "They said it was me. Couple of girls."

Portia glanced up, startled. "Girls? How old were the girls, Jimmy?"

He froze for a moment, his eyes fixed on some point in the corner of the room. "Young—so young. I thought they would be different."

Portia leaned back in her chair, staring at him. Some of the pieces were falling into place. Young girls and old women. Both frail, easy to overpower. Escalating from rape to murder. He'd been looking for victims more helpless than he was. "Did you rape them, Jimmy?" she asked quietly.

He could only shrug. "They said it was me. It's strange, though, ain't it? I never really knew. It was like that about Lizzie, too. What you asked me. They said it, though, and I went along. I stopped thinking about it after a while—what happened with them girls, with Lizzie." All of a sudden his eyes met her own, bright and eager as a child's. "You know what? You want to know something?"

"What, Jimmy—what?"

"I decided when I left that place. I wasn't ever gonna think about it no more. I'll never know the answer. It's like I'm just a ghost. I don't know what happened to me. It might be true or it might not. It don't matter, 'cause there's never any difference between what is real in your head and what happens. It's all the same."

"It does matter, Jimmy," Portia insisted softly. "There is a difference. It does matter."

He held up his hand. "Don't," he answered. "I know about—them murders. I don't remember 'em. But that don't matter either. Even if they give me the death. That wouldn't be so bad. It'd be easier, maybe. Maybe my head wouldn't hurt so much. Maybe she'd finally stop hurting me."

"How come you say that, Jimmy?"

He shifted his bulk uncomfortably and refused to look at anything. " 'Cause even though I keep thinking I'm okay for a while—even though I can get to where I'm sort of—normal, I always turn out crazy in the end. Just like Lizzie. I guess I'm just like her. Fine for a while and then . . ." He met her eyes helplessly. "You know what I mean?"

Portia gazed at the prisoner through a window of hot, sudden tears. "I know, Jimmy," she answered softly. "I know what you mean."

Fifteen

● ●

THREE QUARTERS of an hour later, Portia crossed the wide expanse of green lawn that separated the prison hospital from the rest of the Columbia grounds, grateful once again for the brief sense of freedom that came from being outdoors. Melanie Durant was due to come on duty in less than fifteen minutes. If she hurried, Portia could catch her before rounds began.

The hospital smell assaulted her nostrils as soon as she hit the front entrance. In all of her years working in and out of such places, she had never grown used to it, never yet understood why the oppressive antiseptic odor always lurked in the lobbies and the elevators, seeming to emanate from the walls themselves.

The prison facility was devoid of the falsely cheery paintings and fake floral arrangements that were standard in hospital decor. Here, the walls were painted an indeterminate neutral tone, and the lobby desk had been designed to welcome no one. Portia showed her identification and was directed to the psychiatric wing by a bored-looking security guard who cracked her gum incessantly as they spoke.

The elevator was prehistorically slow, admitting and disgorging hospital personnel and their patients on every floor. An inmate, clearly dying of AIDS, met her eyes and smiled a wan, skeletal smile as Portia edged into a corner to make room for the gurney. He was wheeled off by an orderly, IV tubes swinging, and replaced by a hugely pregnant woman, escorted by a guard and handcuffed at the wrists, wailing away the first stages of labor.

At the floor that held the psychiatric ward, Portia got off and presented her identification at the locked nurses' station. The nurse on duty, a big middle-aged woman with an indecipherable nameplate, looked her up and down from behind a crisscross of wire fence and smeary, inch-thick reinforced glass.

"Durant's not here yet," she offered. "Sit. You can catch her off the elevator if you want."

Portia took one of the two chairs that occupied the tiny waiting area, suddenly aware of how exhaustion tugged at her limbs. The session with Wier had left her elated at first, but now the high of having made an initial breakthrough was wearing off as the full force of his psychosis became apparent. She sat, almost motionless. She heard the distant blare of television from the day room as game shows and soap operas played out in endless hours before a medicated, hollow-eyed audience clad in bathrobes and slippers. Somewhere, a bell signaled and a doctor was paged. She caught the nauseating scent of the lunch carts already on the floor, reeking of macaroni and chemically flavored gelatin.

Portia shut her eyes and shifted heavily in her chair. The surge of confidence she'd felt that morning gave way by degrees to a disheartening reality. For she knew, better than anyone, that all the knowledge and all the morality and all the psychology in the world pointed only to the fact that if justice were done, Jimmy Wier would spend the rest of his days on a ward like this, staring at television and playing solitaire. Because, whatever she could do for him, whatever she might tell the court, whatever breakthroughs he might have in the therapeutic sense, Jimmy Wier could and probably would get better, but he'd never—ever—get well. What she'd heard that morning was only the tip of a terrible iceberg. She knew that much as surely as she knew her own name. But Jimmy Wier's ship had already run afoul of that ice; and no one had been there to hear his cries as he sank into the black waters of mental disease. All she could do now was help him to understand the wreckage. All she could do now was to keep him safe from his own unimaginable pain. Jimmy Wier's future was in this place or somewhere like it. His sickness was one for which there was no cure, caused by a woman who was sick herself. And all that terrible damage had occurred more than thirty years before they'd come together—all done to a little boy's mind before he was five years old.

Portia sighed wearily, causing the nurse behind the glass to glance up and scowl. Even though she would do whatever she could to save him, whatever powers she had at her disposal still wouldn't be enough. For in the end, Wier needed something even the best psychologist could never offer: Jimmy needed more than psychology, he needed magic, the kind of magic that could turn back time.

The elevator doors rattled open and a small blond woman in her early thirties got out, fumbling with a huge set of keys that would gain her entrance to the locked ward. The nurse behind the wall of glass nodded in Portia's direction, and Portia rose unsteadily to her feet.

"Excuse me, are you Melanie Durant?"

The nurse paused and looked at her, and Portia was surprised by how beautiful she was. Petite and trim, Melanie's curly blond hair haloed an almost angelic face marked by lively intelligent blue eyes. "I am," she answered. "Can I help you?"

Portia extended her hand, glancing at her watch as she did so. "Dr. Portia McTeague. They told me you came on service at noon," she said. "It's just ten of. Can we chat a minute? It's about an inmate who was up here for evaluation not long ago. James Wier? I'm working with his defense team."

Melanie's lively eyes clouded uncertainly for a moment before the realization dawned. "Jimmy the Weird?" she asked. "Yeah, he was up here. How's he doin'?"

Portia shrugged. "Good and not good. I've got him on Haldol now, so that helps, but . . ." She faltered and Melanie nodded her understanding.

"Yeah," she agreed. "He's a sick boy, all right. I tried to recommend Mellaril when he was up here, but you know Keene. Nurses' opinions don't count for much with him."

"Have you got a minute?" Portia went on. "I just needed to ask you about something—a note you made in the file."

Melanie swung the door to the locked ward open wide. "C'mon back," she said. "I need a Coke anyway."

Unlike the rest of the floor, the air-conditioning in the nurses' lounge was going full blast and Portia sank gratefully onto one end of a worn sofa, listening to the jangle of Melanie's coins as she fed them to a vending machine. "Here," the nurse said, handing her an icy can of Classic Coke. "You don't mind my saying so, you look beat."

Portia swallowed greedily, thankful in advance for the anticipated rush of sugar and caffeine. "I saw Wier this morning," she said. "It was productive, thank God. But—tough."

Melanie studied her intently. "You have a diagnosis?"

Portia sighed. "I have several, at this point. He's schizophrenic—

dissociative, paranoid, delusional. I think he hears command voices."
Portia set the can down on a nearby table and leaned forward. "This
morning he told me he was at Atascadero for five years. Got sent up
on rape charges."

Melanie cocked a brow. "In California? Atascadero's the big time,
isn't it?"

Portia nodded. "Atascadero is the state facility for the criminally
insane. Maximum security. Very scary place, from what I know."

Melanie eyed her for a long moment. "Well," she went on. "Good
for you, I guess. Seems like you got him to say more than he has to
anybody else. I heard when Keene saw him, he just sat there like a
stone the first time. Then, the second time, Jimmy tried to eat the
plastic flowers they keep in the consultation room. Didn't talk
though. Not to Keene anyhow."

"Did he ever talk to you? You made a note on the chart when he
was up here. Something about a suspected gender-identity disorder? I
wanted to know why—was it related to the murders? Do you recall?"

Melanie Durant emptied the Coke can in a long last swallow and
tossed it into a blue recycling bin against the far wall. "The only things
I know about the murders are what I got off the news," she replied. "I
noted the gender disorder because, well, it was so obvious."

"Obvious?" Portia asked. "How do you mean, exactly?"

Durant looked surprised by the question. "Obvious as in, well—
obvious. Behavior—you know. Stuff he did. How he looked. Especially after he snuck in here and got into Blades's locker. You met
Nurse Blades? Up at the desk? She was fit to be tied, let me tell you. I
wrote that one up myself."

Portia frowned, momentarily bewildered. "Look, I'm not sure I'm
getting this. I've seen all the reports. But I never got any write-up
describing this locker incident."

"That bitch," Durant said irritably. "I wrote it up myself. What
happened was, Wier broke into her locker when one of the others had
us tied up down the hall with a Grand Mal seizure. He took her
makeup case and some other stuff. Underwear mostly. Anyway, when
she and I made rounds after lunch with the meds, we found him all
decked out, lying on his bed. Bra, panty hose, the works. And a big
old erection. So he sees us and sits up, big as you please, and says,
'Nurse Blades, even though we've never met, I want to thank you for
the use of your titties, and I hope you don't mind. I just wanted
Melanie to see how much I loved her.' "

Melanie paused, smiling a little and shaking her head at Portia's astonished expression. "Blades went red as a fire engine," she continued. "I guess I just stood there. It all got worked out. Pretty weird, huh? He told me that he's a lesbian. That's why he was all got up that day. He wanted me to—well—you get the point."

Portia shook her head slowly. "Wow—"

Melanie rose easily to her feet, and Portia followed suit. The nurse glanced at her watch and frowned for a moment, clearly perturbed. "Listen, I've got to report in a minute. I'm sorry the write-up didn't get with the file. I guess Blades didn't want it to show up as a security breach."

Portia walked her toward the door, her eyes intent. "Just let me be clear about this. Are you telling me you think Wier is some sort of lesbian transsexual?" she asked.

Melanie looked at her. "Yes, I guess I am," she said.

A part of Portia's mind began to frantically sort clinical data in the face of this new information. It had to make sense—somehow. She again met Melanie's eyes, trying to understand how the nurse's perspective could add to her understanding of Wier's condition. And no new insight presented itself. A half hour ago, she'd felt as if she'd begun to get a handle on Jimmy Wier. Now, looking at Melanie, she was faced with the unsettling certainty that the puzzle had grown suddenly bigger and more complex than she'd ever imagined.

Together, they made their way into the now-deserted corridor, their footsteps all but echoing in the early afternoon lull of the psych ward. As they reached the locked entrance, Durant reached for a security buzzer on the opposite side of the front desk to release the door to the elevators. Portia paused at the last moment. "Can I have them subpoena you, Ms. Durant? Would you be willing to testify? As a witness for the defense?"

"Count me in," Melanie replied evenly. "I'll stand up and say that man's crazy any day of the week. You see a lot of 'em come through here, but Wier—well now."

"Yeah," Portia agreed. "Well now."

Melanie looked bemused for a moment. "Imagine that. The guy's mind, I mean. I get to see this cross-dressing because he's in love with me, right? You never get to see this stuff and you're the one he really talks to. That's weird, isn't it?"

"Yeah," Portia agreed. "It's weird, all right. We'll be in touch. And thanks, thanks a lot. I don't know what it all means yet, but I know this will lead somewhere."

Melanie waved as the elevator doors slid open. And Portia saw at the last moment before they closed that Nurse Durant was trying to tell her something more, silently mouthing the words "Good luck."

Even before she was out of the prison's driveway, Portia had dialed her office and had Lori on the other end of the line, directing her to leave a message with Alan's hotel in San Diego, with his answering service, and on his e-mail. If Jimmy Wier had been housed at the Atascadero State Facility for the Criminally Insane, his records could be a gold mine of information. Lori, in turn, told her that Royal's office had called several times regarding her report on the Wier case, a fact that made Portia smile for the first time that day. It meant Royal wanted the paperwork. He needed a written report so that he and his crony, Falcone, could work on Falcone's testimony. It meant they were, if not scared, then at the very least deeply concerned about Falcone's evaluation consultation.

"You know what to do, Lori," she told her, still smiling.

"You're not in the office and I don't know when you'll return," Lori rejoined. "Anything else?"

"Jayne Patten—she's got some results for you. Her last appointment's at four-thirty. She wanted to know if you could drop by after that."

Portia smiled a little out over the road. "Great," she answered. "Call her and confirm. Does Dec know Royal's sniffing around for a write-up?"

"Not unless he's tapping the phone. You gonna call him or should I?"

"I will," Portia said. "I've got all kinds of interesting news."

She punched in the numbers for Dylan's office and waited for him to come on the line. She flipped the radio, aware of a feeling of lightness that she had not felt for months—as if the ghosts and worries and nightmares of the past were finally departing her life and her work, allowing her to feel a measure of confidence, even of faith, that somehow, this time, it was going to be all right. The trial date for Jimmy Wier was fast approaching. There was work yet to be done, lots of it— but whatever else had happened that morning, she'd found a thread, right or wrong, and pulled it. Whatever else happened, she'd begun to unravel the mystery that had led Jimmy Wier to murder.

As she made the turn onto the two-lane that would carry her to the interstate, she listened to the radio, feeling the sun through the driver's side window warming her arm and the back of her neck.

And without meaning to, she began to sing.

"Very nice," Dec's voice was amused when he came on the line.

Blushing at being caught in a private moment, Portia answered, "Hey, they say singing lowers blood pressure. You ought to try it sometime."

"Not today. From the paperwork Royal's been sending over, this Wier case is turning into a dogfight. And I, for one, haven't come up with anything encouraging."

"Well, the day's not over yet," she replied happily. "I've come up with a lot. He opened up, Dec. Not the whole way. But he started to talk. It's a beginning—Jesus," she said in the next breath. "I've never felt so sorry for anybody in my life."

"What do you mean, Portia? You got a history?"

Portia tried to come up with a succinct explanation and found she couldn't. "Look," she hedged. "Wier's schizophrenia—if it is schizophrenia—was caused in part by profound early sexual-identity disturbance, probably the result of regular sexual abuse and torture at the hands of his mother. It may have begun as early as infancy, it's hard to say."

"Oh, Christ," Dec breathed.

"There's more to it. Those murders—the old ladies? Part of an escalating pattern of violence. He told me he was sent up on a rape charge in California. He wasn't sure, but he thinks it was around 1980."

"Let me guess—old women?"

"Not this time—young teenagers. Maybe twelve and thirteen."

"What? That doesn't make sense!"

"Sure it does, Dec. Kids and old people. What do they have in common?"

Dec breathed noisily, trying to follow her.

"Helplessness, that's what. With a guy like Wier, rape victims have to be essentially powerless. As powerless as he was when it happened to him."

There was a long pause. "Royal's not going to see it that way, you know. He's going to have a field day with charges like that. Make Wier into the biggest monster since Jack the Ripper."

Portia's tone turned almost wistful. "Well, if he's a monster, somebody made him that way." There was a crackle of static as the telephone signal began to break up. "See if you can get Alan, will you?" she continued anxiously. "I've had Lori leave messages all over out there, but he's got to know Jimmy was at Atascadero. They'll have the paperwork, Dec. I should be able to reconstruct some sort of psychological history from the records."

"Done," Dec answered. "What about test results?"

"I've got an appointment with Jayne this afternoon. Alan is digging up the records on the mother's hospitalizations. I'll be able to give you more when I see them. How long do you want me to stall on a written report?"

Dec took a moment before answering. "We're not going to give them a report, Portia," he answered gravely. "Royal is clamoring for something, but he's not going to get a clue until the trial begins. I've decided to put you on the stand cold. Prosecution gets nothing till then, understand? If forewarned is forearmed, we keep 'em in the dark."

"Dec!" Portia protested. "It's so risky! I should come on in sentencing—not in guilt-innocence. It's not like I can get up there and say he didn't do it. His mental illness is a mitigating factor!"

"If his defense is not guilty by reason of insanity, we have to prove he's insane. It's that simple."

"Shit," said Portia. "You're not the one up there, Dec."

Dec tried to sound reassuring, and didn't quite succeed. "Don't worry, we've still got some time. And we'll start going over your testimony on Friday. We still on for dinner?"

"I guess I have to be," Portia answered sharply. "Thanks for throwing me to the lions, Dec."

"Not the lions," he answered. "More like the dogs. From the way Royal's barking, I'm willing to bet his case won't have much of a bite."

He continued more gently. "I don't have a lot of choice here, Portia. The political climate—it's changing the rules. Warren lost his appeal. They called me this morning. With the admission of his confession, he'll be dead before December." His voice choked with sudden emotion. "I don't want to lose another one."

Portia stared out over the highway for a long moment before answering, thinking of George Warren, his mouth moving in those mad, endless prayers. "I'm sorry, Dec," she answered after a moment. "I'm so—damn—sorry."

Sixteen

• •

JAYNE PATTEN'S OFFICE was close to downtown, near Dec's firm on Morehead Street. Portia enjoyed the neighborhood with its comfortable assortment of 1920s houses and bungalows, and shade trees that lined the boulevards, softening the newer skyscrapers and office buildings of Charlotte's downtown skyline. The majority of Jayne's practice was concentrated in family therapy, and as Portia entered the office, she had to pick her way through the collection of plastic toys, stuffed animals, and cardboard cities that littered the floor of the waiting room.

"She's waiting," the receptionist replied to Portia's inquiry. "Go on back. I'll just let her know you're here."

Portia headed down a narrow hallway lined with the original beech wainscoting until she found Jayne's office behind a heavy carved door at the end of the hall. She knocked and the door swung inward to reveal the long, rangy figure of Dr. Jayne Patten, wearing a handknit cardigan and sporting the biggest shiner Portia had ever seen. It showed against Jayne's fair skin and gray hair with an almost supernatural clarity, and for a moment Portia could only gape at her in surprise.

"God almighty, Jayne!" Portia managed finally. "What the hell happened to you? Please don't tell me you got that testing Jimmy Wier!"

Jayne smiled easily and motioned Portia into a nearby chair. "Wier?" she snorted ruefully. "No way. This . . ." She reached up and fingered the bruise gingerly. "This comes courtesy of a three-year-old. Came in for his first appointment this morning. Kid's got a great arm. Rotten impulse control, but a great arm."

"I'm sorry," said Portia.

Jayne shrugged. "Goes with the territory." She reached across her desk for a creamy manila folder with Jimmy Wier's name printed neatly across the tab. "Wier was a pussycat. I got some good stuff."

Portia reached for the folder. "A pussycat? You mean you didn't get the benefit of lewd remarks and jailhouse machismo? He didn't try to scare you?"

For a moment Jayne looked almost puzzled. "Wier? Why, no. To tell you the truth, he practically cringed when I came in. Cowered. I had to talk to him for a good half hour before his hands stopped shaking enough to do the tests at all."

Portia stared at her colleague, clearly confused. "It only gets weirder," she said after another moment. "As soon as I think I've got a handle on this guy's behavior, he goes left on me."

Jayne shot her a rueful smile. "That's why we call 'em crazy."

"I guess," Portia replied, flipping through the folder. "But why would he be frightened of you? I mean—not to put too fine a point on it—his victims . . ." She glanced at Jayne, feeling suddenly as though she'd backed herself into a corner. Wier's victims had been elderly, white-haired, as Jayne was. It wasn't unreasonable to believe he might have perceived Jayne as a potential victim. That was why she'd warned her about him in the first place.

Then, in the next instant, it began to make sense.

"Oh my God—" Portia breathed. "I get it! He was frightened of you because of your size! Your height! Somewhere in his mind—you scared the dickens out of him precisely because you're not helpless, not frail. If you know what I mean."

"Yeah, I can put the fear of God into multiple murderers," Jayne answered, laughing. "It's the three-year-olds I can't control. But never mind. His being afraid of me probably worked to our ultimate advantage. Once I got him calm, he was a lamb. Did everything I asked. Have a look at what we got, Portia. The MMPI—it's pretty impressive."

Portia flipped through the file to the pages that comprised the Minnesota Multiphasic Personality Inventory, eyeing Jayne's neat scoring and comments with appreciation. "He sure is working hard to look normal," she commented.

"No kidding," Jayne agreed. "But even if he were trying, there's no way he could manipulate the results. It's a valid profile. The schizophrenia and depression subscales are highly elevated. He's practically off the chart."

Portia met Jayne's eyes as the implications of Wier's scores began to register. "Mommie dearest," she murmured.

"No kidding. She must have been something. Nobody can produce a profile like that without having some serious abuse from the primary provider. You can see how early he shut down. Never completed emotional tasks. No coping skills."

Portia nodded. "And all the resulting reality distortion," she answered. "The schizophrenia was essentially a learned response. Because of the abuse—he had to distort reality because the reality was unbearable."

"That's the way it works," Jayne said sadly. "You come up with anything on the mother?"

"Plenty," Portia admitted. "Enough for this to make sense. Perfect sense."

Jayne leaned back in her chair. "How'd he do on the TAT?"

Portia sighed. "No real surprises. Some evidence of sexual abuse. Definite preoccupation with sexual thought and behavior."

Jayne referred her back to the MMPI. "I got that, too. And I'd put money on violent acting out."

Portia nearly laughed. "Keep your money, Jayne. Earlier today, he told me he was at Atascadero. I'm guessing he did five to seven on a rape charge. Kids."

Jayne's eyes narrowed. "When?"

"He wasn't sure," Portia answered, rising to her feet. "Why do you ask?"

"Because if he was there as part of their sex offender program, Portia, you can start smiling." At Portia's confused look, she continued. "You ever hear of their sex offenders treatment program? Bio-psychosocial Rehabilitation. Pretty fancy stuff when it first happened—in the late seventies—maybe eighty. If our Jimmy was one of the first participants, they have that boy documented up the wazoo, I can promise you. The state and the feds needed all the evidence they could get to justify the program financially. They had their inmates documented down to their hangnails."

Portia's eyebrows shot up in surprise as Jayne went on.

"After all, it was pretty radical stuff back then, treating sex offenders like they were actually sick rather than simply horny."

Portia couldn't help smiling. "I got news for you, Jayne. For most people, it's still pretty radical. But thanks—even if I get nothing else from California, I've got this." She lifted the file folder in Jayne's direction. "I can't thank you enough."

Jayne grinned, then winced a little at the sudden ache around her eye. "Any time," she answered. "Just practicing the cardinal virtues. Heal the sick, bury the dead, test the lunatics."

Portia smiled warmly. "Not to mention ducking the occasional fast ball," she said and made her way to the door, leaving Jayne, still chuckling, in her chair as the first long shadows of twilight began to gather in the corners of the room.

Two blocks away, in a tiny office in the old two-story house that was home to Declan Dylan's law firm, Amy Goodsnow saw the same purple shadows gathering in the street as she waited for the day to come to a close. She was looking forward to trying out her new membership at the YMCA gym, a luxury that never would have been possible on an assistant DA's salary. She was just three days into her new job, and there was still so much new to get used to. A brand-new Mac, complete with Windows and a web crawler; the complicated telephone system, even the blessed privacy of her own office—not some divided-up cubicle, but an actual office—admittedly small, but neat and inviting, with a window that overlooked the pleasant mauve and granite skyline of downtown Charlotte.

Most of all, she still could not quite allow herself to believe that she had been hired as an associate by one of the most well-respected firms in the South, a turn of events made all the more miraculous by virtue of the fact that only a few short weeks before, she and Declan Dylan had been on opposing sides of the bench. Amy continued to stare out the window. It was all so unbelievable. Not a week before, Declan Dylan had called to ask if she might be interested in an associate's position. When she'd said yes, Dylan had gone into action, pulling all the necessary strings to free her from the DA's office weeks earlier than she might have hoped to leave. Things had fallen into place so easily, so effortlessly, it made her feel a little like Cinderella. What she didn't yet know was the reason, and the question had nagged at the back of her mind every waking moment. Why would Declan Dylan, a man who had access to all the new legal talent in the country, to say nothing of the means to pay for it, want her, a backwoods graduate like Amy Goodsnow, on his staff?

Her degrees hung in plain wooden frames on one wall above her desk, marking the room as somehow her own. The simple, single reality of having her own office in a firm like this validated her in ways she could not have articulated to anyone. The vague, unfamiliar sense of happiness it gave her was tempered by the not-so-vague sense that if she failed to meet the unspoken standards of this place and its assorted personnel, somehow, without warning, it could all be taken away. Midnight could come at any hour, and Cinderella's dream would turn to ashes once more.

She felt a little flutter of trepidation as the intercom on her desk beeped for her attention for the first time the whole afternoon. She frowned at the new telephone equipment, and struggled to remember just which button it was that would allow her to respond.

She took a breath and chose one. "Goodsnow," she said, inwardly breathing a sigh of relief when a voice crackled a response through the speaker.

"He wants to see you," a woman told her with flat efficiency. "Second door on your right."

Amy stuck out her tongue at the intercom. The location of her boss's office was one thing she was sure about. "Thank you," she replied sweetly. "I'll be right there."

She entered the open door of Dylan's office noiselessly, her feet sinking mutely into the still-rich nap of an old Sarouk, whose navys and rusts and golds seemed to shimmer in the lamplight. Some part of Amy thought of that rug as a magic sort of carpet, as if even being summoned to that office, with its discreet, tasteful colors and polished pecan desk was enough to change her fortunes forever.

Dec didn't look up. "Amy, good to see you. Please. Sit down."

Ashamed of her sudden jitters and the dampness of her palms, Amy took a chair opposite the desk, feeling a little lost in the high leather wingback. He looked so damn normal behind that desk, she thought. So handsome and so utterly at ease. To look at him, you'd never know the kind of private hell he must have been through when he lost the use of his legs. And the thought made her a little grateful as she mutely watched him put the finishing touches on some paperwork. Maybe if you didn't start out with so much, God would not see fit to take so much away.

"So," Dylan said quietly. "Tell me. You getting used to the place? Everything all right?"

"Yessir," Amy replied. "It's wonderful—really. I just—well, I just wanted you to know I'm really grateful. For the opportunity to work here."

Dec grinned easily, displaying white, even teeth and deep dimples on either side of a generous mouth. "Don't be grateful just yet. I haven't even put you to work. Couple of months down the line, you might just change your tune."

Amy smiled back, amazed both at herself and at the way he was able to put others instantly at their ease. No wonder he was one of the most sought-after lawyers in the state. He was good—damn good. "I doubt that, sir. I really do," she answered shyly.

Then, in an instant, everything changed, the warmth of their surroundings replaced by a sudden cold efficiency in his voice and attitude. "They're going to admit the Warren confession. Thanks to your work, I imagine. I got word this morning."

Amy all but shrank into the leather of the chair. She stared at him, uncertain of what response was expected of her. "I see—" she stammered.

Declan met her eyes and held them for a long moment. "Do you?" he asked. "Do you see? The fact is, Amy, George Warren is more than likely going to be executed because of this decision. What does that mean to you, exactly?"

Amy eyed him warily, groping for some response. His expression didn't change. He simply sat there, waiting.

Amy wet her lips and struggled to meet his look without flinching. "I had a job to do," she answered simply. "I did it."

If Dec was disappointed by the reply, he chose not to show it. "Yes," he agreed. "You had a job to do. And you did it very well, I might add."

Amy allowed herself to breathe again.

"Tell me," Dec continued. "Can I expect you to do the same for me? I think it's time I let you get your feet wet."

"Of course!" Amy replied passionately. "I'll do my best! I'll do—"

"Anything?" Dec cocked a quizzical eyebrow. "Good. I need some help on the Wier trial. I take it you're familiar with the case?"

Amy was, but at the same time she was having some trouble grasping just what she might be able to contribute with the trial itself less than two weeks away. "What can I do?" she said aloud.

Dec studied her intently. "You recall Dr. McTeague? From the Warren case?"

Amy sat forward. "Of course." That hearing was the only reason she was sitting in this room at all. Dylan had been impressed with her work in the courtroom. He'd told her that much when he'd made their initial appointment.

"Good. I'm working with McTeague on the Wier trial. I'm putting her up not as a mitigating specialist, but as our key defense witness. And I want you to work with her, Amy. I want you to go after her the same way you did for Warren."

Amy frowned, thinking of the cool expression she'd seen in Portia McTeague's eyes as she'd questioned her. "I'm not sure I understand. You want me to coach her?"

Dec surprised her with another of his winning smiles. "In a manner of speaking. As we go over her testimony for this case, I want you to give her everything you've got. For purposes of our coaching session, you're the prosecutor. I want you to give it everything you've got. Royal's not going to be easy on her, and I want you to be worse than he is. I want you to coach our witness as though you had everything at stake—your life, your ambitions for the future, everything. When you question McTeague, I want you to be hell on wheels. You think you can do that?"

Amy allowed herself a small, pleased smile. He'd hired her to toughen up his witness, then. To play it just as she'd play it in court, as though everything were at stake. Her smile broadened. "Oh," she answered. "I can do that. When do we start?"

"Dinner Friday night," Dec answered. "My house, seven o'clock. Maris will tell you where it is."

Amy rose, suddenly more relaxed than she'd been in weeks. "I'll be there."

As she turned to leave, Dec called after her. "Oh, I almost forgot," he said. "There's another detail I'd like you to see to."

Amy turned to him, her hand on the doorknob. "Anything."

"Dr. McTeague tells me she's been contacted by a former deputy at the Dixon County Sheriff's Department—a man by the name of Justin Chitwood—regarding some information he had about the case. It seems, however, that Chitwood left the sheriff's office very abruptly shortly thereafter. No one seems to know where he's gone, or why."

Amy digested this information. "You want me to find him?" she asked.

"We believe whatever he has to say about the Wier arrest could help the case, yes." Dylan tore a message slip from a tablet on his desk. "I have Maris trying to trace a location through the phone company, but so far, they haven't come up with an answer. I want your input on it. Maybe if we sit down and try to put together Chitwood's possible motives for contacting Dr. McTeague's office, then leaving his job so mysteriously, it will give us some clue to his whereabouts, some means of letting him know we're very interested in what he has to say."

Amy frowned a little at the piece of paper in her hand, the name and number neatly recorded in Dylan's own hand. She looked up and met her employer's bright blue eyes, amazed at herself all over again. It was as though she were somehow inspired by an invisible force that emanated from this man and from these rich surroundings—as though the carpet beneath their feet were imbued with a little bit of magic after all. And all at once she smiled.

"I'll try the Internet," she said. "If he's out there, I bet I can find him."

Seventeen

● ●

J IMMY WAS AFRAID. He paced ceaselessly back and
forth in his cell, peering from time to time through the
two-inch slit of Plexiglas set vertically into the cinder-
block wall that served as a kind of window. He saw the Doctor everywhere, thought it was her crossing the grass to the hospital grounds,
knowing it wasn't as the woman disappeared. He dreamed she came
to him one night, dressed in a guard's uniform and whispering her
endless questions. Over and over, he thought of the things he had
told her. And he thought of the pictures she had shown him, and
what he had said. And it made him afraid that she hadn't been back.
Something very bad was going to happen now—he could feel it. The
voice had been so silent, too, leaving him with a strange echoing in his
head that was ominous and sad.

Something had to happen now. Now that he had told the secrets.
And he waited for his punishment to come.

The She must be very angry now—worse even than before. And
from time to time he would pause in his pacing with his head cocked a
little to the side, listening—waiting for that shrill screaming to begin
inside his head. But there was nothing. And her terrible silence only
frightened him more.

He peered through the window and waited for the Doctor. He
knew there was no one else to save him now. But even the Doctor
stayed away. He thought maybe the She would come back, after the
Doctor stayed gone. But he listened and he could not hear the voice

and it worried him—worried him so much that he sat on the hard edge of his bed and had to squeeze his eyes shut tight as he tried very hard not to cry.

This was very bad, he knew—so bad he couldn't imagine the whole badness of it all at once but could only let his mind skitter around the edges of it like a frightened creature running from the dark. The She had been so quiet—too quiet. He couldn't remember when the She had been so quiet before. And it made him think for a moment that maybe the She was dead, that maybe the Doctor had done some trick and killed her when he wasn't looking.

And he wondered, if that were true, how he would live without her.

He had an idea then, and rose to fumble around in the drawer where he kept the pretties. He slipped her favorite earring on, his trembling fingers missing the hole at first, then finding it, pushing the wire through, unmindful of the blood he'd drawn. The She liked the green one. He knew that. It was shiny and dangly and she liked that kind the best, he knew. The best of any of them. Maybe putting it on would make it easier for her to come back. Maybe if he put it on even before she asked him to, the She wouldn't be angry with him for telling the secret things. Because he had done that. He'd sat with the witch doctor and told the things he was never to tell. Not all of them—maybe not even the worst ones. But he had said the words. It did not even seem to him as if he'd meant to, really. But the words had come out of his mouth. The Doctor had listened and written them down. There was no telling what would happen now. And that was bad. That was the worst kind of bad there could be.

And the enormity of what he had done turned him sick and cold with anxiety. He stood very still, trying to listen, trying to pluck one voice, one note from the ocean of sounds that echoed through the prison walls. And he thought he heard the walls themselves laughing, jeering at him as he waited and listened.

And still the She would not come. She stayed gone, away somewhere he could not find her. He stood very still, not knowing which should make him more afraid—knowing that she was gone or knowing that she was coming back to punish him. The She would make him do something—something terrible. Something too bad to even think about.

He froze at that moment, snared by the slit of sunlight that found its way through the narrow window and onto the floor. He closed his eyes and wore her favorite earring, too afraid now to think or to breathe or even to imagine what would happen when the She came back.

Jimmy Wier stood motionless as a tree, stuck in a fading patch of sunlight that filtered through his cell-block window—a small line of dried blood running down his neck from the torn earlobe where a cheap green glass earring hung forlornly—a trail to match the twin roads of moisture that slid from behind his tightly closed eyes.

Then the sun moved away and he felt the coolness of its absence against his face. The She was gone, leaving only a desolate loneliness behind, a void that was great and black and endless. The She was gone and the Doctor was gone and there was nothing now, save the great howling emptiness inside. And he was cold and alone and there was nobody to save him from the terrible punishment that would surely come.

He wanted to sleep, to make it be done and go to sleep, to somehow end the endless emptiness that stretched out before him. Jimmy Wier faced forever, chilled and afraid in a cell full of dark.

He moved like a sleepwalker to thrust a hand under his mattress. He withdrew a crumpled pack of cigarettes and threw them aside, taking up a forbidden box of matches in his hand. He cocked his head, listening. They would not come too quickly, he knew. If he was lucky, they would not come at all.

Smiling a little bit, he wadded up the single sheet and blanket in the center of his mattress. He tore a few pages from a worn paperback and stuffed them inside the pillowcase. And one by one, he put his whole precious box of matches to the pile, breathing in the acrid smoke like a fine perfume.

Across the tier of the cell block, Judd Wilkins rolled over, blinking in an unfamiliar light. Judd was doing three consecutive life terms and he knew the dangers of too much curiosity about his fellow prisoners. He tried not to turn his head, tried not to fall accidental witness to something better left unseen. But the weird light and dancing shadows troubled him, and he sneaked a glance toward the corridor to see what might be going on.

All at once, he sprang to his feet, his eyes wide and his mouth frozen open as he strained to make sense of the silhouette of the man in the cell opposite, his blank face flickering in the white-orange light of the fire in his bed.

"Holy shit!" Wilkins shouted. "Jesus! Hey, you motherfuckers! Get down here! Fucking maniac's trying to burn us down! Hey! Somebody!"

Wilkins screamed again as he watched Jimmy Wier feeling himself up and down the length of his huge body, saw the way he grabbed hold of his erect penis, poking it in and out of the flames in a parody of a lover's dance.

The thunder of a hundred running footsteps echoed down the corridor in their direction, as the night guards came brandishing black-jacks and fire extinguishers. Wilkins heard the pissed-off rumblings of a rudely awakened cell block as the men struggled out of sleep, yelling threats and cheers and catcalls.

Judd sank back onto his own sagging bunk, shivering as he tried to push away the strange dreamlike image of the killer they called Jimmy the Weird, dancing naked in and out of the flames, as if he was trying to burn his own balls off.

"Fuck," Wilkins said to no one in particular. "Weird is right."

Dr. Harry Falcone was not a bad man. He was not even an especially bad psychologist. But Falcone was a weak man—a person could all but smell weakness on him in the vague scent of last night's martinis, see it in the way he so carefully combed his hair over his balding crown and in the sad timidity that shone from his small gray eyes.

Nor was he a stupid man, though there were some who thought he was, because his propensity for thinking things through tended only to exacerbate the impatience of those made of sterner stuff. Blessed with more than his natural share of IQ points, Harry Falcone had the curious ability to discern all sides of a question without prejudice, unencumbered by personal morality. And it was that same curious knack for viewing reality through a kaleidoscopic lens that had drawn him to psychology. As a younger man, Harry Falcone had believed that a science of the mind would somehow clarify all the subtle demands life made upon the personality—that, once mastered, psychology would manage to dictate all the decisions Harry had never quite been able to make for himself.

And when Falcone had found ordinary practice somehow disappointing because of the terrible sameness of his patients' problems, his curious choice had been to try forensics, an arena where notions of good and evil collided with such regular intensity that it had astonished him. Yet the polarization of opinions in criminal court had not served to define Harry Falcone as much as they had served to highlight his sense of indecision. For all the days he'd spent in court, Falcone had somehow, despite the odds, managed to preserve his perennial inability to come out on one side or another. The court was a world that argued the rights and the wrongs of things, the blacks and the whites. Harry, on the other hand, moved in a world of perpetual gray, where everything was always a little bit true, and what mattered most was who did the talking.

Donny Royal was only too aware of all these things as Falcone entered his office and took a place opposite Royal's bleached oak modular desk. It was the Thursday after Harry had spent two of the more interesting days of his career, chiseling away at the psychological artifacts of a killer named Jimmy the Weird.

"So Dr. Harry," Royal began a little too heartily. "What's the good word on our boy down at Columbia?"

"Rumor has it he tried to set his cell on fire last night," Falcone answered, enjoying the little flicker of surprise and rage that lit up Royal's eyes. Nothing would be worse for the prosecutor than to have a suicide on his hands. Royal needed a conviction. The corpse would come later. "You'll be pleased to know they got the fire out before he did himself any serious damage, though."

Royal tried to conceal his relief and didn't quite succeed. "You get all the psycho tests worked out? Get what we need?"

Harry sipped a cup of weak coffee the secretary had provided and gazed at Royal laconically, knowing in advance that any attempt to explain the real condition of the inmate would be pretty much wasted on the DA. So he confined himself to a nod, halfheartedly lifting an untidy sheaf of papers housed in a soiled manila file folder.

Royal leaned back and rocked slightly in his executive-size office chair, and Harry began to think of how out of place the prosecutor looked in these subtle, meant-to-be-tasteful surroundings. The carefully chosen neutrals of the furniture and bookcase, the spare use of pastels in the sofas, and the abstract prints on the walls clashed somehow with the dark sheen of Royal's expensive polyester suit and the sharp, almost predatory expression in his eyes. He looked, thought Falcone, like a viper on a pillowcase.

"Cut to the chase, Falcone. Is there a chance they can make the plea stick?"

Not guilty by reason of insanity. The M'Naughten rule—designed originally to protect those who had no knowledge of their actions, no sense of right or wrong. It had been designed to instill a measure of mercy in the administration of justice, Falcone reflected. It had never been meant to be used as Royal and all of the others used it, as a definition open to capricious interpretation, where the madness of one could be the excuse of another or the premeditation of a third.

Yet in the end, he supposed it was the fault more of its authors than its interpreters, for they had attempted what Harry Falcone, in his profound disillusion, would never attempt to do, to draw some line between the sick and the healthy, the damaged and the whole, and to define that subtle mystery where madness came to know itself.

"I have no idea," he replied. "I'm a psychologist, not a fortune-teller. 'Course, the attempted suicide don't make it easier."

The truth was, Donny Royal saw little difference between psychology and fortune-telling, but he didn't allow that to show on his face. Instead he offered Falcone a broad smile. Expert opinion was how the game was played these days, and Donny Royal played it to win.

"Well now, you can tell he's not crazy. I mean, that fire could have been accidental, right? Smoking in bed. Wier don't foam at the mouth or eat boogers, does he? I don't want the jury judging on appearances, okay?"

Falcone's small eyes grew somehow smaller as he gazed across the prosecutor's desk. "They've got him medicated," he answered slowly. "He appears fairly functional."

Royal grinned. "That's good. That's very good. What I mean to say is, I just don't want a jury to be prejudiced, that's all. We know Wier done those old women on purpose. I just want them to judge him on the evidence. If you know what I mean."

Falcone smiled thinly. "It's all in the file, Royal. The prisoner shows some evidence of psychological disturbance. I don't know how extensive that disturbance is because I haven't spent enough time with him. We know he was at the scene, the DNA reports link him up to both rapes and murders. He did the crime. Whether or not he knew what he was doing is subject to interpretation."

"And you can say that, right? Under oath?"

Harry deliberated for a long moment, making Royal flush with impatience. "I don't know that I can answer that," Harry answered slowly. "I imagine what I say under oath will depend on the questions I'm asked. I will tell you that it's going to be very difficult to prove that Wier did not have a preexisting psychological condition. If the defense has any idea what they're doing, it's my guess there'll be records—lots of 'em."

"Shit," spat Royal. "What've we got?"

Falcone lifted the file in a halfhearted gesture. "I've got some standard tests, some medication history, and my own opinion."

"Which is?" Royal flushed red at Falcone's waffling. "Now, Harry, you know as well as I do which side you're supposed to be on. The state of South Carolina's the one wrote you a check."

Falcone met his look calmly. "You paid for my opinion, Royal. I don't know that you paid enough for a lie. Jimmy Wier is a disturbed individual. Schizophrenic. A real poster boy. And any psychologist in America who ain't blind and deaf is going to go in there, get the same things I got off the interviews, and come to the same conclusion."

"Goddamn—"

Harry stopped him with a hand. "Now, whether the fact that he is schizophrenic precludes knowledge and premeditation of the murders is not necessarily so. But that doesn't mean that he did know, either. Problem is, we're talking degrees here."

Royal propped his elbows on the dark green blotter that covered his desk. "What the hell does that mean?" he demanded.

Falcone suppressed a little sigh and wished profoundly to be elsewhere. "In the short version, it means that he might have been lucid at the time and he might not. Some schizophrenics know what they're doing a lot of the time. They hold down jobs, stay functional, and raise families. Some can be crazy about just one thing or only under certain circumstances. I can tell you he doesn't have too good an idea of what's going on now, but whether his condition deteriorated after the murders or before is guesswork. There's your loophole. That's where it's open to interpretation."

Royal made a disgusted little noise. Falcone's psychobabble was beginning to prey on his nerves.

"Well, I got the sheriff of Dixon County coming to stand up and testify that Wier was in his right mind at the time of the arrest."

"I daresay," Falcone replied. Of all the players in criminal court, arresting officers were notoriously predictable when it came to swearing to the state of mind of suspects at the time of their arrest. The criminals were very nearly always lucid and able to understand their rights, and they offered full confessions under questioning. Anything else, and the case could go sour.

Falcone met Royal's eyes. "The question is, will it be enough? The sheriff isn't offering a diagnosis. I am. And so will Dr. McTeague."

Royal sighed heavily. The mention of Portia McTeague was enough to start his stomach acids roiling. He knew from experience she was a tough customer, hard to break down on the stand. And the fact that she was a woman presented a real problem. Push a woman too hard and it looks to a jury like you're beating them up—go too soft and they were easily believed—especially the good-looking ones. The best he could hope for was to make her look empty-headed, the beauty with a bleeding heart and a misguided education.

Falcone sat untidily on the other side of his desk, his suit worn at the edges, a dissipated detachment showing out of his eyes. Falcone thought he was too good to make a stand—thought he knew too much to be corrupted. But Donny Royal, for his part, knew enough not to force Falcone's hand at that moment. That would come later. At the trial. He flashed the psychologist an easy, almost conspiratorial grin as he reached for the file.

"I'll have this copied and sent back to you this afternoon, Harry," he said nonchalantly. "Don't worry about it. I know you're gonna do fine up there."

Falcone, relieved that the meeting was apparently at an end, rose stiffly to his feet. "You got any particular line of questioning I ought to think about?" he asked.

"No," answered Royal, coming around his side of the desk. "As a matter of fact, I'm going to play it by ear."

Falcone was immediately suspicious. "It's not for me to say, Donny. But if you want my advice, don't ignore the insanity issue. Admit he has some problems, then minimize them in relation to the crime. Like I said, we're talking degrees here. Guesswork."

Royal walked his guest to the door. Falcone's idea made a certain amount of sense, but Royal wanted more than sense. The case was too big and he had too much to lose. Aloud he said, "I think we're gonna smoke 'em out, Harry. That way, the defense will do most of the work. I don't believe I'll call you at all for the state." He smiled at Harry's confused expression.

"We'll let the lady go first this time. Then, no matter what McTeague comes up with, I can use you for rebuttal. That way, you'll be the one who's fresh in the jury's mind when they go to deliberate, and I won't have to lean on her too bad. Juries like her—doesn't make sense, but they do."

In Harry Falcone's mind, it made perfect sense why juries liked Portia McTeague; there were a thousand reasons why the case ought to be won on the strength of McTeague's testimony alone. Even Royal knew why on some level. That was why he was planning to set Harry up as the rebuttal witness rather than sully his own image in a confrontation. But there was no point explaining any of that to a man like Royal, whose awareness of his own psychology was roughly equivalent to that of the lower primates, so Harry confined himself to a gracious, if halfhearted nod, and made his way to the door.

"Whatever you say, Donny. Whatever you say. You still want me to advise in jury selection? I could, you know. Maybe give you a little edge there."

Royal measured the possibilities. Overexposing a witness, any witness, even one as forgettable as Harry Falcone, was risky. On the other hand, he might be able to contribute to the voir dire in ways Royal himself had no time to anticipate.

"I'll think about that, Harry, I will," he said as he swung open the door to his outer office. "We'll talk in a couple of days."

After he was gone, Royal sat alone in his office, his mind working feverishly, trying to make the details of this newest strategy come clear. Using Falcone as rebuttal for McTeague's testimony still struck him as unduly chancy. Falcone might wind up concurring with her opinions. Or at least sounding as if he did. Shrinks all spoke the same language, had the same vocabulary. And Falcone was a weak witness generally—unappealing and unauthoritative, despite his distant scholarly air.

Royal thought hard. It was risky, yes. Yet, for all of that, the idea still made sense. He could make Falcone's weakness work. The very offhandedness with which Falcone testified, his demeanor, even his clothes, could work to the prosecution's advantage, simply by virtue of the fact that it would weaken the importance of the psychological testimony as a whole—both his and hers. Played down as an issue, insanity wouldn't stick. And Jimmy Wier would be sentenced to die. Royal rose and began to pace the nondescript carpeting. It was a good plan, but full of variables. And Donny Royal hadn't gotten where he was by putting any faith in variables.

His secretary's voice startled him out of his reverie as she informed him of an appointment at three. Royal walked to the desk and irritably punched the intercom button.

"Get the paper machine in motion, Toots," he informed the faceless voice in the outer office. "I've decided to motion that Dr. Portia McTeague be deposed as a witness in the Wier trial."

"How come?" his secretary asked, surprised.

A hundred answers to the question reverberated through Royal's brain. Unfortunately none of them was entirely legal. "Because she's failed to write up her evaluations on the prisoner James Wier," he answered. "If we can't see her findings, I'm going to try and fix it so she can't testify."

Two minutes before the telephone rang at Declan Dylan's office late that afternoon, the fax machine obligingly spat out a copy of Donny Royal's newest motion. Maris Beasley, who had been typing up a brief while nibbling on half a tuna salad sandwich left over from lunch, paused long enough to swallow the last bite of sandwich, finish her sentence, and gather the document before heading for Declan's office. Amy Goodsnow was in the corridor, heading in the same direction, but Maris waved her off.

"I'd lay low for a while if I were you, kiddo," she told Goodsnow matter-of-factly. "There's going to be some fireworks around here in a minute or so."

Amy froze in her tracks as Maris gestured with the paper in her hand. "I just hope he don't shoot the messenger," she said and disappeared through Declan's office door.

Amy leaned against the wall and tried not to look as though she were eavesdropping. Then she heard it—a low string of oaths that gradually rose in intensity as the telephone began to ring insistently in the outer office. She smiled to herself as she headed quietly back to her own office. It looked for once as though the Beasley bitch had been right. Whatever was going on, Dylan was fit to be tied. She smiled a little as she slid into a chair in front of her computer monitor. It didn't matter to Amy. If something had ruined the boss's day, she had something that just might make it.

Maris handed Declan the phone with an expectant expression. "It's him," she said simply, and settled herself in a chair without ceremony. Years of experience had taught her more than a few things about the workings of an attorney's office. One of them was that some shows were not to be missed.

Declan, red-faced yet controlled, spoke into the telephone. "Why, Donny Royal, what a surprise. You calling for a campaign contribution?"

Maris grinned at him from her chair and flashed a thumbs-up sign.

Royal's voice came smoothly back over the wire. "I take it you got a copy of the motion? I hope you don't mind. I tried to get through to Wier's principal counsel, but Mr. Evans seems to be tied up in another trial."

"Uh-huh," Dec answered calmly. Technically, Evans was still Jimmy's attorney, but both he and Royal knew how it would go down in the courtroom. Dec and Evans had already divvied up the witnesses, with Dec getting the principals. Royal was going to put on quite a show, and Declan Dylan with his playboy good looks and his wheelchair made for a bigger impression in a jury's mind.

"They just this moment set it on my desk," Dec continued. "Let's have a look."

He shot Maris a wink as he covered the receiver with one hand and stretched the pause in conversation far longer than was necessary.

"Looks like your paralegal must've made some mistake, Donny," he said finally. "I'm looking at a motion here that says you want to depose my expert."

Royal's voice came smoothly back over the wire. "No mistake, Dylan. I made that motion on the grounds that your expert has failed to supply this office with the necessary written evaluation reports for review," he answered. "You know as well as I do that we're entitled to see that paperwork."

"I believe you're only entitled to see paperwork that's in our possession, Don. And the truth is, we don't have it either. Dr. McTeague is just up to her ears. Busy, busy, busy." Dec managed a mock sigh. "But that's how it is when you've got the best." He paused to let the remark sink in. "Still, I can't very well give you paper I don't have myself, now, can I?"

"Well, find some way to get it then," Royal snapped back. "We're all busy here. You know as well as I do jury selection begins in six days."

"Yes, I do." Dec shot Maris a wink. "But you know, now we're on the subject, I was under the impression that I was to have gotten Dr. Falcone's reports first of the week. I don't believe we've received anything of that nature here." He raised an eyebrow and looked to Maris for confirmation. She shook her head and examined her fingernails. It wasn't going to be as good a show as she'd hoped, but she'd already decided to stick around for the end of the conversation. Doubtless the boss would have something for her to do when it was over.

"Now see here, Dylan. Something like this has got to be done by the book, understand? There's just too much attention being paid to go at it any other way. So we have to nail this down right now. A gentlemen's agreement, you might say. You show me yours and I show you mine."

Dec stifled a yawn. "A gentlemen's agreement," he began. That'll be the day, he added silently. Aloud he said, "Well now, Don, you know I'd like to help you out there. But like I say, I can't give you paper that isn't wrote. Tell you what, though—"

Royal's voice fairly crackled with impatience over the wire. "What?"

"I'll give the doctor a call and see if she can't hurry things along a bit. Course, I can't make any guarantees now. It's a complex case. And I know you wouldn't want to go cutting any corners. Too much hurry-up and our Mr. Wier could have himself cause for appeal going in."

On the other end of the line, Donny Royal paused in passing a comb through his immaculately styled hair. Bastard, he thought. He ducked down to stare for a moment at his own reflection in a small hand mirror perched on the edge of his desk, then forced a smile until it became almost real.

"You do that, Dylan," he answered. "But you know, I was thinking just now. Just occurred to me. Let's say I withdraw the motion to have her deposed. Let's say we just dispense with both the experts this time. You get rid of McTeague as a witness and I'll lose Falcone. What do we need the shrinks for, anyway? They don't add a thing to the process. Just confuse everybody. So, what do you say? You lose the insanity plea, and we agree not to clutter up the works."

At the sudden change in Dylan's expression, Maris sat forward in her chair. Maybe it wasn't going to be such a bad show, after all. The boss was looking as if he'd just been force-fed a handful of nickels.

Dec struggled to keep his voice calm. "Now why in the world would I do that?"

"Because," Royal answered. "We come to an agreement, maybe I can give you a break in jury selection. No old ladies, maybe. What do you think?"

Dec looked up frantically at Maris, and passed a hand across his throat in an abrupt, horizontal motion. Immediately Maris was on her feet. She thumped a button on Declan's phone console producing an entirely satisfactory bleep.

"Sorry to interrupt, Mr. Dylan," she intoned in a high nasal tone. "I have an emergency call on three." She hit the button and it bleeped again.

"Sorry to cut this short, Don. Emergency. You take care, now, hear?"

"But what about—"

"—What? Oh, your half-assed deal? Oh, Don," Dec replied, smiling, "I don't think so."

Maris looked at her employer for a long moment after he'd hung up the phone. "How's Mr. Royal?" she asked.

Dec glanced up, a mixture of distraction and puzzlement and glee moving over his chiseled features. "Desperate, I think," he answered. "Either that or he's gone crazier than Jimmy the Weird."

"Hmmph," offered Maris in a noncommittal tone. "Well, I hope for your sake, he's gone crazy."

Dec glanced at her. "Why do you say that?"

She looked at him for a long moment. In a way, it had never been a mystery to her that Declan Dylan, for all his privilege and looks and brains, had wound up as he had. A tragedy maybe, but no mystery. He never saw things coming. Declan Dylan went through life thinking God was on his side, and maybe God even was. The problem being that Dylan had such an excess of faith he never quite paid attention to who might be fighting for the other side. He wouldn't know the devil if he came up and bit him on the butt.

"Because," she answered. "Crazy people are easier to beat." She waggled a manicured finger at the fax sheet still perched on top of the nearest pile of papers. "You want me to call her?"

Dec smiled. "Yeah," he said. "Yeah. And make sure she's coming for dinner Friday night. Tell her no excuses. We've got to discuss the—uhh—motion."

Dink, thought Maris. Why don't you just call her yourself? "I'll do what I can," she promised. "By the way, that new girl was loitering outside your door a while ago. Seemed all excited about something. Shall I send her in?"

Dec frowned a little. "Goodsnow? Yeah, why not? I've got a minute."

Maris, back at her desk with the telephone tucked firmly under one ear, watched as Amy emerged from her office a few moments later with fresh lipstick and newly combed hair. Her time at the firm seemed to have breathed some new life into her wardrobe. Amy moved toward Dylan's office in a well-styled gabardine skirt and silk blouse that showed off more by way of slim young curves than Maris thought entirely appropriate for office wear. She even caught a whiff of flowery perfume as Amy moved down the hall and Portia McTeague's office picked up on the other end of the line.

Dink, she thought. And he'll never see it coming.

Eighteen

● ●

J IMMY WAS WAITING. It seemed to him as though he
had been waiting for ages before she came to him. He sat
alone in the stifling conference room, waiting for her.
They'd uncuffed his hands in anticipation of the visit, and again he
marveled that she would be able to make the guards obey her wishes,
even from afar. He'd seen the clock as he passed their station on his
way into the little room. Just a few more minutes, he told himself. A
few minutes more and he would see the lady doctor and make her
explain what had happened to him. Just a little while and he would
finally be able to ask the question that had first puzzled him, then
worried him, then had taken root in his mind like some miracle demanding explanation.

And so he waited, wishing the Doctor's footsteps down the corridor, wanting—no, needing—the reassurance that she would come at
last to relieve the terrible anxiety that had settled on him like a shroud
since their last meeting.

Jimmy sat alone, trying not to be afraid. He needed to see the lady
doctor with the bag full of tricks and the sad green eyes. He needed to
ask her, fearing already the answer that might come, and the terrible
power over him that was hidden somewhere in the things she had to
say.

He stared at nothing for a long moment, ceaselessly flexing his
hands in the dim light. A picture swam up in the back of his eyes, and
he froze instantly. His hands. He remembered. His thumbs pressing

deep, crushing something. Muscle against bone. There were blond hairs curling on his knuckles and a roaring in his head, and something in him shivered. Then the picture was gone and there was only silence in his mind, and flashes of light and dark where the image had faded behind his eyes.

Jimmy began to rock, tortured again by the terrible urgency he felt as he waited for the Doctor to come. He needed the answer. Needed it so much that the need itself turned him cold with its power.

The Doctor was coming. He needed to ask her—

What had she done with the She?

He heard it then, the sound he had been waiting for, so faint at first that he could not be sure it was real. The footsteps stopped at the security station near the end of the hall and he thought he might have heard her voice, picking it out of the endless dull roar on the block. Please, please, he prayed silently. Let it be her—let it be real.

And then—magically—she was there, and he could see her standing in front of him, with her sunglasses pushed up into her curly hair and her face looking down at him. Dr. Tricks had been a real thing after all—real enough now to reach across the narrow table and take his hand.

Jimmy began to tremble, the question already boiling up inside him. But the Doctor's mouth was working and he had to try hard to focus until the sounds in the room sorted themselves into a word or two.

"Hi, Jimmy," Portia said. "How are you doing?"

He gazed up at her, slack-jawed with some unnameable gratitude. "You came back," he said.

Portia settled herself into the opposite chair. "Of course I did, Jimmy. You knew I would."

Jimmy licked his lips. His mouth was dry, his tongue suddenly thick and clumsy as he struggled with some reply. "I did know, I guess. But I wanted—I wanted it—you to. So because I wanted it, I couldn't—be sure—if it would happen."

She looked at him and he blushed for no reason under the bright intensity of her gaze. "I'm sorry," he finished.

Portia smiled kindly. "Jimmy, you don't have to be sorry. I'm glad you wanted me to come back. I'm glad—"

"Wait," Jimmy interrupted.

Portia paused, her pen poised above the yellow of a blank new page of legal pad. "What, Jimmy, what is it?"

He shivered a little, trying to quiet the sudden roaring in his ears. "What have you done to me?" he blurted. And despite himself, his eyes filled with sudden tears. He thumped the table in frustration, the need within him so great now there was no point even trying to keep it hidden. His voice shook with effort, rising in the tiny room like a cry.

"What did you do with her? How did you make her go away? She's never been gone this long before. It's—too quiet. In my head. I like it . . ." He was rocking furiously now, the words tumbling over one another. "But I don't like it. I'm afraid. Something very bad is going to happen when she comes back. You wait. You just wait and see."

Portia could only look at him in astonishment. "Who are you talking about, Jimmy? Who is she?"

Jimmy glanced furtively toward the door, as if hearing the name spoken aloud would summon some physical presence there. His voice dropped. "I did a bad thing," he whispered. "I made a fire. See? He held up his knuckles. "I thought they'd told you I was bad. I thought you weren't ever coming back here."

Portia stared at his hands, feeling an uncomfortable rush of sympathetic response in her own skin. Silently, she cursed the prison system. Why hadn't they called? She should have been informed of any crisis in the prisoner's behavior. "No, nobody told me. But, Jimmy, why? Why did you start the fire?"

He stared at her incredulously. "Because—I don't know. I thought if I got hurt, the She would come back. And the She likes fire. I know that. I was scared."

Portia struggled to place this new information, barely able to contain her excitement. Gender-identity disorder, chronic schizophrenia, and now this—she. What was it? A command voice? Some new delusion?

"Tell me about her," Portia managed finally. "The—she."

Jimmy hesitated. "I mean—I don't know too much. The She thinks I'm too stupid to know anything. But I know some things."

Portia never took her eyes from his face. "What things? Does the she talk to you? Like a voice in your head?"

He glanced at her distrustfully, suspecting that the question might be another trick, yet knowing, somehow, that there was no returning to the place where his secrets could be kept. A sigh escaped him and he went on. "She tells me what to do," he answered, as though it were somehow obvious. "And She punishes me—sometimes. The She takes care of me—always. I listen to her. I try to make her happy." He glanced up and looked at Portia helplessly. "I'm lonely without her— I'm afraid."

With that Jimmy bent double in his chair and his huge shoulders hunched in agony as wrenching sobs overtook him, hoarse and uncontrollable, shaking his great frame like a series of physical blows.

Some part of Portia wanted to run at that moment, horrified all over again at being witness to such pain, feeling the tug of responsibility for having somehow caused it. But even at that she sat quietly and allowed his sobs to continue, all too aware that the pain in Jimmy Wier had to be released. He was no threat to anyone now. He was lost and alone, grieving and afraid.

After a few more minutes, when he had quieted, she steeled herself and went on, her voice sounding unnaturally soft. "How long, Jimmy—how long have you known about her?"

Jimmy sniffled noisily, wiping his tears with the back of a beefy hand. "Don't know," he answered. "Long time."

Portia felt an iron bar of tension settling across her shoulders. "Does she know what you tell me?"

"Yes."

"Does she know what I tell you?"

Despite himself, Jimmy's eyes welled once more with unbidden tears. "Yes, that's why I'm so scared. You did something to her. You made her go somewhere . . ." He trailed off, somewhere between despair and resignation. "When she comes back, I'm in trouble."

Portia took a momentary refuge in scribbling notes, trying to hide the sudden trembling of her hand. She'd found the gold she was digging for in Jimmy Wier. For the first time, the fragments of Jimmy's diagnosis began to make sense. Durant's guessing he was a transsexual lesbian, the schizophrenia, and now the She—another piece, perhaps the last piece of the puzzle that was Jimmy Wier.

She wrote three words in the center of the page in front of her, underlining them so deeply that her pen would leave an impression through half the tablet. Dissociative Identity Disorder. She'd never seen a case firsthand, but once the idea came clear, it seemed so obvious that she was almost ashamed of herself for not having suspected it earlier. This "she"—whatever it was—was where Jimmy Wier had placed his unspeakable pain, the humiliation he had been made to feel for being born a male. Another part of her mind frantically began to sort through the things she knew about the disorder. Severely abused individuals always developed fragmented personalities. In DID, those fragments assumed identities of their own, sometimes capable of acting without the knowledge of the core personality, and sometimes even controlling it entirely. The tragedy was that all too often a person with the disorder had a control personality that was nothing more than a highly successful re-creation of the principal abuser.

Portia studied Jimmy intently, her mind in turmoil. The question now was one of degree. Had Jimmy's gender-identity problems manifested in a full-blown alternate identity, or was the "she" simply a command delusion capable of directing Jimmy's actions? And who had committed the murders? Whose idea had that been?

If Jimmy Wier did have an alternate personality, it was one she had still never met. And so the problem now became more one of strategy than it was of therapy. How to smoke out this "she" without invoking the wrath and punishment Jimmy so feared?

Portia took a deep breath and prayed silently for some inspiration. She was so close to the truth, she couldn't afford to say the wrong thing. Jimmy's eyes were dry again for the moment, but brimming with pain nevertheless. She managed a wan smile.

"Maybe she's quiet because she wants you to be in charge for a while," she offered gently.

Jimmy frowned and shook his head. "No—no. That isn't true. How could it be true? It's never happened before. Never. Not even when . . ."

Portia saw the instant of hesitation and pounced. "Jimmy, tell me the truth, do you remember killing those old women?"

Wier folded his arms across his chest in a gesture of unconscious defense, protecting himself now, almost shrinking from her quiet insistence. He lowered his eyes. "No—not really—a little maybe. Before you came, just now. And last night, in the fire. I thought I could see some of it then. I think I was there, when they died. My hands were there. But . . ." He faltered and coughed uneasily. "My head hurts—hurts to think about it."

"Try to think about it, Jimmy. You have to try."

"My hands—I could see them. Like this." He held his hands up, fingers curled, thumbs perpendicular, pressing savagely against the empty air above the table. Portia set her teeth against the picture those jerking hands painted in the air, feeling her own throat contract instinctively.

Jimmy dropped his hands, a sheen of sweat breaking out on his forehead. "They were my hands," he said helplessly. "I could see them. So it must have been me." His eyes moved restlessly toward the door and over the table and then the floors, finally coming to rest on her face.

For a moment, Portia saw something flicker in the back of his eyes, something she had seen before—hypnotic and bottomless and insanely seductive. "Don't remember," Jimmy insisted. "Don't. Can't."

He was seized by a violent trembling then, sobs tearing at his voice. "Poor old ladies. Poor, poor things. But—She—something happened. I thought I could tell you—but—don't remember. She was yelling at me—so mean. So mean." He began to rock, moving his great hands in the air like someone drowning, his voice dropping to just above a whisper—low and hoarse and taut with anxiety. "They're so easy to break. Just like eggs. Oh God—I thought it was—I thought I knew them. She told me—She told me I needed to make sure Lizzie was dead. And I thought I did, but then my real mama came. And I needed to make sure—I had to fix it—so there wouldn't be any more babies. Don't you see?" The tearing sobs overcame him completely as he surrendered to the agony inside.

And Portia could only watch helplessly as Jimmy Wier went to pieces before her eyes. He was a man so damaged that only a touch—only a moment of trust and contact—had brought him to this—snot-nosed and sniffling, all two hundred and fifty pounds of him shaking uncontrollably in an agony of remembering. She wanted—needed—to go on, and she could not find the strength to do it, could not make the questions come. He was slipping beyond her, and she could not make herself bring him back. She could only watch, stunned by his pain and confusion, feeling his sobs reverberate deep within her own body.

Portia sat very still, feeling as if she, too, might shatter at a touch, feeling Jimmy's cries reaching deep into her own darkness, beckoning her secrets into the light. And in that moment they were so very much the same, joined together by their awful secrets—by the image of a pair of hands strangling a handful of air.

Portia glanced down at her half page of notes, trying not to let him see the awful sadness that rose up within her at the sight of him wiping his nose on his sleeve. After some minutes he looked at her, his eyes showing nothing but a terrible exhaustion—one that echoed through her own limbs like a sedative, as though they might both slump back in their chairs and fall asleep like two lost children.

"I thought they were my mommies. But they weren't, were they?" Jimmy asked.

Portia swallowed the sudden lump of emotion that rose in her throat. "No, Jimmy. They weren't."

But there was more—there was always more. Even now she could not leave Jimmy Wier alone. Even now she had to put her own weariness and disgust and pain aside to ask the questions that would make up a history for the jurors who were going to decide his fate. She had to go on. She managed a weak smile and tried to sound reassuring.

"Jimmy, I—need to be able to tell the court some more. Just—just tell me what you remember. Don't worry about the rest."

Jimmy nodded and gazed disconsolately down at his hands lying motionless in his lap. "I never did get to see her dead was the thing."

"Who, Jimmy?"

"Lizzie—my mama."

"When did she die?"

"In the summertime. Nineteen eighty-eight. I was in jail. Parole violation. They told me she was dead—but they wouldn't let me see her. And then I could hear her sometimes—talking. I thought if I got to see her dead it would stop."

He met the psychologist's eyes, his own filled with an awful resignation. "I thought it was her. She was yelling—and she . . ."

"What, Jimmy? Did you think Ms. Mooney was your mama?"

He stared at her for a long moment. "It must have been her. She didn't have no babies of her own."

Portia wrote hastily. "What about Ms. Bennet?"

Jimmy shrugged, offering only a long inappropriate yawn. "I don't know. I don't remember that. Nothing."

Portia studied him, thinking of how to continue. The yawn had signaled something. She couldn't push, though. If she did, he'd slip away. She decided to take a new tack. "Jimmy," she went on. "Remember when we talked about families? And how the pain comes from that sometimes? Tell me some more about what it was like. Tell me what you remember."

Jimmy shifted uneasily and began to pick nervously at the tabletop. "Horace left us," he said. "I think maybe that was the worst part. Then there was nobody anymore. Just me and her. And she just took up with anybody, any kind of man, after that. I guess she was a whore, maybe. I don't know. But the men would come and then sometimes there was money. Mostly there wasn't. Maybe they were sorry for us."

Portia glanced up, noting the change as his voice grew distant. His whole affect flattened—face, arms, shoulders—slack and leaden as Jimmy the Weird began to spin out his terrible secrets in an apathetic monotone.

"I went down on them for food money. And Lizzie would watch and make sure they didn't give me more than they gave her. Sometimes they didn't give money. Just took me in the ass. First her, then me. Like we were the same."

Portia wrote, struggling against the numbness that had settled over her in the aftermath of his tears, against the low hypnotic tone of his voice. "How old were you when your parents split up?"

"Five. I was five when the others started coming. It hurt at first, but Lizzie showed me how to make it easier. She worked me with the broom handle, you know, till I got loosened up. She told me that was what it felt like to be a girl. And it hurt, but I got to where I liked it. That feeling."

"What happened when you went to school? When you didn't have to be around Lizzie so much?"

"She tried to hide me. She kept me in the house so the school people wouldn't find me and make me go. But they did, I guess. It was always like that. I kept trying to stay hid, but they still found me."

"Who, Jimmy?" Portia interjected, urgently now. She could see him, feel him slipping out of her reach, off to the only place where he had ever succeeded in hiding from the demons that pursued him.

He glanced at her, as if surprised she was still there. "The men," he answered simply. "By the time I was maybe eleven, I couldn't walk down the street without some guy offering me a ride, some money. You'd be surprised."

"Oh, I don't think so, Jimmy," Portia answered sadly. "Did you tell anyone—a teacher maybe? Did you tell anybody your mama was hurting you? That those men were hurting you?"

"Hurting me?" Jimmy shook his head in a vague way. "No, I didn't tell. I didn't know it was hurting after a while. I didn't feel—anything. I thought they knew. I thought they could tell about me. Anybody who wanted a fuck knew right away. Guys would always come around and find me, and I would do what they wanted. I didn't think I needed to tell. I thought everyone knew."

"Why did you go with them, Jimmy? Those men?"

Jimmy shrugged. "Different reasons. Maybe I just thought somebody might love me a little. And sometimes I went because she told me to."

"Who, Jimmy? Your mother?"

Jimmy did not answer, only stared into space at something Portia couldn't see, his mouth curving in an odd smile.

"She always thought it was funny," he continued. "You know, that the guys thought they were doing a guy. Only they were really doing her. The way she liked. On my back and through the legs—like a woman. She liked that—fooling people. She thought it was funny. It was like Mama said."

Suddenly, the big man's chin began to quiver and tears threatened once again behind his eyes. The monotone gave way to a single high, helpless note. "Please . . ."

Portia bit her lip in an effort to control her own emotions. If he wept again, she wasn't sure she could stand it. "What, Jimmy, what? How was it like your mama said?"

He did not cry out this time, but only sat staring into his lap, his huge head moving back and forth. "I can't—do—this." The four words came with a terrible effort, more grunting than speech.

"You have to try, Jimmy." Portia leaned forward, trying to close the space that suddenly gaped between them. From somewhere deep inside the prison, she heard a shout that barely registered, so intent was she on keeping Jimmy tied to the bits and pieces of memory that floated up from the black, stinking waters of his torment. She reached out to touch his shoulder, and he shuddered at the contact as if he'd been scalded.

Wier moaned and held his head between his hands. The words came again, uttered in short, choking gasps. "My mama—men hurt us. Her daddy, her brothers—her husband. They all hurt us and then left. All those men. But she kept going back. So I had to. It was like we were always looking for men. And I had to do what she told me. I needed her. I was a boy—I was bad—but—she kept me. My real mama didn't. And Lizzie—tried to make me see it—how bad it was— to be a boy. Only—only—only . . ."

"Tell me, Jimmy. Don't stop. It's all right. You don't have to be afraid." Portia tried to reach for his hand, and again he threw off the touch in an agony of self-loathing, folding into himself, away from his pain.

"All those men—all so bad. And then I couldn't tell if I was bad or if they—made me bad. But—when she made me a girl—it got better for a while. It made her into a man—sticking things in me. And I didn't understand it until—the other one came. The She explained it. She—understood. She knew what to do. But now . . ." Jimmy shivered helplessly.

Portia tried to speak, fighting back the sick despair that had closed around her heart. Jimmy couldn't stand much more. The things he had told her were tearing him apart.

Jimmy nodded vaguely, fading visibly as fatigue and confusion all but overcame him. "Bonnie Jean," he called dreamily. He fell silent for a long moment, his breath coming shallow and fast, as though he'd been running.

Portia let him rest and worked on her notes, the words swimming up at her from the page. Everything was there, hidden somewhere in the disjointed phrases and snatches of Jimmy's history, couched between the lines of his tortured confession. And everything was hidden, even now. The internal reality of the things Jimmy had endured were recorded in this sad collection of sickening details and fragments of his understanding. Yet, the facts of his life—the names, the dates, the frame for his tormented life were lost, perhaps forever, in the wreckage of his mind.

As she wrote, she became aware of something, some sudden indefinable change in the room, like a drop in temperature or a dimming of the lights. She shifted in her chair, still writing, then paused all at once, possessed of the peculiar certainty that she was being watched. She glanced up and what she saw looking back at her took her breath away.

It was the same Jimmy, in the same orange jumpsuit, perched in his chair with his huge hands hanging down. It was the same face, the same mouth. But the eyes that had watched her, that now held her own, were bright and utterly changed, gleaming with some mad excitement—vicious and cunning and howling with rage. His tongue came out, wet and shining, and he ran it easily, wetly, over his mouth as he looked at her. Then he stretched his lips and pursed them, a liquid sucking noise filling the room as the thing that sat before her offered an obscene parody of a kiss.

And the laughter, when it came, was high and harsh and weirdly familiar, and Portia drew back as the figure in the chair began to stretch and preen itself in the mirror of wonder and fear reflected in her eyes. And then the eyes locked on her own, and Portia's confusion fell away as she found that she knew them—knew that she had looked into those eyes before.

And the voice was ripe with hatred when it spoke to her.

"You want to know something, cunt? Witch doctor. Priss doctor. Why don't you ask me?"

And then she knew—the force of the knowledge hitting her like a blow as amazement caught up to reality and screeched to a halt. She knew before she could form the words or the thought, or find even a moment to be a little afraid.

This was not Jimmy at all.

Nineteen

● ●

THE THING that was inside Jimmy Wier fixed Portia with voracious eyes. "Leave him alone, you hear me? You fool! You'll kill him if you keep this up, can't you see that?"

Portia was frozen in quiet horror, awed by the transformation. She could only gulp for a moment before forming a response. "Are you— her? Are you . . ." Her mouth formed Jimmy's phrase clumsily. "The She?"

The voice cackled its derision, sending a chill to the pit of the psychologist's stomach. "Very smart, shrink," it answered. "Who the fuck else would I be? I have a name, though. It's Bonnie. Bonnie Jean."

Portia fought back a hysterical little giggle at the incongruity of the alter's choice of a name. Looking into those bottomless eyes, it seemed almost silly. Like finding out the devil's name was Bob. She eased imperceptibly toward the door, sliding her chair a half inch backward. Some part of her mind registered that the prisoner's hands were uncuffed. She needed to know she could get out. Yet her response, when it came, was studied, almost casual in tone. "So how come I get to see you now? Why not before?"

The bottomless eyes narrowed as they looked at her. "I've been here the whole time, watching you—and him. I even spoke out loud once. And you didn't even know it." The thing smiled unpleasantly, puffy lips curving over big, unevenly spaced teeth. "You and those lawyers and the whole fucking dog-and-pony show. I was here from day-fucking-one."

Portia mentally resolved not to be intimidated, and almost succeeded. "Still doesn't answer the question," she responded mildly.

The huge hands slapped across the narrow counter between them with the force of a thunderclap, making Portia jump.

Bonnie Jean leaned forward, the icy eyes now alive with rage. "You think I don't know what's going on? All that lah-de-dah shrink talk and that little Miss Priss routine doesn't fool me. Trying to be so fucking kiss-my-ass sweet. Sharing the pain. What a load of horseshit! I know what you are, bitch doctor. You think I can't see through you? You and old Jimmy boy here are members of the same club. You're just as fucked up as he is."

Portia met the other's eyes. "Maybe we are," she replied, strangely calm. "All I'm trying to tell Jimmy is that he can get better. Is that why you decided to show up? Are you afraid he'll get better?"

Bonnie Jean laced her huge fingers together and laid them on the tabletop in a gesture at once so feminine and so sinister it made Portia go cold inside.

"The only reason I came out is because you're stupid. You're going to kill him, you know that? With your shrink talk and your questions. He can't take it—Christ! He'll kill himself if he ever figures it out. He dies, I die. And frankly, you stupid cunt, I don't intend to die."

Portia considered this. "You think if Jimmy remembers the murders you're going to die?"

The answer was taut with fury. "He doesn't remember shit! I do. I was there! Not him!"

"You killed those women?"

"Brilliant! Did you just figure that out? Wowee!" Bonnie Jean grinned maliciously. "And you call yourself a doctor. I'm more of a doctor than you are. At least I take care of the big, stupid idiot. I had to do it. He was too weak to do it himself. Call it self-defense."

Portia poised her pen above her page of notes and looked at Jimmy, feeling as if the huge body were indeed some masterful disguise for the person she was addressing, as if that masculine frame and blond beard and wide jaw would begin to dissolve in the next moment, revealing the face of the woman underneath.

"How do you mean?"

"Because he was too far gone—because. Look . . ." For the first time, Bonnie Jean faltered. "Jimmy can't help you, I can. So I help and you lay off the tricks, get it? You work for the lawyers, right? So do your fucking job. You're supposed to save his ass. Not kill him. And believe me, he will kill himself. He would have that day. Maybe he even would have done the old broad and then offed himself. I was just the insurance."

"How do you know that?" Portia insisted. "How do you know he would have killed somebody? Or himself?"

Bonnie Jean shook her head. "Take my word for it, okay? Like I said, I was there. As for killing himself, he tries it every time one of you quacks tries to get him to dredge up all that crap about his pathetic childhood. He's tried it lots of times. So leave his head alone, bitch—that belongs to me."

Portia silently weighed the odds on pressing for more and decided against it. It was clear that whatever Bonnie Jean's reasons for showing herself, they had nothing whatever to do with feeling the need for therapy. "What do you want from me?"

Bonnie Jean snickered. "Since you can't be any smarter, I'll settle for your being a messenger."

"I'm not sure what you mean," Portia said.

"I need to tell you about those bitches we did, okay? So you get it right before the trial. So you and his bleeding heart lawyers don't screw up our chances."

Portia nodded. "So, I'm listening—" she said. "What happened?"

Bonnie Jean leaned forward in a conspiratorial way, the high harsh voice dropping to just above a whisper.

"His asshole boss was giving him shit about being a queer, that's what started it. I got dressed up the night before and Jimmy forgot he had on an earring of mine. But Jimmy isn't a queer, I am—see? I'm the one who likes men. So when I'm out, that's who I go with. And that makes Jimmy the fag, don't it? Only he don't want anybody to know what a dirty boy he is. Gets real uptight when somebody figures it out."

"Let me see if I understand," Portia said slowly. "You like men, so that makes Jimmy a homosexual."

Bonnie Jean smiled her satisfaction. "He's the one who does the do, Priss. I just tell him who. A woman's got needs, after all."

Again the tongue flicked in and out, and Portia averted her eyes, refusing the alter's obvious attempts to bait her. "But you said just now—you said you were—homosexual. I talked to Melanie Durant. The nurse at the hospital. She told me you wanted her."

"Homosexual," Bonnie Jean mimicked, lisping. "So what? I do men, I do women. I do 'em all. Sometimes, like that day, I do young ones. Real young."

Portia's expression did not change. "What do you mean?"

"Jimmy had a delivery that day—earlier. There were these kids all over. They had the measles. I hate kids, but there was this one little boy. Maybe six, maybe eight. Nice and tight. I saw him and I got to thinking. Talked to Jimmy about him, too. Did a little whisper in his ear."

Portia shuddered inwardly. Dear God. "What happened?"

Bonnie snorted. "He got all weird about it, like usual. But I didn't push him. I don't like to push him. Then he don't cooperate. But when we got back to the grocery store, and Derman started in on him about that earring and being a queer, it flipped him, you know? He thought Derman could, like, read his mind or something. It always flips him when he thinks shit like that."

Portia paused in her frantic efforts to record this bizarre conversation for her notes. "So what about the murders?"

"I'm sayin' he was already out of it when he got over to the bitch's house, right? He's so fucked up, forgets the earring. The old biddy starts screaming at him when she sees it. Calling him a pervert. And then there's all these fucking violets, see? All over the house. Hundreds of 'em." Bonnie shrugged nonchalantly and went on.

"I had to come out and do the bitch when I saw those. I mean it. Jimmy was flipped out. He wasn't gonna make it. He drops the bag of groceries and she's screaming and he like—he thought he was home, you know?"

"So it was you, not Jimmy, who killed Lila Mooney?" Portia asked, resisting the idea. "Did you rape her too?"

Bonnie smiled, almost sheepishly. " 'Course." The big body leaned so close Portia could feel the breath on her cheek. A tongue flicked lasciviously from between the lips.

"No titty like an old titty, I always say."

Holy shit, thought Portia, looking resolutely down at her notes. There's a twist. Her wrist ached from writer's cramp as she began a new sheet of paper, her thoughts reeling. Her eyes told her she might be looking at the first case of alternate identity she had ever seen, but her mind could not help but shy away. Of all the possible diagnoses for Jimmy Wier's condition, multiple personality was possibly the worst. It could be the kiss of death for his case, the kind of trick that was only pulled from the hats of quacks and movie-of-the-week psychological experts. Or so she'd thought until now.

"What about the other victim? Jimmy doesn't remember anything."

Bonnie Jean made a dismissive gesture. "Easy. We're in the kitchen, doing the deed. She comes up to the front door and barges the fuck in, right? Knocks once, then just walks her fat ass right in like the place belongs to her. And since all of a sudden there's this witness, I figure—what the fuck? Let's party!"

Portia drew a long breath and kept writing. "So you killed her, too."

There was an answering chuckle. "She was so sweet. I kept her alive while I was on her and then cut her when I came. It was sweet. So sweet to be rid of them."

Portia glanced up, careful to keep her voice steady. "Is that all?"

Bonnie Jean smiled almost lazily. When she spoke again, the voice was so rife with hatred and triumph it raised the hair along Portia's arms.

"Lizzie raped us with broom handles and bottle necks and I got her good. I got her back. I stuck her the way she stuck me. And it was so fucking sweet."

The voice dropped another notch, turned suddenly dreamy and far away. "The bitch who bore us and left us like a sack of garbage. She came to the door squealing like a pig. I cut her up so she couldn't have no more babies—not ever. It was so sweet. It was payback time. I sliced off the tits they made me suck, and it was sweet . . ."

Bonnie Jean returned to herself, fixing Portia with a wary look.

"Jimmy started freaking when he saw the blood. He wanted to come back. He started screaming. So I had to keep him—like—busy, you know? Shut him up. Give him something to do. I made him take the jewelry and the bitch's grocery bag. Make it look like a robbery. I had him lift the flower, too. I wanted it. Christ, it was a fucking trophy."

Portia jumped at the sound of a soft tapping at her back. A guard outside the door held up his watch as a signal that her time with the prisoner had come to an end. She shot Jimmy a glance, and he was as he had been, sitting in his chair, huge hands folded on the table. She glanced back at the guard, realizing in a kind of wondrous haze that he couldn't see it from where he was standing—the triumphant madness that glittered in Bonnie Jean's eyes. All he saw was Jimmy sitting there. And that was all he'd ever see, unless Bonnie Jean decided otherwise. The thought made her suddenly giddy. That guard didn't know how lucky he was.

She nodded toward the window and held up a single finger, requesting another moment with her client. When the guard had moved safely away, Bonnie Jean glanced up once more, grinning like a hyena in the face of fresh kill.

"Okay," she said. "No more. Jimmy won't know about this, so don't even ask him. You have what you need, girlie. So get your shit together. Do your job. I don't want to be fucking executed, got it? It doesn't matter what Jimmy wants. I call the shots. And this is my game, now."

Portia dared herself to meet Bonnie's leering grin full on. "Then come out before the jury. Show them what you are, just like you showed me. Show them you're crazy."

The laughter, when it came, was rich with contempt. "Oh but, Doctor," Bonnie Jean purred. "I'm not. Jimmy's the one who's crazy."

The guard returned, handcuffs jingling, and Portia stepped out into the hallway as he secured them around Jimmy's wrists. Her own wrist pulsed with cramps, exhausted by the note taking. She stood motionless, watching the back of the prisoner as he disappeared through the heavy doors at the end of the corridor. She felt numbed by what she had seen and heard—numbed, yet possessed of a strange excitement.

After another moment she turned and headed to the opposite end of the hallway, her mind running through an endless loop of names for the madness that was Jimmy the Weird. Gender Identity Disorder. Dissociative Identity Disorder. Schizophrenia. Paranoia. Delusion. Just names, really, all seeming inadequate and coldly clinical in the face of the transformation she had just witnessed. There was no adequate way to describe that, no way to explain.

Yet something in her was almost grateful to the monster that called itself Bonnie Jean. For it was thanks to her that at last Portia had something. Enough, finally, to go to court. For the rest, she could only pray that Bonnie would be there, too. A multiple personality, she thought as she made her way toward the security station. A dual one, at any rate. For the first time in her career, she understood why so many of her colleagues wrote the disorder off as an insupportable diagnosis—as simply unbelievable. Even now, some part of her mind was trying to convince her Jimmy's transformation was preposterous. And yet, for all of that, she knew it was true.

Somewhere inside Jimmy the Weird was a female self, twisted and distorted into the vengeful beast called Bonnie Jean. Portia's heart sank as she found herself unable to deny the reality of what she had witnessed. For in a few short days she would have to stand up in court and testify as to her diagnosis of Wier's condition—a disorder that nearly everyone had heard of, yet one so poorly understood that few believed it was possible. And she was the one who was going to have to make them believe Jimmy suffered from a form of mental disease so rare that one part of him had come out to kill without his even knowing what had happened. Portia would have to make the jury believe it had happened just as Bonnie Jean had said.

Because if she couldn't, Jimmy Wier was a dead man.

She was so preoccupied she barely nodded to the unfamiliar face at the security station down the hall. She never noticed the guard behind the desk as she scrawled her name and made for the coffin-sized elevator. She was too busy frowning over her notes and scribbling an addition here and there. She never saw anything unusual in the way he punched the elevator controls. And when the doors closed, Dr. Portia McTeague was so enthralled with the mind of Jimmy Wier that she was only dimly aware of the elevator's beginning its slow, silent descent. She never noticed anything at all—until, in a single instant, the dim light above her flickered and went out, plunging her into a sudden, terrifying blackness. She had been through so much that day, she would not have believed she could have been frightened any more. Until the blackness was upon her and she heard the tired little ventilator fan grind to a noisy halt just as the tiny car lurched in a single, nauseating bounce.

And stopped.

Twenty

● ●

J USTIN CHITWOOD sat on the front porch of a log-
faced cabin deep in the Blue Ridge Mountains looking at
nothing but the long shadows on the hillside as the afternoon marched to a slow close. A lethargic sadness settled over him as
he sensed his wife, Meg, moving around inside the house, busying
herself with the never-ending series of tasks she seemed to find to fill
her days. He felt, rather than saw her presence as she came and
watched him through the screen door, silently, patiently, waiting for
him to do something—anything—that would justify their leaving
South Carolina.

He'd had to hand it to Meg; she'd never asked too many questions
when he'd quit his job and announced that he needed to go home to
Virginia. She'd never argued or accused him of being rash or of gam-
bling with their lives. She had accepted his explanation and given him
his space. But now, with the first hints of autumn showing on the
hillsides, and the first chill of winter threatening at night, he knew, as
Meg did, that this small interlude in their lives was coming to a close.
And still she waited every day—waited for his next move, or some idea
to come to him that would restore him to himself. She waited and was
patient and still he would not move.

After almost two months, Meg was beginning to feel the way she
did during the seemingly endless winters of her college days in Bos-
ton, when cabin fever hit and she yearned for human contact. That
was where she had first met Justin. He was so alive, so full of purpose,

ready to battle injustice and the threats to human rights that he saw all around. Seeing him now through the screen, sitting motionless, staring into space for what seemed like hours, filled her with a combination of sadness and rage. She had to do something to snap him out of it. Whatever his past had been, his future was with her. It was time to get on with their lives. She glanced again at the sheet of paper she'd printed out from the computer. It was the fourth such e-mail they'd received. She took a deep breath and headed out onto the porch where her husband sat like a stone, staring at the sad Virginia twilight. Meg Chitwood was resolved—if Justin didn't answer this time, she would answer it herself. They had to get off this mountain before they both went insane.

"Hey," she began gently enough, settling at his feet, raising her knees and wrapping her long arms around them.

"Hey, yourself." Justin answered. "I was just thinking—"

"You do a lot of that these days, Justin," she answered mildly. "So how about some talking?"

He said nothing at first, betraying his agitation only in the way he gripped the rough-hewn arms of his old bentwood chair. "So, what do you want to talk about? I quit my job, okay? And we came up here for a while. You hated that burg as much as I did."

Meg looked at him. "You quit because you were scared. And you ran up here because here is where you always run when you're scared."

Justin got restlessly to his feet. "Look—I don't need this, okay? I need some space. Time to think things out."

My butt, thought Meg, not unsympathetically. Aloud she said, "She wrote again. That lawyer. Amy what's-her-name. On the e-mail. She knows you're connected with that case, Justin."

Justin shook his head disgustedly. "Not anymore."

The self-contempt in his voice was too much for Meg. She jumped to her feet, swinging him around by the shoulder until they were eye to eye. "How can you say that!" she demanded. "How? You of all people! My God, Justin. You saw what happened. You know that bastard forced the confession—tampered with evidence!"

"I don't care—"

"The hell you don't! You do care! You've always cared, dammit. You took your own father in when there was nobody, you fought for him, got him to a hospital. You cared then."

Justin stared miserably out over the purpling landscape. "He's dead."

"So?"

Chitwood shoved his hands deep into the pockets of his jeans. "So nothing. So just because my old man was nuts doesn't mean I have to rescue every schizo on earth, does it? I did my time with the old man. And he . . . and he . . ." All at once, Justin faltered, turning away as his eyes burned with unexpected tears.

Meg reached out to put a hand on his arm. "He killed himself," she finished, following her husband's tortured gaze to the place where the soft purple eased into indigo and finally, a velvety black down in the valley.

It had happened just a few months after their first anniversary. Justin's father had been a fairly successful real estate developer, one of the few to see the potential of housing developments in the Virginia countryside. He had also been a paranoid schizophrenic, possessed by demons that drove him first to succeed and then to fail as they took his successes away, one by one. The scandals had been few at the outset, easily quieted. Then the desperate, elder Chitwood had had a series of psychotic breaks, attacking and nearly killing a stranger at a traffic light. He was convicted on charges of assault and the nice Southern family in which Justin Chitwood grew up fell entirely apart. Only Justin had been there as his father made the long slow descent into madness. Only he had cared enough to fight for his father's rights as old associates and even family members came out of the woodwork with endless lawsuits and liens, helping themselves like vultures at a feeding, wanting to extract their revenge for the madman's mistakes.

In the end, Justin had managed to save only this cabin, a modest little place in the mountains, the only remaining scrap of what had once been an empire. He and his father had used it as a hunting camp, he'd once told her. It was a place where they'd always been happy. He'd salvaged it from the scrap heap of his father's fortune after they'd committed him to the state hospital in the hopes that his father would live there when he was well enough to come home. He'd even taken the job in South Carolina to be near enough when the time was right. But Justin's father had killed himself two months after he went in. Before he ever got to see again the way that twilight fell on that mountain in a hundred shades of purple and blue on an early autumn evening. Justin's father was never coming home.

Meg stared up at the silhouette of her husband's profile in the gathering dark. She only knew that much of the story, how his father's illness had shaped so much of his destiny, turning him from a bored student in the Harvard business school to an expert in criminology, computers, and even psychology, as he gave up so much of his own life trying to save a lost man. She knew as much as she could know, and shared the guilt of that final, awful decision to have him committed. She knew, too, how Justin feared the specter of his father's illness even more than the dangers of law enforcement. And yet, she thought as she stood silently beside her husband, there was so much she would never know, there were some pains too secret ever to be shared.

Her voice came softly into the darkness. "You can't hide up here forever, Justin. You have to tell what you know."

He sighed heavily. "I can't. I get up there and squeal on Glass and it's over. Everything."

"It is not!"

He turned to face her once again, his eyes gleaming miserably. "It is, Meg. Either way. I accuse Glass of screwing up the biggest case in South Carolina, I never get a job again. It's a small network, and the word will be out—can't trust Chitwood. End of career. And I deserve better than that. So do you. Besides," he finished sadly, "it's his word against mine."

"What about Jimmy the Weird?" Meg almost shouted. "What does he deserve? You're no better than anybody else, Chitwood."

He turned to her, startled. "What is that supposed to mean?"

"It means you're just trying to save your own ass. You know as well as I do that your testimony could change Wier's chances. That maybe he'd get into a hospital instead of a death house. You know that better than anybody. Only you don't give a shit. You're so preoccupied with your image and your fucking career prospects that you're gonna hide up here and keep your mouth shut till it all blows over. Shit!" she exploded. "You liked your stupid job that much, why did you quit? Why didn't you just go on licking Sheriff Glass's big black boots?"

"I had to quit—"

"No you didn't," she shot back. "It's not like you've got the strength of your convictions, is it? Why not just stay there and keep your stupid mouth shut? Yuck it up with the rest of the boys?"

"Meg—please. I had to quit—because of us. I knew—because—"

She stared him down, fury and frustration and love all dancing in her eyes. "Because why?" she demanded.

He came to her and placed his hands on her shoulders, squeezing tight in a combination of strength and terrible need. His eyes, when they met hers, were still filled with pain but alive with some new feeling she could not at first identify until the words came, low and strained and shaking with intensity.

"Because I know how dangerous he is. Royal's got him in his pocket."

Meg looked at him. "So what? Royal's got half of South Carolina in his pocket."

"Unless there's some kind of miracle, Royal's going to the Senate," Justin answered. "And when he does, Glass is suddenly going to come up in the world. Who knows? Maybe Royal appoints him a judge. The more power Glass has, the more dangerous I am to him."

Meg narrowed her eyes. "And what about the power he'll have over other people if that happens, Justin? Think about it. You really want to see Dwight Glass on the bench? You're not the only person in the world. It's not all about you. It's about a whole lot of other people. You just happen to be one of those who can try to put a stop to things before they get worse than they already are."

Justin shook his head uncertainly. "You can't change the way the world works, Meg."

She sank to the top step and took a long look out over the mountain. "Maybe not," she replied. "Maybe you can only try."

He turned away then and made for the screen door, opening it half way and stepping over the threshold. Inside, the cool blue light of the computer monitor threw eerie, beckoning shadows on the walls of the next room.

"Where are you going?" Meg asked him, empty now of anger, yet still straining to reach across the gap of understanding that lay between them.

Justin glanced back over his shoulder, his mouth a sad, determined line, his eyes unreadable in the dark. He did not answer, but only moved farther into the house.

And still she called after him, wanting—needing—desperately to know her husband's mind.

"Are you going to tell?"

Twenty-one

• •

I T WAS like a dream . . .

For a moment, Portia froze, unable to comprehend the sudden blackness and the terrible silence inside the elevator. By reflex, she fumbled for the left wall, anxious fingers running over the surface. And then she remembered, there was no control panel, there was nothing at all.

She began to sweat, trying to think what might have happened, struggling to quell the flutter of panic that beat its way up through her innards and into her chest. She tried to get her bearings in the dark, aiming her voice toward the single small grate that housed the now-silent ventilator fan.

"Hey!" she shouted, her voice sounding high and unnatural as it reverberated in the small space. "Hey! Somebody. I'm in here! In the elevator!"

But there was only silence. A scream rose up in her throat and she leaned against the wall to stop it, feeling her breath begin to come in short, sharp gasps. And claustrophobia closed all around her, as though the walls themselves were shrinking and folding in. As though the dark were made of something solid that pressed closer and closer.

"No!" she gasped aloud. "Stop it, Portia. Stop it!" She bent double and drew in great gulps of air, forcing them deep into her diaphragm. "Breathe, damn it! It's only an elevator—it's only the dark. Think of something, think of something else," she chanted and squeezed her eyes shut tight, her fingers closing hard around the legal pad she held close against her chest. Think of Jimmy. Jimmy, that's it. Think of Bonnie Jean. Remember what she said. There was something—something she said. Remember.

She felt her knees go weak as she leaned farther into the wall. Still gasping a little, she recalled that she ought to sit down. If the car began to fall, she ought to be sitting down—to lessen the impact. And so she eased quietly into a corner and sat, alone and sweating and gasping for breath, with her pad of session notes clutched against her like a shield. She had to wait, that was all, she told herself silently. They would come for her. All she had to do was wait. Stay calm—and wait. And breathe. She had to breathe. She had to think of Jimmy—of Bonnie Jean.

And so she sat, alone in the black, bathed in sweat and breathing and waiting for something to happen as the minutes were eaten up one by one in the dark. Five, ten, fifteen. She squinted in vain at the face of her watch. There was no time, no space, no air. There was only waiting in this small eternity of dark.

"Hey!" she called again, thinking she had heard the barest noise somewhere far above her. "I'm here! Hey?" Her voice rose uncertainly and died. Maybe there had been no noise. Maybe they did not know.

Think about something else, she told herself. Anything. Think about Jimmy. Think about the case. And her mind went reeling back as she tried to recall that face, that voice that called itself Bonnie Jean, her mind seizing upon odd details, working desperately to push away the chattering terror that crowded at the edges of her thoughts.

And the minutes fell away and the air grew stale and close and hot and . . .

It was like a dream.

The hatred in that voice echoed down to the marrow of her bones. Bonnie Jean knew all about her. Bonnie Jean had been there all along—watching, waiting, knowing how stupid she'd been, how inept, as she tore at Jimmy's mind with clumsy fingers. Waiting for her to make some mistake, waiting for her to go too far. Jimmy would kill himself, that's what she'd said. And still Portia had pushed for the truth, hoping that this time the truth would set them both free.

Bonnie Jean had known it, known it all along. Of course she did— they were members of the same club. That club whose members were all the same—damaged and ashamed and full of secret need. They could see it in each other's eyes, know it in the way they moved. The club was secret, you had to be a member to know. And Bonnie Jean had known about her from that first day. Bonnie Jean had watched and waited because she had known. Because all the members of that club knew each other, didn't they? All tied together by the rules of secret shame, bound up in an infinite network of guilt and lies. There was no point pretending otherwise—she and Jimmy and all the rest were inescapably the same.

Portia leaned against the wall in the suffocating dark all alone, with the voice of a madman screaming in her head and her eyes leaking tears as the memory of that voice gave way to another secret, even more unspeakable memory. And then terror and grief and unendurable regret came bursting from her tortured heart.

And it was like a dream.

That other box, like this box, black and hot and full of smothering dark. Buried somewhere in the sweet soft earth. No light, no air, just the hot, awful dark. And the voice—another voice, all but forgotten—chiding her from somewhere above.

"Are you going to tell?"

No!

"If you tell, I'll bring you back and leave you here. I swear I will. I'm the only one who knows about this place. They'll never find you—never! You'll rot in there. The air's gonna run out soon. You're gonna die. So you better say it, girl. You gonna tell?"

She was so young, crying hysterically, shivering in the damp and the dark. Her legs cramped in that tiny tomb, still bleeding between, still raw. Then she was pushing away the awfulness, fighting, trying to thrash her way out.

"Leave me alone!"

And, laughing so loud, his hatred finding its way even to where she lay trapped. "That what you want, girl? I thought you wanted out."

And she knew then, there was no room inside that box for fighting. There was barely room to breathe.

Her own voice came echoing out of her memory, high and childish, begging him across the years.

"Please—I won't—I won't tell. Nobody. Please—just—just let me out!"

More laughter above, enjoying her pain, her confusion. "Say it! Promise!"

"I—promise." Panting now, trying to breathe. "Please. Let me out."

Cackling—then another sound, low and strange and unrecognizable as she lay motionless in the dark. A scratching that worried the surface of the box somewhere above her head. Movement. She could not dare believe it was over, that she might be freed.

"Hey, cousin," the voice called. "I don't think your air is running out fast enough, you know? I don't believe I'm gonna let you out after all. But I don't want you dying slow. That wouldn't be right, would it? So I tell you what, cuz, I'm gonna make it easy. Here's a little present to keep you company."

An instant of blinding light, then dark again as the lid of the terrible box slammed shut once more. Something on top of her, heavy and writhing. A terrified scrambling as claws and teeth sank deep into her arms and legs. Her own hands, closing in horror around a furry neck, trying to pull it away, trying to save herself and feeling her thumbs as the bones of its neck snapped and gave way. And her cousin had sat there for another whole hour, on top of that trapdoor hidden in the earthen floor of an old outbuilding on a farm in Mississippi. As she and a dying kitten screamed together in the dark.

And then a voice calling softly, just once more.

"Are you going to tell?"

After an eternity of darkness and remembering, they found Portia McTeague hunched in a corner with her session notes spread out over the floor, her arms wrapped around her knees, and her face wet with weeping.

"Ma'am, you okay in there?" She lifted her head, blinking as the elevator doors slid open, revealing a sea of troubled faces crowding in for a closer look. One man broke loose from the throng and came forward as two prison guards helped her shakily to her feet.

"You all right, Dr. McTeague? You want some coffee?" He handed her a styrofoam cup, filled with weak, steaming liquid and she drank greedily.

"Warden Jack Nagle," the man went on as they eased past the gathering of curious guards and visitors who crowded the small hallway.

Portia blinked at him. "I know—" she said. "How long—?"

The warden glanced sheepishly at his watch. "Well, it's about three hours now. We had a power failure in A block. That's where the elevator runs from, the A block circuits. Damnedest thing. One of the boys up there tried to drown his radio in the toilet bowl. Shorted out the whole wing." Jack Nagle smiled sheepishly. "I can't apologize enough for this, ma'am. It's a terrible thing. But I want you to know we did our best to get you outa there, ma'am. Just as fast as we could. Problem was, we didn't know anybody was in there right away."

Portia stared up at him, her relief at being freed slowly replaced by a cold suspicion settling somewhere deep in her gut. "Why did it take so long to get the power back on?"

Jack Nagle's smile froze for just a moment. "Regulations," he replied. "Anytime we have an incident like that, we have to lock down and investigate. But you know that, right? I mean, with your reputation and all. But we got you out just as soon as we could, ma'am. And I do apologize for the inconvenience."

Portia rose suddenly to her feet. "Right," she answered. "I take it I can go now?"

"Well sure, but I wish you'd take a moment. Are you sure you're all right to drive? You look right peaked."

"I'm fine, thanks. I just need to get home. Where are my notes?"

A guard slid forward, handing her a ragged sheaf of yellow legal papers, now smudged by a single footprint and an inexplicable coffee stain. She flipped through the pages, silently counting. Somebody had read them. The thought fled as quickly as it had come. She took a second look to convince herself. It was all right; they were all here.

"You were up there with Jimmy Wier, weren't you?"

Portia eyed him warily. Of anyone in the prison, Jack Nagle would know what she'd been doing there that morning.

Jack Nagle's smile spread like an oil slick over his broad face. "Big case," he said. "Coming right on us, too."

"Yeah," said Portia. "Jury selection starts Monday."

Nagle's smile did not change, but his eyes seemed to turn inward as he looked at her. "Will you be back again, to see Jimmy I mean? Before the trial?"

"I'm not sure," she replied, meeting his eyes. "I do expect to be informed of any crisis in his behavior, however. Like that fire last night."

Nagle managed to look almost contrite. "Yes, well. The truth is, I just heard about that myself." He paused, rubbing his chin. "Fire last night, today this radio thing. Must be the full moon."

"Full moon or not," Portia replied evenly, "I should have been informed. A failure to cooperate with Mr. Wier's defense team could result in a mistrial, Warden. As I'm sure you are already aware."

The warden smiled while his eyes called her a meddling bitch. Portia didn't care. She was entirely too tired to care.

"Well, I hope this unfortunate incident won't keep you from coming back to see us again, Doctor," Nagle went on. "Now, are you sure you're all right? You don't want the infirmary folks to look you over?"

Portia shook her head. "I'm quite sure. I'm fine. I'd just like to get home, if you don't mind."

Nagle was still smiling. "You drive safe now," he said. "We can't have you getting yourself in some accident. It'd go hard for Jimmy—losing his expert."

She looked at him. There was nothing in his face but concerned solicitude. He looked like an undertaker.

Portia smiled a bleak good-bye and headed through the main doors. Someone had gotten her briefcase and car keys from the Visitor's Center and had brought her car from the main parking lot. It was waiting a few steps from the front door. She slid behind the wheel and sank into the seat gratefully, turning the ignition key and rolling down the windows from the panel on the driver's side. Never had sodden heat and humidity smelled so sweet, never had she so enjoyed the rush of air through her hair as she swung the car out of the gates and onto the highway. She breathed and breathed.

Once on the open road, she found herself worrying over the afternoon's events, arranging and rearranging them in her mind. The terrible length of time it had taken to free her from the small prison of the elevator car, the sheaf of yellow sheets next to her with their odd coffee stain. Had somebody read them? Mentally she tried to relive those last moments in the elevator. They pried the door, a hand came through the opening and pulled her toward it. She'd walked out, dazed. Had a guard gone to retrieve the notes as she recovered herself in the confusion of prison personnel gathered outside the car? An image flashed into her mind. They'd given her coffee. Had she spilled some herself?

She glanced again at the ragged disarray of papers on the seat beside her. It was too confusing; there was no way to be sure. Royal probably had people all over the inside. Pilfering a few notes from the opposition was minor compared to what might have been arranged. She silently thanked herself for the foresight to have developed her own peculiar form of shorthand long ago. If Royal did have somebody nosing around, he hadn't gotten much. Nevertheless, the unspoken suspicion nagged at her. The revelation of Bonnie Jean followed so closely by those hours in the elevator, the smudged and stained notes. It all seemed too coincidental to be mere coincidence. She frowned uneasily. Was someone trying to frighten her? To keep her from testifying? The thought astonished her.

And yet, she was more surprised by the realization that if her time in the elevator was meant as a threat, its purpose had been wasted. For she had just spent the afternoon with demons more terrifying than any that anyone else might have dreamed for her. She had relived a terror more completely than she could have believed possible. She had tried to forget it for years, even believed that she had forgotten. But she had forgotten nothing—nothing save the feelings that went with that memory, emotions so powerful they had left her helpless there in the dark. As helpless as she'd been before. For three hours that morning she had been eleven years old. She had remembered and felt all the terror and rage and grief she had felt so long ago.

For the first time in what felt like forever, she integrated the emotions of that long-ago afternoon in Mississippi with the pictures that had haunted her memories since. And there in the car with the wind in her face and tears rolling like rivers down her cheeks, she faced those long-buried demons down.

She knew then why she'd worked so hard to force Jimmy to remember—knew why she made all of them look and remember and face the terrible pain of their histories. She was looking for the truth—her own as well as theirs. She had always been looking for the truth. But getting at the truth was only half the battle. Telling it was the other half. Experiencing it, feeling all the pain and terror that went along with it. Needing to feel it again, if only to be whole. Knowing the truth of the emotions and keeping them hidden, that's what kept you a member of the club—forever.

She plucked up her car phone and dialed Sophie's office number. She wanted to schedule an appointment as soon as she could. Yet she smiled as the receptionist said there wasn't an available opening until her usual appointment on Friday, realizing with a start that tomorrow was Friday. That would be soon enough, she thought. Soon enough to tell the things she had kept hidden for so long.

She smiled at nothing as she hung up the phone, filled with a wild sense of wonder. It had been a day of revelations. With time, for both her and Jimmy Wier, more revelations would come. And she marveled a little at the strange convergence of circumstance.

Portia McTeague smiled as she drove the wide lanes of the interstate, utterly exhausted yet alive with a new kind of hope. After so many years, and so much pain, she had begun to be free of her fear of the dark.

It was time to tell.

Twenty-two

• •

PORTIA MADE the turn into the old Dilworth neighborhood in Charlotte less than two hours later. She drove slowly, her eyes hungrily seeking out the hundred-year-old houses, the wide boulevards, and the stately shade trees. After her day of awful confinement and the hours on the interstate, her neighborhood came to her like an oasis. In the last light of the afternoon, her neighbors were involved in the blessedly normal activities that punctuated their days—barbecue smoke curling lazily from behind one picket fence; shouts from a father-son game of one-on-one; a silver-haired couple taking the evening air. As she swung the Volvo around the curving streets, she thought she had never loved a place as much as she did this neighborhood of well-kept lawns and sprawling Victorian mansions and cozy brick bungalows.

She barely noticed the unfamiliar car with a small trailer attached parked at the corner. She had no reason to, really, for her thoughts were fixed not on her own house, but on the one next door, where her daughter Alice was playing outside with her best friend, Jessica. As Portia pulled the Volvo into her own driveway, she grinned at the sight of the two of them, absorbed in a game of Pogs, their heads bent low over the top step of Jessica's walk. Alice's dark, curly head stood in such contrast to Jessica's blond waist-length hair, it put Portia in mind of an old fairy tale, "Snow White and Rose Red."

"Hey," she called softly as she came up the walk toward them. "How about a kiss for your mommy?"

The girls' heads rose in unison. Alice smiled, then frowned as she looked at Portia. "Where have you been?" she demanded suspiciously. "I was waiting and waiting."

Portia eased herself down to the steps, until she was at eye level with the little girls. "I got stuck in an elevator," she said. "It took a long time to get me out."

Alice's and Jessica's eyes went wide with surprise. "Cool," said Jessica.

"Was it scary?" asked Alice.

Portia nodded. "Pretty scary," she agreed. "But I'm okay now, so let's go home."

Aggie, Jessica's mother, appeared behind the screen door. "Look what the cat dragged in," she offered mildly.

The image was more ironic than it should have been, and Portia felt a little bubble of laughter rise in her throat. "Hey, thanks, Aggie, for picking up Alice from school."

Aggie only shrugged. "No problem," she answered. "You know these two. Joined at the hip. Did you see your company?"

Portia looked at her. "Company?"

Aggie squinted through the screen. "Yeah," she answered. "That's his car, the one with the trailer. He showed up about an hour ago. He'd been traveling awhile. Said you were expecting him. Something about a delivery."

But Portia was already on her feet. "Where?" she asked.

"I didn't feel right about letting him in. So I set him up with some ice tea out on your patio around back. I've been keeping an eye on him through my kitchen. He's sound asleep. In your hammock. He said his name was Alan something."

"Oh my God," breathed Portia. Alan. He must have driven cross-country. "I've got to see him," she said to Aggie. "It's about a case. Can you keep Alice for a while longer?"

Alice glanced up. "I'm staying over," she offered matter-of-factly. "Me and Jessica are going to have pizza."

Portia raised her eyebrows and glanced at Aggie. "I told her it was okay with me if it was okay with you. Like I said," Aggie shrugged, "joined at the hip."

"Well, all right," Portia agreed, torn between her desire to spend a normal, quiet evening alone with her child, and the curiosity that consumed her. Alan had driven from California. What in the world had possessed him? "You sure, honey?" she said to Alice.

Alice looked up at her with wide brown eyes. "Course," she answered. "Jeez, I'm not a baby."

Portia grinned. Sure you're not, she thought, looking down at her daughter with a mixture of pride and helpless love. Until the next time you want to be. "Okay," she agreed. "But you be good, okay? I'll see you in the morning. Give me a kiss."

Alice obediently went to give her mother a polite, little girl kiss that smelled of bubble gum and playground dust. Portia responded by wrapping her arms tight around her, making Jessica giggle.

"Mom," Alice protested and wriggled to get free.

"All right, all right," Portia grinned, releasing her to her game. "Thanks, Aggie."

Aggie smiled. "Enjoy your evening. And get some sleep. You don't mind my saying so, you look like a good match for your friend over there. Exhausted."

Portia waved as she crossed the adjoining stretch of lawn and headed back around her own house. Alan was here, she thought. Alan.

He lay with his arms folded across his chest, two day's worth of blond beard glinting in the rosy glow of the sunset. His shirt was rumpled and his hair mussed with sleep. He lay snoring softly, rocked gently in the little breeze that sang in the shade trees on either side of the hammock. Portia watched him in silence for a moment, not knowing how he did it. For Alan Simpson, incorrigible as he was, managed to sleep with the same easy sensuality that he did everything else. And after such a long, strange day, that peaceful sleep was a sight she found strangely comforting. He looked so—normal. So uncomplicated. Part of her wanted to let him rest there awhile. But part of her could not.

She crept silently across the grass, pausing a few feet in front of the hammock. "Alan?" she called softly.

He did not move, so she edged closer still, placing a hand lightly over one of his own. "Alan? It's me, Portia."

His eyes, startlingly blue, blinked back at her, and he struggled to sit up. "Hey you," he said, leaning from his place in the hammock to kiss her cheek. "I made it."

She couldn't help smiling. "Yeah, you did," she agreed. "But Aggie said you'd driven from California. What on earth for?"

He swung his long legs easily over the side and jumped to his feet. "Long story with cargo shipping. Believe me, it was easier this way. C'mon," he said, taking her hand and tugging her toward the garage. "I've got a surprise. You didn't see it yet, did you?"

"See what? Alan—"

"Shh!" he commanded. At the side entrance to her garage he released her hand and swung the door inward. "Close your eyes," he said, gently pushing her forward.

"Alan, I—"

"Close 'em," he commanded. "Okay?"

She heard the overhead light switch flick on and waited, feeling a little silly.

"All right, my dear one. Now open your eyes and see what Uncle Alan has brought you from California."

She opened her eyes and stood, transfixed by what she saw. For inside her garage, neatly stacked from floor nearly to the ceiling, were rows and rows of cardboard file boxes. There were at least fifty, maybe closer to seventy-five or as many as a hundred of them lining the walls. For a moment she could only stare.

"What in the world?" she began. Then, as she moved to a nearby group of boxes stacked higher than her head, she caught the neatly typed caption on a yellowing label:

James Wier
Psychiatric Treatments
June 1976–January 1977
Atascadero State Facility for the Criminally Insane

"Oh my God," she breathed, looking to Alan's delighted face for confirmation. "These are all about Jimmy?"

Alan grinned. "Yup. They're mostly from Atascadero. There are other places, too—criminal court, some outpatient stuff—but mostly Atascadero."

Portia stared around her in disbelief. "How long was he there?"

"Six years," Alan answered. "He was sent up to participate in their pioneer sex offender program in seventy-four. Rape charges. Two assaults on minor females."

"Minor females," Portia murmured. "All this for two minor females? Christ."

Alan shrugged. "You don't know the half of it. Seems our Jimmy attacked two teenaged girls in separate incidents. In each case, he starts coming on to them, telling them how sweet they were, etc. Then he gets rough. Real rough. One of them got away with no rape per se, but a broken collarbone. He beat the other one half to death. She had four different operations to reconstruct her face."

"Oh God," Portia said. "Bonnie Jean."

Alan looked confused. "Say what?"

Portia ran her hands over the nearest of the file cartons, as if to make sure they were real. "Yeah," she told him. "Unless I miss my guess, our Jimmy is a bona-fide case of multiple personality. Or what used to be called multiple personality. These days, those of us in the trade refer to it as Dissociative Identity Disorder. Whatever you call it, I think he's got it. Big time. I met her—and the control is a her, by the way—today."

She almost smiled at Alan's bewildered expression. "Believe me," she said. "You're not half as surprised as I was."

Alan sat down heavily on a nearby carton. "Wow," he breathed. "Up until this moment, I thought the folks at Atascadero had it all," he continued. "But they got nothing on this diagnosis."

Portia glanced at him. "You mean they don't have him on record as a multiple?"

"Nope." Alan hesitated for a moment, as if trying to decide what to say next. "You sure he's not faking you out?"

Portia sighed. "I know what you're thinking. A diagnosis of DID could be the kiss of death for an insanity plea. But no, from what I saw today, I can't believe he's faking. Nobody's that good."

"But it is a kind of an eleventh-hour appearance for this alter, isn't it? Eve of the trial and all that. Not to mention the proverbial noose around his neck."

Portia stared unseeingly at the cardboard mountain in front of her. Alan's comment, though well intentioned, annoyed her a little. Yet, annoyed or not, he was only pointing out what she'd been telling herself a few hours before. And it was an issue she didn't feel she could afford to overlook.

"I don't know, Alan. I can't believe he manufactured this character for my benefit. For one thing, Jimmy's not that smart. According to his test results, he doesn't have the IQ points to pull it off. Maybe the alter manipulated her appearance to come at a point where it would have the most effect on me." Portia paused, frowning, as she glanced at her companion.

Alan cocked an eyebrow. "I take it it worked? You seem pretty affected."

Portia shook her head slowly. "Among other things, I was scared shitless. DID is a risky diagnosis to make, I know. Juries hate it, lawyers hate it—even a lot of psychologists hate it. But in terms of what I know about his background, it's not as weird as it sounds."

Alan shifted stiffly, still feeling his hours behind the wheel. "Fill me in."

"An alternate personality develops as the ultimate defense—it's a protective device. As Jimmy and I got further into his history, he began to visibly deteriorate. He can't handle talking about his past. He lost affect, the whole nine yards. And then he remembered the murders. Well, he remembered being there at least. Then, before we could go any further, this alter came out. Told me to back off or he'd kill himself. And she knows everything about what happened. She wanted me to know the facts, if only so Jimmy would have a shot at the insanity plea."

"I don't think I'm following," Alan said.

Portia laughed ruefully. "I don't blame you. It took me a few minutes to catch on myself. The fact is, Jimmy is so sick—so miserable—he doesn't care if he lives or dies. But the alter cares. And she is not about to be executed." She paused for a moment. "The problem is, if I stand up in court with a diagnosis like this, Jimmy may very well die."

Alan shot her a sharp glance, skepticism written in his eyes. "Then why go with it?" he asked. "Look. I'm not saying the guy's not sick, I'm just asking if you're sure about this multiple personality thing. It's damn hard to prove."

Portia nodded gravely. "I'm not sure of anything, Alan. Every time I think I've got a handle on this guy, something new turns up. I swear, I'd rather offer a PMS defense. At this point, even that's got more credibility." Abruptly, she lightened her tone at Alan's answering chuckle. "What about you? Did you go over any of this stuff?"

Alan stood up, thumbs hooked in the belt loops of his jeans. "His criminal record starts with a bunch of juvey convictions for burglary, car theft, the usual. Then a few assaults, then the first rape. Then, less than three weeks after he gets out on probation for the first one—the second. The first conviction got him the standard sentence; he was out in eighteen months. The second was what got him a six-year stint at the Hotel Atascadero. Oh yeah. I nearly forgot. He went after the second victim in drag."

Portia looked up at him, a sudden wild grin spreading over her face. "Did you say drag? Oh my God! Alan, that's wonderful!"

"Kinky," he replied dryly. "But yeah, drag. Wig, hose, the works. Is that supposed to mean something?"

Portia turned and made for the inside door that led to the kitchen. "Maybe it means this alter business isn't so eleventh hour after all," she told him. "C'mon, you look done in. Why the hell did you drive, anyway? And why didn't you call somebody? I must've left a half a dozen messages out there. Dec, too."

Alan followed her into the pale, butter yellow kitchen and sank gratefully into a chair. "Like I said, long story."

She turned to face him and saw the lines of fatigue etched deep into his handsome features, his blue eyes slightly bloodshot in the light. For once, he wasn't smiling.

"So fill me in," she continued. "You first, then me. You want some dinner? A drink?"

"Desperately," he answered. "Your very nice neighbor got me some tea, but frankly I could use something stronger."

"I'll join you," Portia replied, searching through the kitchen cabinets until she found a bottle of Kentucky bourbon. "It's been that kind of a day. Rocks?" she asked, holding it aloft. "Soda?"

"Just rocks. Thanks." He sipped the drink she handed him gratefully, as she slid into the chair opposite him. "Cross-country road trips are either for very young twenty-somethings or retired folks. Unfortunately, I don't qualify in either category."

Portia sipped, studying him carefully. She could feel the events of the day beginning to catch up with her. "So, tell me what happened. Why didn't you call?"

Alan shot her a long, appraising look, as if trying to decide if she could handle what he had to say. "Atascadero was the gold mine," he began. "Sawtelle's deposition was only the beginning. I've got pretty much the same story from three other family members, and I ran down Elizabeth Sawtelle's hospitalization records like you wanted. But at Atascadero, they had everything else. And I mean everything. They'd just started the sex offender program when Jimmy came in, so they were real serious about the record keeping."

Portia felt the bourbon's welcome warmth spreading through her insides. She smiled. It was just as Jayne Patten had promised—documentation up the wazoo. "How far did the records go back?" she asked. "Did you see any school records?"

Alan nodded a quick assent. "I skimmed some stuff about two outpatient trips to the local mental health depot back in high school.

Wier was referred by a guidance counselor or something. The first time, he showed up by himself. The second time, he had Mommie Dearest with him. Some CSW recommended them both for the funny factory. But they never came back for another appointment."

"And nobody in Social Services followed up?"

"Not that I could see. Looks like Jimmy just"—Alan made a vague little gesture—"fell through the cracks."

Portia was silent for a moment, hearing Jimmy's own words echoing in her thoughts. *I thought everybody knew . . .*

Alan went on in a tired voice. "Anyway, to answer your question, the folks at the sex offender program hunted up everything there was to find on our boy. They've got stuff that dates back to elementary school. Even report cards."

"You have school records? That's fantastic!" Portia rose to unexpectedly rubbery knees. The day and the drink and the slow elation of the knowledge that she had records to bring to court all began to catch up with her. Somewhat unsteadily, she began to move in the direction of the pantry cupboard. Never much of a cook, she nevertheless managed to unearth a box of pasta from the shelf and a selection of salad makings from the refrigerator.

"From what Jimmy has told me," she went on, "he's been sick for a long time. His home life was hell—abuse, poverty. School records will reflect that—something, anyway. Teacher comments, grades. Somebody will have noticed what was going on with this kid. I can use all of that to support a diagnosis of schizophrenia resulting in Dissociative Identity Disorder."

Alan nodded tiredly. "Whatever you say, you're the expert. Only—"

"Only what?"

He shrugged noncommittally. "Only he never got that diagnosis anywhere else. I went through some of the records, Portia. He was treated for fetishism, aggression, substance abuse—mostly booze. They even had him in group therapy sessions for transvestites. One shrink out there was pretty convinced he was a pedophile. But no schizophrenia. And no multiple personalities."

Portia paused in her activity, freshly rinsed lettuce dripping unheeded onto the floor. "Shit," she said. "Okay, maybe they could have missed this other identity, but schizophrenia? Even an undifferentiated type. How could they have missed that? The man tries to eat plastic flowers, for God's sake!"

Alan leaned back comfortably in his chair, watching her move around the kitchen. Though they'd worked together for years, he'd never before seen her in her own house, her own element. Even tired and disheveled, she was beautiful, and somehow more relaxed than he'd ever known her to be. He blinked and shook his head, blaming the bourbon for the sudden image that had risen in his mind. He found her looking at him, an amused little smile replacing her burst of annoyance, as if she'd somehow heard him thinking.

"What?" she asked.

"Nothing," he answered. "I was just—distracted. Anyway, it makes a certain amount of sense that nobody found the guy was schizo. The program at Atascadero was for sex offenders, remember. It was new. Lots of funding, all the bells and whistles. Jimmy was a rapist. That's what got him in there and that's what they treated him for." Alan helped himself to another shot of bourbon.

"You're right," Portia admitted slowly. "I guess that is hindsight on my part. It's just that once I got a look at this alter, it was so clear. It was like everything about Wier began to make sense." She finished slicing a tomato onto the salad and filled a pot of water, suddenly keenly aware of how Alan was following her with his eyes.

She put the water on to boil and sat down once again. "This alter is for real, Alan. She calls herself Bonnie Jean. Very aggressive. So full of hatred. It's like his body is still there, but there's a different person inside of him. It's incredible."

Alan leaned his elbows on the table. "Look, you're the doctor. You saw what you saw. But you have to admit the multiple personality thing is one old chestnut, especially when it comes to the insanity plea. You don't have to convince me, but you will have to find a way to convince a jury."

She turned to him, misery written on her face. "I'm not sure if I can," she said uncertainly.

Seeing her change in attitude, he stood and placed his hands on her shoulders. "Of course you can. I'll be there rooting for you. Just—be careful with it, okay? Talk it through with Dylan. Talk to me."

Portia nodded and moved restlessly away from his touch, making her way to a cupboard. "Bonnie Jean is the part of Jimmy that houses all his sexuality. Because he was so horribly abused as a kid, sex came to be equated in his mind with pain. How does somebody fake a psychosis like that? Anytime he feels attraction, Bonnie Jean apparently comes out to fulfill the sexual experience. To hurt—then kill."

Alan had returned to his seat and was listening, fascinated, though whether by her explanation or by Portia herself was unclear. "So Jimmy feels the attraction, Bonnie Jean comes out and gets off, whoever's on the receiving end gets hurt or killed."

"Right."

"Jimmy wakes up, doesn't remember what happened, and takes the rap." Alan shook his head. "So if the guy isn't faking this alter, tell me this. Why do you get to see her all of a sudden? Jimmy have the hots for you?"

Despite herself, Portia could feel a blush creeping up her neck from her collar. "Very funny. But no, at least not that I'm aware of. The alter wants me to save Jimmy. And her. Period."

Alan smiled hazily. "Then all I can say is, he really must be nuts."

Portia faced him, smiling as she took down dishes. "Men," she said. "You get a woman standing around in the kitchen and all of a sudden you're in love."

Alan interrupted with a huge yawn. "I beg to differ, Doctor," he answered. "I was in love long before I saw you in the kitchen."

Portia blushed furiously this time, at a loss for a reply. His tone said he was kidding, but there was something in his eyes that told her he was not. She suddenly felt a delicious, electric charge of possibility in the air. And it astonished her.

"Looks like I better get some food into you before you embarrass yourself completely," she went on, a little too brightly. "How long did it take you to get here, anyway?"

"Few days," he answered, watching as she set the table with some blue and white Italian spongeware, silver, and—as an afterthought—cobalt-stemmed glasses and a bottle of California Chardonnay. He eyed the wine speculatively. "Madam," he said with a trace of humor, "are you trying to get me intoxicated?"

"You're a big boy, Alan," she answered coolly, scooping pasta with butter and cheese onto his plate. "You don't have to drink it all. I thought it might be nice to act like civilized people for a change. You know—all the amenities. Especially after today. On top of the singular experience of meeting Bonnie Jean, I was stuck in the prison elevator for almost three hours. Some kind of power outage."

Alan paused in opening the wine as she brought the salad to the table. "Three hours? Jesus—I'd sue."

She shook her head, chewing appreciatively. "They had to lock down to investigate. Some prisoner tried to electrocute himself by putting his radio in the toilet bowl. They didn't get me out because I guess nobody knew I was in there. But there's no point making a fuss about it. You know the game, Alan. Make trouble for prison officials and they make trouble for you."

Alan frowned over a forkful of steaming pasta. "What if somebody *was* making trouble, Portia?"

"How do you mean?"

He began to eat thoughtfully. "Out in California, after I got to the folks at Atascadero, things started getting weird. That's why I couldn't return your calls right away. I couldn't be sure . . ." He faltered.

She looked at him. "Alan, stop talking in riddles. What happened?"

He stared at her for a long moment, his blue eyes troubled. "That's just it, nothing happened. It wasn't something I could ever put my finger on. But I got the distinct feeling somebody out there was—well—investigating the investigator."

"You mean you were being watched? Followed?"

He shrugged. "Interfered with is more like it. Getting these records was like pulling teeth. One day the releases were in order, the next day they'd be lost somehow. Misplaced. And we'd have to go through the whole shebang again. Showing the identification, getting Dec's office to fax duplicate paperwork." He paused in his discourse. "I thought you might know all this already," he went on. "Didn't Dylan tell you?"

Portia shook her head. "We've both been swamped," she replied. "Dec doesn't even know about my breakthrough with Jimmy. We're going to get together tomorrow night and catch up before jury selection begins on Monday. We're having dinner."

Alan smiled thinly. "I'm glad I beat him to that, anyway."

She smiled back. "You never quit, do you?"

Alan raised his fork and pointed it in her direction. "You'd better be glad of that, dearie. If I were a quitter, you wouldn't have those records in your garage right now. As I started to explain, I'd arranged for shipping via cargo plane. Then the flight was canceled. Some mechanical failure. They caught it at the last second while the plane was still on the ground. If they'd allowed the thing to take off, all documentation on Wier would have been blown to kingdom come. Maybe I'm just paranoid, but with all the tail-dragging that was going on—the releases disappearing and the rest of it—I just felt weird about taking a chance having them shipped. Call it instinct. So I got the trailer and drove them here myself."

For a moment, Portia could think of no response. "Who do you think was trying to interfere with the investigation?"

"I don't think anything. As a matter of fact, once I got the stuff in the trailer and out on the road, I'd pretty much decided it was all in my head. But when you told me about this elevator thing— well . . ." He paused to pour them both another glass of wine, allowing her to draw her own conclusions. "Let's just say that if I was thinking, my money would be on Donny Royal. He's got a long reach. And deep pockets."

She turned to look at him. "I thought the same thing myself this afternoon. It looked as though somebody had been through my session notes with Wier. I can't prove it, but that's how it looked. But, Alan, I can't believe he'd try to interfere with evidence!"

She glanced up as Alan cut loose with a belly laugh. "That's what I adore about you," he told her.

"What?"

"You're so—innocent. Here you are, mucking around with some of the most hopeless, vicious lowlifes the planet has produced. They tell you things that would give me nightmares for weeks, and yet you still can't believe Royal would tamper with evidence! Good lord, Portia. That's what lawyers do! Rearranging the information is what they do. They sin by omission. And most of them, including our Mr. Dylan, would sell their grandmothers to win a case!"

"He would not," Portia insisted. "And all I meant was, I can't see Royal getting involved in anything illegal. No matter how much he wants to win this one. Besides, who would help him?"

Unexpectedly, Alan half-rose and kissed her on the forehead. The sensation of it lingered curiously on her skin as he resumed his seat and continued eating. When he looked at her again, the twinkle of amusement in his eyes did little to mask the gravity of his tone.

"I met the Sawtelles, remember? We're talking about folks who'd kill for a hundred bucks, okay? Sure, I got some depositions, but there are a few more family members out there who wouldn't talk to me. You have to allow for the possibility that somebody else got to them first. And there's a whole lot of boys on the other side of the fence at Columbia who do the same kind of work. I don't think the theory is too farfetched, do you?"

She looked at him, her eyes gone dark and troubled. "Maybe not," she agreed. "I guess I was so preoccupied with Jimmy. And something . . ." She trailed off uncertainly.

"Something?" he prompted.

"Something personal. Something I found out about myself in that elevator today." She paused, blinking, horrified at the tears that welled in her eyes. She uttered a short, self-deprecating laugh. "Amazing what a little sensory deprivation can do for you."

Alan was out of his chair. "Portia, what is it?" He draped an arm around her shoulder and she could not help leaning into it, needing the warm reality of that touch, the quiet strength behind it. She was so tired, so drained from the day's events. And Alan was so completely there, so ready to hold her.

After another moment she broke away, taking up her glass as she ushered him through the kitchen door and into the living room.

He followed her in silence as she walked easily over to a soft leather sofa the color of butterscotch and settled into one corner, letting him choose where to place himself. He took a seat next to her, searching her eyes.

"Portia, hey? Talk to me."

She laughed a little ruefully. "Sometimes I don't think I know how. I'm sorry, Alan. Maybe I've just had too much to drink."

He leaned back against the couch, never taking his puzzled eyes from her face. "Baloney," he replied. "You've done this more than once. And you were cold sober. Or have you forgotten that little drive we took? You start to open up, and it seems like you want to." He reached down and took her hand, and again she felt the charge of attraction between them. "But as soon as I think I've got my signals straight, you just—go away. Why?"

She could not look at him, but instead fixed her attention on some far point in the corner of the room. "Fear, I guess. Isn't that the usual explanation for that kind of behavior?"

Alan leaned toward her, an urgent light in his eyes. "When are you going to give yourself permission to have a personal life?"

She glanced at him, offended. "What's that supposed to mean?"

"It means I'm not talking to some shrink, now. I'm talking to you. What happened to you in that elevator today? You started to tell me and then—this. I'm here, Portia. I'm listening. Maybe I'm not a shrink, and maybe I'm not perfect. Maybe you don't have any reason to trust me. But I am here, right now. I'm your friend."

She stared into the depths of her glass, swirling its contents as though she were some fortune-teller reading the signs. "I don't have a real good history with male—friends, Alan. I don't have a good track record. It's hard for me to be as attracted as I am to you, without some conflict. It's hard for me to feel anything without analyzing it. To just—feel. That's part of what happened to me today in that elevator. I felt some things I thought I'd never have to feel again." She lifted her glass to her lips, her hands shaking uncontrollably. "I'm not sure I like it," she finished lamely.

Wordlessly, Alan reached for her free hand and she felt his vitality surging through her, giving her a new sense of strength. She took a deep, shuddering breath. "I was abused. Back in Mississippi, where I come from. My family life was—quite violent. It's affected me. Naturally. It gets in the way of how I do my work—my relationships—and so I go in and out of therapy. And I work on it. But I'm damaged, Alan. Damaged goods. You don't know—I'm not any different from any of those criminals I evaluate. They're just like me. Same backgrounds. Same damage. I manage to live and to function and to get through the days, but—I'm still screwed up. And I'm afraid of that. I'm afraid to let anybody get close."

She began to cry helplessly, tears falling in twin rivers down her cheeks.

Alan looked at her for a long, silent moment. "God, woman," he said, smiling gently. "You have everything going for you. Everything. Looks, brains. And all you want to do with that is beat yourself up for not being perfect."

"But—"

"Shh—shh—"

And then Alan's arms were around her and she clung to him with all that was left of her strength, feeling the hot hardness of his muscles through the thin fabric of his shirt, catching the spicy scent of lust and road dust and sweat that rose from his skin. She took his kisses like a drug, drowning in the sweet gratitude that flooded her body after being alone so long. And time itself fell away in those next precious moments, their bodies meshing in a secret synchronicity that was beyond words, beyond any need to explain anymore. He kissed her hair, his lips murmuring soft, unidentifiable sounds of comfort. His mouth moved down the side of her face, to her neck, sucking and biting, soft as a newborn kitten on her chin, her throat. His tongue flicked hotly in and out of the secret hollows of an ear, sending fiery shivers of need from her loins to her breasts.

She arched her back and turned to him, and their mouths met instantly, taking in the sweet unfamiliar taste of one another, reveling in the meeting of tongues and lips and hands that roamed one another's flesh, exploring all the curves and planes and softness and heat as they fell together in mute mutual need—joyful and overwhelming and terrifying all at once.

She broke away from him, gasping. "Wait—"

He looked at her, blinking and laughing a little. "Don't tell me to stop—I don't think I can."

"No, no," she answered, panting a little, even now reaching for the expanse of his chest, covered with golden hairs that showed from his unbuttoned shirt. "It's just that—oh, damn it, Alan. Let's go upstairs. If I'm going to do this, I want to do it right."

He was instantly on his feet, grinning and pulling her to her own. "All this and a real bed, too? God, life is good."

She kissed him hard on the mouth. "Second door on the right. I'll be two minutes."

And later, she thought it could not have been more than that as she moved through the few downstairs rooms switching out lights and locking the doors, feeling a little foolish. She knew it could not have taken her long to climb the stairs and pause, just for a moment, in the bathroom to run a comb through her tangled hair and spritz a quick spray of perfume over her neck—less than a second perhaps to grab a condom from a four-year-old box she kept tucked high on a shelf behind the towels in the linen closet, and to head down the hall to her own bedroom, her heart thumping in a wild combination of anticipation and relief.

It was not a long time since she had left Alan, but it was somehow enough. For when she swung the door open, he was sprawled unceremoniously over the wide bed, clad only in his underwear, one arm thrown back across his eyes. It took a moment for her to register what had happened, to identify the soft sound emanating from the long-limbed figure on the bed.

Alan Simpson, the only man she had even considered going to bed with in more than four years, lay on his back, snatched away by a need more urgent even than sex.

He was snoring, sound asleep.

Another woman might have let him lie there, knowing how far he had come for her in the past hours. Another woman, or even another psychologist, might have read that sudden sleeping as evidence of a need for distance or even as performance anxiety. Still others might have seen it as some sign of rejection, now that the prize was all but won. Certainly they would not have stood there in the doorway as she did, grinning so delightedly at the sight of those long, golden, muscular limbs spread-eagled over her linen sheets. They might have turned and shut the door before their eyes had drifted to the enormous, curved erection that poked so bravely from the bulge of his underwear. Another woman might not have lingered, nor felt the warm, answering slickness between her own legs as she pulled off her clothes and kicked them to the side.

But Portia McTeague was not another woman. She was only blessedly, blissfully, completely herself as she made her way to the wide bed and the man who lay on it, waiting for her like a gift.

Four years, she thought as she ran her fingers lightly up and down his torso in a wicked little tickling designed to rouse him.

Four years is long enough to wait for anything.

Twenty-three

• •

ALAN FOUND HER in the garage the next morning. Though it was only a little before six, Portia was bent low over an array of open boxes, so intent on her reading that she didn't notice him at first, not until he stood almost next to her, his blue eyes crowded with a mixture of hope and concern.

"Hey," he said softly.

She lifted her head to look at him, and he was surprised at the sudden vulnerability of her face in the early morning light. He pulled over a box and sat down.

"Morning," she answered, returning her eyes to the page in front of her. "There's coffee in the kitchen. Help yourself."

He looked at her for a long moment, unsure of how to continue. "How long have you been up?"

She shrugged. "Awhile, I guess. I needed to get started on these." She indicated the boxes of records with a wave of her hand.

Alan sighed, smiling wistfully. "I—uhh—you. Last night. Portia, I don't know quite what to say."

Portia glanced at him uneasily, a flush of unwelcome color creeping up her neck. She looked as though she wished the floor might open up at that moment and swallow her whole. "Alan—please don't. Really. I—just don't want to talk about it."

"But I want to talk about it, Portia," he went on earnestly, reaching for her hand. "I want to tell you how incredible you are."

Abruptly, she snatched her hand away. His touch had sent an answering tremor of delight through her limbs. "Alan. Honestly it was—great. But last night was last night. This is today."

"Meaning?" he asked, the word sounding harsher than he'd intended.

She would not look at him, unable to face the bewildered expression on his face. "Meaning nothing. I don't know! I need time. To think things through, that's all. Yesterday was so confusing. So much happened. The day—the wine—I just—" She paused and took a deep breath, struggling to keep her tone cool and uncaring. "I think maybe it was a mistake, that's all."

He stared at her, anger and hurt darkening his features. "You call what happened between us last night a mistake?"

"Oh, Alan, I didn't mean it like that. I just—look, give me some space here, okay? I'm not like you. I don't just go falling into bed with people."

"And I do?" Alan rose and drew himself up to his full height. "Oh, Portia, don't be such a ninny. We're both grown-ups here. We know the difference between a little pat and giggle and what happened last night."

She was silent, shaking her head slowly.

"Don't we?" he insisted.

She was on her feet then, trembling. "I don't know anything! Okay? That's what I'm telling you. Give me some damn space!" She stopped in mid-speech, her mouth open, astonished at the tumult of feeling that raged through her. "I can't deal with this now, Alan. I've got this trial to think about—please. You said you were my friend. Let's just keep it that way, okay?"

He could have slapped her. Instead, he stood rooted to the spot, his hands balled into fists at his sides. "Whatever you say," he managed after a moment.

Portia nodded, as though that somehow settled things. "And, Alan it was—kind—of you. To deliver all this yourself. Thank you for that. For everything. These records are going to make a big difference at the trial."

He turned away, stung. "Let me get this straight. Last night you made love like no one I've ever been with, and this morning I'm back to being the hired help. Is that about right?"

She ran a hand through her hair distractedly. "Alan, that's not fair!"

"You'll forgive me if I wasn't aware that fairness was playing a big part in this conversation." He moved toward the door.

"Look, all I meant was that last night neither of us was thinking straight. We had some drinks, we had some fun. Can't we just let it go at that?" She stared hard at his back, her green eyes gone emerald with emotion.

"I don't want to let it go, Portia," he answered softly. "But you've made it pretty clear you do." A little rush of air escaped him as he turned once more to look at her, her auburn hair catching the fiery early morning light. "It's always the same story with you, isn't it?"

Portia was shaking now. Things had been so clear before he came downstairs. And yet she felt herself being irresistibly drawn by the sheer physical presence of the man standing not three feet from her. It made her want to scream with frustration. Why couldn't he see it?

"I don't think you know me well enough to know what you're talking about," she answered bitterly.

"And you don't know me well enough to know whether I'm thinking straight," he countered. "I'm a big boy, Portia. I'm not one of your damn patients. I think I know what's going on in my own head. I make my own decisions." He faced her squarely, his blue eyes mirroring the torrents of emotion in her own. "And I've just decided to get the hell out of here."

"Fine," she snapped.

"Fine." At the last moment, he turned back, pausing at the door that led outside. "I always wondered why it was that a woman like you, with everything you've got going for you, would spend half her time locked up in prison. Now I know why it doesn't bother you. You're already in prison, aren't you? What difference do a few bars make?"

"Leave me alone!" she shouted at him.

Alan flashed a bitter smile as he turned to leave her. "You want space? Hey, you've got it. Think of me in light-years."

And in the next moment, he was gone, heading down her driveway. Portia stared after him for a long moment, her vision blurred by the hot tears that rolled unheeded down her face, torn between rage and hurt and reason and a deep, unspoken desire that had nowhere at all to go.

The slam of the car door resonated in the confines of the tiny garage, making her jump. And still she stood watching, willing her feet to move, to run after him, even as she saw the eggplant-colored car disappear around a curve and out of sight, unable to stop him, unable to make herself move.

She turned around, numb. She was suddenly overwhelmed by the mountains of paper stacked all around her. She had to go through it all—as much as she could—before her meeting with Dec that evening. Alan would have to wait. She perched heavily on the edge of a box, taking up a sheaf of files in one hand trying to ignore the ache of desire that lingered in the cold light of the garage. Alan.

She stared into space for a long moment, unable to stop thinking of him, feeling all over again his passion, the unexpected sweetness of lying in his arms. There had been so many Alans in her life. Too many. So wrong, most of them. And some . . .

Some.

"Shit," she said to no one. And began to read.

Two hours later, already jittery with caffeine, she checked in with the office. She was curious to know if there had been any further messages from Donny Royal's office.

"Not a thing," Lori answered in response to her inquiry. "As a matter of fact, all I've heard through the grapevine is that he's all backed up on his homework. My sister-in-law knows a paralegal who works down at his office. Says he's got them running morning and night."

Portia pondered this news, not knowing if it boded well or ill for the approaching trial. "Anything else?" she asked after a minute, hardly daring to hope that Alan had somehow seen through her terrors and called. A sudden loneliness overwhelmed her as Lori's voice came back over the wire.

"Just a message from Dr. Stransky's office, canceling for today. She was called out of town for a funeral. She's not due back until next Tuesday, so her office said they'd just keep your regular appointment for next Friday."

After leaving a few miscellaneous instructions, Portia hung up, suddenly despondent. She'd been looking forward to her session with Sophie—there was so much to talk about. Alan, the DID diagnosis, the trial. So much that she needed to integrate somehow. But Sophie wasn't there. Sophie was at a funeral. The thought made Portia shiver unexpectedly. It wasn't fair. She—of all people—knew it wasn't fair to expect that her therapist not have a life of her own. It was ridiculous to believe that Sophie would always be there, as if she somehow existed only in that hour they met on Friday afternoons. But that knowledge did not stave off the wave of disappointment that swept over Portia as she stood in the middle of her kitchen, feeling lost and alone. She had so much to think about, so much to examine—she wanted someone to confide in. And yet, when Alan had offered to be that someone—if only for a little while—she had pushed him away.

And on the heels of that thought came another, one that made her go cold with foreboding. The trial started Monday. There would be a day, maybe two, of jury selection. And then the trial itself. She would have to face it alone—without Sophie's calm support. Without her encouragement and insight. Without even the promise of Alan Simpson's nonchalant humor to cheer her along as she testified to one of the toughest diagnoses she'd ever had to give.

There was only Dec left to guide her. Only Dec, who in the midst of a trial grew increasingly remote and out of reach, putting all his own needs and emotions on hold as he got caught up in the game—a game he always played to win. She'd seen him tear up a witness's testimony like so many tissues, and seen him turn away with a smile on his face. Not because he was bad, but because he believed he was right.

Thinking of Dec did little to hearten her as she moved back toward the garage and the mountain of records that served to chronicle the mental and criminal history of a little-known madman named Jimmy Wier. She would talk to Dec tonight—maybe not about everything, but some of it. She knew she could share at least the final pieces of the puzzle that had fallen into place. She glanced at her watch, a new idea taking shape in her mind.

If she hurried, she could make Columbia by noon and be back at Dec's in time for dinner. It would mean canceling her weekend appointments and reading all night, but if she left now, she could still make it.

She had to see Jimmy once more before the trial began. And if possible she had to see again the monster that called itself Bonnie Jean.

Whatever else happened, she had to be sure.

· · ·

Three hours later, she scrawled her name into the visitor's log. The guard on duty eyed her quizzically as she checked her purse and car keys, taking only the pen and yellow legal pad that were allowed her.

"Didn't expect you back so soon after yesterday," he said by way of conversation. "Damn shame about you getting stuck that way."

Portia looked at him. If he knew more about her time in the elevator than the remark indicated, it showed nowhere on his face. "Didn't expect to be here, actually," she answered brightly. "Something came up." She left the Visitor's Center and headed out into the sunshine, making her way up the long familiar walk to the prison's main building. She presented her pass and identification to a faceless guard in the booth.

"Prisoners are in the cafeteria now, ma'am. I'll have to send word."

"Fine," Portia answered. "I'll need a conference room." She strained to make out the man's eyes behind the tinted window.

Unexpectedly, the guard picked up the phone and murmured into it, a brief set of instructions that she could not quite make out. A door to her left emitted the sounds of tumblers turning in their locks. Another guard approached her, round face smiling with an even rounder belly straining at the buttons of his uniform. The man behind the window nodded to her. "Second floor," he said. "Jenkins'll walk you upstairs. Elevator's busted."

Portia smiled broadly as she turned to follow Jenkins's wide behind up the gray-painted service staircase that led to the second floor. Thank the lord, she thought. Or the warden.

They brought him to her fifteen minutes later, shackled hand and foot. As they undid his handcuffs, Jimmy glanced sheepishly at her, wiping self-consciously at a smear of ketchup on one side of his mouth. "They didn't let me finish my french fries," he said by way of greeting.

And she saw that it was, indeed, Jimmy, not anyone else. He looked so vulnerable sitting there, so shyly pleased to see her again so soon. His blue eyes held none of the venom she had seen yesterday, none of the monstrous hatred that was Bonnie Jean. The man in front of her was gentle, simple in his acceptance of her presence. Any resistance Jimmy held had crumbled with his awful confessions. He faced her now with an expression so full of trust that it unnerved her, so open it was almost childlike. She wet her lips, her mouth suddenly dry. How could she ask him to give way to the thing she had seen yesterday?

"I wanted to see you again, Jimmy," she began. "I need to talk to you about some things. Before the trial."

He nodded gravely. "Okay. I guess it's okay. I was feeling pretty bad, but that lawyer came to see me this morning. Not the one in the wheelchair. Evans. He told me it was going to be all right. I guess I believe him."

He glanced at her as if for confirmation and Portia suppressed a sigh. She could only hope Evans was right. She studied Jimmy closely for another moment. Gone was the gray doughiness she had seen in their first sessions, the bizarre behaviors. And not for the first time was she struck by the irony of a system that provided prisoners with a decent diet and needed medications as a prelude to a sentence of death. Her eyes drifted to the prisoner's hands, where the line of burn blisters still glowed angrily along his knuckles. There was little time for sentiment. Jimmy might indeed be responding favorably to prison life, but that didn't mean he was sane. From what she had seen yesterday, the chances were slim that Jimmy Wier would ever be whole.

She coughed nervously and began again. "Do you remember what we talked about yesterday, Jimmy?"

He cocked his head to the side, thinking hard. "We talked about the ladies." He paused and stared down at his hands, and began to pick uneasily at one of the blisters. She stopped him, catching him by the wrist, forcing him to look at her.

"Yes, Jimmy, the ladies. And you told me you remembered that your hands were there, at Lila Mooney's house. You remember telling me that?"

Jimmy shifted his bulk uneasily. "I guess . . ."

"And you told me about being at Atascadero. In the hospital? Why did you have to go there, Jimmy. What did you do?"

He frowned. "It was a long time ago," he said uncertainly.

"That's not good enough, Jimmy. We got the records. You were sent up on a rape charge. Assault. A teenaged girl. She was the second, Jimmy. The one you beat up. You remember?"

"No," he answered simply.

She peered at him, struggling to make sense of it all. If he was telling her the truth, it would fit in with a DID diagnosis. Patients with no real knowledge of an alter would report segments of missing time. Carefully, she probed for more.

"Jimmy—what happens to you when the She comes? How do you feel?"

He met her steady gaze uncertainly. "I told you. She's gone. She didn't come back."

The hell she didn't, thought Portia, and made a notation. "But when she did come, what happened? What was it like?"

He shrugged and made a confused gesture. "I would just hear her . . . sometimes. The She would talk to me."

"What about?"

Jimmy considered the question. "Hurting," he managed finally. "I would get to where I hurt and hurt. Until it was like I couldn't hurt no more. And the She would come and talk to me. And then something would happen."

"What happened, Jimmy? What would happen when the She came?"

He could only look bewildered. "Different things. A fuck maybe. Or I'd have some money. Sometimes I'd wake up in jail because something else happened. You know . . . the usual stuff."

Portia bit her lip. Those last three words told her more about Jimmy's life than he could know. The usual stuff. And yet she could not put aside the questions that must have answers before they went to court. Questions to which the man in front of her more than likely had no real answers. Jimmy Wier was as much a victim as those two old women had been, caught as he was in the nether land that lay between the terror that was his reality and the horror that was Bonnie Jean. She took a long, shuddering breath, steeling herself.

"I want to talk to Bonnie Jean."

To her utter amazement, Jimmy began to giggle, cautiously at first, then erupting into something that was almost like honest laughter, save that it was punctuated by a series of shrill uncontrollable snorts. The kind that come from people unused to laughing. She stared at him. It was Jimmy and Jimmy alone who was overcome by this fit of mirth. Of that much she was certain as he leaned back and clumsily wiped his eyes.

"Jimmy, what happened just now? What's so funny?"

He sputtered and stopped, seeing her expression. "You. You said you wanted to talk to Bonnie Jean." He shook his head, as if unable to believe the sheer absurdity of the request.

"But why is that funny?" Despite herself, Portia felt her shoulders suddenly relax, as if someone had just let the air out of her someplace.

"Because you can't," Jimmy replied, chuckling. "She's dead."

"Dead?"

"Oh, yeah. She's dead, all right. As a doornail."

"But you said her name," Portia insisted. "Yesterday. You called Bonnie Jean. And then you . . . you sort of fell asleep. Remember?"

His blue eyes were wide and utterly innocent as they met hers. "Naw. I mean, I don't. But if you say I did . . . well. Maybe I was dreaming or something. I still have dreams about her sometimes. Even though she's dead."

Momentarily bewildered, Portia fixed her attention on her notes, trying to decide what to ask next, as if the right question would produce an answer she hadn't yet thought of. "But who was she, Jimmy? A friend? Somebody in your family?"

He studied her patiently, as if their roles had been suddenly reversed, as if she were sick and confused and he were the one making a diagnosis. A small knowing smile played around his mouth. "Bonnie Jean was my dog," he explained. "My dad, Horace, he gave her to me when I was just a little kid. Before he left us. It was a kind of a shepherd, maybe. A mutt. He brought her home one day and said I could give her any name I wanted. And—I don't know. I couldn't decide between the name Bonnie and the name Jean. So I named her both things. Bonnie Jean." He nodded slowly, still approving the choice after all these years.

Portia listened. And when she managed finally to form a question, her voice cracked with unexpected emotion. "Tell me about her, Jimmy."

Jimmy shook his head again as he stared unseeingly over a distance of years. "She was a real one-person sort of dog. Mean, though. Truth is, Bonnie Jean was about the meanest dog that ever lived. I guess it was just her nature. But she loved me. She protected me. Truly she did. No matter what was goin' on, Bonnie Jean was there. Couldn't nobody lay a hand on me when Bonnie Jean was around."

"What happened to Bonnie Jean?"

Jimmy's face contorted with pain. "Oh," he breathed softly. "I killed her. I had to. They said it was the only way." He closed his eyes tight against the memory.

Portia's voice was barely a whisper. "Who?"

Jimmy shook himself, as if awakening from some dream he'd had, sitting there. "That's funny. I don't know who made me do it. I remember that Bonnie was lying there, on her side. She was breathing real hard. She was sick from something—I don't know. I can see the gun in my hand, though. It was so heavy. I didn't even think I could lift it. I was so—small. But whoever was there with me said Bonnie Jean was dead anyhow. And since she was mine, I ought to be the one." Jimmy shuddered, suddenly overcome. "And I did it. Pow! Right in the head. I know it was me that killed her. But I don't know who was there with me. I don't know who made me shoot that dog." He stopped, looking into Portia's glistening eyes, as though he might find some answer there. "That's funny, isn't it? That I can't remember?"

Twin tears rolled down Portia's exhausted face as she clutched his blistered fingers and tried very hard to smile. "Never mind, Jimmy. Never mind. It's okay—okay. You don't have to try to remember any more."

Twenty-four

● ●

S HE LEFT JIMMY an hour later, after doing her best to
reassure him about the upcoming trial. But she pulled
out of the parking lot and drove the long miles back to Charlotte with
a heavy heart, her mood matched perfectly by the thick gray storm
clouds that clotted the horizon to the north. She had gotten what she
wanted in her last interview with Jimmy Wier before jury selection
began on Monday. It was finally, irrevocably clear to her that he knew
almost nothing about the existence of Bonnie Jean. In his particular
case, her diagnosis of Dissociative Identity Disorder was completely
valid. But the knowledge that she happened to be right did nothing at
all to improve his chances at trial. If anything, it made things worse.
And neither those thickening clouds nor her state of mind had lightened by the time she turned the car once more onto the winding
streets of Dilworth two hours later. It was as if the world itself were
held in some oppressive stasis as the same old questions repeated
themselves in endless litany. If Jimmy Wier was insane—and she could
prove that he was—why was there any question of putting him to
death? How much proof did the people need? And why would killing
him make it better? What did it fix?

As she wearily showered and changed for her dinner with Dec, she
continued to turn the problem of a DID diagnosis over in her
thoughts, trying to anticipate Dec's reaction to the news. She knew
the sheer dramatic impact of an alternate personality would appeal to
the showman in him—the actor that lurked in the hearts of all trial

lawyers. But she also knew that Dec was too good a lawyer to risk jeopardizing Jimmy's life with what many people in that courtroom would almost certainly perceive as crackpot theatrics. As she brushed her hair and put the finishing touches on her makeup, she met her own tired eyes for a long moment in the mirror. Her mouth twisted in an ironic sort of smile. The fact was, this should be an incredibly exciting moment in her career. She'd found the kind of case that most clinicians and forensic profilers only got to read about. A psychological disorder so rare most shrinks would never see it up close. And yet Portia was nowhere near excited, she was heartsick. For she knew the only real way to convince a jury of Jimmy's insanity was for them to somehow see for themselves what happened when Jimmy became Bonnie Jean. Yet, if a jury saw what she had seen, the rage, the viciousness—the vengeful glee—it would be everything but the signature on Jimmy Wier's death warrant.

She smacked her lips to blend the color and shot herself a last appraising glance. She looked terrible. Evidence of the emotional and physical strain of the last few days showed everywhere in the lines and shadows of her face. She'd been able to hide things like no sleep and truckloads of worry at twenty-five—even at thirty. At forty, the strain was visible in ways no makeup could really disguise.

"Christ," she said to no one, taking up an enormous batch of files and her car keys. "I've got to get out of this business."

Declan Dylan's house was huge, a rambling two-story gray stone monument on Colville Road in the exclusive Eastover section of town. It was set off by sweeping lawns and two enormous magnolias that shaded the front porch, a picture that sent an unmistakable message of quiet elegance and understated old money. The wide porch was lined with enough intricate, Victorian-style, white wicker rockers and swings to start an old folks' home. Once, early in their friendship, Portia had chided Dec for hanging on to so grand a place, insisting that it was far too much house for a man so wedded to his work. He was practically never home. But Dec had been born in that house and somehow he managed it all, keeping track of the repairs and maintenance and landscaping chores with all the delight of a general directing a small domestic army. Most especially, Dec loved the rockers. They gave him a break from his wheelchair, and he could easily get them in motion with his sinewy, well-muscled arms. Sitting on the porch of that house on long mild evenings gave him both a sense of a freedom and a sense of belonging that, she imagined, it was hard for him to find anywhere else.

He frequently entertained at home, organizing a mix of personal friends and professional associates with an efficiency and ease that had always astonished her. An expert chef, he preferred to dine on his own creations than out in restaurants. There were two kinds of people in the world, he said, people who cook and people who eat out. She happily put herself in the latter category—especially when she got to eat out at Dec's.

She parked the Volvo a little off to the side of the house, sliding from the front seat and waving as she headed up the broad front walk, an armload of case files at her side.

"Hi, stranger," he said. "Where's that gorgeous child of yours?"

Portia shrugged, shifting the heavy files to her other arm. "She stayed at her friend Jessica's house last night. According to my neighbor, they're inseparable. Apparently it's true, because they came back from school and insisted that tonight they were staying over at my house. I fed them hamburgers and fries and turned them over to my sitter. They're probably all glassy-eyed with videos even as we speak."

Dec patted the chair next to him and pointed to a small bar set up at one corner of the porch. "Try the Merlot," he urged. "It's extraordinary."

Portia frowned a little at the selection of beverages and helped herself to an ice tea instead. "Maybe later," she said, settling herself in a rocker next to Dec's. "With food. I haven't eaten yet today. Wine will just make me giddy. Besides, I had more than enough last night." As soon as she turned to face the too-interested expression in Dec's eyes, she could have bitten off her tongue.

"I don't know if you've spoken to him," she continued hastily, "but Alan drove all the way across country with those records. There was some problem with shipping. And he knew we were running out of time. Anyway, he was beat and I was, too. We had some drinks—dinner." She trailed off uncertainly, turning away and fixing her eyes on some point on the lawn. The other things she'd shared with Alan Simpson were made somehow very obvious by the awkward little silence that followed.

His bark of laughter startled her. "You? Too much to drink? Giddy? Sorry, but Portia McTeague and giddy are two words I don't think I'd ever use in the same sentence." He laced his fingers together as if to contemplate the issue, his eyes alive with a curious fire Portia could not—or did not—want to identify. "Portia—giddy. Nope," he finished. "It's an oxymoron, or something."

She looked at him, strangely offended by the remark. "Did Alan call your office?" she asked uneasily, as if saying the name aloud might conjure the man's presence at her elbow.

Enjoying her discomfort, Dec smiled thinly. "That's my girl. All business. Tell me, does our gumshoe playboy appreciate your ceaseless dedication, or does he get to see an aspect of you I don't?"

Portia stared at him, color creeping up her neck from her collar. Nothing in the mildness of Dec's tone betrayed anything. Yet his eyes flickered with some unspoken passion. Never had she wanted so much to talk to a friend—to confide in someone like Dec, a man who probably understood her better than anyone else. And never had she realized with such utter clarity that this was one instance where talking could only make the situation worse. And so, for a moment, all she could do was look at him, imploring him with her eyes to understand.

"Dec," she managed finally. "Something new has come up. I've waited to tell you until I was sure. The diagnosis. It's . . . complicated. More complicated than I'd thought."

Dec's eyes narrowed, his feathers still clearly ruffled. The knuckles of his fingers, laced thoughtfully under his chin, were white with strain. "So what is it? According to Simpson, we're going in with some very serious documentation."

Portia motioned to the pile of records she'd brought with her. "There's some of the highlights," she said. "I have truckloads more. But, Dec . . ." She paused, the prospect of having to explain the intricacies of a DID diagnosis more daunting than she'd imagined it would be. She rose abruptly from her chair, making her way back to the bar. Wine suddenly seemed like a very good idea. She poured herself a glass of the Merlot, staring into its ruby depths a moment before going on.

"The hell of it is, Dec, Jimmy Wier is—well—controlled by an alternate personality. Somebody called Bonnie Jean. She's the real killer."

Dec leaned forward, his face drawn taut with concern. "Portia, what are you saying?"

She could only nod. They both knew how grave things suddenly looked for Jimmy. There was no need to say it aloud. "Apparently," she continued after a moment, "he developed this identity fairly early on. He created this . . . woman, if you want to call her that, as a place for his sexual impulses, his rage, et cetera. She's so well established he's only dimly aware of her. When she comes out, he dissociates. He wakes up with very little, if any, memory of what happened while she was in control."

"Multiple personality," Dec murmured. "Jesus."

"The official name is Dissociative Identity Disorder. It's rare, but it's out there. And Jimmy's got it. I'd stake my reputation on it."

Dec scowled over the failing light that crept through the long shadows on the lawn. "Good God," he breathed tiredly. "Royal's going to shit his britches."

"I know, I know," Portia protested. "I know what a diagnosis like this can mean to an insanity plea! That's why I went back this afternoon. I had to be sure."

Dec shifted restlessly, and she knew that if he could have gotten up and paced the length of the long porch, he would have.

"What about the schizophrenia?" he asked. "Isn't that what the drugs were for? Isn't that why he got better?"

Portia made a feeble little gesture. "Dissociative Identity Disorder may or may not be a type of schizophrenia. Opinions differ. What the Haldol did for Jimmy was to reduce or eliminate symptoms, bizarre behaviors, and command voices. He even told me that the voice he called the She had disappeared. Only she hadn't gone anywhere. She simply stopped communicating with Jimmy at any level he was aware of. Instead," she finished tiredly, "she came out to talk to me."

Dec was staring at her, clearly confounded. "Explain."

Portia rubbed her forehead and sipped her wine. "Think of it this way. Somebody's got a voice in their head, right?"

"Right," Dec replied.

"So, pretend that this voice is coming in on a sort of radio wave. Sometimes it just interferes with normal perception—whispers, static, that kind of thing—like a station that isn't quite tuned in. And then other times, during a full psychotic break, that voice is the only thing the person can hear. It's loud and clear, directing the person's thoughts, actions, whatever."

"A command hallucination—" Dec interjected.

"Exactly."

"So what did the drugs do? For Jimmy?"

Portia sank wearily into the nearest rocker. "They turned the volume down on the voice. All the way down, according to Jimmy. Only they didn't cure him. Not by a long shot."

She glanced up unseeingly as a small white compact turned into the driveway. "What I didn't know until yesterday was that there was more than a voice in Jimmy's head. A whole lot more. There's a whole other identity in there, Dec. And believe me, she's somebody you don't want to meet."

Dec rocked forward, planting his feet in front of him as the small white car came to a stop behind Portia's Volvo, effectively blocking her in. "Regardless of that," he said, "here's someone you do want to meet."

Portia glanced warily at the approaching figure, dimly conscious of the fact that there was something oddly familiar about the blond hair and the set of the shoulders. She turned to Dec, who was busy hoisting himself from his rocker into the waiting wheelchair.

"I told you I hired a new associate, didn't I?" he went on in answer to her puzzled expression. "I asked her to join us tonight. She's going to be really valuable in going over your testimony."

"My testimony?" Portia shot him a backward glance as good manners fought with annoyance and won a temporary victory. She rose to her feet and came to the railing as Dec wheeled to the edge of the top step and waved at the young woman crossing the lawn, flashing Portia a series of nervous smiles.

"If you wanted me over here for a coaching session," she growled under her breath, "all you had to do was ask. You didn't have to make dinner."

"Nonsense, Doctor," he answered through his teeth. "If I told you, you'd never have showed up."

Portia was about to protest when suddenly the odd familiarity of the young woman now climbing the wide stone steps gelled into a shock of recognition.

Dec turned to Portia and smiled so graciously that a person would have had to know the man as well as Portia did to notice how much he was enjoying his little surprise. Enjoying it so much, in fact, that there was a light of something like glee in his eyes as he presented the young woman with all the warm familiarity of an old friend.

"Portia, surely you remember my associate, Amy Goodsnow? Amy was with us at the Warren trial, weren't you, Amy?"

And Amy smiled at her with a cold studied grace that belied the casual twist of her hair and the long, flower-printed chiffon dress that flowed around her slender body in a softly perfect curve. She offered Portia her hand, a gesture Portia chose to leave floating in the air.

Portia glanced at Dec, then back to Amy, smiling bravely as she choked back the hundred snide comments that arose in her mind. "I never forget a prosecutor," she managed finally. How the hell did you manage to worm your way into Dec's firm? she added silently.

Amy hid her unshaken hand in the folds of her skirt.

"I was so impressed with Amy's work, I figured I'd better hire her over to the other side while I had the chance," Dec offered nonchalantly. "Wasn't I, Amy?"

Amy's thin smile never wavered as she met Portia's glittering eyes. "Yessir," she answered firmly.

"Amy has an extraordinary trial ability," Dec went on. "I figured, with her questioning you in the role of prosecutor, we could polish up her technique and your testimony at the same time. Kill two birds with one stone."

If they all got through dinner, Portia thought bitterly, birds might not be the only casualties of the evening.

"Well," Portia responded brightly, taking up her glass as Dec led the way toward the wide front door. "They do say politics makes for strange bedfellows."

He turned and met her eyes then as Amy preceded them into a grand foyer, lit by the thousand crystal lights of an elaborate chandelier. And a person would have had to know him as well as Portia did to see behind that handsome smile, and know that there was something other than a well-played trump card that fueled the light behind his eyes. It was something more than the usual spark of Machiavellian excitement that criminal lawyers brought to the shaping of a witness's testimony—even if that witness was supposed to be a friend.

Someone would have had to look quite closely to see the odd coldness of Declan's smile and the sadness underneath it, all wrapped in tattered payback for her night with Alan. A person would have had to look more closely even than Portia did to see the wasted love hidden there. Portia lingered on the threshold behind them for a long moment, trying to put a name to the look in her old friend's eyes, a look she was not sure she had ever seen there before, and was very sure she did not ever want to see again.

Something almost like revenge.

. . .

They went in, crossing a foyer done in sea greens and grays to the dining room, where quiet gold and rose shades played with the quieter light of another chandelier. The mahogany table was set simply for three. Or as simply as it could have been in Declan Dylan's house, Portia thought, mentally contrasting her own preferences for hand-painted stoneware to the almost translucent bone china with its thin, gold edging. Crystal goblets and sterling reflected in the polished tabletop like jewels. A small silver vase filled to overflowing with miniature lavender roses from the gardens served as a centerpiece, and Portia caught the heady scent of them as she sneaked a look at Amy, who was trying very hard not to gawk. Portia took a place on Dec's left, and the two women faced each other eye to eye as Amy took her place on his right.

"No wonder you like to dine at home," Portia said. "It's beautiful, Dec." And she added, for Amy's benefit, "As usual."

"Surround yourself with only the best," he grinned. "Fine food, fine wine, and fine-looking women. Just excuse me a minute while I get us started." He wheeled through the kitchen doors while Portia frowned after him, wondering if all the noblesse oblige crap had been solely for her benefit, or Amy's.

She smiled thinly across the table. "So how do you like your new position? It must be quite a change."

Amy's eyes never wavered. "It is," she answered simply. "But I believe I'm up to the challenge." Then, without hesitation, she added, "I'd like you to fill me in on anything you've discovered about Mr. Wier. It will save us some time if I'm brought up to date."

Portia glanced down at the beautiful place setting in front of her, very nearly ashamed of herself. She should know better than to try and second guess Declan Dylan, especially when it came to judging legal talent. Amy was clearly intelligent, straightforward, and had enough grit to make the grade. If anything, she was more poised than Portia herself, at least at that moment. If a former prosecutor was even willing to help prepare Portia for the grueling circus this trial promised to become, she ought to be grateful. The next smile she offered across the table was more genuine.

"Hey you two, come get these appetizers," Dec called from the kitchen and the two women rose simultaneously. Portia laughed a little. "Looks like he's got us both well trained, doesn't it?"

When they were all seated once again, Portia began to fill Amy in on the specifics of a DID diagnosis, and the dangers of bringing such a diagnosis to trial. She paused momentarily and took a small bite of the delicate ravioli in front of her, watching Amy curiously. For all her sawmill accent and cheap shoes, the girl had amazing table manners, choosing the right pieces of Dylan family silverware with no hesitation at all.

Amy's eyes deepened in the soft light, turning them an almost attractive blue. "Tell me, just what did the records turn up?"

"A long and interesting criminal history, among other things. Evidence that he was escalating in his levels of violent behavior for years." Portia paused and glanced at Dec. "We have to be prepared, Dec. Royal's going to come at you with both guns blazing over that record. Burglary, assault, attempted rape, and finally, these murders."

Dec folded his hands reflectively, propping them under his chin. "He always does," he answered. "The old hardened criminal routine. No redeeming social value, etcetera. Point is, from what you tell me, there's a clinical history to offset that, right? So we say he tried to get help; he just didn't get it."

Portia sighed as she continued. "He was in and out of treatment programs as he drifted east from California. Local clinics—short-term stuff—even some substance abuse programs. He was a member of AA for a while before he came here. Only he was never treated for schizophrenia. I think that's the key. Nobody who saw him figured out what he was. Even at Atascadero, they were only treating symptoms, not the disease. Wier is more than a "multiple." He loses touch with reality. He has delusions he can't separate from what's real. He's never had anyone help him put his fantasies back into the context of the normal world."

It unnerved her a little, glancing from Amy's face to Dec's and back again as they plotted moves, their expressions nearly identical—each face betraying all the emotion of two people working out a mathematical formula.

Dec turned to Amy as she sipped the last of her Merlot. "What're you thinking?"

Amy laid her hands on either side of her plate, looking as if she might begin to fidget, but didn't. "There are a number of judicial precedents for a diagnosis of this kind as a basis for an insanity plea," she said after a long moment. *People v. Thornton,* for one. That trial took place just over in Tennessee. I'm not sure of the date—nineteen-eighty, I think. But it was a murder case. Thornton got sent to the state hospital. It's tricky, but it has happened."

Dec pushed his small appetizer plate aside. "Not good enough," he said, shaking his head. "Times have changed too much since eighty. People are more—"

"Vengeful?" offered Portia cynically.

Amy fingered her napkin. "I can't agree," she rejoined softly. "Maybe it isn't just vengeance."

"Meaning?" Portia asked.

"They're more frightened is all. People have less of a feeling of—control. Over their lives. They don't feel safe. I think the key to the whole defense may be to identify the things that people are the most frightened of and to present Wier's illness as far outside of those fears as possible."

Portia looked across the table with new respect dawning in her eyes. Whoever Amy Goodsnow was, and wherever she'd come from, the girl had brains. She turned to Dec, who'd begun the second course and was eyeing his new associate and chewing like a satisfied cat on some meal of canary. "Go on," he said.

"The question is," Amy continued reflectively, "how do we go about that? Can we let the jury see this Bonnie Jean?"

Portia shook her head. "Won't work. First, she's too damn scary. And second, she's the control. She only comes out when she wants to."

"What about hypnosis?" Amy asked. "Hasn't that been used elsewhere?"

Portia sighed heavily as Dec interjected. "Also risky. I don't think Royal would go for it. Besides, last trial I heard about used that, the prosecution took the defense completely apart. Had all sorts of statistics to prove that people were more fantasy prone under hypnosis."

Amy's thoughtful expression didn't change. "Are you sure Bonnie Jean is his only other personality?" she asked softly.

Portia paused in her eating, her fork in mid-air. "I can't say. Frankly, it never occurred to me to look for more. Certainly there's no other I've seen. But it's possible, I suppose. Anything's possible."

Amy resumed eating. "I was only thinking," she went on, "about people being frightened. It was the vulnerability of the elderly victims that upset people. We need to counter that with something. Childhood, for example. If old people are vulnerable—Wier's defense will have to go to the other end of the spectrum."

"That's at least part of the reason he chose those victims," Portia explained. "He felt they were more vulnerable than he was."

"I understand. But somehow we have to make Wier completely nonthreatening. More vulnerable than each and every juror in that box feels themselves to be. As long as they aren't personally threatened by him or his case, we can still win."

Portia shot her an amused glance. "You wouldn't happen to know how to do that, would you? I could hang up my shingle."

But all attempts at humor were pretty much lost on Amy. "I think we have to ask ourselves what it is that scares people. That is why I was thinking about another alter—maybe a child. The things that happen to a child are far more frightening to most people than an older person's death. Anyway, I just thought something like that might help strengthen the case." Amy fell suddenly silent and shrugged her narrow shoulders, almost as if she were embarrassed at having made so long a speech.

Portia stared at her, open-mouthed with admiration. "You really are good."

Amy appeared neither flattered nor flustered by the comment. "Just keep the child idea in your head when you testify," she instructed gravely. Glancing at Dec for confirmation, she went on. "Defense's line of questioning should play to that, of course. But prosecution's won't. My guess is that they're prepared for you to play up his mental illness. But no matter what happens don't allow yourself to be steered from the child angle. People don't care about insanity."

Portia nearly snorted. "Tell me about it. Just one more reason I love my job."

If Amy understood, she didn't show it. Clearly she didn't consider this conversation an opportunity to make friends. "My point is that insanity is just a word to most people. It's not something they know how to care about. They care about their kids—they're worried about the future, keeping them safe. So I think you have to talk about Wier as though he were a child. Maybe even one of their kids. Be as emotional as you can. No matter what they ask you."

"I don't know," Portia responded uncomfortably. "I have to answer the questions they ask." Privately, she was feeling a little defensive, wondering if odd little Amy Goodsnow wasn't more of an expert on the workings of the human psyche than she herself was.

"I don't think Amy's talking about your answers, but about how you answer," Dec added mildly.

Portia flushed in the soft light. "It's not as easy as it sounds."

"Nothing is," answered Amy. "But make him as vulnerable as you can. Don't talk about him like he was crazy. Don't even talk about him being sick. Just . . ." She paused and made a futile little gesture. "Just be him."

She met Portia's eyes, and in that moment there passed between the two women a silent understanding. For Portia realized all over again what she had seen the first time they'd ever laid eyes on one another at the Warren hearing. She suddenly held the certainty that behind the efficient, almost robotic exterior of Amy Goodsnow, she too was a member of the club—the club whose members understood like no one else could, all of the terrible things that can happen to children. What's more, Amy's pale eyes recognized the same in Portia and were pleading with her to do more than be an expert or craft her testimony, or even save the life of a man she'd never met. Those eyes spoke volumes across the bone china and the crystal goblets, for they were asking Portia McTeague to speak for all of them, all the members of that terrible club who were able to recognize one another without a word. All bound together by their unspoken memories, their awful secrets written in blood. Portia looked away reluctantly and Amy did too, each aware of just how much that was to ask of anyone.

"We've been doing all the talking, Dec," Portia said after a moment. "What're you thinking?"

He raised his eyebrows, as if he'd just remembered she was there. "Me? Oh, jurors," he answered.

"What did you have in mind?"

Dec bit his lip in a way that Portia knew very well. "A black or two, I think. I'm not sure. Maybe somebody with mental illness in the family." He turned to Amy. "What's your opinion, Amy? It's how I was going, but this vulnerability angle has given me some new material."

"I'm not sure," Amy said. "I had been thinking of jurors in more general than specific terms. I'm sure you'll make the right choices, though."

"Never mind, Amy. Dec only asks questions he already knows the answers to anyway," Portia advised, smiling a little.

Dec smiled back and she suddenly forgave him for his attitude earlier in the evening. They both knew he'd made no mistake in bringing Amy into the mix, even if she was looking at him with a combination of seriousness and awe that was difficult for anyone but a man like Dec to miss.

"Royal offered to make me a deal," Dec went on. "Did I tell you? I turn over a written report from you for Falcone to go over in exchange for no old ladies on the panel." Dec grinned gleefully. "I turned him down."

Portia nodded. "Lori told me about some messages from his office. We ignored them, as usual."

"Good," Dec responded. "I was thinking older women might be a good choice here. More sympathy, you know. More perspective."

"More religion," Portia interrupted. "More of that eye-for-an-eye philosophy."

"Can't get around that, hon. Goes with the territory. But don't fret. I'll throw in a ringer somewhere. Trust me. I'm a pretty good judge of character."

Like hell you are, she thought, but didn't say. Dec faced the beginning of every case with the sort of confidence reserved only for fools and visionaries, and there was no point in deflating that confidence now. There were plenty of juries to do that for him.

"You want me to help in selection?" she asked instead. "I could give you an idea of the subtext during the selection."

"No way," he responded immediately. "I've asked Amy to give me a hand."

Amy looked at the wall, as if hearing her name spoken aloud by her employer had temporarily robbed her of her senses.

"Besides, you're my star witness. I want them to be properly awed and impressed. By the way, wear that blue Armani suit, won't you? I want you to look absolutely perfect for this one. Falcone's going to turn up in his usual J.C. Penney special and I think it would make for a good contrast. Besides," he finished, smiling gleefully. "This one's on camera."

"Terrific," she said bleakly. "Tell me, Amy, does he enforce a dress code in the office, too?"

"Excuse me," Amy said. "But I'd go with something else."

Dec stared at her, obviously a little taken aback at being contradicted. Seeing the look, Amy colored uncomfortably. "I'm sorry," she murmured. "That is, I don't mean to disagree, but Dr. McTeague, well . . ."

"Well what, Amy?"

This time Amy did give in to the temptation to fidget, nervously plucking at the handstitched hem of her napkin. "Dr. McTeague will look fine, of course, whatever she wears. But Royal is aiming to get elected as a man of the people. And if she's going to speak to Wier's vulnerability, well, she just can't look so . . . unapproachable. I've faced you on the stand. And you were very . . . intimidating. Perfect, even. But not accessible. You know what I mean?"

"I think so," Portia replied slowly.

Amy searched Declan's face anxiously. "I just think it would be to her advantage to wear something more . . . ordinary. Earthier, or something."

Dec laughed aloud, causing Amy to blush even more furiously. "How about it, Portia, something in gingham?"

You idiot, thought Portia. Sometimes she wondered how a man as smart as Dec could possibly be as insensitive as he had just betrayed himself to be. Whatever else was going on with the thoroughly surprising Amy Goodsnow, it was clear to Portia at least that Dec's new associate was half in love with him.

"Snob," she told him. "Amy was simply saying that I ought to make an effort not to project the Snow Queen image you seem to like so much."

"Yes," Amy breathed gratefully. "It's just that, really. Like, wear your hair down or something. People will be more willing to listen to what you have to say if they can relate a little better to how you look."

"Okay, but I draw the line at polyester," Portia answered dryly. "Besides, Armani himself said fashion is dead. I saw it on TV."

Dec shrugged and uttered a long, mock sigh, while Amy contented herself with merely looking worried. "Rest in peace," Dec offered, raising his glass. "But I did like that suit."

Maybe I'll give it to Amy, Portia thought silently. She can wear it to the office. Aloud she said, "Listen, I've got to get home to my sitter. She made me promise to get back by ten. She's got a late date or something. Do you two need me for anything else? Anything else I need to think about?"

Dec looked up at her from his place at the head of the table. "Are you sure? I thought we might have a chance to go over some of your testimony. Have Amy ask you some questions."

Amy met Portia's look and came to her rescue. "We can make an appointment for that next week," she interjected. "If that's all right with the doctor."

Thank you, mouthed Portia. "Great," she said. "And a great dinner, Dec. As usual. Thanks. And, Amy, thank you. You've given us veterans a lot to think about. Right, Dec?"

When Dec didn't immediately answer, she pinched the back of his arm to prompt him. "What? I'm sorry—of course you have, Amy. Yes. Thank you."

Portia offered them both a small smile. "Well, Amy, let's let Dec do the clearing up. I've got to ask you to come and move your car."

Amy scrambled to her feet. "Of course. And I'll be back to help with the dishes."

Portia kissed Dec lightly on the cheek as they left the room. "Find me some good jurors," she told him. "See you next week."

"I will," he promised. "Just be a good witness."

The two women headed out into the warm autumn evening in silence, oddly reluctant to engage in small talk without Dec to buffer their conversation. It had been an evening of surprises, not the least of which had been Amy herself. Humorless and gritty as Amy was, Portia couldn't help being curious about the life and the background that had formed someone of such intelligence and ambition. Amy's outsides contradicted her insides, that much was sure. But then, that much could be said about most people. It was just that, in Amy's case, the contrast was more marked than in most people.

When she'd moved her car out of the way, Amy crossed back in Portia's direction, a curling sheet of fax paper in her hand. "Oh God," she said worriedly. "I can't believe I forgot. Mr. Dylan's going to kill me."

Portia laughed. "I've known Dec Dylan for years, Amy. He's never killed an associate yet. What did you forget?"

"This," Amy answered as though it were somehow obvious. She lifted the fax in Portia's direction. Portia took the paper in her hand, but failed to make out anything in the darkness.

"Well, go in and tell him about it. I'm sure he'll understand. What is it, anyway?"

And the oddly surprising Amy Goodsnow offered the last surprise in that thoroughly surprising few hours, her eyes shining as Portia handed the paper back.

"Oh, I found him, that witness. Mr. Dylan asked me if I could track him down and I did."

"Witness?" asked Portia, suddenly interested. "Which witness?"

Amy frowned distractedly, as if she were impatient to be done with this unnecessary digression in the conversation.

"Justin Chitwood. I tracked him down on the Internet, just like I promised. He's posted on a BBS somewhere in Virginia. I sent a whole lot of inquiries to his e-mail address, but he never answered. I wasn't sure if he didn't want to, or if he just hadn't been online for a while. But this afternoon," she said, her pointed features shining with elation, "this afternoon it came. This—he sent his deposition."

Portia shook her head, blinking. "He gave you a deposition? What does it say?"

"It tells what he knew of Wier's actual condition at the time of the arrest. It was weird, really. When they picked him up, Wier was wearing panty hose."

"Oh my God," Portia breathed. "That's not in the arrest report."

And even Portia could see Amy smiling broadly in the dark, glancing down at the sheet of paper in her hand. "Oh, I know," she answered. "There's a lot that didn't make it into the arrest report. That's why I thought he'd make such a good witness."

"Well, get in there and get Dec to subpoena him, Amy."

"I can," Amy answered uncertainly. "It's just that I'm not sure he'll show up."

Portia slid behind the wheel, squinting at the outline of Amy's slender form in the darkness. "Just get him to do it. And tell Dec I said so."

"Okay," Amy replied. "I guess we can hope he'll show up."

Portia waved as she pulled out and down the long drive, glancing back at the young woman making her way up the wide porch steps.

Hope is right, she thought.

Hope.

Richland County Courthouse
Columbia, South Carolina
People v. James B. Wier

Twenty-five

● ●

D ONNY ROYAL was in rare form. He faced the panel
of jurors with just the right mix of righteousness and
understanding playing across his lean features, as though he could not
himself decide why they all had gathered there that day—as though
this were one particular cup of justice he would have preferred could
pass from them all. He met each set of eyes in turn as he began his
opening remarks, looking only long enough to establish contact before moving on, as though he and the panel were all locked in some
necessary but nevertheless tragic complicity.

"Ladies and gentlemen," he began. "I just want to say a couple of
things. The case that we are about to put before you constitutes perhaps the most horrendous crime I have ever seen. And I've been at
this business a long, long time. I've seen a lot. Murders, rapes, child
molestations. And I've done my level best to see that each and every
one of the criminals in those trials was brought to justice. Sometimes I
won and sometimes I lost. And I guess that's true of any of us. But
never—ever—in my entire career, have I so deeply believed in the
guilt of an accused man as I do in the case of James Wier. Never have I
so felt the need for justice as I do today."

Royal began to pace slowly, as if fueled by some inner fire the rest of
them could not see.

"James Wier has been accused of three things—the kidnapping, the
brutal rape, and finally the murder of two elderly women. He's accused of kidnapping because those ladies were tied up; he's accused of

rape because those helpless women were viciously and brutally raped and mutilated. And he's accused of murder because those two women, Lila Mooney and Constance Bennet, are dead—gone forever from the life of their communities, their churches, and their families."

He paused and leaned heavily on the podium, as if the burden of the knowledge itself might, in the end, prove too much to bear. "Now, I didn't know those women, but I can tell you they loved their lives. Constance Bennet was almost ninety years old, ladies and gentlemen. Ninety. Lila Mooney was eighty-three. And though each of them was frail, though each of them had gray hair and stiff knuckles and some wrinkles here and there, those ladies were still here, loving every day they had in this world—treasuring it, and using it to enrich the lives of those around them.

"And each of those long and fulfilling lives ended in unspeakable horror and pain." The District Attorney paused to snatch a linen hankie from over his heart, mopping his brow with a sad and studied resignation, glancing heavenward where the ceiling fans whirred, trying to circulate the collective breath of a courtroom packed to the rafters with spectators and press. He caught the eye of a group that looked like law interns in the loft and nodded sadly before going on.

"Now, the accused has come into this proceeding today pleading not guilty by reason of insanity. Fine. It is this man's right as an American to plead any way he wants. Advising him on the wisdom of that plea in this instance is not my job—that is the job of his defense team. And, ladies and gentlemen of the jury, I want you to know that Mr. Wier's defense team is going to do their darnedest to convince you that the accused is not guilty by reason of insanity. But I want to just take a moment here and think about what that means. Not guilty by reason of insanity.

"According to the guidelines set down for us in the M'Naughten rule, not guilty by reason of insanity means that the accused—one"— Royal held up a hand in front of him, spreading the fingers wide— "does not know right from wrong. Two, the accused had no sense of what he was doing, and three, because of his mental state he was incapable of premeditation. That's the gist of it, folks. And I guarantee you, that man's defense team is going to try and prove those things to you. They're going to try and prove that James Wier was out of his mind at the time of two murders that took place within fifteen or twenty minutes of one another one day last May at the home of Lila Mooney. They're going to try and prove that James Wier was insane when he committed those crimes. They should, that's their job. And whatever your opinion of the accused and what he may or may not have done that day, I want you to remember that he's an American, just like each and every one of you. And as an American, he's entitled to counsel."

At this juncture, Royal allowed himself the first in a series of troubled smiles. "All I have to do is show that this man is guilty of the crime of which he has been accused. And I can do that. He has been placed at the scene of the crime; he was in possession of some of the items taken from Ms. Mooney's house; and, yes, he has been identified as their killer from a DNA match of blood and semen samples."

Royal moved away from the podium and spread his arms wide. "So you see, I haven't got very much to do here, have I? Mine is the burden of proof. And we have that proof. I have more proof than I honestly know what to do with. I have more proof that James Wier committed these crimes than I want or need to present in this courtroom. I just don't see the point. To bring out everything the state can throw at this man would just be a waste of your time, and mine, and that of the taxpayers of the great state of South Carolina. And I just don't see the point. The prosecution's case against James Wier is clear. And I intend to keep it that way. I hope you all will help me do that when it comes time to decide this case.

"But as we begin these proceedings, ladies and gentlemen of the jury, I would ask you something on behalf of those two ladies, Lila Mooney and Constance Bennet—those ladies who are no longer with us. As you listen to the defense lawyers as they bring out their witnesses, their experts, and their paperwork, I would ask you to be a little bit tolerant of some of the things you're going to hear in this courtroom. Those ladies would want you to, and so do I. I want you to remember that this man is entitled to a defense. And in this instance his defense is not guilty by reason of insanity.

"Only as you listen to these proceedings, I want you to ask yourself some questions. Questions that are, perhaps, at the very heart of this case. Ask yourselves why—if the accused was truly not competent at the time of the murders—why he has a criminal record that stretches back almost twenty years. Ask yourselves if you know, or have ever heard of anybody, no matter how emotionally disturbed, who doesn't know right from wrong? Who doesn't have a sense of their own actions? Who has no idea or plan of their movements from one moment, or one murder, to the next? Have you ever seen anyone that crazy?

Have you ever known or heard of anybody who does not know good from evil? I have not. And I do not believe that is the case with Jimmy Wier.

"I believe that Jimmy Wier knows all those things; I believe he knew them even on the day he committed this crime. But Jimmy Wier went over the line, ladies and gentlemen. He turned his back on all the values society holds dear the day he went to Lila Mooney's house. He crossed that line of his own free will and he became a monster. What did those women ever do to provoke such a vicious, animalistic attack? Nothing. Why did they, of all people, deserve to die that way? We know they did not."

Royal's voice dropped to just above a whisper as three hundred people held their breath.

"I believe maybe only God knows all the things they suffered before they died. And maybe only God can know for certain what went on in the mind of Jimmy Wier that day. But I know one thing, ladies and gentlemen, when Jimmy went in there that day—when he went over the line that divides us from the beast—he gave away more than his knowledge of right and wrong or time and place.

"He gave away his soul."

Portia shivered as a murmur of admiration swept through the courtroom. She sat in a far corner, away from the other witnesses. She kept to herself, pretending to review her files as she hung on Royal's every word, mentally punctuating his speech with her objections. As the ocean of restless coughs, movements, and rustling of papers subsided, the bailiff announced that opening remarks for the defense would be made by Mr. Dylan.

Unable to see very well above the sea of spectators, she closed her eyes and pictured him, swinging around the table, making his slow way to the jury box, looking like some fallen hero. It was always a dramatic moment, and Dec had always played it to the hilt. She held her breath along with everyone else as he cleared his throat and began to speak, her own nervousness falling away as she felt herself drawn back to this battle they had no choice but to fight together.

His voice, soft and cultured, came drifting like a spring rain through the room. Portia strained to listen, marveling at the way that soft tone managed to come across like the voice of Reason itself after Royal's folksy oratorical style. She could tell Dec was smiling as he began, imagining the bemused friendliness on the face she knew so well. And yet, after only a few moments of listening, she began also to be keenly aware of much she did not know about him—of all the secrets they had so successfully kept from one another over the years.

"It's interesting to me that Mr. Royal should choose to speak this morning on the issue of choice," Dec began. "I've had a lot of occasions to think about choice and the role it has played in my own life— the lives of some of my clients. And I think I know better than most people how some events are not at all an issue of personal choice, but a question only of tragic circumstance. Choice is a luxury, ladies and gentlemen. Free will is a gift."

Dec centered his wheelchair directly in front of the jury box. And there he would stay, his voice still soft, managing nevertheless to reach every corner in that courtroom. He would stay in that spot until he was done. Moving around would be distracting; keeping still drew every set of eyes.

"Yes, free will is a gift," he went on. "But the notion that everyone is able to use that gift is a mistake. And the idea that we are all able to change our lives and circumstances simply by making the right choices is nothing but a lie.

"I know it is a lie, because if we could all change our lives just by an act of will, I would be standing here talking to you today instead of sitting in this wheelchair. I would like to change that, but I cannot. And all my choices and all my prayers and all my free will won't make any difference. My body has sustained irreparable damage. I can get physical therapy, I have tools to help me get around and live my life. But I won't ever walk again."

He paused a moment, fixing the jury with an unwavering gaze. "Understand that I don't say these things to gain your sympathy, ladies and gentlemen. I am simply stating a truth. A fact. I am damaged in my body. Just as the accused is damaged in his mind.

"Mine is the kind of damage you can see. I sit in this chair. But Jimmy Wier's kind of damage is harder to see. It has been there, with him, since he was a little boy. And the record will show that throughout his life, he called for help, tried to get help. Jimmy Wier displayed evidence of serious mental illness by the time he entered the first grade, ladies and gentlemen. He needed help. Only Jimmy Wier never got that help—he never got the therapy, he never got the tools to help him live his life in spite of the damage he had sustained.

"He never got the help he needed because all throughout his life people looked at what was happening to Jimmy Wier, and then they looked away. Just as people sometimes avert their eyes when they see me in this chair. They did not want to see what they didn't know how to help. And because it's so much easier sometimes to pretend the problem does not exist. I do that myself."

From her chair, Portia McTeague listened and thought of Dec out on his porch in a white wicker rocker. And her eyes filled with tears.

"And so," Dec continued, "as people turned away, Jimmy Wier became the kind of man invisible to most of us—drifting, trying to hold down jobs, moving from place to place. Nobody knew him and nobody cared. And Jimmy continued to deteriorate in his mind because he had no help. This tortured, damaged man was invisible. All the way up to the day he killed Lila Mooney and Constance Bennet. The day when Jimmy Wier could not hide his damage anymore.

"Ladies and gentlemen of the jury, I want you to understand that there is no one in this courtroom who is going to try and prove to you that Jimmy Wier did not commit these crimes. He did. But we do intend to prove that these murders were not the acts of a sane man, a competent man, a man in control of his thoughts and actions and his choices. We will show that Jimmy Wier's history reveals a mind so damaged that it can no longer distinguish delusion from reality, much less right from wrong. We will prove to you, ladies and gentlemen of the jury, that Jimmy Wier's mind is irreparably damaged—unable to distinguish the issues of right and wrong and choice and free will that we as sane people so take for granted. We will show you a man who killed not by choice, but because he had no choices at all."

Dec took a long pause, allowing his statements to sink in. When he spoke again, his voice seemed filled with a new sadness, one that Portia could not recall having heard before.

"Finally, ladies and gentlemen, Mr. Royal spoke to you of Jimmy Wier's going over the line when he committed those murders. I don't believe there is a line that divides us, one from another. I believe that we are all the same, black or white, rich or poor, man or woman. And if there are differences between us, I believe that those differences only serve to define us, not divide us.

"So I ask you to consider something for me. I ask you to consider the possibility that you were in my car the day I had that accident. Given the same circumstances, it would be you in this chair instead of me. Your legs damaged instead of mine. And then I want you to ask yourselves, as you listen to the evidence in this case, as you hear about a hell that few of us can imagine, whether you would not suffer the same mental and emotional damage that Jimmy Wier sustained. Your legs would be damaged, just like mine. Minds can be damaged, just like a pair of legs. There is no line that divides us, ladies and gentlemen of the jury. We are all the same. I ask you to remember that as we enter into these proceedings. And I ask you—just this one time—not to look away."

Dec turned and wheeled slowly back to the defense table, catching the bright-eyed nods of admiration that both Evans and Amy Goodsnow tossed in his direction. He noticed also that Donny Royal had chosen that moment to rise to his feet as a young intern approached his side, a yellow paper fluttering in his hand.

Minions, Dec thought bitterly, deliberately chosen to distract the jury at a critical moment. He slowly swung his chair around and back to his own table, taking his place next to the one where the defendant sat, motionless as some great lump of clay. And without meaning to, Dec wondered if it had been too great a risk, trying to draw the parallel between them, if it might not prove off-putting to a jury, calling attention to himself and his chair.

Yet, as he noted the appearance of the prosecution's first witness, he knew there was no turning back. Any life was worth a risk—even Jimmy Wier's.

In the front of the courtroom, Sheriff Dwight Glass took the oath with all the grave intensity of a man summoned to the pearly gates. And Donny Royal approached the witness box with a relaxed little smile.

"Thanks for coming up here to be with us today, Sheriff," he began. "As the officer in charge of the apprehension of the accused, I was wondering if you could just fill us in on the events that transpired."

Glass shifted a little in his chair. "Well, the call came in that two of my deputies had picked up the defendant about five o'clock in the evening. He was sitting under a tree. Had blood all over him. The officers also found an African violet that had been removed from the victim's house, along with Ms. Bennet's bag of groceries. They read him his rights and took him off to the jail."

"And you handled the questioning yourself?"

"Yessir."

"And what," Royal went on, "did Mr. Wier say during the time he was questioned about those events. Was he, in your opinion, coherent?''

"Oh, yeah—he was crying a bit, but he was coherent."

"Did he confess to the murders at that time?"

Glass shook his head in disgust. "Not exactly. He said he'd been at Miz Mooney's though."

Royal walked the sheriff through the details of the arrest without fanfare, pausing only to submit and circulate photos of the murder scene through the jury box. Dec watched the faces of the jurors carefully as the photos made the rounds, trying to gauge reactions. One juror closed his eyes, two more covered their mouths. The foreperson made the sign of the cross. And yet, Dolores Baxter, a black woman in late middle age and a key bargaining chip in the battle for jurors, showed no expression at all as she examined the police photographs. Dec frowned uncertainly as he studied her broad implacable face, third from the left, second row.

Just at that moment, Dec was confronted unexpectedly with a minion of his own, a small note passed to him, scrawled in Portia's hand.

"Nice job for openers," it read. But it was the signature that made him smile—Pokey. He glanced up as Royal turned over the witness for cross-examination and Evans rose to his feet. Evans was a good, dedicated attorney, but not a courtroom star by anyone's definition. Nevertheless, Dec's smile did not fade as Evans pounced on the sheriff with a series of rapid-fire questions.

"Sheriff Glass, it's true that you and Mr. Royal are personally acquainted, is it not?"

"Yes, sir. I've known Mr. Royal for some time. Since our college days."

"I see," Evans went on. "Are you friends?"

Glass considered it. "Well, yes. In a manner of speaking."

Evans glanced up, his bald pate catching the light. "And what manner is that, Sheriff Glass? Do you see each other socially?"

"Not really. Not for a while, anyhow."

"So you're professional friends? Cronies?"

Royal's head shot up from his notes. "Objection!"

"Sustained. Mr. Evans, where is this going?"

Judge Raymond Johnstone looked up from his notes, peering over the glasses that perched dangerously close to the tip of his nose. Middle-aged, paunchy, slightly balding, Johnstone had presided over dozens of murder trials in his twelve years as Resident Circuit Court

Judge. A Columbia native, Johnstone was the product of an "old money" Republican banking family. He had spent the early years of his legal career defending insurance companies against malpractice claims. Though personally conservative, he had long been known as compassionate, thoughtful, and fair, publicly championing the rights of the poor to have access to adequate legal representation. Twice he had served on the Board of Directors of the Richland County Legal Services program. Dec had thanked his lucky stars when Johnstone was assigned to Wier's case.

"I'm trying to establish complicity between the law enforcement officials and the prosecution, Your Honor," Evans answered evenly. "I believe it may bear upon the defendant's cause."

"That's ridiculous!" Royal blustered. "The only complicity involved is keeping the laws that govern us all, Your Honor. The fact the sheriff and I attended the same college is completely irrelevant."

"Mr. Evans, I'll have to agree."

"Very well," Evans answered. "Sheriff Glass, I have a deposition here where a former deputy of yours has sworn that when Mr. Wier was arrested, he was wearing a pair of panty hose, an earring, and had on what appeared to be lipstick. Can you tell me, sir, why none of those things were recorded in your arrest reports?"

Glass flushed but his eyes never wavered from the attorney's face. "I wouldn't know," he answered easily. "I didn't write up that report."

"Who did?"

"Why it was Justin Chitwood. He was a deputy down at my office before he up and quit."

"I see," Evans went on. "What would it mean to you, Sheriff, if I told you that Mr. Chitwood has filed a copy of his original report with this court, and that in comparing the two documents we have discovered several discrepancies?"

Glass squinted. "How do you mean?"

"I mean that discrepancies of this kind could indicate other discrepancies, Sheriff Glass. I mean that if one of the deputies involved says the defendant is wearing a pair of hose when he's arrested and those hose aren't anywhere among the defendant's personal belongings, that might very well indicate that evidence had been suppressed in this trial." Evans went on brandishing the official reports. "There has been no hose found among Mr. Wier's personal effects." He glanced up, seemingly puzzled. "Why is that, Sheriff Glass?"

The sheriff did not appear to be especially perturbed by the question. "I can't say," he answered. "I'd just arrested a killer. I wasn't paying too much attention to Mr. Wier's undergarments."

A ripple of amusement swept through the spectators. Evans didn't bat an eye. "Yet your officers were apparently aware of the stockings, Sheriff. Even though you were not."

"I guess—"

"What happened to those stockings, Sheriff? Between the time Jimmy Wier was picked up and the time you sat down with him for questioning. One minute he is said to have had them on. Then, they disappear. What happened?"

"I don't know," Glass answered. "I told you, I never saw 'em. Why don't you ask Chitwood? Maybe he was trying to plant evidence. He put the whole works on computer anyway, didn't he? And everybody knows you can change that stuff every which way. Any time."

"Objection," Evans interrupted. "The witness is speculating."

"Sustained," Judge Johnstone intoned. "Sheriff, just confine yourself to answering the question, please."

Evans nearly smiled. "Sheriff, I'd like your opinion on something. Do you think that wearing panty hose could be considered relevant to the accused's mental state at the time of his arrest?"

"Objection," Royal called out. "Calls for speculation on the part of the witness."

"I asked for his opinion, Your Honor," Evans answered. "As a law enforcement official of some years' experience, I believe he is qualified to offer an opinion."

Johnstone sighed heavily. "Okay," he said. "Answer the question."

Glass faced the attorney, his eyes hard and unyielding. "I don't have any idea," he said.

Evans took his chair. "No further questions."

And so it went throughout the morning. The coroner took the stand to establish the time of death; Ed Derman, wearing a suit he reserved only for funerals, took the stand to verify the approximate time of the grocery delivery. An expert from the state lab went on for some time as to the variety and veracity of the forensic evidence—fiber matches, hair matches, and finally blood and semen matches.

Back in her corner, Portia listened to it all, drifting in and out of the testimony as she divided her attention among the various witnesses, her own sheaf of reports, and the cold anxiety that crowded her heart.

Though she knew from experience that the prosecution had all its ducks in a row, it didn't help that the facts and the statistics, paraded in such detail before the jury's eyes and ears, could so utterly indicate a man's guilt. She stared uneasily down at her sheaf of psychiatric reports. Jimmy Wier was guilty of the crime of murder. It was just that his guilt wasn't the whole story. And because of that, it was going to take more than facts to win this one.

Dec had known that going in, and that was why he'd found the wherewithal, at the last moment, to draw attention to his own ruined legs. It was why he'd found the courage to take the risk of comparing his own life to that of Jimmy Wier.

She sat back, glancing around the room, and thought she caught Alan Simpson's profile high up in the gallery. She couldn't be sure. Lulled by the ongoing drone of testimony, she found herself drifting back to the other night, Amy Goodsnow's words echoing in her mind. Talk about the child—just be that child. Only Amy hadn't known what she was asking—how much it would take for her to feel those emotions here, in this so terribly public place—what it would take for her to meet the eyes of each and every one of the jurors in that box and talk about that kind of pain. And do it in such a way that they would understand the child Jimmy Wier had been without making them afraid of all that he had become.

Somehow—some way—she was going to have to reach deep inside herself and find the courage to do just that when the bailiff called her name.

Twenty-six

● ●

WHEN THE COURT RECESSED for lunch, Portia searched the sea of faces flooding into the corridor for Declan Dylan, only to be sighted herself and confronted by a flurry of reporters.

"Dr. McTeague!" one of them shouted as she hustled through the throng. "Dr. McTeague! We've heard that Wier is a hermaphrodite. Is that true? Dr. McTeague! Do you care to comment on that issue? Dr. McTeague!"

Far down the hallway, caught in the light of a television crew, she saw Dec moving slowly toward the entrance. His profile stood out in sharp relief as he offered the usual no-comments, and the sight of her old friend, being escorted out into the daylight by the slim silhouette of none other than Amy Goodsnow, left her suddenly defeated.

"Dr. McTeague!" The clamor of voices around her rose in intensity. "As Wier's psychologist of record, what's your opinion of the prosecution's case? When will you testify, Dr. McTeague? Why did he do it, Doctor? Do you think he'll get the death penalty? Dr. McTeague!"

She pushed through them, desperate to get away, reaching the ladies' room at the far end of the hall just as Donny Royal exited the courtroom and the throng turned to follow him, like lemmings, out onto the courthouse steps.

She stood before the empty stalls, enjoying the sudden ring of silence in her ears. No matter how many cases she was involved in, no matter how many were lost or won, or called a draw, her sense of foreboding was always the same. The psychologist of record ran restless fingers through her hair, rehearsing for the hundredth time the words that would serve to tell the story of Jimmy Wier. She smoothed the perfect lapel of a dress bought off the rack at the Southpark Mall, and wondered about the image she would project into a courtroom already primed by the press for blood and revenge. What if Amy Goodsnow was wrong? What if the jurors would find her no easier to relate to than they ever had?

And yet, here alone in the deserted bathroom, she knew that Amy had been right about one thing at least. All the records and the facts and statistics were not the real story of Jimmy Wier's life. The real story was about a little boy, hurt and confused and in terrible pain, playing in a patch of sunlight all those years ago.

And as she walked out again into that now-deserted hallway, the heels of her shoes clicking against the floor, she thought about the infinite prisons of the mind. Hers was a dark box buried in a shallow grave back in Mississippi, and a promise, made so long ago, to keep a terrible secret. Jimmy Wier had a warden by the name of Bonnie Jean. The differences in their cases had served, somehow, to define them.

But there was no line between them. There was no line at all.

She caught sight of two male figures farther down the hall, heads together, deep in conversation. It was Donny Royal and Harry Falcone, so intent on what they were saying they seemed unaware of her approach. She edged closer, and backed into a doorway out of sight as their voices rose, echoing eerily in the deserted corridor.

"You're next up, Harry. I need you. I want you setting him up as being sane as you or me."

Falcone's voice was measured, almost calm in his reply. "I can't do that, Donny."

Royal's voice dropped menacingly. "Listen, Falcone, you've been paid to testify. And that means you say whatever I want you to say."

"I've been paid to evaluate a criminal," Falcone replied in the same measured tone. "You want me to give the results of that evaluation, I do it. You want me to be a party to a lynching, Royal, and I just won't play."

"What the fuck are you talking about?" Royal's voice dropped again.

And Harry Falcone's voice came back to the place where Portia was hidden, slow and measured, the words bringing a smile of sheer amazement to her face, as though she'd somehow become the solitary witness to a miracle.

"You've already lost, Donny," Falcone said. "Wier's sick. He's insane by every available definition of that term. And they will prove it. Hell, I can prove it, and haven't spent half the time with him that McTeague has."

"You'll pay for this, Falcone. I'll go after your license."

"You can't. Not unless you're willing to expose yourself. You may be willing to get up there today and commit professional suicide, Royal, but I'm not. And if you put me on that stand you better be willing to listen because the jury will be."

But at that moment, Portia was the one listening, still smiling widely, as Falcone's footsteps echoed down the corridor. After a few moments so did Donny Royal's, heading hastily in the opposite direction.

After the lunch recess, the trial reconvened at two o'clock that afternoon. Portia took a seat. She hadn't been able to find Dec during the recess to tell him what she'd overheard.

"You may call your next witness, Mr. Royal," the judge announced.

Portia pricked up her ears. According to the roster, the prosecution's next witness was Dr. Harry Falcone. She allowed herself a small inward sigh. Whatever his diagnosis of Wier, it was a pretty safe bet he hadn't come face to face with Bonnie Jean.

At the front of the courtroom, Donny Royal rose to his feet, looking first to the jury, then to the rest of the room with an open, almost benign expression. "The prosecution rests, Your Honor."

A collective gasp of surprise rose from the spectators. Royal held up a hand for silence. "I see no point in wasting the court's time and the taxpayers' money with further testimony, Your Honor. I prefer to let the facts of this case speak for themselves."

The lawyers for the defense put their heads together at the news. It was both an unexpected turn and a brilliant piece of courtroom strategy. It meant that Royal was trying to score with both jurors and voters by keeping his case short and sweet, all but guaranteeing a wave of public approval and lots of press coverage. It also meant he was saving his bigger guns for cross-examination and rebuttal. By forcing the defense to play their cards earlier than they'd planned, he was increasing his chances of a win. Above all, Portia knew, Falcone wouldn't testify.

Jimmy Wier, on the other hand, didn't even look up.

"Well," the judge replied, "as you wish, Mr. Royal. Mr. Evans, Mr. Dylan—is the defense ready to proceed?"

"We are, Your Honor," Dec answered. In truth, they weren't, but both lawyers would rather have lain down and expired than admit it, so Dec calmly rolled his chair in front of the witness box.

"The defense calls Dr. Portia McTeague."

Portia jumped at the sound of her own name, feeling every eye turned toward her as she made her way to the witness box in a stupor of apprehension.

Dec eyed her for a long moment after she was sworn in and seated.

"Dr. McTeague," he began mildly. "Please tell the court a little about yourself and your credentials."

He walked her through the basics of establishing her status as an expert, the two of them falling into the comfortable routine of question and answer that they both knew so well. She glanced at the jury now and again, long enough to establish that Dec had at least gotten his way in some respects. There were several black members among the panel of seven men and five women. Most appeared to be between thirty-five and sixty. That was good; while younger jurors tended to more liberal views, they also tended to push for quicker decisions.

"Now, Dr. McTeague, will you tell the court, please, how you came to be involved in this case?"

I was snookered into it by a lowlife lawyer, she thought. "I was contacted by the defense and asked if I would conduct a full psychological evaluation of their client, James B. Wier. His attorneys were concerned about his psychological state at that time, during the evaluation period, and about his psychological state at the time the offenses occurred."

"And were you able to evaluate him successfully?"

"I was able to arrive at a general clinical impression. An actual diagnosis took somewhat longer."

"Now, when you first started this case, you were well aware of the crimes attributed to the accused, were you not?"

"Yes," Portia answered. "I was familiar with both the police reports and with what psychological records were available through the South Carolina prison system."

Dec feigned surprise. "And is it usual practice for people charged with a crime to be referred for psychological evaluation by the prison system, Dr. McTeague?"

"No," she answered firmly. "It is not. Mr. Wier was referred initially because there was concern about his competence to stand trial."

"And what did those initial reports illuminate about the defendant's psychological state?"

"He was judged competent on two occasions and medicated with Benadryl, which is a drug that has sedative effects."

"And on your first consultation with Mr. Wier, what was your impression of his psychological state?"

Portia glanced at the ceiling, then toward Jimmy Wier, who was sitting motionless at the defense table, his head bent low.

"After meeting Mr. Wier," she went on after a moment, "I recommended that he immediately be evaluated for antipsychotic medication to improve his reality orientation, his psychomotor function, and his speech."

"And did he improve on this medication?"

"Dramatically. After two weeks, he became oriented, able to communicate, and showed no sign of the bizarre or repetitive movements he had displayed previously."

"Dr. McTeague," Dec went on in the same mild tone, "are you in the habit of recommending courses of antipsychotic medication for clients who are not psychotic?"

She couldn't help smiling a little as she shook her head. "No, sir, I am not."

"And in addition to the records you were familiar with at the outset, you used other sources to help form your opinion of Wier's psychological condition, did you not?"

"Yes. I used a variety of records that became available to me through the California state penal system at Atascadero. These records came from Mr. Wier's schools, his clinical experiences, and from various hospitalizations and treatments he underwent while incarcerated for six years in a sex offender program at Atascadero. And, of course, I relied on my own interviews with him."

"And how would you characterize Mr. Wier's psychological condition?"

Portia took a deep breath. "Put as simply as I can, Mr. Wier suffers from Dissociative Identity Disorder, a mental illness that is characterized by the development of an alternate or control personality as a result of the severe and repeated sexual and emotional abuse he suffered as a child and adolescent.''

Portia all but held her breath and shot an anxious glance in the jury's direction.

"Explain for the court, if you will, how a person might develop such a disorder.''

Portia wet her lips. "It's a kind of coping mechanism, really. When a little child is forced to grow up in an environment that is . . . crazy, that literally threatens his survival, it interferes with normal functioning. The child develops a way for his world to make sense.''

"Can you explain that further, Doctor?''

Portia took a long breath. "People—children—aren't born crazy, unless there's some organic condition. But when the people upon whom that child depends most for survival, for safety and for love, hurt and threaten and belittle that child—when the adults in the child's life are crazy—the child believes those adults, and learns from those adults. He has no choice. Their view is the only view of the world the child knows.''

"So you're saying Jimmy learned to be insane?''

"In a manner of speaking. As a little boy, Jimmy Wier had to find a way for his world to make sense. He had to develop a way to cope with the adults, specifically his adopted mother, so that he could survive.''

Dec's next question came softly. "Dr. McTeague, I want you to tell us, not in clinical terms now, but in human terms, just what it was like to be a child in Jimmy Wier's house.''

"Objection!'' Royal called out. "That question calls for conjecture on the part of the witness.''

The judge peered down at Royal from his position on the bench. "Mr. Royal, the witness has established herself as an expert. She's supposed to know how these things work. So let her tell us how they work, all right?''

Royal sank back in his chair, and from her place on the stand Portia caught the barest hint of Declan's smile. "Proceed, Doctor.''

"Jimmy Wier was adopted at the age of six months by a disturbed woman, herself the victim of childhood sexual abuse. Elizabeth Wier was raped and tortured repeatedly by the male members of her family and was committed to a mental institution sometime in her early adolescence. There she was sterilized because her relatives believed her to be mentally deficient. She married a man who gave her the name Elizabeth. Up until that time, she had never had one.

"The couple was given the infant by a neighbor. His adoptive mother told him that he was unloved by his real mother. Unwanted. That his real mother had left him on the adoptive mother's table like a sack of garbage. Jimmy's earliest memories of his adoptive mother are of a disturbed and abusive personality. Elizabeth told him from the time he could first remember that she loathed boys—that boys were dirty and disgusting and wanted only to hurt women. She would make fun of his genitals; she would display herself to him in a sexual manner and then punish him for responding by tucking his penis up between his legs, taping it down, and dressing him like a girl. She told him what a nice girl he would have made, and that she wished she had been able to get a daughter, but that she was stuck with him. I'm talking now about events that all happened before he was five years old. He's not yet begun school."

She paused and took a sip of water, aware of a sudden uncontrollable trembling throughout her body. "He was raped repeatedly, anally and orally, both by his mother and by her male friends, throughout his early childhood. He reports that his mother stuck broom handles, bottle necks, and other objects in his anus to stretch his body to accommodate anal entry by her male sexual partners. He also reports performing oral sex on men for money to buy food. After the departure of his adopted father, the family was destitute. He believes his adoptive mother was a prostitute, but he cannot be sure. He knows that he and his mother shared the same bed until he was twelve or thirteen years old. He suspects that he may have had sexual relations with his mother, but he is not sure."

Portia turned and looked at the jury. "We have to understand that this child is less than five years old. Think of your own children. Babies—toddlers—don't know the difference between right and wrong, they don't know the difference between reality and fantasy. Normal children believe in the tooth fairy—in Santa Claus. They have to be taught that those things aren't real. But Jimmy Wier never had any of those things to believe in. Imagine lying in your mother's arms and not knowing from one moment to the next if she's going to kiss you or burn you with a cigarette. Imagine getting up in the morning and not knowing if she would dress you like a boy or a girl. Imagine asking for something to eat and never knowing if you'll get fed. Imagine being told as a little child that boys were ugly and disgusting, and that your body, your genitals, were some kind of mistake. Think about just wanting to be held, to be touched, to feel safe, and knowing that a pat on the head meant your mother's boyfriend was going to rape you. Because the only time anyone noticed you was when they wanted to beat you or rape you or make you ashamed. Imagine what that does to a child. Try to pretend your own child was living in that terrible house, being told those terrible things. Try to imagine yourselves as children and think about what that would do to you."

Portia paused, suddenly, horribly aware of the tears rolling down her cheeks. "I'm sorry," she murmured. From his place at the table, she could see Jimmy staring at her, his blue eyes full of pity for them both.

The judge's face was solemn as he looked at her. "Dr. McTeague, do you want a recess?"

Portia shook her head. "No," she answered firmly. "I'm fine."

Dec's eyes shone with pride as he looked at her. "What did it do to Jimmy Wier, Doctor?" he asked her softly. "What did living in that house do to Jimmy Wier's mind?"

"He dissociated. He found a way to escape by creating another identity, someone who understood—someone who was stronger than he was, who could handle the abuse he couldn't handle. Someone who would fight to protect him when every adult person in his world only wanted to hurt him. As he went out into the world, away from his home, that personality came with him."

"Why is that, Doctor? Why was this alternate personality so essential once he was removed from that house?"

"Because it was what he had learned," she answered simply. "For the same reason that we all try to teach our kids things at home that they will be able to carry with them throughout their lives. His alternate personality didn't go away just because his circumstances changed. She had already become essential to his functioning."

"She?" Dec prompted.

Portia swallowed hard. "Because of the nature of the abuse that Jimmy Wier suffered, his control personality is a female identity who commands and controls his violent and sexual impulses. An identity who was, in my own opinion, responsible for the murders."

A murmur swept through the crowd. From the corner of her eye, Portia saw Amy Goodsnow slowly shake her head.

"Objection!" Royal cried out. "Nothing in the record indicates the presence of this so-called 'other personality.' Without some evidence, the witness is presenting mere heresay!"

Judge Johnstone frowned. "Overruled."

Dec shot Portia a small conspiratorial wink. "When you first met Mr. Wier, was he aware of having committed any crime?"

She shook her head and reached for a sip of water. "Not immediately. As I continued my sessions with him, he began to have vague memories of that day, but that's all. As we got nearer the actual events, his psychological condition began to deteriorate. That was when the alternate personality first revealed itself. She spoke with me and informed me that, in fact, she had committed the murders."

"Objection!" Royal bellowed from across the room. "This is the purest fantasy!"

"Overruled!" Johnstone shot back. "Sit down, Mr. Royal."

"Dr. McTeague, is it your opinion that Dissociative Identity Disorder is a serious enough condition for us to call Jimmy Wier insane?"

Portia did not hesitate. "Yes, it is."

"And is it also your opinion that Jimmy Wier"—Dec paused and pointed to the prisoner seated at the other side of the room—"that this man was not aware of his own actions at the time of the murders, and that his actions were, in fact, controlled by an alternate identity of which Mr. Wier is only very dimly aware?"

"Yes," Portia answered. "That is what I know."

"Thank you, Doctor. Is there anything else you'd like to add?" Dec's eyes were shining as he looked at her, sending a sudden flood of emotion through her body. He had so much courage, so much confidence—it was though he had never been afraid.

"Just that Jimmy's disorder—his mental illness—can be controlled with medication, with therapy. But he will never be normal in the sense that he will be free of this degree of personality damage."

The silence in the courtroom was punctuated once more by a wave of motions, coughing, and the rustling of three hundred bodies shifting in their chairs.

"Mr. Royal," the judge intoned. "Care to cross-examine this witness?"

Donny Royal rose to his feet, a small thin smile playing around his mouth. "Absolutely, Your Honor," he replied. "Absolutely."

He strode easily to the witness stand, coming closer to Portia than was usual, closer than was necessary. She could see a thin line of beard stubble where he'd missed a place on his neck shaving that morning, and though his proximity was doubtless meant to unnerve her, the sight of that stubble just under his chin was one she found curiously calming. Even Donny Royal could make a mistake. She searched his face for some sign, some indication of Falcone's defection. But there was none and she braced herself.

"All right then, Dr. McTeague," he began. "This . . . disorder you've been telling us about. It's very rare, isn't it?"

"Relatively rare, yes," she answered cautiously.

"And there's some controversy about whether it even exists at all, isn't there? Even among professionals such as yourself?"

"Yes, there is."

"Uh-huh," Royal murmured reflectively. "Well, all right then, presuming this rare disorder you describe actually exists in the first place, it still doesn't explain why, does it?"

Portia faced him squarely. "I'm not sure I understand the question."

"Why did Wier kill those old women, Doctor? Why did he tie them up and rape them and—"

"Objection!" Dec's voice rang out. "This calls for speculation on the part of the witness."

"Rephrase the question, please, Mr. Royal."

Royal merely looked bored. "I want you to tell us, in your own words, based upon these records here and your own interviews with the accused—I want you to explain just exactly why one person who has a hard time growing up doesn't ever kill anybody, and yet somebody else does. How does psychology explain that, Doctor?"

She took a long shuddering breath, keenly aware of the faces in the courtroom. "I can't speak for all psychologists," she replied slowly, "but there are any number of reasons. Individual personalities, circumstances, the degree of mental illness involved, even intelligence. They all play a part. As well as the fact that some people simply get help—the help they need—before they commit violent acts."

"But the fact is, some abused individuals turn out killers and some don't. Right?"

Portia clasped her hands together. This was the line of questioning she'd been dreading. And yet, she had no choice but to answer. "That's correct."

She paused and took another drink of water as waves of restless motion swept through the room, punctuated by uncomfortable coughs, throat clearings, and whispers. From his place at the defense table, Jimmy Wier looked up and met her eye.

Royal bared his teeth like some terrier smiling over a bone. "Wouldn't you say, Doctor, that the reason is because some people choose to kill and some don't?"

Portia thought long and hard over her answer. "We're all individual people. Some people might not kill, but they might rape or be raped. Some people might allow themselves to be hurt rather than hurt someone else. Every personality will develop coping mechanisms for dealing with abuse and pain. Those mechanisms are as different as people are. In Jimmy's case, his abuse was so severe that his personality fragmented. That was the only way he could cope. A normal child in normal circumstances might develop an imaginary friend. That's normal. But Jimmy had to have more than a friend, even when he was very young."

"Your Honor, please instruct the witness to answer the question," Royal interjected nastily.

Portia stiffened in her chair. "If I haven't answered adequately, it's because there is no single answer. It's like asking why some people get cancer, or heart disease—why some people die of those things, but others don't. Yes, there are causes. And we know some of them, but we don't have all the answers, not by any means."

Royal backed toward his table, but never lost his oily composure. "You don't know why some abused individuals will commit the act of murder, and yet you're willing to stand up and face the good people in this courtroom and tell us you are certain you know the reason why that man there is accused of doing what he did?"

"Yes," Portia answered. "I am."

"But how can you be sure, Doctor? How can you know that Jimmy Wier was not aware of his actions that night at Lila Mooney's house? How can you be sure? If you, by your own admission, don't have all the answers, what makes you so sure you have the answer for that?"

There was a short pause. She waited for Dec to object and the objection did not come. He was bent low over a sheet of yellowed paper, oblivious to the beating she was taking on the stand.

"Because I asked him," she managed finally. "Because I asked Mr. Wier to trust me. I offered him help when nobody else did. He told me the truth because he wanted that help. Because he needed it. And I believe him."

"So you're the answer to Mr. Wier's cry for help, are you?" Royal turned to the jury as if to see how much of this preposterous story they might actually swallow.

"Why didn't he get some help before you came along?" he asked. "Why didn't he tell somebody else? You two have some kind of special rapport or something?"

"Objection." Portia was startled to see that Evans had raised the objection, not Dec. In fact, Dec was nowhere to be seen. Nor was Amy Goodsnow.

"Overruled," the judge answered. "Answer the question."

Portia drew a deep breath. "He was just a little boy . . ." Her voice broke, but she went resolutely on. "For most of his life, he didn't know things were supposed to be different. He didn't know there was any other way. And the world—the rest of the world— didn't want to see what was happening to him. He didn't get help because nobody knew he needed it. And if they did, they didn't try to give it to him."

Her voice dropped a notch, and she stared for a moment at her hands. "You see, Jimmy had given up. The world was just like his mother said it was. The only reality he knew was crazy. And knowing that made him insane, and the only way for him to cope was to try and hide his insanity from everybody else. That's what his alter was for. That's where he kept all his craziness."

Her eyes searched the room for a long moment before coming to rest on Jimmy Wier's face.

"But why didn't he get this help, Doctor? His records show he has been in various treatment programs. Seems like any competent psychiatrist might have been able to see what you did. Unless, of course, you only saw what he wanted you to. Unless you were simply manipulated."

She ignored the implication. "From what I can determine, Mr. Wier has never been treated for his principal disorder. Mr. Wier is a schizophrenic. The other disorders that have been specified in his records are symptoms of his core disorder. Without proper treatment for the disorder itself, he may improve from time to time but will always eventually deteriorate under certain circumstances and stresses. There's just a whole lot he'll never be able to handle."

Royal took a long, almost leisurely breath. "I guess that brings us back around, doesn't it, Doctor? Why did Jimmy Wier kill Lila Mooney and Constance Bennet?"

"Objection! Mr. Royal continues to ask for speculation on the part of the witness, Your Honor." Evans's bald pate was red with indignation.

"Overruled," sighed Johnstone. "You may answer if you know. Mr. Royal, let's move along now. You're trying my patience."

"The alter took over. He—they—were killing his mother," Portia announced in a clear voice. "Jimmy's hatred for her was such that he felt impelled to fix it so she couldn't have any more babies that could be hurt the way he had been hurt. He removed her female organs because Elizabeth Wier had been sterilized as a young girl. But Jimmy Wier had two mothers to kill: the one who bore him and the one who raised him. He hated them both for what they had done to him. He believed at that moment that those two women were his mothers. We know that was a delusion, but Jimmy didn't know it. He needed to see them die."

For the first time, Portia allowed herself a small smile. "I think that fact can only help the court to understand that Jimmy Wier did not know what he was doing when he murdered those two women."

Johnstone sat back in his chair, his face troubled. "Mr. Royal?" he inquired.

Royal's face had gone oddly pale, clearly aware of the damage that had been done. "I have no further questions at this time," he offered in a carefully nonchalant tone. "Given the hour, I would move for a recess, Your Honor. Let's all start fresh tomorrow."

Johnstone concurred. "You may step down then, Doctor. And this court will recess until nine o'clock tomorrow morning."

Portia rose on rubbery legs as the judge left the bench and Jimmy was led away in shackles. She made her way toward the defense table, trying to catch Evans's eye.

"Hey," he said, placing a hand on her shoulder. "You were something else up there today. Good job."

"Thanks," she replied distantly. "But tomorrow's going to be worse. Where's Dec?"

"Not sure," Evans answered. "They brought him a message. I think he went off to chase down that witness Goodsnow dug up."

Portia's eyes went wide. "Chitwood? You mean they actually got him to respond to the subpoena?"

Evans sighed wearily. "Actually, I don't think they did. I think he was coming and then punked out. That's what sent them running this afternoon. But hey," he said at Portia's crestfallen expression, "for what it's worth, my money's on you."

"Till tomorrow anyhow," she answered ruefully. "Royal's not through with me yet."

The next day dawned gray and rainy, blanketed in an odd chill that Portia could not seem to shake from her bones. She arrived a few minutes late and had no time to talk to Dec before the session began, though she was grateful to see he was present. Amy Goodsnow, however, was nowhere in sight.

Portia hurried to the front of the room as her name was called, catching another all-too-familiar profile out of the corner of her eye, one that sent a little flutter of excitement through her as she made her way to the witness chair. Alan Simpson was seated in the second row, near the aisle.

"I will remind the witness that she is still under oath. Mr. Royal, you may proceed."

Royal offered her a slow, sly smile as he approached the stand. "Dr. McTeague, we all heard you testify yesterday that the defendant, Mr. Wier, was the victim of childhood sexual abuse that resulted in his becoming, in your opinion, mentally ill. Is that correct?"

"Yes, it is." Portia eyed him warily, uncertain of what to expect. Royal was puffed up like an adder, ready to strike.

"I see. And you maintain that, because of that abuse, he developed a split personality disorder and that this other personality came out and killed Lila Mooney and Constance Bennet. Is that correct?"

"In a manner of speaking," she answered slowly. "I maintain that the alter was in control of Mr. Wier's personality at the time the murders were committed."

"Fine. Now, Doctor, tell me something if you would. Are you schizophrenic?"

Somewhere in the back of her mind, a red flag went up. "No, sir—"

"Are you suffering from this"—he glanced down at his notes—"Dissociative Identity Disorder?"

"No—"

"Objection!" Dec's voice rang out. "What is this about?"

Raymond Johnstone stared down at them. "I'd like to find that out for myself," he answered. "Overruled. Mr. Royal, you may proceed, but do get to the point."

Royal's eyes were like daggers as they caught and held her own. "Dr. McTeague, have you ever been raped?"

She glanced away, thunderstruck.

"Objection!" roared Dec. "The doctor's personal history is completely irrelevant to the matter at hand."

Royal lifted his hands. "Your Honor, if it is the witness's hypothesis that rape makes people schizophrenic, I think her own history is very relevant. And I have here a police record from nineteen seventy-six, stating that the witness was the victim of a sexual assault in December of that year. It's a matter of public record."

Dec wheeled sharply around to come up at Royal's elbow. "Let me see that!"

"Gentlemen, approach the bench." Johnstone's voice dropped a discreet notch as he turned to address the District Attorney.

"Mr. Royal, this is highly irregular."

"Perhaps, Your Honor, but I believe it is relevant nonetheless. The witness's own history has certainly influenced her testimony in this case."

"So what?" Dec rejoined. "Your Honor, this is preposterous. To ask a professional woman to resurrect this sort of incident is beyond low, it's—"

Portia's voice interrupted their angry whispers. "Never mind," she hissed. The three men turned to look at her, startled. She met Dec's eyes, then Royal's, and at last searched out those of Alan Simpson.

"I have nothing to be ashamed of," she told all of them at once. "I'm comfortable answering the question if His Honor would instruct me to do so."

"All right," Johnstone intoned. "But I warn you, Mr. Royal, you'd better not belabor this."

Royal paced a small circle in front of her. "Dr. McTeague, I'll repeat the question. Have you ever been raped?"

"Yes. I was in college. I was attacked on my way home late at night."

"So you were a victim, Doctor? Just like you say our Mr. Wier was a victim?"

She faced him coldly, knowing suddenly where this was going. "Yes, I was. Mr. Wier, of course, suffered abuse that was much more serious. And his abuse began when he was a tiny child. The degree of damage would be much more severe for him."

"What kind of irreparable personality damage did you suffer as a result of that attack?"

"Objection." Dec, having returned to his place, wheeled around the table to register his protest.

"Sustained. You want to rephrase that, Mr. Royal?"

"Did you suffer any psychological repercussion as a result of that attack?"

Portia looked out over the crowd. "Of course I did. But I managed to get therapy to help me through it."

"So the damage you suffered as a result of this attack was not irreparable, was it?"

"I hope not."

"And your rape did not result in permanent psychological damage?"

You bastard, she thought, cut to the chase. "I'm not sure what you're asking me, Mr. Royal. I don't think it's possible to ever completely overcome the scars created by that kind of trauma. An individual can learn to function in spite of those scars."

"So, if you did it—if you learned to function—why couldn't our Mr. Wier?"

"As I tried to make clear in my earlier testimony," she replied in a voice gone cold with anger, "Mr. Wier never got the necessary help. His personality damage was far more pervasive than mine, and I was fortunate enough to have options he did not have."

Royal continued smoothly. "Do you carry a certain amount of rage at your attacker, Doctor? To this day?"

She faltered a moment. "Yes, I suppose I do."

"But you didn't go out and find and kill him, did you?"

"Objection! Not only have we addressed all this yesterday, Mr. Royal is badgering the witness."

"Sustained. Mr. Royal, please."

Donny Royal smiled briefly and tried not to gaze at the light from the video camera whirring just above his head on the far wall. "Very well, Your Honor. Dr. McTeague, would you say that your own history influenced your choice of psychology as a profession?"

"Yes, I would." You idiot, she added silently.

"Would you say that your own background of rape influenced your diagnosis of Mr. Wier's condition as well as the diagnoses of many others you've treated?"

"No, I would not."

"No?" Royal inquired. "Are you sure? Are you certain you're not viewing all such cases through your own psychological lens, Dr.

McTeague? Trying to win victories for them that you couldn't win for yourself?"

Portia hesitated, caught off guard by the question. She gave Royal a long penetrating stare. And then she smiled, inspired suddenly by a knowledge that she had carried within her, something she had not been aware she knew up until that moment. And her fears fell away.

"I'm able to relate to some cases, including Mr. Wier's case, on the basis of common experience. I can offer to share his pain because in some ways I have experienced that same pain myself."

And from somewhere, high in the gallery, came a little ripple of applause.

"Order please." Johnstone turned to face Donny Royal, something very like contempt showing in his eyes. "Mr. Royal, are you through?"

"Yes, Your Honor," Royal answered. "Yes I am. I have no further questions."

Portia looked for Alan as the crowds flooded into the corridors for the noon recess, but couldn't catch sight of him. Dec reached her in his wheelchair just as she was turning to leave, making her slow way to a side exit. She didn't want to deal with the press at that moment.

"Hey," Dec began in a tone that belied his concern. "You okay?"

Portia fixed her eyes on some point far away and smiled ruefully. "Yeah, I guess."

"Pretty tacky move, that," Dec went on. "Want me to beat him up for you?"

"Can't argue with the public record, Dec. Royal didn't find anything somebody else couldn't have found. Besides," she shrugged, "it's okay. Not completely, maybe, but okay. I just hope that little circus in there this morning helped Jimmy's case, that's all."

"You sure?"

"Yeah," she said, smiling bleakly down at him. "But what about Chitwood? Is he coming?"

Dec averted his eyes and sighed. "I sent Amy up there to talk to him. And I gave it my best shot over the phone. But I don't know. He's scared."

"Dec—" Portia began, knowing how much the ex-deputy's testimony could mean to the case.

He flashed a weak imitation of his presidential grin, one that did little to hide how discouraged he was. "Look," he said after a moment, "you've been through the mill. Go home. Take a couple of days off or something. Bake cookies. See your kid. You've heard all of it before, anyway."

"You sure you don't need me here?" she asked, tempted by the offer and yet torn.

For some reason he refused to meet her eyes. "It'll be all right," he told her. "I'll call if anything changes."

A long slow parade of defense testimony and witnesses filled the next two days. Melanie Durant, a former doctor from Atascadero, even one of the Sawtelle brothers flown in from California, freshly shaved and in a suit purchased for him by Declan Dylan's seemingly bottomless defense fund. Alan testified as to his role in the discovery of Jimmy's background and criminal history. Together they made a convincing case for Wier's insanity. And still, on the eve of closing arguments, no one knew if it would be enough.

On Thursday morning Donny Royal presented his closing remarks. True to his word, he kept it brief, pausing to deviate from the facts only long enough to mention that his expert had never even been called because there was no point in further stating the obvious— Jimmy Wier was sane, sane enough to make choices, sane enough to know right from wrong, and sane enough to pause to rob Lila Mooney after he had killed her, proving that the acts were premeditated and duly planned.

Thursday afternoon, Dec, with deep lines of strain and fatigue etched in his face, addressed the jury in his closing remarks. Like Royal, he kept them brief and to the point.

"Jimmy Wier is not sane, ladies and gentlemen. He was not sane at the time of the murders and he is not sane now. We are all charged here with a great responsibility, and yet, that is not to define the line between sanity and insanity, or to draw a boundary between yourselves and the unfortunate man accused of this crime. Because each and every one of you, had you been subjected to the tortures that he was, would suffer the damage same as he has. Maybe you wouldn't have a split personality, maybe you wouldn't have killed. But you would not be sane, you would not be competent, you would not be able to distinguish right from wrong. Had you or your child or any other child been raised as Jimmy Wier was raised, you or that child would be equally and irrevocably damaged.

"And so I can only remind you of that, ladies and gentlemen of the jury, as we bring the first phase of this trial to a close. And remind you also that you are charged with a rare and meaningful responsibility as you face deliberations in this case. That responsibility is not to divide us further, one from another, it is not to draw a line between yourselves and Jimmy Wier. Rather it is to recognize that we are the same underneath, that our development and our emotions and our ability to know right from wrong or good from evil, rest upon many things that we take for granted. Values that were taught to us and values that we teach our children. Those are values Jimmy Wier knew nothing about.

"Your responsibility now is to extend a measure of justice to one of our own—a measure of mercy. There is guilt in this case, there is responsibility. But it is not all Jimmy's. We share that guilt and that responsibility. We share it because we live in a world that raises new Jimmys all the time. And we turn away. Don't turn away, ladies and gentlemen. Not this time."

Twenty-seven

● ●

THERE WAS NOTHING to do now—nothing but wait. Friday was as brilliantly sunny as Thursday had been gray, and Portia headed out to the Volvo after getting Alice off to school, enjoying the balmy breeze and the sweet scents of the coming autumn. The radio said there was a hurricane moving up the coast and she felt the excitement of the approaching storm deep in her limbs, despite the glorious morning. She slid behind the wheel and drove slowly out of Dilworth toward the old Victorian house at the edge of downtown. It seemed to her as if Sophie had been gone for months, rather than just a week, as if the days and hours she had lived since their last meeting had taken place in some other part of the world, one that was brutally removed from the part she shared with Sophie Stransky.

And yet, she thought as she stopped for a traffic light, now—more than ever before—it was time to unite those parts of her world. Time to bring together those elements of her life that had seemed so disparate it had been impossible to reconcile them. All that had changed, beginning with the dark memory that had surfaced in the prison elevator, through her emotionally wrenching testimony on Jimmy's behalf. And finally, even through the spiteful implications of Donny Royal's cross-examination. She had told the truth; she had acknowledged being the victim of a sexual assault in a courtroom full of three hundred curious faces. She had even seen the headlines of the past week, screaming tales of the psychologist with the murky, troubled past.

She parked near the curb and made her way up Sophie's walk, where marigolds lined the borders in yellow and gold rows, Portia knew she could only be thankful it had been so easy. For what Donny Royal had discovered was only a glimmer of the truth. There were harder truths than that buried in her past. And it was time to face them, too.

She rang the bell and waited, just as Sophie came around the corner from the garden, wearing a floppy straw hat to keep off the sun and carrying a pair of shears.

"I thought I heard you drive up, my dear," she greeted Portia warmly. "Come, let's go around to the garden, shall we?"

Portia followed her down the steps and back to another of the many surprises in and around Sophie's house and office. For the backyard was planted almost entirely with a riotous sort of garden, of roses and sunflowers and zinnias, and hollyhocks all blooming wildly on both sides of a brick walk that ended in a gazebo grown over with a sort of a grapevine.

Sophie turned to her. "Do you mind if we talk out here?" she asked. "I have a great weakness for my garden, I must confess. With the cold weather coming, I think we ought to enjoy it while we can, don't you?"

Portia heartily agreed. "After the courthouse, this is like a vacation."

They settled themselves easily on the cushioned benches inside the gazebo, and the sounds of the city disappeared. Portia listened to the wayward warbling of a nearby songbird.

"I was sorry to hear you'd been called away, Sophie. For you, I mean," Portia began clumsily. "Was it—anyone close?"

Sophie smiled sadly. "My brother," she answered. "And no, we were not close. As we all know, sometimes circumstances prevent families from closeness. Still, he was my brother, so I went. But never mind that," Sophie went on, smoothly steering the conversation away from herself and back to her client. Her dark eyes were serious. "How are you? I've been following the trial."

Despite herself, Portia smiled ruefully. "Then you've doubtless heard about the scandal surrounding a twenty-year-old rape," she replied. "It was headline news."

"I did," Sophie said mildly, worrying the petals of a nearby blossom. "So? You want to talk about it?"

Portia leaned into the seat cushion. "There's nothing much to say," she began. "I was in college. It was late at night. I was alone crossing the common. A boy I knew from a seminar came at me from behind. He was wearing a ski mask. He dragged me into some bushes. I didn't scream, I didn't fight. I didn't feel anything."

"Did you get counseling?"

Portia smiled oddly. "I'd already been in counseling, Sophie. But yes, I did. The women at the rape crisis center on campus talked me into pressing charges. And that's what happened." Portia paused, lost in the memory, her eyes far away.

"You know, I think that was the first time I ever testified on a witness stand. That's funny, isn't it? And they tore me apart. I was good-looking, so I asked for it. I was sexually active, so I was a tramp. The boy's family was rich, powerful. So was mine, but I was the one who was humiliated."

"I'm sorry," Sophie replied gently.

"Don't be. You have to understand . . . something. Something about me."

"What? My dear, what must I understand?"

Portia rose to her feet and began to pace restlessly, wrapping her arms around her body as if suddenly taken with the cold. "As terrible as that experience was, it was a major step for me, charging that boy with rape. It was horrible, yes. Humiliating. But that was the last time I have been raped in my life. The last time. But it wasn't the first, Sophie, not by a long shot."

Sophie closed her eyes in empathy and nodded. "You've carried this around with you a long time, Portia. Tell me."

"I honestly thought I had forgotten, you know? For a long, long time. I knew things had happened to me, but I thought I knew what they were. I thought I had it sorted out."

Portia looked at Sophie and she nodded. "Yes . . ." she urged.

Portia raised her hands helplessly. "But I didn't—I didn't know everything that had happened. I didn't feel anything. Not until last week. I got trapped in an elevator during a power failure at the prison." Her rush of words stopped as suddenly as they had begun.

"I grew up in Mississippi. Old family, fine Southern stock. Full of secrets, lots of social standing. We lived in the biggest house in the county. My father was a very rich, very weak, alcoholic. My mother—

my mother was a beautiful, bored social climber who married for money. They didn't love each other and they didn't love me. I was raised by nannies and governesses and riding instructors. I was this—perfect—stupid, shallow little addition to the family tree. I was born to become a member of the Junior League. I even won a little girls' beauty contest."

Portia laughed harshly, painfully, as she went on. "And then, when I was eleven and he was fourteen, my cousin started raping me."

Portia began to cry hoarsely, her sobs echoing out over the garden. "I didn't know . . . anything. I didn't really know what was happening to me." After long minutes, she paused to wipe her nose and eyes, fumbling for a tissue in her handbag.

Sophie listened, her face lined with concern. It had been so long in coming, there was nothing to do now but let it come.

"It was in a sort of barn. One of the outbuildings on our property. There was this box built into the floor. Shallow, very cramped. So dark. It had been used in the slave days. He called it a punishment box—a killing box. They threw slaves in there when they tried to run away. Sometimes for days. Some of them died in there, I know it. It smelled . . . like death. My cousin raped me and threw me in there and made me promise not to tell anyone. He kept me there for hours . . . I don't know. But I never told. I don't know why." Portia sighed and looked out over the garden. "It went on for years. All through high school. We went to the same dances, saw the same people. And he was always there. He was like me—privileged, handsome. He gave me to his friends like a party favor. I'd get drunk or high on something and I'd do it. Anything with anybody, any time, anywhere."

Portia met Sophie's bright eyes for a long moment. "They called me 'Pass-Around Portia.' I think the whole town knew, everybody except my parents—my family, his family. I couldn't tell anyone, you know? Because, well, because there wasn't anyone to tell." She glanced up, meeting Sophie's eyes. "In my senior year I got pregnant. I was so out of it, I didn't even know. Not for a long time. Not until it was too late. When I told my parents, they wrote me a check for ten thousand dollars. I took it. And I never went back."

Portia bent her head, tears falling unheeded into her lap. "I don't know if it was his. I've never been sure. But I knew I could not keep that child. Not if there was even a chance it was his. I was afraid I might do something . . . terrible—if it was his. I gave it up. I didn't want to see it, didn't want to hold it in my arms. I've always thought that made me . . . deficient somehow. I pushed that baby away. Just like I push everyone away. But I couldn't—you understand? I—just—couldn't—"

She bent double then, her fiery hair falling over her knees as she rocked back and forth in agony, weeping uncontrollably. And the silent flowers fell witness to her pain.

"You felt what you needed to feel," Sophie interjected sadly when Portia had quieted somewhat. "You cannot go back and do it over. You can't make the decision over again. You were a teenager, Portia. Not an adult. You have to start to forgive yourself for the things you could not know."

Portia breathed deeply of the soft, sweet air. She paused for another long moment, fingering a clump of ripening grapes in her hand. "It's funny, how this all came together. I can't explain it."

Sophie leaned forward. "How do you mean?"

The younger woman shook her head wearily. "This trial, these memories. I listen to myself and it's like I'm listening to Jimmy. To so many others. I always thought I was different, somehow—luckier, maybe. Smarter. But I'm not, am I?"

"You're the same in the sense that we are all the same—we suffer the same emotional pain, the same problems."

"It's so strange," Portia went on, exhausted, but strangely relieved. "On some level, I was looking for that sameness. It's as though I got involved in this kind of work because . . ." Her eyes were dark and troubled as she stared out over the garden.

"Because why?" Sophie prompted gently.

"Because maybe I relate to people like Jimmy Wier better than I relate to normal people. Maybe I'm willing to look at cases like his because they make my own problems recede. They make me feel . . . cured. And I can go right on pushing people away, because of my work."

Sophie shook her head. "Oh, my dear, you've come so far in such a short time. You've revealed so much. Back up a little bit. You've just opened a lot of old wounds. You've only just started to deal with some of your own pain. You don't have to know what it means yet."

Portia uttered a long sigh. "I don't know, Sophie," she said. "I just know that it was only when I allowed myself to experience Jimmy's pain . . . emotionally, that I could allow myself to experience some of my own. He made me ready, somehow, to face myself. Back there in that elevator."

Sophie's bright birdlike eyes were fixed on a point somewhere out in the garden.

"What are you thinking?" Portia asked.

"I was thinking of a passage from a book I read again recently. A book of wisdom. I was listening to you and a particular phrase from it came to mind." She turned and faced Portia, her eyes burning with some secret understanding. "It says that we are all teachers. And what we teach is what we have to learn. So we teach it over and over again until we learn it. Do you understand?"

Portia looked down at her hands. "Yes," she responded after a moment. "I think I do."

"So. One part of our work ended today, I think. And another has begun. Do something for me, won't you? For next time?"

Portia looked at her with tired, swollen eyes. "What?"

"Read Portia's great speech from *The Merchant of Venice*. You were named for her, I think." Sophie smiled gently. "She was a spokesperson for mercy. And so are you. She recommended forgiveness, and so do you. Maybe that is your job as a teacher, Portia. To teach us all about mercy. And maybe that is what you need to learn as well. How to forgive yourself."

Portia stood to leave, anxious in some unnamable way to return from her past—and move into the future.

At the last moment, she turned and saw that Sophie had a worried expression.

"What is it?" Portia asked.

Sophie dismissed the question with a little wave of her hand.

"Nothing," she answered. "I just wanted to say—good luck. With your Mr. Wier, I mean. I hope it goes well."

Twenty-eight

• •

T WO BLOCKS from Sophie's house, Portia's car phone beeped, and Lori's voice came gravely over the wire. "I've been calling all over," she began.

"What is it? Is there an emergency?"

Portia could hear Lori's sharp intake of breath on the other end. "Dylan's office called. You better get down to the courthouse in Columbia. They reconvene at one sharp. The jury sent word. They're coming back."

Portia hung up. So soon, she thought wildly. How could they be back so soon? They'd only received instruction that morning. What had it been, one hour, two hours of deliberation? God, that was barely enough time to go over the paper. She swung the car into the choked lanes leading onto the interstate, her mind senselessly repeating the words in a kind of mantra of anxiety. The jury is back. The jury is back the jury is back.

She drove wildly, thankful for the unseen guardian that kept her from a wreck. She had to be there—for Jimmy, for Dec. For all of those who had worked so hard and so long on this case. And she drove and drove and tried to believe it was not lost. She tried to believe the twelve people on that panel had, just this one time, seen what was so obvious. That they had seen it and voted—just this once—not guilty by reason of insanity.

The area in front of the courthouse was clogged with the curious as she parked the car and ran across the square, sweating heavily in the tropical depression that hung over the Carolinas like a blanket. The hurricane was coming, she thought wildly. Could it really be as simple as that? Had they voted just to get it over with? To get home before the storm came?

She pushed through the crowds, oblivious to the cameras flashing in her face. The next day, a number of them would carry the same shot—a photo of her, disheveled and puffy-eyed, elbowing her way through the crowd: Psychologist Weeps at Verdict, the captions would say.

Only Portia didn't know that yet.

She found Dec outside the courtroom, a worried little line etched between his brows.

"Dec, for God's sake! How could this happen? How could they come back so soon?" He studied her, searching her eyes for answers to all the same questions. Wordlessly, he took her hand. "Portia, listen. We think they made a deal, and if they did—"

But he was never able to finish his sentence, for just at that moment the doors to the courtroom opened wide and they were all but run over in the rush to get a seat.

"Pokey," Dec began, lifting her hand to his lips for the barest breath of an instant. "Don't worry, it'll be all right. Either way. It'll be all right." He let go of her hand and left her standing there, bewildered, lost in the crush of people.

The bailiff announced the judge a few moments later, and then the jury filed in. "Mr. Foreman," the judge asked, "has the jury reached a verdict?"

"We have, Your Honor."

"May I see it, please?"

The paper was passed from one hand to another, opened, read, and folded again. Portia, from her place at the back of the courtroom, could only fix her eyes on the back of Jimmy's head as he sat at the defendant's table, big and boneless-looking as he waited, along with the rest of them, for what would come.

"Will the defendant please rise?"

Jimmy loomed from his place at the table, and Portia felt a little shiver go coursing down her back.

"Mr. Foreman, please read the verdicts."

The foreman's tenor rang out, high and self-conscious as he read the verdicts.

"As to the charge of first-degree kidnapping, we find the defendant, James B. Wier, guilty as charged."

"As to the two counts of rape in the first degree, we find the defendant guilty as charged."

"As to the two counts of assault with a deadly weapon, we find the defendant guilty as charged."

"As to the two counts of murder in the first degree—

"We find the defendant guilty as charged."

The foreman sat down, not looking at anything. And the silence in the room was deafening. After a long pause, the judge cleared his throat. "Thank you, ladies and gentlemen of the jury."

He took a long moment before he spoke again, as if he were too stunned to speak.

"James B. Wier, you have been found guilty of the crimes of which you are accused. Do you have anything you wish to say?"

Jimmy raised his huge head, and looked around the courtroom. And as she watched him, Portia knew that it was not Jimmy at all—it was that other.

"Very well," the judge continued. "As you know, the state of South Carolina requires that we move next into the sentencing phase of this trial. Sentencing hearings shall convene one week from this day on the morning of—"

Portia never heard the rest. From her place at the back of the courtroom, she simply stopped listening.

As the courtroom doors swung open, she moved with the rest of the throng like a sleepwalker, flashbulbs popping in her face. As the press struggled for position near the doors and on the courthouse steps, she ducked through a doorway to avoid them, and found herself back in the courtroom. Two prison guards were flanking the huge figure of Jimmy Wier, ready to take him away. He looked as though he were holding court for the small congregation of lawyers that moved around him, Dec and Evans and Amy Goodsnow and even Donny Royal, who was moving up to the defense table, smiling and offering to shake someone's hand. She pushed her way from the back of the room toward Jimmy, straining against the tide of bodies trying to get through. She had to see him to say something, anything, to offer him comfort on this terrible day.

Something was wrong. She stared at him and the guards, at the little audience of lawyers, and she knew it was wrong even before he saw her coming. Even before he lifted his great head in her direction and fixed her with that terrifying gaze. Even before she saw that Jimmy was laughing.

It was like a dream. Her tired mind registered what it was in the few short steps it took to reach him. But there was not even time to give a name to the thing she knew had possessed that body. She could only push the others aside as she ran toward him, as she screamed for Jimmy and was answered with a bellow of rage.

And it was like a dream when she saw the flash of silver slipped from a sleeve even as the guards piled on the prisoner, attempting to restrain him, their blackjacks and pistols aimed at his head. But it was no dream when that blade met her flesh in the single instant before they got him to the ground, leaving a long thin wound that bubbled bright with blood.

Then the whole world went spinning with shouts and warnings. Portia turned, staggered long enough to see Donny Royal's mouth fall open with surprise, and fell to her knees. Somebody caught her, then the world spun again and faded into darkness. And somewhere in the darkness Bonnie Jean screamed.

Twenty-nine

· ·

T HE DEFENSE calls Portia McTeague."
She made her way slowly up the aisle, conscious of
hundreds of pairs of eyes upon her as she took the witness stand,
swearing the oath with her left hand, as her right was bound up in
bandages and a dark length of sling. Wier had nicked an artery, neces-
sitating quite a few stitches, but other than that, the witness appeared
entirely intact as she settled herself easily in her chair. The sentencing
hearing had been plodding along for days as jurors heard evidence of
mitigating circumstances.

She glanced around. Jimmy sat like a statue in his place at the
defense table. Shackled with his hands to his waist, his legs to the
chair. His chains made an eerie sound as he turned to face her, his eyes
miserable and sad. She smiled at him, letting him know it was all right.

Declan looked up at her, trying to reassure her with his eyes. "Now,
Dr. McTeague. Everyone in this courtroom knows you were attacked
by the defendant on the day the initial verdict was passed down. The
circumstances have been in all the papers and on the television news.
There's no point at all in going over it again."

"No," she agreed. "There isn't."

"And the jurors here have had a chance to go over your expert
credentials and your expert testimony. I think they're smart enough
people to understand the connection between the defendant's state of
mind and the crimes themselves." Dec laced his fingers together under his chin. "But there's something I don't understand. You have

yourself been attacked by this person—this monster," he went on. "He's clearly dangerous. And yet, you're recommending mercy in this instance. You'd like to see him hospitalized rather than executed, is that right?"

"Yes," she answered, smiling a little. "I don't know how I could be who I am and recommend anything else."

"Why is that?"

"Because Jimmy Wier is sick. He is insane. And if he is a monster, it's because he was made a monster. By his family, by the system, and by this society. By anyone who even suspected what was happening to him and turned the other way. Nothing he has done changes that."

Dec's face shown with pride. "Thank you, Doctor. Thank you for being with us today."

"Mr. Royal?"

Donny Royal allowed himself a long look at the jury box, only to meet the eyes of a middle-aged black woman, third from the left, second row. She lifted her chin defiantly as she stared down the prosecutor, her eyes blazing, her mouth set in an intractable line. And for a moment Portia watched along with everyone else as the plump middle-aged juror and Donny Royal engaged in a silent battle. It was clear from her expression what he could do with a death penalty.

All at once, the prosecutor looked away. He had lost. A death sentence required a unanimous vote. And, looking at Dolores Baxter for those few silent moments, he knew it would never come.

He glanced back around the courtroom as if he had suddenly realized they were all still there.

"No questions," he mumbled and sat down.

Portia stepped down and made her way toward the back of the room. She was about to leave when Alan Simpson, from his place on the aisle, gently pulled her into the seat beside him. "Stick around," he murmured. "You're not going to want to miss this."

"Who's the juror?" she wanted to know. "And what the hell was that look about?"

Alan smiled tightly. "Dolores Baxter," he said. "Head of the local Mental Health Association. Her son's a schizophrenic. Seems like Royal didn't do his homework."

A voice came from the front of the room. "Next witness?"

"The defense calls Justin Chitwood."

Portia swiveled her head in the direction of the tall, good-looking man who made his way toward the witness stand.

And from that point it was like a dream come true.

The papers would call it the most damning piece of evidence in the trial. Not only had the infamous panty hose been destroyed, other pieces of evidence, including the earring Jimmy had worn to Lila Mooney's, had also mysteriously disappeared under the direction of Sheriff Dwight Glass.

Chitwood told everything he knew. The arrest reports had been falsified to reflect the changes in the police inventory; there was tampering, perjury, and his own eyewitness description of the defendant's state of mind at the time of arrest.

But there was one further, final piece of news that forever put the seal on the fate of one little-known killer named James B. Wier.

For near the end of that testimony, the attorney for the defense asked Justin Chitwood a final critical series of questions.

"Mr. Chitwood, was Jimmy Wier of sound mind the night he was arrested?"

"No, sir. He was not."

"And are you aware, Mr. Chitwood, of the diagnosis of Mr. Wier's mental illness?"

"Yessir."

"Do you agree with that diagnosis of this alleged alternate personality?"

"I do. Yes."

"Can you tell us why?"

Justin Chitwood had flushed red, coughed, and answered, "Because I saw him . . . change. Into that other person. That woman. She, uhh, came on to me. She wanted me. She asked if I would help her. Be her big strong man. She told me that all her life she'd wanted somebody like me. Somebody to take care of her. She . . ."

Here the witness coughed and sipped at a glass of water.

"She told me she could love me, if I only gave her a chance."

And that was when Donny Royal had risen to his feet. "Your Honor, may I approach the bench?"

"Mr. Royal, there's a witness giving testimony here!"

"I know that, Your Honor, but I must make the request. A conference. In chambers."

The judge peered down at Royal. "Mr. Dylan? Mr. Evans?" he asked, never taking his eyes away from Royal's face. "Are you all right with that?"

Evans rose. "The defense is amenable, Your Honor."

"All right, the jury is to be removed. Gentlemen. In my chambers."

The minutes ticked slowly by as the principle players filed from the room, leaving the spectators to murmur restlessly among themselves. Portia glanced up to find Alan looking at her. "What's that about, do you suppose?"

Alan flashed a sly smile. "Who knows?" he said. "Lawyer stuff. I've missed you, Portia."

She ducked her head. "I guess I was an ass, Alan," she answered slowly. "But, for what it's worth, I've missed you, too."

They fell into a silence that was both awkward and easy, not knowing what their future might hold, but knowing that at least it held something.

Twenty minutes later, the judge filed in, followed by the attorneys and the jury. From her place among the spectators, Portia anxiously searched Dec's face for some indication of what had gone on behind the closed doors of the judge's chambers, but there was none.

A gavel banged to bring the room to order. "Ladies and gentlemen of the jury, the state has just recommended that the death penalty be withdrawn as an option for sentencing in this case. I must say I agree with that decision. Therefore your job here is finished. I thank you for your time. You are free to leave now if you wish."

And so, the Honorable Judge Raymond Johnstone banged his gavel, scanning the courtroom with his penetrating gaze. "Very well. James Wier, please rise, sir."

Jimmy rose to his feet, his lawyers on either side.

"It is the decision of this court that you be remanded to the custody of the state of South Carolina Department of Corrections for the full term of your sentence allowable under the law. And it is further recommended by this court that you be incarcerated in a facility that is adequately equipped to deal with the mentally ill."

Portia felt the room swim as she leaned against Alan. He was going to live, she thought. He was not going to die. They were sending him to a place where finally Jimmy Wier could get the help he had needed for so long.

The rest of it passed in a blur as the spectators and reporters and witnesses all fell over one another trying to get out of the room. Portia and Alan moved slowly toward the defense table, fighting against the flow of bodies. It was over. They had not won, but they had not lost.

Dec glanced up as she came to him, his eyes twinkling in spite of the fatigue that was so clearly written over the rest of his features. "I told you it would be all right," he said. "Thanks to your gumshoe here, we got Chitwood. And Royal, when he heard about Chitwood, he threw in the towel."

Portia turned to meet Alan's eyes. "Gumshoes aren't all bad," she answered. "I did a little detecting myself. Remind me to tell you about Falcone."

Dec frowned. "What about him?"

"Later," she assured him. "We'll do the postmortem later. Right now, I want to go out and celebrate."

"Speaking of later," Alan interrupted. "I'm outa here. I need to go take a sauna someplace." He leaned to offer her a polite peck on the cheek. "Glad to see you're okay."

She grinned as she met his eyes. "I'll call you," she promised. And meant it.

Portia fell into step beside Dec as he made his slow way down the aisle. "I still don't get it, really," she said. "Royal, I mean. He wanted a death vote, he had the witnesses. I can't believe he'd give up the show."

"He took a little persuading," Dec admitted. "But you see, we had Dolores Baxter."

Portia glanced at him, perplexed. "Alan told me. Dolores Baxter."

"Third from the left, top row. Her son was committed to the state mental institution. She was the dealmaker. Conviction yes, but no death. From that look she gave Royal, it was pretty clear that hell could freeze over before she went for death. Between her and Chitwood, I believe our Mr. Royal began to think he'd better cut his losses." Dec looked at her and held her eyes. "Either that, or the son of a bitch might actually have been convinced. You put us over the top, Pokey. I'll always believe that."

She took his hand in silent thanks and smiled. "Practice, practice, practice."

Together they headed slowly out of the courtroom. "Come on," he told her. "I want to go home and cook something."

Unexpectedly she laughed. "You just saved a man's life, and you want to cook!"

Dec smiled a little as they headed out into the charged air of another storm front. "I don't care," he said. "Living well is still the best revenge."

Portia paused for a moment, watching the flight of some birds heading west—away from the big rains and wind that were coming in. She loved the big storms of autumn, and even now the electricity in the air charged her with a new kind of excitement—a new kind of hope. Rain washed the world clean; it made it possible to start over.

They stood together, two old friends, knowing perhaps that they had not won, but at least, this time, they had not lost. Justice had blinked, but in the end it had not been blind. It had not turned away. She watched as the birds fought the rising wind, seeing the last of the sun reflected on their wings as they soared above the turmoil of the world below.

And she felt free.